# THE ROMANOV CONNECTION

# THE ROMANOV CONNECTION

## A NOVEL

## William M. Green

BEAUFORT BOOKS, INC.
New York

Copyright © 1984 by William M. Green

Library of Congress Cataloging in Publication Data

Green, William M., 1936–
The Romanov connection.

1. Soviet Union—History—Revolution, 1917–1921—Fiction.
2. Romanov, House of—Fiction.   I.  Title.
PS3557.R3757R6   1984       813′.54       84-6368
ISBN   0-8253-0221-8

Published in the United States by Beaufort Books, Inc., New York.

Designer: Cindy LaBreacht

Printed in the U.S.A.

10  9  8  7  6  5  4  3  2

TO
LINDSAY
AND
ROSS AND NANCY

# BOOK ONE

I n April 1918, three months before Tsar
Nicholas II of Russia, his wife, his daughters,
and his son were executed by a Bolshevik firing
squad, an audacious and enigmatic figure rode
into the Siberian town in which they were being
held prisoner. He persuaded the commandant to
place the royal hostages in his custody, took them
by sleigh to a nearby railroad junction, and started with them on an eastbound journey by train
that might have led to freedom. His true identity
and motivation remain a mystery to this day.

In that almost forgotten incident lies the germ of
this novel.

# CHAPTER ONE

The Grand Duchess Anastasia, twelve years old, youngest of the Romanov sisters, the one they called The Imp, sat with her knees drawn up to her chin on the wide windowsill of her upstairs bedroom in the Catherine Palace. Barefooted and nightgowned, she was determined to resist the sleep that it had been decreed all children absolutely require. From under leaden eyelids she watched the dancers on the lawn, fancied herself in their midst, and composed mental notes for her little girl's private journal. It was the final night of the Summer Fête, the year's climactic social event, for which the royal houses of a dozen nations had gathered in this most splendid setting in the northern world. And the spirited little girl had resolved that despite banishment to her bedroom, she would not miss a single moment.

From her high window she was able to isolate her sisters among the dazzling crowd in the great, gardened forecourt. A platform for dancing had been laid down upon the jade green lawn; an orchestra played inside a raised and blossom-festooned pagoda at its center, the hub of a wheel of whirling dancers. Tatiana and Marie, her two middle sisters, could be clearly seen gliding and turning dutifully at arms' length from princes of the blood whose company she knew they dreaded. Olga, the oldest and shyest of the three, with something of her mother's reserve, stood off to the side near an ornate pavilion, dutifully sipping punch with a slack-jawed Hapsburg.

Whirling uniform coats of scarlet and supple white gowns of silk began to meld before the little girl's sleepy eyes until the whole scene looked like a great spinning bowl of strawberries and cream. Her chin dropped against her chest. Her journal slipped to the sill with a thump. Anastasia jerked her head up and blinked herself awake. And saw,

1

standing without a partner at the edge of the dance platform, the beautiful Englishman, Aldonby—Marie's good friend, Marie's dear admirer—taller, straighter, more princely than any of the royal sons. If ever she had an admirer like Aldonby, Anastasia resolved, she would run away with him and let the gray-bearded statesmen worry about duty.

For duty was what these gay August gatherings were really all about. As the merchants and tradesmen of nearby Petersburg promenaded their marriageable daughters before the city's eligible sons each spring, so the royal houses and their hangers-on sent their princesses and pretenders to Tsarskoe Selo for the Summer Fête. Ten days of picnics and games, dinners and balls, informality, elegance and purposeful frivolity. The younger generation of Romanovs, Hapsburgs, Saxe-Coburgs, Bourbons, Hanovers, and Savoys could introduce themselves anew, refresh old acquaintance, determine who had grown beautiful, who had grown strong, whose family's power and influence had waxed, whose had waned. The senior members of the great households could look on approvingly and plan for their posterity, making matches in their minds for the yet to be born offspring of these still unmated pairs.

Charles Aldonby, despite Anastasia's adoration and Marie's secretly avowed love, was not one of the contenders here. He was a member of that corps of second and third cousins once or twice removed, the sons and daughters of courtiers, black sheep uncles, and scandal-haunted distant aunts, who had no chance at the great awards in this mating dance and knew it, but who were valued for their energy and imagination and for the service they might one day render in administering the realms of their more thoroughly blue-blooded kin.

At twenty, Aldonby—whose Romanov connection was through his Russian-born mother—already exuded that special aura of competence and authority that marked him as one destined to win most of the prizes that life had to offer, except one; the prize that he coveted above all others would be forever beyond his reach. Marie Romanov, the summertime playmate and fairy princess of his childhood, was now a radiant young woman of seventeen. Sweet of temper, graceful of bearing, lovely, gay, and wise, she was a prisoner of the circumstance of her birth. That love and lifetime of allegiance that she would joyfully have given to Aldonby was not her gift to give. She was the daughter of a tsar and one of her country's national assets, as were her sisters. And Aldonby had no empire, no provinces, no precious natural resources, or warm-water ports to offer in exchange for her hand. The games they had played in childhood during his annual summer-long visits to his mother's homeland had been inspired by the fables of Hans Christian Andersen and the nameless bards of chivalry and bore no relation to the hard realities of life as they approached young adulthood. With each passing summer the calendar of events seemed malevolently designed to afford them fewer and fewer moments together. And as this August's festival drew to a close they both sensed that even those odd moments would no longer be theirs to share. Marie might be spoken for before the year was out.

The waltz ended. Anastasia noticed that Marie had begun to separate herself from the crowd on the dancing platform, threading an irregular course toward the lawn, stopping briefly to exchange a pleasantry, continuing on in the direction of the perimeter of the throng, yet always facing the orchestra and the center of activity. At ground level it must have seemed that she was still a part of whatever was going on. Only from Anastasia's elevated vantage point was it apparent that she was moving farther and farther away, in the direction of the pavilion at the end of the palace. And then she disappeared around the side. Behind the palace lay the park.

At almost the same moment another countermovement in the crowd caught Anastasia's eye: Charles Aldonby, making his retreat from the center of activity in much the same manner as had her sister. Anastasia pressed her hand to her lips as if to hold back a cry of delight, as she considered the thrilling possibilities. Barefooted, she fled her room, crossed the mirrored corridor and entered the dressing room with a window facing the park. Heart pounding, she parted the drape in time to see the Englishman moving quickly across the grounds toward the maze.

Designed for the amusement of Catherine the Great, the maze had baffled and entertained visitors for more than a century. Though its outer dimensions were only fifty meters on each side, individuals had been known to pass through its innocent-looking portal of holly and then be lost for hours, finally having to shout for help from one of the groundskeepers outside who had been entrusted with the maze's secret.

From her high angle Anastasia could see the moonlight glinting on Aldonby's gilded shoulderboards as he plunged like Theseus into the labyrinth. Only she suspected that if he found his way, no Minotaur, but her lovely sister Marie would be waiting for him at its core.

Aldonby shot a quick glance backward before entering the maze to make sure that he hadn't been followed. Then he chose the right-hand pathway, as Marie had instructed. At each of the next four left-hand options he would have to follow her directions scrupulously or, instead of spending the next stolen hour with her, he might spend the rest of the night thrashing aimlessly about in the deeply shadowed alleyways between the tall yew hedges that formed the labyrinth.

Stumbling over exposed roots in the deep shadows, groping like a blind man for openings in the shrub, he found his first left turn and then his second. And finally, heard Marie's anxious whisper: "Charles? Is it you?"

"Yes," he responded. "You sound so close." No more than a few arms' lengths away, separated from him only by the widths of a few hedges. But that was the grand deception of the maze. He would have many tortuous meters yet to go through the dark alleys before he found her.

"Don't miss your next turn," she urgently warned.

He had to watch for one more turn left, and then a right. His heart skipped; he had all but passed the left turn before he realized it was there. It had been so close to the previous one. And then he was abreast of the final option, the one he would have to take to the right.

Suddenly the confining hedge walls were behind him and he found himself in the large, moonlit oval that was the heart of the maze. And Marie was there, a discovered treasure, dimly shining in her rose-colored gown, bare shouldered, shimmering, waiting apprehensively beside a backless marble bench.

They moved toward each other and she placed her lace-gloved hands in his. He could feel the tremor that ran all the way down through her arms.

"It would be a scandal if anyone ever knew," she whispered.

"They'll never know from me," he promised.

"Not even your classmates at Sandhurst?"

"I swear."

"And when you have become a famous general and won many battles and set down your hero's life in memoirs?"

"Never. But I'll never forget."

"What?" she asked insouciantly.

"What?" he echoed, puzzled.

"What will we have done that we are swearing never to forget?"

"Come here? Alone?"

"And kissed?" she asked, challengingly.

"But we haven't kissed," he indignantly declared.

"Will we have?"

"*That* would be a scandal."

"Have you ever kissed?"

He hesitated.

"I won't be angry," she promised.

"I'm a man," he explained.

"Then at least one of us will know what to do." She drew closer to him, tilted her face, and offered up a fragrant cheek. He leaned over and touched her with his lips. She suppressed a giggle. "I hope it will tingle like that when my husband kisses me."

"I don't," he grudgingly blurted.

She smiled. "Would you deny me that small pleasure?"

"I already envy the king who will have the pleasure of pleasing you."

She led him by the hand to the bench. They sat down side by side and she folded her hands primly in her lap and stared straight ahead. "I envy the lady you have kissed. Did you pay her? I've heard that some men do."

"I didn't. She wasn't that kind of lady."

"Was she a married lady?"

"No."

"I'm glad. Because that would have been a sin. But—if she wasn't a married lady—did you teach her?"

"She taught me."

"And she wasn't married? Where did she learn?"

"From a man. As you're learning."

"What sort of lady was she? A countess? A peasant?"

"A dancer."

Marie gasped in astonishment at his having had a liaison with anyone so daringly employed. "Then she must have been very experienced. Was she a prima ballerina?"

"Just a member of the corps."

"But older than you?"

"Just a month or two."

"But she was able to instruct you? I thought men knew more about such things."

"What they know they learn from women—a little older or a little more experienced or both. And they pass on what they have learned to other women—a little younger or a little more naive—"

"Or both?" She shot him a quizzical look. "If we kiss mouth to mouth what happens to the noses?"

"They sort themselves out."

"I wouldn't want to damage your nose."

"My nose is as strong as your nose."

"Shall we see?"

He placed his hands on her bare upper arms and turned her to him. And pressed his lips to hers. She drew back reflexively and stared at him wide-eyed.

"Forgive me," he apologized.

"I just didn't expect—"

"We'd better leave." He stood and took her hand to help her up.

"Would you? Again?" she asked, her eyes fretfully searching his face.

"Forgive me."

"But I want you to. It was just a surprise. No man has ever kissed my lips before. The noses do sort themselves out, don't they?" She tilted up her chin and closed her eyes. And waited.

"We're too far apart. I'll have to come closer."

"Then do." Her eyes were still closed.

"I'll put my arm around you," he told her. He didn't want to startle her again. "It will be as if we're dancing. Only closer." He enfolded her in his arms and pressed her gently to him and fitted his lips to hers. He could feel her arms pulling him closer to her with astonishing urgency, and her mouth began to work on his. This time he drew away, but gently. She clung to him. "We'd better leave," he said.

"So soon?"

"We'd better leave before neither of us wants to leave at all."

"Could that happen?"

"It's happening already for me. Shall we go?"

"Shall we first kiss once more?"

"What will you tell your husband when he asks where you came by your experience?"

"I'll recall how I was before we came here. And I'll deport myself in such a way that there'll be no question. But in my heart I'll remember."

Aldonby's features clouded over. "There's something else you must remember. Should you ever need a friend and not know where to turn, know that you can turn to me."

And she promised that she would. It was one of those futilely sincere promises that lovers often make on parting, a benignly deceptive denial of finality that makes it possible to say good-bye. Tomorrow they might face the bleak truth that in all likelihood they would never meet again except at arms' length across the abyss of a reception line.

They left the maze, as they had entered, separately and unobserved, even by little Anastasia, who had fallen asleep with her head resting on the cushioned windowsill.

They met again, four years later, in circumstances that would have been too horrifying to contemplate by anyone present that night at Tsarskoe Selo.

# CHAPTER TWO

The Peter and Paul Fortress squatted like a sumo wrestler on its island at the gateway to Petersburg, a sullen, hulking mass in the river Neva, impassive and impassable. In the misty copper light of dawn its very stones seemed to sweat.

Anatoly Darabny, working his herring skiff through the slack tide around the seaward side of the Fortress, shuddered and recalled a time when the place was not so ominous a presence. Imposing? Yes. And awesome in its bulk. But in those days not so long ago, as recently as six months ago, the Fortress had echoed with the sounds of life: the chiming of bells from the spire-topped church inside, the clatter of well-shod hooves and the clash of sabers in the cobbled courtyard as the Emperor's cavalry formed up for its morning parade, the two hundred boot heels of the infantry striking the stones with one resounding crunch, as if they were a single pair of feet belonging to a giant, the singsong litany of shouted commands drifting over the water.

In those days passing the Fortress at dawn on his way to the herring grounds was like passing a stadium instead of a tomb. They had promised a lot, the Comrades had, but things hadn't changed much at all. Sure, their Commissars soaked themselves in the Tsar's golden tub, but for common folk like Anatoly the necessities of life were as scarce as ever. Only the lines were plentiful—for bread, for milk, for whatever one needed for survival. Thank God he was a fisherman. As long as he had his boat and the seas were filled with water, there would always be food on the table.

The bow of the little boat thrust upward and then fell with a hard slap against the water. He could feel the tickle of a breeze behind his left ear. The mist had burned away and an exhilarating vista of open sea lay before him.

"Wake up, you lazy boy," he shouted to his son, Misha, who was dozing on the forward deck. "We've cleared the harbor; let's raise the sail."

"Is the wind up already?" Misha yawned and stretched, wishing for one of those mornings of dead calm when he could sleep all the way to the herring grounds.

"Had you not been dreaming you'd not have to ask," Anatoly shouted back. He tucked the tiller under his arm and clapped his hands for emphasis. "Turn to! Turn to! Petrol is as scarce as bread. And twice as dear."

Anatoly steered his little boat before the breeze and watched approvingly as Misha set the mainsail. He would make a good fisherman one day, that boy; thank God he was only twelve and too young for the war. Thank God that he, Anatoly Darabny, was too old. And thank God that his other two children, aged fifteen and eighteen, were girls. There were families he knew who had been wiped out by three years of conflict on the Western Front. Fathers, sons, all—vanished, maimed, ground to dust. Fortunate were the ones who had the wherewithal and the courage to leave, to flee. Like the refugee, Malenovsky, who was hidden in his hold, dressed in borrowed fisherman's clothes. The man had offered him gold for a passage across the Gulf of Finland. Not rubles, which grew more worthless every day, but gold. The herring grounds were just a few kilometers from the Finnish shore. And the gold that the refugee had offered in exchange for his secret passage would buy enough fuel to keep his boat running through whatever windless calms the summer might bring. A nobleman the fellow must have been. A boyar; his bearing testified to it and his manner of speech. An officer of high rank? A courtier? The heir of a prince of industry? Maybe even a cousin or nephew of the Tsar himself huddled in the herring hold. Who could tell precisely who anyone was anymore? All signs of rank had been effaced. Gone by revolutionary edict were the golden epaulets, the scarlet sashes, the rainbows of ribbons, the glittering medals. Everyone looked the same. And everything had turned to the color of dung. And still the war went on, and still there was no bread. And now, instead of hussars who had been responsible to someone, hooligans roamed the streets armed with cast-off and confiscated weapons, responsible to no one; for the Revolution had led each man to believe that he was a tsar unto himself. Pedestrians were robbed of the clothes off their backs; homes were looted at will. And when the looting was done, the looters robbed each other.

And the poor were treated no better than those who once had been wealthy. Only yesterday he had heard of a poor babushka, an apple seller on Voinova Street. Two members of the Red Guard shot her in the face rather than pay the price of an apple, and then strolled down the Prospekt eating their purloined fruit and left her to bleed to death in the gutter. And nobody stopped them or even shouted a reprimand. Would a reprimand have been worth another life? In a land where there is no law what constitutes a crime? If some young thug with a rifle should choose to confiscate his boat one day, Anatoly wondered, would he dare to defend it? What recourse did a simple fisherman have in a land where the mutilated bodies of fleet admirals, butchered at the whims of their crews, could be found floating in the Neva on any morning? In a world like this who was safe?

When the revolution had come Anatoly Darabny had been swept along on the tide with all the others. It had seemed to be a tide rolling in the right direction. And then it had turned rogue and had swamped everything. Someday soon he would have to find the will to turn his back forever on the city and the river he loved, on cousins, uncles, aunts, friends. With his wife and his daughters in the hold, he and Misha would sail the boat out past the Fortress of Peter and Paul and never come back. He could use the gold that the young refugee had given him to help start a new life across the Baltic . . . in Sweden perhaps, or Norway. There would be a livelihood for a good fisherman there. But it would have to be soon—before the short summer ended and the winter set in and the sea turned treacherous. Soon. Before winter. Because by next spring it might be too late. Yes! Anatoly Darabny decided. Soon. The fugitive boyar shuddering down in the hold had shown him the way.

"Misha," he shouted. "Come back here and man the tiller for a while. Your papa has to take a leak."

Andrei Malenovsky, the refugee in the fisherman's boat, was no boyar. No nobleman's blood flowed in his veins. He was a pedagogue, a tutor to the Tsar's young daughters, a student of history—not necessarily one of those actually cut out to live it. So, what was he doing here?

Down in the herring hold of Anatoly Darabny's skiff he sat huddled like a beetle, his back fitted into the curve of the boat's hull, his knees drawn up tight against his chest, wrapped up in the soiled and salt stiffened blanket that the fisherman had given him. It didn't help much; he was still cold. And why not? The hold was made for herring, not men. The chill had got inside him; his teeth were clicking together so uncontrollably that he was afraid they might shatter. And maybe it wasn't the cold alone that had him shivering; maybe it was the fright. The darkness down in the hold isolated him; the metronomic slap of water against the boards at his back terrified him. It was as if the sea with all its crushing weight was importuning for entry. There was barely a half-inch of soggy timber between him and the smothering mass of the Gulf of Finland. He could feel the strakes flex with each roll of the hull. He had been on boats before—riverboats—in cabins high up and well separated from the water. He had never realized how hostile the sea could be. And the smell of herring exuding from the boards and beams all around was doing nothing to quiet his roiling stomach.

As the hours passed and the afternoon sun warmed the deck above him, the chill in the hold abated somewhat, but he kept the blanket around him and shuddered only a little less than he had earlier in the day. The fisherman had come down twice and brought him something to eat and had informed him of their progress. The heavy, dark bread had somehow ballasted his stomach, but the news that they were almost across only gave birth to fresh anxiety. When they put him ashore, dressed like a vagrant and smelling like a fish, what then? His odyssey would have barely begun.

He had gold coins sewn into his shabby trousers, enough for new clothes, bribes, and overland passage across Finland. Then there would be the sea to face again, across to Sweden and again the sea from Norway to Britain. It would take weeks of the most unpleasant kind of travel. And for all that, the whole miserable journey upon which he had been launched might prove to have been unnecessary. Robashevsky, a former captain in the Imperial Guard and a man well suited by nature and training to the uncertainties of clandestine missions, would surely in just a few days' time have accomplished the simple rail journey from Petersburg to the British base in Archangel.

Why then had they seen fit to send him, Andrei Malenovsky, the least likely of couriers, off in another direction? In case Robashevsky could not get through? If Robashevsky could not get through on a simple overland route, then how could they imagine that Malenovsky could make it over treacherous waterways and around war zones clear across Northern Europe? How unkind the fate that had thrust upon his frail and shaking shoulders such a mission. Fate be damned. It was the Tsaritsa herself who had insisted. So how could he refuse? It was the

Empress who had insisted that at least three couriers be loosed, like a flight of arrows, in the hope that at least one of them would reach the target. And in the Imperial household the Empress even more than the Tsar had the last word.

At least he had been spared Krasnov's route to the very ends of the earth, clear across Siberia to Vladivostok on the Pacific coast, where an American expeditionary force was believed to be encamped. A journey like that would take months . . . or forever. Andrei Malenovsky shuddered at the thought of it and pulled the smelly blanket a little tighter around his shoulders. Winter would set in before Krasnov would have gone halfway to the Pacific, and he would freeze to death. Pity Krasnov. Pity him: he was not much better off. And both he and Krasnov were superfluous anyway. Robashevsky had the most sensible route. Robashevsky would be in Archangel in two days' time.

# CHAPTER THREE

Thanks to the pair of sturdy, fur-lined boots he had chosen expressly for his journey, Krasnov would be spared a slow death by freezing and starvation in the icy Siberian wilderness. In a land of discomfort and deprivation a fine pair of boots was a commodity as valuable as gold.

He had been on the road for less than half a day when he stopped at a farm and bought some food from the peasants who now owned the field. The boots were appraised by covetous eyes. And while he ate his lunch at the roadside, Krasnov was jumped by three stout thugs who, without ceremony or apology beat him to death and stripped him to his skin. Two of the louts got one boot each and ran off in different directions with their treasure. The third murderer got a broken nose inflicted by one of the other two in the squabble over the spoils and wound up with little to show for his trouble except Krasnov's old clothes—the ragged shirt and trousers he had hoped would serve as a disguise.

Krasnov's mission had been aborted abruptly but relatively painlessly. Sitting by the roadside in the sunshine as if upon a picnic in his childhood, he had barely felt even the initial impact of the hoe blade against his skull. Robashevsky was not so lucky.

They had picked him up on the north platform of the Finland station at four o'clock in the afternoon. He had been dressed as a factory worker and maybe that had been a mistake. Clothes were one thing, bearing was another. He was an officer, not an actor, and a lifetime's attitudes, moving, standing, speaking, could not be erased in a day. In any event he should not have been on the platform at four o'clock in the afternoon; he should have been on the train, and the train should have been hours away from Petersburg on the way to Archangel. But there were strikes and counterstrikes, and equipment failures, and nobody to make repairs, and no spare parts, and one could spend days in a station waiting for a train to leave.

And there was the rumor of a trainload of fresh meat coming up from the south, and the station had become so mobbed with people that nothing could move. When the freight cars, covered with signs reading FRESH MEAT arrived in the yards and the station guards slid open the doors, they found the boxcars packed from floorbed to roof with corpses: Red Guards killed by White Monarchists in a battle hundreds of miles to the south—a savage joke, and one that had cost Robashevsky dearly.

The delay caused by the jammed trackyards had forced him to spend more time than prudence would dictate in and around the station. True, there were thousands of others chaotically milling about, and their number had multiplied as the rumor of the impending arrival of fresh meat had spread across the city. But when the benighted freight train came into view and the empty-bellied masses surged out of the station and into the yards to meet it, Robashevsky was suddenly alone on the platform and alarmingly conspicuous.

He backed away from the tracks toward a pillar and slipped down onto his haunches: he tucked his head down between his knees and pretended to be asleep and hoped to attract no more notice than any other weary vagrant. The city was crawling with them.

But he had made his move too late. One of a half-dozen Red Guards on the opposite platform had evidenced a singular interest in the elegant derelict across the way. Minutes later Robashevsky, head still down between his knees, felt the toe of a boot prodding him roughly in the ribs.

"Comrade!" More a command than a greeting.

Robashevsky raised his chin and rolled his eyes upward, attempting as best he could to appear vague or dull or both. He was surrounded by four Red Guards, all callow, all intense, all armed. His expert eye could tell at a glance that the rifles were so old or so ill-kept that it was questionable if they could fire. But even if they couldn't shoot it didn't matter: they had him securely hemmed in. One of them seemed barely able to contain his excitement as he spoke.

"Former Captain Robashevsky . . . " he placed the emphasis on the word *former*. "I am Tarpov. I was in your regiment on the Austrian Front."

Robashevsky couldn't place the name or the face; there had been so many in two and a half years of war. This one had been a nonentity, had distinguished himself in no particular way. Robashevsky had a sinking feeling that this Tarpov was about to attain a small measure of notice for the first time in his miserable life.

"You are out of uniform, my *former* Captain," Tarpov tauntingly declared.

Robashevsky shrugged. "There's not much future in being attached to the retinue of a deposed Emperor, living under house arrest in a disused palace. I'm a soldier, not a nursemaid."

"You don't much look like a soldier now, former Captain."

Robashevsky nodded resignedly, but inside he was seething. Not long ago he would have horsewhipped this young lout for such effrontery. Not long ago? A lifetime ago.

Robashevsky let his head loll until his chin was again resting on his knees. He hoped that they would be satisfied that he was a beaten and helpless man, entertain themselves with a few verbal insults, take their delight in this evidence of how the mighty had fallen, and drift away, laughing.

A sharp kick in the ribs painfully disabused him of this hope. In an instant he was on his feet, governed by an uncontrollable reflex, lunging at the youth who had assaulted him. And then he was stumbling forward under the impact of a rifle butt against his right kidney, sinking to his knees, drowning in pain. And the strident-voiced Tarpov was standing over him again and crowing.

"We've been told to keep an eye out for you, former Captain, you and two others. Do you think our officers can't count? Three were not among those present who should have been present in Tsarskoe Selo early this morning." And then to the others. "Get him on his feet. I know somebody who will be happy to see what we've caught here."

The corridors and rooms in the police station on Marinsky Square had been stripped of almost anything that could be moved. A few bare benches and desks remained. The paneless windows gaped; the walls were a snake's nest of graffiti; the corners stank of urine; the paint itself appeared to have been stripped from the rooms.

While he waited on a bench in a windowless anteroom, Robashevsky tried to think of a way to destroy the message written in her own hand by the Empress. It had been sewn into the lining of his jacket the night before by Demidova, the Empress's personal maid. On the paper had been inscribed a plea for rescue, in English, which had always been her language of preference in correspondence. She preferred it to Russian, which was not her native tongue, and dared not use German, which was. She had also drawn on the paper a diagram of the palace and the park and its points of easiest access and entry. Both the Tsar and Robashevsky had tried to dissuade her from committing her plea to paper, but she had been adamant, insisting that without credentials the messengers and their motives would be open to question. They might be treated as agents, provocateurs sent by the Reds to embarrass the British royal family. The Tsar had acceded to her arguments as was his custom, and Robashevsky and the other couriers could only act in accordance with their monarch's wishes.

Now, in light of his present predicament, Robashevsky realized that taking the trouble to secrete the message in the lining of his jacket had only compounded the folly of committing the message to paper in the first place.

Had he the piece of paper loose in his pocket he might somehow have disposed of it in the initial scuffle with Tarpov and the Red Guards. But how does one dispose of a sheet of paper sewn into the lining of one's jacket when one is subjected to unrelenting surveillance? They had even followed him to the toilet and watched him while he relieved himself. Maybe, he decided, the only way to lose the paper would be to lose the jacket.

It was warm in the windowless anteroom—not stifling, but warm. He looked at the guard standing near the doorway and smiled uneasily. Then he took out his handkerchief and patted his forehead as if there were sweat there, and worked his fingers around under his collar, as if he were uncomfortably hot. After a while he worked his arms out of the jacket and folded it up by his side at the end of the bench. A little while later he lay down on the bench, using the folded jacket as a pillow. He hoped that in time the guard would no longer think of the jacket as part of Robashevsky but would accept it as part of the room.

They came for him an hour or two later; he had lost accurate track of time. He couldn't see a clock, and he had lost his timepiece in the scuffle at the station. In all the hours he had spent there nobody had questioned him; nobody had even spoken to him. Had it not been for the fact that they had never taken their eyes off him, he might have thought they had lost interest in him entirely.

When they took him from the room, he left his jacket behind, folded like a pillow on the end of the bench. He simply got up and left it there without a backward glance, as if it were part of the furniture. He had no delusions about the jacket going unclaimed: clothing was precious. Maybe the guard at the door would take it. Maybe he'd had his eye on it since Robashevsky had taken it off. Maybe that was why he hadn't reminded Robashevsky that he'd left it behind. Whoever took it, Robashevsky hoped that its origins would soon be forgotten, along with the paper sewn into its lining.

The sun was setting as they hurried Robashevsky down the front steps of Police Central and into a waiting car. One man took the wheel, another sat beside Robashevsky, revolver drawn. Two Red Guards mounted the running boards, one on either side of the car, rifles slung. They started off with a jerk and careened precipitately through the streets. The guards on the running boards hung on for dear life and grinned and shouted at the passersby. They loved these motorcars that they had taken from the rich. They loved their power and their speed. One could see them racing wildly up and down the boulevards, going nowhere in particular, draping themselves on the running boards, red handkerchiefs waving like banners from the bayonet mounts on their rifles.

They cornered, skidding tires squealing onto the Petrov Embankment Bridge, and Robashevsky's heart sank. He knew with dreadful certainty now what he had previously only suspected; they were taking him to the Peter and Paul Fortress, the lair of Georgi Borodnev, Commissar of Public Safety for the Petersburg district. Since the February revolution very few who had entered there had ever been seen again. In its cellars, under guard and restraint, lay curdling the cream of the former aristocracy and bourgeoisie of the great city: the nobles, the merchants, the lords of industry. Whether they were alive or dead was a topic of speculation. It was known only that they had last been observed entering there under guard.

As they came careening off the bridge, Robashevsky prayed that his lunatic driver would turn the car over; he might, if he weren't killed, have a chance to escape.

They skidded to a halt in front of the gate to the Fortress. The driver leaned impatiently on the horn. Robashevsky decided that once inside his best hope would be to plead that he was a victim of a mistake. He could not deny that he was a former officer in the Tsar's body guard. But that in itself was not necessarily a crime. Scores of former officers as well as enlisted men by the thousands had defected to the side of the revolution. Indeed, without them the revolution would not have been possible. The fact that he had been discovered in mufti in the railroad station might merely mean that he had turned his back on the royal entourage; it might even be considered to his credit that he had finally seen the light and fled Tsarskoe Selo. Without his jacket and the note sewn inside he might be just another displaced person.

As the gate to the Fortress swung open, Robashevsky's despair turned to hope; he had always been an optimist. He decided that he would be one of the few who would come out through that gate again.

Across the yard from the gate, on the top floor of the Fortress, Georgi Borodnev stood at the window of the office-apartment that was his private aerie.

Squinting through his one good eye, he watched as the car drove in and as Robashevsky was rushed across the yard into the guardroom. He had been expecting Robashevsky, indeed had been restlessly awaiting his arrival, ever since the officer in charge at Police Central had telephoned the news of their catch. The long wait in the police station had been in accordance with Borodnev's instructions. And now the guards in the Fortress would continue to pluck at the strings of their prisoner's anxiety. Robashevsky would be locked in the guardroom, alone, and would be informed that Commissar Borodnev was especially interested in his case and would come personally to interview him as soon as he, Borodnev, had finished his dinner. None of this apparently casual conversation was without design.

It had been learned that Robashevsky had not eaten since the night before when he had left Tsarskoe Selo. Surely, while he waited alone in the dark, his discomfort and apprehension would be augmented by visions of his interrogator languorously ravishing a dinner. And though Borodnev's name had been dropped with artful offhandedness, its mere mention should certainly start Robashevsky's empty stomach churning.

Yes, Borodnev decided, another hour or so of waiting should soften Robashevsky up very nicely. Meanwhile, there was no reason why he, Borodnev, should also suffer hunger pangs. He called down to the kitchen and ordered a plate of hot rolled cabbage, then squeezed his porcine body into the chair behind his desk, and reviewed again the dossier on Robashevsky, most of it from the official army files of this former officer of the former Tsar.

Borodnev was too important a figure in the district hierarchy to be dealing with a simple case of vagrancy or flight. If his intelligence was correct and this Robashevsky was involved in an escape plot, he might have found the lever to force the Provisional Government to take an action that should have been taken months ago.

Borodnev believed that Alexander Kerensky was soft, wavering of purpose, a positive threat to the spirit of revolution, empathetic to the plight of the former bourgeoisie, and downright cordial to the ex-

Imperial Family. It was almost as if he were trying to insure against loss in an historic gamble. Borodnev suspected that Kerensky, unchecked, would have allowed Nicholas and his spawn to leave the country months ago for a life of opulent exile. Borodnev, had he had his way, would have erased them all on the morning after the coup.

In Borodnev's one good eye there gleamed the fearful incandescence of the zealot. One doesn't launch a new society encumbered with the barnacles of the old. Borodnev wanted a clean sweep, and if Kerensky lacked the nerve to wield the broom he, Borodnev, would do his damnedest to see that Kerensky was swept out with the rest of the imperial garbage.

To Borodnev's mind the fiery polemicist Lenin might be just the right person to replace the placid Kerensky. True, Lenin had been a target of ridicule and abuse since he had slipped back into the country from his exile in Switzerland. But he was made of iron, and the Duma, made up as it was of as many former bourgeoisie as laboring class, was hardly the kind of governing body one would wish for in a revolution; they were infected with the same softness of mind and outlook as was Kerensky. What a half-assed revolution it had turned out to be, Borodnev thought bitterly, a kind of belch in response to the great dyspepsia of the time: no discipline, no sharply focused objectives.

The trouble with Kerensky was that he hadn't bled at the hands of the Tsar as had Borodnev, hadn't seen a brother hacked to death by cossack sabers and trampled to a pulp under horses' hooves, hadn't had an eye smashed, as Borodnev had, by a rider's spur.

This Lenin was another story, and Trotsky too. They were like twins. They each had a ball of bitterness burning in their guts, hot as molten iron. They had suffered; they had bled; they had lost dearly in the name of the cause. Forged in fire, they were what Borodnev was and what Kerensky with all his mushy humanitarianism was not—true revolutionaries. And their day would come. If Borodnev had anything to do with it, their day would come.

There was a knock at the door.

"Enter!" Borodnev barked.

A kitchen helper came in bearing a plate of stuffed cabbage and a pot of tea on a tray.

"Ah!" Borodnev noisily smacked his lips. The kitchen helper set the tray down on a side table and left. Borodnev picked up one of the cabbage rolls in his fingers, shoved it into his mouth, and tore it apart with stainless steel incisors.

The phone rang. Borodnev muttered an oath. He wiped his hands on a handkerchief, swallowed his mouthful of cabbage, rice, and beef, and picked up the earpiece.

"I'm having dinner," he growled.

"It's the Police Central. They say it's urgent."

"What isn't?" Borodnev grumbled. "Put them on; my food is congealing on the plate."

In the guardroom Robashevsky lost track of time again. He had been left alone in the shuttered, locked cubicle for a little over an hour; it might have been ten. He was feeling weak and light-headed from lack of food and water, and his nerves were tight as an E-string. When the key was thrust into the lock, he jumped. He struggled to achieve an air of composure; if they found him on the verge of exhaustion and hysteria, they would have the battle of wills half won. By the time the door opened, he was able to present a reasonably tranquil facade.

Two men entered. The first was an armed guard who took up a position just inside the doorway. The second, squat and keg shaped, he recognized as Commissar Borodnev. He had seen him once or twice at Tsarskoe Selo, ostensibly checking the security of the park but actually doing his best to bedevil and harrass the Tsar, despite Kerensky's orders to the contrary. The boarlike countenance and milky blind eye were unmistakable. Most men would wear a patch over such a disfigurement. Not Borodnev; he displayed it as if it were a medal, a souvenir of his time on the battlements. He covered it only when he was wenching, a concession to the sensibilities of certain females. A woman always knew when Borodnev was casting a lustful eye her way: the blind one would be decorously covered with a patch.

"Good evening, Captain," Borodnev greeted him. Absolutely matter-of-fact. No warmth, no hostility.

"Former Captain," Robashevsky ventured to correct him. "As you can see I have unfrocked myself."

"Former. Ah, yes. Of course. Everyone is former something or other nowadays, aren't we. Revolutions will do that." He was carrying, tucked under his arm like a soccer ball, a parcel wrapped in brown paper and secured with twine. "You are a former officer; once you took an oath of allegiance to the man who is now a former Tsar; even I am a former . . . revolutionary. Representing as I now do the regime that has come to power, I am no longer a revolutionary, am I?" Borodnev grinned agreeably, displaying a neat row of steel teeth on the side of his face that bore the blind eye. Robashevsky wondered if the same blow that had smashed the eye had also knocked out the upper teeth.

"But tell me, former Captain, when was it that you decided to divest yourself of your uniform?"

"Last night." Robashevsky felt that there was no harm in telling Borodnev what he must already know, which was that he had been reported absent from Tsarskoe Selo in the morning. "I had made an oath to serve the Tsar. Since Nicholas was no longer a Tsar, I was no longer bound by my oath."

Borodnev nodded agreeably. "And so you threw away your uniform and left Tsarskoe Selo. Did you do this alone?"

"Yes and no." Borodnev must also have been aware that three men had been reported missing that morning.

Borodnev looked at him quizzically. "Yes and no?"

Robashevsky thought it might be safe to muddle the truth a little here. "I met one other, like myself, outside the gates this morning. We went our separate ways. Surely we aren't the first to have abandoned Nicholas."

"Did you know the destination of this other individual?"

"I'm sorry to say that we did not completely trust one another. He went his way; I went mine."

"I have been informed that three men left Tsarskoe Selo without authority last night."

"That may be. I met only one other. There may have been a dozen. One might compare the Tsar to a sinking ship. More and more it is becoming a question of every man for himself."

"Did *you* have a specific destination in mind when Comrade Tarpov found you in the train station?"

"I had hoped to find transport to the Caucasus. My family is there." A half-truth. He had no intention of heading for the Caucasus. But his family *was* there. Borodnev might attempt to check that.

"You realize, of course, that you were on the wrong platform for a train to the south."

Robashevsky tried to achieve a look of chagrin. "I didn't. There was great confusion in the station this afternoon."

"Yes. The episode of the fresh meat. The sort of brutality that one can expect of the monarchist gangs."

Borodnev dropped the brown paper parcel on the bench beside Robashevsky and said, offhandedly, "You left this at the Police Central."

Robashevsky's heart skipped. But there had been no indication that Borodnev attached any special significance to the bundle. "My jacket?" Robashevsky asked.

Borodnev shrugged. "They just sent over the parcel." Robashevsky relaxed.

"It was very warm there; I took it off. I must have left it behind. Please thank them for sending it along. Clothing is dear."

Robashevsky picked up the package and held it in his lap. Borodnev appeared to be disinterested, as if his mind were already on more important matters. Borodnev started for the door and then turned. Robashevsky had a very strong feeling that he was about to be set free. "You'd better open it up and make certain it's yours," Borodnev said. "As you said, clothing is dear."

"Of course." Robashevsky wasn't in the least interested in the jacket, but he thought it wise to make a show. He began to fumble with the string. Borodnev watched, curious.

Robashevsky folded the paper away from the jacket and held up the garment. To his great relief it appeared to be intact. The lining had not been torn out. "Yes," Robashevsky said. "Thank you. And will I be able to leave tonight? There might be a train—"

"That will depend."

"On what?" Robashevsky's empty stomach was beginning to knot.

"On how thoroughly you cooperate with us."

"I've done the best I can." His voice was growing hoarse; he couldn't seem to control it. His voice was betraying him.

Borodnev gave a disinterested shrug. "May you can do a little better."

"I'll try. But I really don't know how . . ."

"To begin with, you can tell me about this letter." He reached into his pocket and held up the plea for rescue written by the Tsaritsa. "Tell me how a letter signed by the German bitch, our former Empress Alexandra, came to be sewn into the lining of your jacket."

Robashevsky stared dumbstruck at the incriminating sheet of stationery. He could feel his stomach's sour juices rising up, burning his throat. He swallowed hard to keep from gagging. Borodnev had slammed a gate down between his mind and his tongue, had cut off the vocabulary of evasion. He was ripe for plucking.

Borodnev turned to the guard at the door. "Take the prisoner down to the cellar. Interrogation chamber number three. I'll be along presently." He looked at Robashevsky and shook his head despairingly. "We have a long night ahead of us. I, for one, can think of better ways to spend it." He reinforced his allusion with an obscene gesture. "If you know what I mean."

Robashevsky lay on his back on the stone floor of a fetid cell in the bowels of the Fortress, spread-eagled, as if the palms of his hands and the soles of his feet had been staked to the granite, as if he had been crucified there on the ground. But no nails of iron were needed to hold him there on his cross; pain was his pinion.

Borodnev had been true to his word; the night had been long and arduous. It had cost Robashevsky an eye, the fingernails on both hands, and a half-dozen teeth, which had been drawn out, one by one, with pliers. He had fainted and been rudely revived countless times during the proceedings. He couldn't remember how often. After some hours his body had become such a single roiling mass of pain that he could no longer feel the individual insults that were being administered to him. Because of the blessed and pervasive numbness, he had begun to think that he had beaten them. But he had been mistaken.

They could see that he was no longer reacting properly to stimuli. They were wasting their energy, and they were wasting him; an individual had only so many organs and extremities to tamper with. They dragged him to a cell, pitched him on the stone floor, and locked him in.

In the morning, at about the same time that the tutor Malenovsky crawled into the herring hold of the fishing boat, Robashevsky began to revive. The great tide of pain that had engulfed him had receded; individual points of agony had begun to assert themselves: each finger, each sucking hole in his jaw, the empty socket where his eye had been. And at that moment, as if his tormentors had sensors out monitoring his feelings, they came for him again.

He knew what they would do to him today. The whole procedure had been diagrammed on a chart before they had begun last night. They had made a point of letting him see it, so he would know what awaited him. Anticipation was half the battle.

As he shuffled, was half dragged between his guards down the long stone corridor, he knew that if he survived the day it would only be because he had broken and told them everything they wanted to know. And it would end anyway with a bullet through the base of his skull. He knew of only one way to be sure that he would not betray Krasnov and Malenovsky.

As they approached the ominously narrow flight of fourteen stone steps that led like a funnel to the inescapable horrors of the interrogation chamber, he shrugged off the guards' supporting hands and straightened his back. He knew what he had to do.

"I can walk on my own," he told them, mustering all the dignity that his ruined body could command. Then he hurled himself, headfirst, down the flight of stairs.

There was an astonished shout from the guards. As for Robashevsky, he remained silently, triumphantly airborne for the briefest of moments, like a champion diver executing the swan, and then he plummeted like a shotgunned bird and struck the unyielding granite floor. The crack sounded like the splitting of a tree. The guards clattered down the stairs in his wake, knowing already that there was nothing they could do except prepare to face the blast of Borodnev's fury when he learned that they had allowed former Captain Robashevsky to escape.

# CHAPTER FOUR

*From the journal of Anastasia Romanov*

They shot a family of deer on the lawn this morning, tame deer who have made the park here their home for as long as I or my sisters can remember. Three of the soldiers who guard us did it. I saw it from the window after the sound of the first shot and ran out into the park and begged them to stop. My distress amused them. They told me that we were lucky it was not we rather than the deer they were shooting.

My father and Olga and Marie, who had also heard the commotion, came rushing across the lawn. (Mama told me later that my screams were so alarming that they thought I was being molested. A line of soldiers appeared and barred their way, and the next thing I knew Leonid was half carrying me, half dragging me from the scene . . . all the while begging my pardon for handling me so roughly and pleading with me to be quiet lest my cries further enrage the three drunken louts who were doing the shooting. And through it all I could see the startled and betrayed look in the eyes of the dying deer that were our pets. And their blood was splattered on the leaves and the trunks of the trees. May I never be witness to such a sight again.

Later, Leonid, who is only two years older than I and who is my friend, though he is one of the soldiers who guard us, apologized and told me that he had learned that the deer had been shot for food, there being a grave shortage of meat. That being the case I shall become a vegetarian and urge my brother and my sisters to do the same for, God knows, otherwise I could never be sure that the meat I was eating might not be the flesh of those gentle creatures who were murdered in the

25

park. But I also wonder if what Leonid has told me is absolutely true or if he did not make up that story in order to make less odious the behavior of those men whom he calls Comrade. I think that they did the killing simply out of drunkenness or meanness or as a deliberate affront to us.

Things have become much more difficult for us in the past month, in fact, since the night that Mama sent the couriers. There are more soldiers on the grounds than ever before, and the new ones are not nearly so decent in their behavior to us as the old ones have been. For this Mr. Kerensky has apologized to Papa. But, he says, there are certain things over which he has little control and that sometimes, for political reasons, he must look the other way when the cruder elements behave badly.

Lately everything that we possess has been subject to new and revolting examination. Toothpaste tubes are probed and jars of yoghurt are explored with filthy fingers, and chocolate bars arrive half-eaten (their way, we are told, of examining them for contraband). We shall all fall ill from it.

And the popgun that Alexei gave me for my birthday was confiscated, as were all of his toy guns. Though, he tells me, he has managed to keep one hidden.

Papa spends his time planting vegetables and cutting wood. He seems to be almost content, as if he should have been born a peasant rather than a tsar; though Mama stills plays the Queen.

Mr. Kerensky, with whom Papa has formed a most sympathetic friendship, finds all of this odious but declares that he must allow it . . . in our own interest in a strange way. It is a valve, as it were, through which his people can let off steam and hostility. Better, he says, than to allow the pressure to build up to an explosion. He is under great pressure, too, from the District Commissar of Public Safety, a Mr. Borodnev. All these unfamiliar names, all these people of whom no one has ever heard before, administering an empire more vast than that of Alexander the Great. God grant them the wisdom for such a task.

I begin to think that what has happened is that the emissaries that Mama sent have all been caught and this Borodnev knows what we had planned. And if that is the case, I wonder what hope there is for us now.

I express my fears to Leonid (though I do not tell him about the emissaries) and he assures me that for as long as he is my guard no harm will come to me. And I am sure that he is sincere. But Leonid is not much older than I am. And even if, as he swears, he acts as my protector, what of the rest of the family?

# CHAPTER FIVE

S ara McKenzie, like many of her generation, had put her life in a state of suspension for the duration—maybe forever. Tall, lithe, slender, she had abandoned her studies at London's Royal School of Ballet in favor of full-time work as a volunteer in the War Office. After two years behind a desk as a confidential secretary in the Ordinance Division, she still had the look of a dancer: it was there in the turned-out walk and the proud set of her delicately sculpted head. But in her heart she knew she would probably never dance again, not as a member of a first-class company; her body had lost its discipline, its finely tuned edge. At twenty-two she doubted if she could bring it back again. Not that the loss troubled her too greatly. She had Charles. The fact that she had so willingly abandoned her career for Charles—or anyone— led her to suspect that, promising though her talent had been, she had lacked that single-minded dedication, that self-centered tunnel vision that was essential to true artistic achievement.

She had gone to work in Whitehall a week after he had crossed the Channel for France, believing that somehow her work would shorten the distance between them. He hadn't been gone for long. He had returned to England on a litter six months later, shattered. It had taken the surgeons all these many months to piece him back together. And now that he was almost whole he would need her more than ever, she felt, to help him over the last and most difficult hurdle, the restoration of his self-esteem.

In her small office down the hall from the General's suite, already feeling enervated at half past nine in the morning by the heavy July humidity, she began reviewing the previous night's dispatches before putting them in order for presentation to the Brigadier. The news from the Western Front was not good. She wished she could suppress it.

27

In their flat in Sheffield Terrace, Charles would read about it in the afternoon paper and it would increase his despair. When she got home in the evening, she would be greeted by silence, as if he were ashamed to speak, as if yesterday's losses at Ypres were his responsibility, because he hadn't been there, as if his terrible wounds had been self-inflicted, as if he were a deliberate malingerer.

She knew that his silences and sullenness had nothing to do with her, had to believe it or she couldn't go on with him, had to believe that as his physical wounds mended the mental lesions would heal. The only trouble was that when it happened, and if the war were still on and it seemed that it would go on forever, he would return to combat. He wouldn't be required to in view of what he had suffered, but he would be impelled to for the sake of his peace of mind. And then she might lose him totally and forever.

But even at that she must, despite her frustration and despair, consider herself more fortunate than many; she had him now, if only part of what he had been; she had the privilege of caring for him, which was more than so many young women of her age had—of caring for their lovers—and the war *might* end before he could be returned to the front.

Her shirtwaist was growing clammy with perspiration. She went to the window and drew the shade part way, to block the sun. The intercom box on her desk sputtered.

"Sara? Are you there?"

"Yes, General. I'll have the dispatches for you in a moment."

"Never mind the dispatches. I have Arthur Craig on the line in my office. He's called and asked to speak to you."

"I'm sorry, General. He should have . . ."

"Quite all right. We also serve who pass along messages. Please hurry, now."

She picked up the folder of dispatches, let herself out of her stifling little cubicle, and hurried down the corridor.

Charles and Craig had been at Sandhurst together, their relationship marked by that abrasive friendship, or simmering rivalry, that often sprang up between achievers. At one point she had been its point of focus, though she had never been romantically interested in Craig at all. And she wondered if Craig's interest in her arose solely from the fact that Charles possessed her. Once, in a fit of unmotivated jealousy, Charles had maintained that Craig had chosen intelligence work in order to escape combat and that it therefore served him right that he now daren't sleep with a woman for fear he might compromise military secrets.

She tapped lightly on the General's door and entered. He took the folder of dispatches from her, pointed to the telephone, and left the room. He didn't seem to mind the interruption at all.

"Arthur? Sara here."

"Good morning, Sara. Apologize for the interruption."

"Don't apologize to me. Apologize to the General."

"Not to worry. Had some business to discuss with him first. Maybe it'll inspire them to install a telephone in your room. How's Charles these days?"

"Doing very well, thank you."

"Still have the cast on his leg?"

"Yes. But he gets around quite well with the crutch."

"Glad to hear it."

What? she wondered. That Charles was still in a cast or that he was getting around a bit? What was Arthur after?

"Mental outlook improved any?"

"Nothing wrong there that getting back on his feet and back into action won't cure." Why go into all the gloomy details with Arthur? Why provide fuel for club-room gossip?

"Something's come up that he might help us with. Might do him a world of good to be able to be of some service, don't you think?"

I think, Sara thought, that I detect a snotty, patronizing note in your voice and I don't like it at all. But she said, "Well, he's not exactly sitting around twiddling his thumbs, you know. He's got plenty to keep him busy." Which was a fib. "He certainly doesn't need any make-work projects."

"Sorry. Didn't mean to imply anything of the sort. Do you suppose he's fit enough to meet me over in Clerkenwell for an hour or so? Or—I could pick him up in my car."

"He can take a cab," she said, defending Charles's independence. "What's it all about?"

"Nothing strenuous," Craig replied, both slipping the question and restoring Charles to his invalid's category. "Just a matter of an identification."

"Well, Arthur, I'm sure Charles would be delighted to help you. Shall I ask him tonight?"

"Not necessary, thanks. If it's all right with you, I'll ring him up myself. Good speaking to you, Sara." And he rang off, leaving her with a strangely empty feeling. For the first time in more than a year she wouldn't know exactly what Charles was doing. And, as for Craig— even though she found him insufferable, he might at least have shown a *little* interest in her.

In a chair by the window in their Sheffield Terrace flat Lord Charles Aldonby disconsolately leafed through the day's newspapers. Strong, young, born to lead, trained at Sandhurst in the science of war, he had been reduced to the status of a spectator, a twenty-four year old invalid, following the disheartening progress of events on the front through Reuter's reports and the news that Sara brought home at day's end. None of his training, none of his skills had been validated by a single moment in combat. On the eve of the great push on the Somme, a vagrant artillery shell had caved in his bunker, concussed him, crushed his rib cage, punctured a lung, shattered his right leg, mangled his left arm, and left him floundering in delirium, helpless prey to the bone saw and the knife.

They had managed to piece together the leg, but the arm was a lost cause, the nerve connections having been irreparably damaged; it would never again be anything more than a decorative appendage.

While the surgeons at a field station near Arras made the first of what would be a long series of surgical maneuvers to make him whole again, his second-in-command led *his* troops in the great assault he had helped to plan. Two weeks later, when a savage counterattack threw his regiment back to its original position giving the sum total of the intervening bloodshed a value of zero, Lord Charles lay bedridden in the lush, verdant bosom of the family estate in Kent, recuperating from his wounds and awaiting the next surgical encounter. Remorsefully and erroneously he felt that had he been there when the counterattack had been launched his presence might have made a difference.

In the ensuing months, as the sequence of follow-up surgery had begun to restore function to his leg and as he had learned to maneuver with the aid of a crutch, he had followed in the daily press the see-sawing fortunes of his regiment as it was relentlessly ground to dust. A year and a half later they were mired in the same position they'd been in on the night he had been wounded, and though the regiment bore the same name and insignia, not a man of that original force remained. He began to arrive at the gloomy conviction that if it went on this way, the war would end in a stalemate for want of whole men to fight it. Lately, with the collapse of the monarchy in Russia, he began to fear that there would be an ending more calamitous than stalemate. All those German armies currently bottled up on the Russian Front would be free to roll westward. The Allied lines in France would be swept away by the juggernaut and that would be the end.

Aldonby became aware that the phone was ringing, had been ringing for some time. If he didn't pick up quickly, Sara would be rushing home in a panic to see if he hadn't fallen off his chair, toppled no doubt by the weight of the plaster of paris on his left leg.

"I'm all right," Aldonby snapped.

"Charles? This is Craig." He sounded puzzled, as if he'd reached the wrong party.

"Oh! . . . Arthur." Nonplussed. He had been so sure it would be Sara.

"Are you all right?"

"Of course I'm all right!"

"The way you answered—"

"I simply stated that I was all right." Belligerently.

"If you'll forgive me, it's not the sort of statement one is accustomed to hear as a preamble."

"Surely you didn't call to inquire about my health."

Thank God, no! Craig thought. "A little matter related to military intelligence." He could almost hear Aldonby's interest quicken. "You spent a summer in Petersburg a few years ago, didn't you, Charles?"

Craig would have his file open, would know the answer before he asked the question. "I spent a month of every summer there. From nineteen nine through thirteen." Milestones on his way to manhood. And 1913, the year he was twenty-one, the best of all.

"You were acquainted with the Imperial Family?" Craig asked rhetorically.

"Yes." Marie had been seventeen then. And when they danced, she had squeezed his hand. And their eyes, under the eyes of the chaperons, had carried on a secret dialogue.

"And, I suppose, various members of the household staff?"

"Some of them." The simple mention of Petersburg never failed to kindle a yearning in him.

"Good. I'm at St. Bartholomew's Hospital. There's a chap here who claims to know you. Actually, he named half a dozen of you who spent summers in Petersburg, but we can't reach the others. Two are still at the Front, and the others are dead."

Aldonby stiffened, cautioned himself against a recent disposition to interpret innocent comments as deliberate affronts, and composed himself. "What's his name?"

"Malenovsky."

"The girls' tutor?"

"So he claims."

"What's he doing here?"

"That's quite a story. And, if it's true, a war secret. Let's just say he has a confidential letter for His Majesty."

"Is it possible for me to see him?"

"Not only possible. Absolutely necessary. Before we go about delivering potentially volatile messages to His Majesty, we'd better be damned sure this fellow is who he says he is."

"What hospital did you say?"

"St. Bartholomew's."

"What's the matter with him?"

"Flu."

"Bad?"

"Quite."

"I'll get right down."

"Would you like me to pick you up?"

"Not necessary, thanks." He almost bridled again.

"I'll be waiting."

Aldonby hung up the phone, twisted around in the chair, and reached for the crutch that was leaning against the wall nearby.

Craig was waiting at the hospital entrance when Aldonby's cab drove up; he stepped quickly down to the cab and had the door open before the driver could get around. Aldonby thrust his crutch out and Craig offered a hand for support and then thought better of it.

"Which way?" Aldonby asked when he was up on his feet with the crutch securely wedged into his armpit.

Maneuvering expertly with the crutch and his good leg, he followed Craig through the main door and past the admissions desk. Craig measured his pace and glanced to the side now and then to make sure Aldonby was all right.

"Don't worry about me," Aldonby grumbled. "I'll keep up."

"Not worried about you at all, old boy. You handle that equipment like it was part of you."

"Yes, isn't it a shame; just when I've got it mastered, they're threatening to take it away from me."

"Oh! That's good news. Cast coming off?"

"In two or three weeks, I hope."

As they moved through wards redolent of antiseptic and sibilant with the sounds of breaths painfully drawn, in low tones Craig filled Aldonby in.

"He was in this rundown hotel, putting in calls to the palace three and four times a day. He must have been half delirious even then. Insisted he had to speak to the King. And you know how sinister any foreign accent sounds these days. The switchboard at the palace began to wonder if they didn't have a madman on their hands, or an assassin. Bomb-throwing anarchist type, you know. They got the name of the hotel and sent around security officers.

"They found him in a semicoma, still muttering about a message for the King. Sewn into his clothing.

"They took him here, tore his clothing apart, found a letter. Signed by Alexandra, Empress of Russia. Addressed to her dear kinsman, George, Rex."

Craig stopped before a wood-framed door with a frosted glass panel in the center. "Here we are. We moved him into a quarantine room, just in case."

"In case, what? Half the people in the ward out there must be down with the flu."

"In case he is who he says he is and not an agent provocateur or a madman." Craig opened the door and stood aside to let Aldonby pass through.

Dead silence . . . and the cloying odor of putrification. Dingy gossamer curtains billowed feebly in the breeze, stirred by the opening of the door, and then came to rest, like a sigh. The air in the room was tepid, drenched with humidity like the atmosphere in a greenhouse. And the still figure in the enameled steel hospital bed appeared to be wrapped in cellophane, like a prize yellow rose, cut and waiting to be delivered.

Aldonby glanced inquisitively at Craig.

"Oxygen," Craig said. "But he's still alive."

Aldonby leaned on his crutch, swung his leg, and moved farther into a position near the sick man's head. Aldonby was certain he was dying.

"Do you recognize him?" Craig asked.

"Yes." Aldonby's voice was heavy with grief. "It's Malenovsky."

"Well, I'll be damned."

Malenovsky's eyelids moved, the barest fraction of an inch—not really open but not sealed shut as they had been. There was the faintest trace of animation in the heretofore dead face under the cellophane canopy.

"I'm afraid I've wakened him," Aldonby said.

"Maybe he heard you speak his name. It would do him a world of good, for his peace of mind at least, if he knew that he had been recognized and that the letter will be delivered."

Malenovsky tried to open his eyes, but it was as if they were coated with lead. Aldonby could sense the effort.

"Professor Malenovsky," Aldonby softly called out in Russian.

It seemed that labored minutes passed until finally the eyes were open, almost halfway, staring expressionlessly in the direction of the ceiling.

"It's Aldonby, Professor. Charles Aldonby. Do you remember?"

The watery blue pupils shifted slowly in the direction of the voice, coming to rest at last on the young officer's face.

Aldonby removed his cap to make recognition easier. Thank God he isn't nearsighted, Aldonby thought, and waited, nodding his head encouragingly.

The vacant, watery eyes appeared to remain unseeing and un-focused, but the corners of the mouth began to stir, settling finally into what might pass for a smile.

"Your letter will be delivered, Professor," Aldonby said, enunciating with great care, as if he were speaking to a backward child.

The eyelids slowly lowered and were laboriously raised again. That was the best that Malenovsky could do to let Aldonby know that he understood and was grateful before he slipped back into unconsciousness.

"Is there any hope for him?" Aldonby asked, after they had left the room.

Craig shrugged. "I'm a soldier not a physician."

A captain of statistics and file cards, Aldonby thought bitterly, a paper pusher by choice rather than by circumstances. "I'd like to keep in touch, do whatever I can to help him."

"I'll give you the name of the doctor."

"Thank you. He was truly a dear man, you know. The girls adored him."

Craig grunted. "I wouldn't have taken him for a ladies' man."

"I didn't mean that. These were his pupils, the Tsar's daughters. They adored him in the way that adolescent girls, even Grand Duchess-es, would adore a gentle but stimulating teacher. In a way he is the first man who opens them up, reveals to them the possibilities within themselves and in the world outside." Aldonby stopped, and shuddered. "I'm talking as if he were already dead. How do we get out of here?"

Craig led the way. As they retraced their route through the corridors and wards, Aldonby was moved to further recollection. "You know, on my last visit there he staged a reading of one of Chekov's plays: *The Three Sisters* with Olga, Marie, and Tatiana in the leading roles. Little Anastasia raised a fuss because she was too young to appear. And the Empress raised a fuss because the Tsar took the role of a servant. Maybe it was prophetic."

In the vestibule, while they waited for Aldonby's cab, Aldonby asked what the message was that poor Malenovsky had carried so far.

"I'm afraid we can't discuss it," Craig said. "Official Secrets."

"Do I look to you like a German spy?"

"Sorry, old chap. Rules are rules. We're at war, you know."

"Yes," Aldonby replied. "I know."

The cab drew up and Craig hurried ahead to open the door. "I'll see what I can do to get a clearance for you in this matter," Craig volunteered.

Aldonby was surprised but grateful. "Thank you. I have more than just a passing interest in that man and that family, and I doubt he put himself to the risk of a journey across Europe in the middle of a war to deliver a simple greeting from the deposed Empress of Russia to her cousin the King."

# CHAPTER SIX

When Aldonby limped into the flat that evening, he found Sara noticeably distraught. Half relieved, half enraged, she came storming at him like a nervous young mother whose child had just wandered away: "Where have you been? I've been home for over an hour and no word of you." She stood combatively in the foyer, blocking his way, feet apart, hands on hips, chin jutting.

Aldonby blinked, nonplussed. "Sitting in the park."

"At this hour?"

It was only eight o'clock and the light was still good. "Just some thinking to do."

"You might have telephoned."

"Lost track of time. Sorry."

She rushed to him and embraced him, awkwardly, the crutch getting in the way. There were tears. Hers. He couldn't understand what all the fuss was about.

She bit her lip. She had almost spoiled it. For the first time in months he had taken independent action, and she had reprimanded him for it. "Nothing to be sorry about. It's a lovely evening. Why shouldn't you sit out? I've just had a beastly day," she fibbed. "Nothing to do with you at all."

She slipped her arm through his and walked with him to the rear of the flat, continuing to make apologies for her assault on him.

Over dinner he told her about his visit to the hospital with Craig. About Malenovsky. About how even here he felt cut off from events. Malenovsky had carried a message with him. Craig had stood on form.

"Rotten of him," Sara said.

"That's Craig. Of course one can guess. They're asking for help."

"How fortunate that you were able to identify him," she said pointedly.

"I suppose." And then suddenly, bitterly. "Been invalided for two years so that I could be on hand to identify Malenovsky. How nice to know it's all been part of a great plan."

The bitterness came in waves, unexpectedly, but Sara was used to it by now. She let it pass without comment, which she had learned was the best way.

"Will they get help, do you think?"

"I can't imagine otherwise. The shame of it is that they should have had to ask. Never mind the family connection, the King being their cousin; they have been the staunchest of allies. I would venture to say that it was Nicholas's determination to abide by the terms of the alliance, to hold the Bosh on his front at any cost, that cost him his crown. To turn our backs on him now would be nothing less than craven."

When it was time for bed, Aldonby excused himself. He wanted to stay up for a while and think. He lowered himself into his chair by the window, propped his crutch against the sill, and stared out into the darkness, recalling summers past in Petersburg: hazy, warm days; languorous, cool nights. Times filled with gaiety, activity, laughter, and lingering twilights that seemed to meld with the dawn and the sound of string orchestras. Cantering through the park at Tsarskoe Selo. Boating on the river, fencing on the lawn, and the lovely young Grand Duchesses, cheering for their favorites, giggling, comparing—like schoolgirls anywhere.

When he and Marie had danced, at the required arms' length, the airspace between them had seemed to be statically charged like the air around a meadow before a lightning strike. Was it only his imagination, or had she felt it too?

One of the other young aristocrats there had warned him not to let it go to his head; it was just Marie's way. She was blossoming and beautiful and trying on her womanhood. Still, he had believed that her feeling for him was special. Fantasy? Maybe.

Not that it would have mattered. A Grand Duchess, a Princess, was too precious a commodity to be allowed to be ruled by her feelings. How ironically sad that now that she was no longer a Grand Duchess she would be free to follow the dictates of her heart. Why not allow his imagination free rein? The fact that Marie's mother, the Tsaritsa, was his own mother's cousin needn't stand in the way. In the circles in which he had moved, everyone was somebody's cousin. Germany, Russia, Britain, they were all linked through the genes.

And they were all killing each other off. A household gone mad. It may have been some Prussian cousin of his who had ordered the shot that had crippled him.

He was startled out of his reverie by the touch, however gentle, of a hand on his shoulder. "Charles."

"Yes."

"It's very late." She brought the crutch to the chair and helped him to his feet.

Later, when she bent over his bed to kiss him good night, he drew her down to him. Through the awkward, passionately explosive time of their coupling, neither of them was aware that they were bringing to its climax an encounter that had begun in Petersburg four years ago. What Sara blissfully mistook for a new beginning really marked the onset of the end.

# CHAPTER SEVEN

*From the journal of Anastasia Romanov*

TSARSKOE SELO
JULY 27, 1917

We had our chance and we lost it. Papa promises there will be other chances. I wonder.

A week ago, Mr. Kerensky came for one of his frequent meetings with Papa; they were locked in the study for almost an hour. When he left, Papa called us all together and told us that we were to prepare to leave. We were to think carefully about those things that we wished to take, as we would be allowed only what could be carried by hand. We would leave in approximately forty-eight hours; a special train was being assembled to take us to Archangel. The pressures on Mr. Kerensky have grown so great that he fears he can no longer guarantee our safety. He had attempted this once before, but word had leaked out and the railroad lines had been blocked by radicals. This time he planned to operate in utmost secrecy. After we were safely under the jurisdiction of the British expeditionary force in the north, he would make a public announcement that we had been sent off in disgrace, condemned to exile. Papa accepted this. In the first place, he had no choice. In the second place, it might have been the only way we could ever leave here. It might have been. But the moment has passed. And we are still here. And the fault is mine.

When Papa made the announcement to the family, I felt nauseous and hot. I thought it was because I knew that once we left we would never see Russia again. The next morning I broke out all over with nasty red spots. Measles! Mama was beside herself. Even while she ministered to me and tried to bring my fever down, I could feel her

39

deep resentment over my becoming ill. Or could it have been my own guilt and resentment, which I imagined I saw reflected in her eyes? I had not conspired to become ill, but that did not diminish the anguish I felt. Dear, faithful Dr. Botkin declared that I could travel only at the gravest risk. I cried and cried and begged them to promise that they would not leave me behind. Papa most urgently asked for Mr. Kerensky to come and meet with him. Our flight would have to be postponed. "We would all leave together," Papa firmly declared, "or we would not leave at all." Can I ever forgive myself? Well, at least the blame had to be shared; the next day Alexei fell ill with the same wretched ailment, and most secretly and to my eternal shame, I thanked God that I was not the only one responsible for having spoiled our chance for escape.

The horrible rash is almost all gone now. And we are all well enough to travel. But the moment has passed. The railway line between Petersburg and Archangel is no longer open. Our escape route has been closed off, forever I fear.

Mr. Kerensky expresses his deepest regrets. He fears that we cannot safely remain much longer anywhere in the vicinity of Petersburg. His regime is under extreme pressure from Bolshevik extremists on the left. He must move us, he feels, but he doesn't know where.

And to make matters even worse, Leonid, who had sworn to protect me, is gone. (Is it a sin for me to be so concerned about myself?) *He* became ill with measles two days ago and has been sent off to hospital in Petersburg. And the guard who has taken his place is a vulgar lout who whispers filthy things to me when no one else can hear, as if it were my fault that I was born an emperor's daughter.

Oh! Sweet Jesus! Will our prayers be answered? Did any of our couriers get through?

# CHAPTER EIGHT

They buried Malenovsky a week after Aldonby confirmed his identity: he never regained consciousness. Nor had Aldonby, without security clearance, been allowed to visit him again. He received his clearance on a Tuesday afternoon, coincidental with a call from Craig informing him that Malenovsky had died the day before and that if he hurried he might be in time to attend the burial . . . if he cared to.

He stood at the graveside with Craig while the men with the shovels and an Orthodox priest put Malenovsky away.

"Thoughtful of you to get the right kind of clergy," Aldonby said to Craig when it was over.

"We try to do the right thing when we can."

"I don't suppose there was anything I could have done even if I had the proper clearance last week."

"He was comatose the whole time."

Aldonby shrugged. "And now I have a clearance."

"We'll ride back in my car. We can talk about it if you like. But it's really all over."

Aldonby dismissed his driver and worked himself into the backseat of Craig's Austin.

"Will you join me for a drink at my club?" Craig asked.

"Not today, thanks," Aldonby replied, wondering if Craig would have extended the invitation had he not so recently been validated as "secure."

"Sheffield Terrace, then," Craig called out to his driver just before he slid shut the glass screen that separated the backseat from the business end of the car. Ritually he peeled off his dress gloves and dropped them into the upturned cap resting on his knees.

"Very well, then," Craig said. "Business at hand: that intelligence for

41

which you so urgently required a clearance. I doubt you'll find it was worth the effort." It was evident that Craig resented the ease with which Aldonby had acquired secret's clearance; it rendered the fraternity to which he belonged that much less exclusive.

Aldonby waited, engaging Craig's eyes with his own, knowing that eventually Craig would feel compelled to speak. "Yes, of course," Craig muttered after a brief interval and shifted in his seat to avoid Aldonby's gaze. "You see, he was carrying this letter from the Empress Alexandra to the King."

"Yes. You told me that much before I had clearance in the matter."

"Of course. Merely recapping for you. Anyway ..." and now he began speaking rapidly and practically inaudibly, as if he were embarrassed by what he had to say. "The Empress asked if, in light of the deteriorating situation, His Majesty would consider mounting an effort to deliver the Imperial Family from the hands of their captors."

"I'd guessed that much, Arthur."

"Oh? Really? Well, then that's all there is."

"And what has the decision been?"

"Regretfully, no."

Aldonby stared at Craig incredulously. "Regretfully, no? Like turning down an invitation to a ball?"

"That's not entirely fair. The plea was given exhaustive consideration. But you can see why this information is classified most secret and must never be revealed."

"Who made this decision?"

"It was made at the very highest level."

"The King?"

"No."

"I didn't think so. The Prime Minister?"

"Yes. But with the King's ultimate concurrence. The decision was not made lightly, I assure you. You know what the military situation is. Beyond that the P.M. is afraid that to offer that autocrat sanctuary here might so enrage labor that the war effort would suffer."

"Where are they being held?"

"A place called Tsarskoe Selo."

"I know Tsarskoe Selo very well. It's very close to the Gulf of Finland. I don't think they've properly considered it. We could be in and out with a small, fast boat before anybody realized what was happening."

"Aldonby! The decision has been made. We dare not antagonize the Provisional Government. They are our allies."

"So was the Tsar."

"We didn't advise him to abdicate."

"No, he was forced to. But largely because of his loyalty to us. His people weren't so much fed up with him as with the war. How long do you think this Kerensky will last if he doesn't make peace with the Kaiser?"

"Who can say? But every day he stands fast is to our advantage."

"The war is bleeding his country. He can't hold the line forever."

"Nor can we in those bloody trenches. But maybe we can hang on until the Yanks get some troops over here. In any event we daren't do anything to antagonize the Russians."

"But Kerensky himself was willing to let them go, I'd heard."

"The situation has changed. He can't anymore, not even if he wants to. And even if he did, the left wing of our own Trade Union movement wouldn't hear of it, wouldn't allow us to give them sanctuary. We are in extremely treacherous waters; let's not muddy them."

Aldonby had nothing more to say. He sat rigid and silent in the seat beside Craig, eyes narrowed, looking straight ahead, jaw muscle twitching.

"You do understand?" Craig asked, a note of warning in his voice.

"Only too well."

It began to rain as the car crossed the Thames by way of Blackfriar's Bridge and turned left into the Victoria Embankment. Pellets of water set up a racket on the Austin's canvas top, pelting the murky river, turning it to the color of mud. Aldonby watched gloomily as men and women in the streets in their khaki service kit scurried for cover, forming dun-colored clots in doorways. Such was his state of mind that the universe seemed on the verge of dissolution. Leaves on the trees in the park, going brittle and dry in the last gasp of summer, were torn loose from their branches under the hammer of the rain and fell spinning to the muddy ground like machine-gunned infantry. Malenovsky in his freshly dug grave would be turning to mud. And the flower of the Commonwealth crouched in the trenches of Picardy. All would be turning to mud. His world was foundering. Why should the powers in Buckingham Palace, Parliament, and Whitehall concern themselves with the fate of an Emperor who had been too weak and too unresourceful to keep his crown?

# CHAPTER NINE

I n the columned Malachite Chamber of the Winter Palace, Kerensky
stood with his back to his desk gazing out across the Neva, framed by
the huge window, like an actor centered beneath the proscenium arch,
eager for the curtain to rise, the scene to begin.

The anxious young woman sat very still and straight in the visitor's
chair, her hands tightly clasped in her lap to keep them from shaking.
Deliberately averting her eyes from the preoccupied Kerensky, she
stared at the crystal tea glass in a silver holder that had been placed
before her on a napkin near the corner of the desk. The tea, which
Kerensky himself had poured for her, had long since grown cool, and
she had not tasted a drop of it. The sugar, so generously ladled in, had
settled unstirred at the bottom. Such had been the state of her nerves
that she feared that had she tried to raise the glass to her lips her hands
would have trembled and, to her eternal embarrassment, would have
spilled the once scalding liquid all over herself in front of the head of
the government. Not that she felt that he would have reproached her.
It was his surprising kindliness, his gentleness of manner that had
given her the courage to see this through.

Kerensky suddenly turned. Apprehensively the young woman
raised her eyes. Kerensky was looking at the clock on his desk; the
moment was almost at hand. Borodnev had scavenged a prize position
for himself in the bureaucratic debris that had lain in the wake of the
Tsar's abdication and had used it as a base from which to undermine
Kerensky's authority. He had plotted with the Bolshevik subversive
Lenin, had inflamed the mobs at Tsarskoe Selo, had cut the rail line to
Archangel, had entertained ambitions to replace the old emperors with
kings of his own making. And he had managed to remain untouchable.
Camouflaging his treachery, using his position to destroy substantiat-

ing evidence. Only his depraved personal appetites had left him vulnerable, would have, had there been witnesses, but none had survived . . . until now.

"He will be here any minute," Kerensky said.

The young woman smiled. It had always been her nature to smile easily and, despite what had happened, the instinct was still there. But her smile was no longer natural. She made a conscious effort to keep her lips pressed tightly together to avoid revealing the gaping space where her upper front teeth once had been. Her fine-featured good looks and carefree smile had once been the envy of her classmates; now she had the nose of a pugilist, the mouth of a hag, and scars on her body that would never be erased.

"A little more tea?" Kerensky asked, aware that she hadn't touched what he had already given her but anxious to make her as comfortable as he could. She shook her head no with almost imperceptible side-to-side movements. Only the eyes remained lovely in that ruined face.

"Shall I take your glass, then?"

She nodded imploringly, relieved at last to be free of responsibility for her undrunk tea.

Kerensky removed the glass and said, "I think that when he comes you should be in *that* chair." He pointed to a ladder-backed chair in a shadowy corner of the huge room. "You will be behind him when he enters and on his blind side. I don't want him to see you until the moment is right. And you will be ten meters from him; I would like that distance between you."

Her brow became furrowed with concern and the lovely eyes looked troubled. The phone rang. Kerensky listened and hung up.

"He is in the building now," he told the young woman. "Just a few more minutes."

He took her protectively by the arm and led her in an almost courtly fashion across the room to the chair in the corner against the opposite wall. As they approached the chair he said, "As you see, there is a door just beside you." He turned the knob and opened the door just a crack so that she could look out. "And two strong men just outside the door." He nodded to the two powerfully built soldiers standing guard. "They are here to see that no harm comes to you. There are two more men of equal size and capability at the side door at the far end of the room. And, after he comes in through the center door, there will be two strong men behind that one as well." Gently he pulled the door shut.

She sat down, timorously, in the chair beside the door. "I still don't understand. Why are you going to all this trouble for me?"

"In all honesty, my dear, I am doing it for me. And maybe for Russia. Now be calm. You'll not have to say a word."

Kerensky gave her hand a reassuring pat, turned, and strode back to his desk. He sat down and composed himself for the meeting at hand. His agents had done well. Gossip had brought the incident of the young woman to their attention. They had traced the rumor to its source, the poor girl's parents, and found it to be verifiable. They had found her in hospital, in such battered condition that the doctors were not certain she would live. They had informed Kerensky, who had told them to attend to nothing else until the young woman was well enough to speak, to make a statement in her own words. They had waited for weeks, while her body healed and the wires that held her jaw together could be removed. And Kerensky sweated. Because Borodnev was pressing him, stoking the fires of the radical left, conspiring to erode the base of his support.

There were two sharp knocks on the center door.

"Come!" Kerensky called out.

The door swung open. Borodnev stood framed for a moment by the doorway and the malachite columns: stolid, defiant. Then he stepped forward into the room. The door swung shut behind him.

Kerensky, out of the corner of his eye, saw the girl wince and go rigid in her chair. With a spastic movement, she brought her fingertips to her mouth, trying to contain her fright. For a moment Kerensky was afraid that she would cry out.

"Comrade!" Kerensky expansively greeted Borodnev, trying to keep Borodnev's attention focused on him.

"Comrade," Borodnev sullenly replied, advancing warily toward the desk. The girl maintained her silence, and Borodnev remained unaware of her presence.

Kerensky gestured for him to take the chair at the side of the desk.

"Tea?" Kerensky asked.

"You said this was important," Borodnev rudely replied. "If it's to be an afternoon social, I'll have to cancel some important business of the State." He sat squarely in the chair, heavy arms overflowing the armrests, fingers curled around the knobs, knees straight out, heels solidly planted on the carpet. He looked like a stone figure.

"A little courtesy, a little civility doesn't necessarily interfere with the business of the day, Georgi," Kerensky lightly taunted him.

"Horseshit! Let's get on with it."

"As you wish." Kerensky sat down and tilted back his chair. "Georgi, I'm going to send you to the Urals."

Borodnev looked as if he'd just swallowed a rancid herring. "The Urals. The security is good in the Urals. They are rock solid for the revolution. Why there?"

"Because I don't want you here."

Borodnev's knuckles went white around the ends of the armrests. He pressed himself back deeper into the chair, as if preparing to spring. "Why not Siberia? Do you think you can ship me into exile without a fight?"

"Ekaterinburg is not Irkutsk. You should be grateful. In my degenerately decent way I am offering you a way out."

"Nine hundred miles from Petrograd?" Borodnev was on his feet, fists on the desk, leaning menacingly toward Kerensky. "A way out of what? My precinct? The center? Power? A way out of your hair? Do you think I am a fool? I have six men, armed and ready, waiting for me in the corridor."

"I know, Georgi. They have already been disarmed and placed under arrest."

Borodnev wheeled toward the center door and roared, "Guards!" A fine aureola of spittle erupted from his mouth, forming a brief, glistening halo before dissipating in the slanting golden light of late afternoon.

The door burst open and two khaki-garbed soldiers armed with submachine guns stepped two paces into the room. Kerensky held up his hand in a pacific gesture. "It's all right. Comrade Borodnev was just rudely wakened from a kind of dream." Kerensky's soldiers turned and left, closing the door behind them. And then, facing as he was the rear of the room, Borodnev saw the girl, saw her, but at first didn't recognize her. He turned to Kerensky accusingly.

"Do you have her taking notes?"

"Look again," Kerensky suggested. The poor girl seemed to shrink in her chair. "You might recognize her. She looks *almost* as she did before you took her to your quarters. I am hoping for all our sakes that she will not be required to tell her story before a court of inquiry. I would prefer that no word got out about certain degenerate and disgusting acts on the part of a man responsible for maintaining the security of the Revolution. I would rather see you leave quietly than be dragged down in public disgrace, because your disgrace ultimately will be our disgrace."

Borodnev turned again to face Kerensky, breathing hard, fists clenched, head thrust forward. For a moment Kerensky thought that Borodnev might lunge at him. If he did, he might very well break

Kerensky's neck before the guards outside could come to his assistance. In that moment Kerensky considered shouting for help before it was too late. But he knew that if he did that, he would have lost, even though he'd won. Kerensky waited out the moment, holding Borodnev's eyes with his own. And then the moment passed, and Borodnev dropped back into his chair.

"Six guards will accompany you to your quarters, Georgi. The public, if they should see you, will think the guards are your own cortege. I will make the announcement of your new posting. You will leave tomorrow."

"Why are you doing this to me, Alex? Surely not for the sake of that slut?"

"I was getting a stiff neck, Georgi. Always having to look over my shoulder to make sure you weren't there waiting to stab me in the back."

"You're imagining things, Alex, that's not a good sign." Borodnev turned away from Kerensky and stared menacingly at the girl. "I should have killed her when I'd finished with her and fed her to the fish in the Neva."

"It wouldn't have been the first time, Georgi."

"This is my reward for my benevolence. I'll remember."

Kerensky's guards accompanied Borodnev from the room, and the poor girl went home, warmed with whatever comfort she might have taken from witnessing Borodnev's undoing. Kerensky stood alone in the Malachite Chamber, gazing out at the Neva and the Admiralty Spire through windows that had gone gray for want of washing, and wondered how long he could hold on before the Borodnevs brought him down and effaced his bright dream of a Russia governed like the great democracies of the West.

# CHAPTER TEN

They sat on a bench in St. James Park and tossed bread crumbs left over from lunch to the ducks in the pond, and kept their eyes on the sky. They might have been off in the Cotswolds instead of just a few hundred yards from Whitehall, these two young men. Except for their clothing. One wore banker's grey and a bowler hat, the other military drab, a walking stick leaning against the bench near his thigh: Heckart, the Prime Minister's man, and Aldonby. Former classmates, old school ties. There was no one else about on this bright first afternoon in August. The park had been deserted. Traffic had stopped. Pedestrians had fled into basement rooms and Underground stations. Except for an occasional helmeted warden blowing his whistle excitedly and herding stragglers into shelter, there was a dreamlike stillness everywhere.

Ten minutes earlier the siren had sounded and the streets had emptied like a basin full of flotsam and suds draining itself dry.

"Zeppelins, do you think?" Aldonby had asked as they crossed the park on the way back from lunch. The walking stick that he employed with considerable panache with his one good arm had become more vestigial than necessary.

"Zeppelins at two, cocktails at four, bloody way to fight a war," his companion droned. "Cheeky of them, don't you think, showing up in daylight like this."

"Maybe they've lost their way. Or maybe they thought they'd catch our lads napping. Let's see."

Aldonby's companion took off his bowler hat and, using it to shade his eyes, scanned the sky above the city. "I don't see anything. But maybe we'd better head for the shelter, anyway."

"Too nice a day for the shelter. There's a bench over there by the pond, and I've got a pocket full of crumbs for the ducks."

So they sat on the bench, heads thrown back like hungry sparrows, while they watched the sky and tossed crumbs to the ducks. And soon they saw it, a bloated, wallowing thing, floating ponderously across the southern horizon trailed by three or four dancing dots, which must be pursuit planes, darting toward the cumbersome creature and then away again, like dogs snapping at the heels of a sow.

"Do you think they'll make it?" Heckart casually asked, as if he were watching a soccer match instead of an orgy of steel and fire.

"Not without help," Aldonby replied.

"Then they won't make it. No escort plane can fly such a distance and return."

"I wasn't thinking of an aircraft; I was thinking of a boat. A fast boat. A torpedo boat."

The aerial battle was drifting closer now, and they could hear the intermittent sputtering of the Vickers guns, like bacon spattering on a grill in a faraway kitchen.

"A boat? What on earth are you talking about? I'm talking about that Hun up there. Oh! For God's sake, Charles, you've got to get your mind off those damned Russians. Oh! Look at that, will you. One of our lads has given up. He's flying away."

"Guns must be jammed. Or he's out of ammo."

"Well, the others had better make a hit soon or we'll have that fat Bosh sitting right on top of us."

"Shall we go?"

"Damn it, no! I want to see the end of this. Do you suppose our lads have been sabotaged?"

"What do you mean?"

"Their ammo belts filled with blanks or some such mischief. Happens more often than the public is aware ..."

"If only the P.M. hadn't been so stiff-necked about it," Aldonby bitterly declared.

"Oh, God, Charles! You're talking about those Russians again. Forget it. I did my best for you with the P.M., but he'd have none of it. You must remember he is a coal miner's son is our Lloyd George, and his constituency is labor and he is not at all interested in committing a British force to the rescue of a Russian autocrat."

"And his family, Alfred. And his family. The Tsar is not alone in his predicament."

Heckart shrugged. "They shared the good times; they'll have to share the bad."

"Nicholas may have been an autocrat, but he was not a tyrant. He deserves better than to suffer a tyrant's fate."

Heckart threw him a sidelong glance. "You've got it wrong, old boy; tyrants don't suffer at all. Everyone's too scared of them. It's the poor bastards who reign in the wake of tyrants: the relative humanists, the softies, if you will. Like Nicholas's father and now Nicholas, who get it in the neck. In a land that's been ruled by the whip for centuries, God help the man who for reasons of conscience, convenience, weakness, or whatever dares lay the whip down. You can bet the mob will pick it up and apply it with vigor to his back."

Aldonby sighed. "Then how is one ever to do the right thing?"

"I'll leave that to the philosophers. I'm just a humble civil servant. But maybe we could put it this way: tyrants once established doom their sons to be tyrants . . . or to be sacrificial goats."

There was a sudden, soundless conflagration in the opalescent summer sky.

"There she goes," Heckart commented, without excitement but with some satisfaction, as the German dirigible erupted in flame and began to come apart like a paper lantern that had been touched by a match. "And none too soon." The dirigible would have been over the city in five more minutes. "Do you suppose the Heinies have those parachute things?" Sound followed sight as a thump like the sound of a gas stove being lit reached their ears. "Well, show's over. Back to work." Heckart tossed the rest of his bread crumbs to the ducks and stood up. "Coming?"

"I'll stay a while longer, thank you. I have some thinking to do."

"Not about that crack-brained stratagem of yours, I hope."

"Not so crack-brained. If no torpedo boat were made available for a trip across the Gulf, we could go by land. A fast motorcade through Finland carrying enough specially trained troops to effect the rescue would take us to the very outskirts of Petersburg. Just a skip and a jump from there to Tsarskoe Selo. We'd have to get a man in there in advance of our arrival to alert the family to be ready to move. We pick them up and go out by the same route. Once we're over the border into Finland we're as good as home."

"What makes you think the Finns will let you through? Going or coming?"

"The Finns have no love for Russia; they're just about ready to make a declaration of their independence. What better way to underline it than to let us through?"

"The Finns have no love for the Romanovs either. It was the Romanovs, not the Reds, who kept them under thumb for centuries."

"It's possible they would let us through in exchange for our agreeing to recognize their independence."

"You're dreaming again, Charles. Remember the P.M. He wouldn't consider antagonizing the Reds." Heckart had been sky-gazing all the while he spoke. "Parachutes are supposed to let a man down easy from any height. But everything up there seems to be falling so slowly I can't separate the debris from the men."

"Thanks anyway for your help, Alfred."

"That's what friends are for. Now do me a favor and forget it. There's no use growing morose over what might have been."

"We'll see, Alfred."

"Be careful, Charles. You're still a soldier. There are penalties . . . Oh! Look at that, will you? Do you see it? Like a white brolly. I think that must be one of those parachutes."

"I might arrange to be demobilized."

"The P.M. would block it."

"On what grounds? The leg's healed, but the left arm is useless. It was only family influence that kept me from being demobbed in the first place."

"Be that as it may, you're in for the duration now. As long as you're in uniform, the P.M. can control your activities . . . and he knows what you're up to."

"There's a connection with the King."

"The King is powerless, Charles, which is why he is still a king. He can't authorize a military mission."

"No. But he could arrange a civilian leave for me. I would be on my own then."

"Charles, since you have a clearance in the matter, I will tell you something in the hope of ending forever these fruitless speculations. Your torpedo boat plan is no longer practicable, if ever it was. Nor is the overland trip . . . even if you could get the consent of the Finns. According to the latest intelligence from our Consul in Petersburg, the Romanovs are going to be moved. To a place called Tobolsk."

Aldonby looked dismayed. "How soon, Alfred?"

"Nobody knows for certain. It's just in the air."

"I don't know Tobolsk; I'll have to check the maps."

"Save yourself the time. Tobolsk is inland. Far, far inland."

"How far? Do you know exactly?"

"Not exactly. I'm told it's in Western Siberia. Oh! I say! Look at that parachute thing. It's caught fire."

Bits of flaming debris were drifting down from the sky like hot chimney ashes caught in an eddying wind. Heckart planted his bowler on his head, nodded to Aldonby, and walked away from the bench.

Aldonby sat there for some time longer. He would have to get hold of a good map of Western Siberia. If a fast boat was no longer practicable and if an overland run through Finland never had been, there must be some other way.

# CHAPTER ELEVEN

*From the journal of Anastasia Romanov*

I wonder where Professor Malenovsky is today? Surely he would have a fit if he saw the state of my handwriting at this moment. In the first place I cannot use pen and ink at all for fear the ink might wind up in my lap instead of on the paper. Letters that should be round come out square. Words are broken in the middle. The dot that should decorate an *i* appears over an *o* half a page away. And my pencil wiggles and wobbles across the paper as if it were in the hand of a victim of the palsy or of one who had too much wine, neither of which is the case. It is simply that we are on a train, a very bumpy train. Papa says it feels as if the tracks have not been tended in months. A shame, he says; this was once a scrupulously maintained line.

Papa is very sad these days—quietly sad. He does not speak to us of his sorrow, but it is written on his face, and there is no way that he can hide it. His eyes and his mouth droop at the corners so that, forgive me, he has acquired the look of a beagle. It is as if his features were melting. He tries to smile, to hide his sadness from us, but when he smiles it is worse, though we have not the heart to tell him so. When he smiles, he looks as if he is in pain. In the last week, when we were still at Tsarskoe Selo, he never went out at all—not to tend his garden, not to chop wood, not even simply to walk about the grounds as was his custom. The shouts of the mob at the gate were too distressing. He could hear them wherever he went, yelling insults, calling for retribution against us.

I think it is our plight, not his, that is destroying Papa. He blames

54

himself for what we are now forced to endure. He feels that had he ruled with a gentler hand things might have been different. But he doesn't know how he might have accomplished that. He gave up to the people certain prerogatives that no Tsar had ever relinquished. He feels that he moved too slowly . . . or that the world changed too fast. Mama feels that he did too much, gave up too much, cared too little for the responsibilities he was born to and forfeited them almost with relief. She is most outspoken on the subject, which is no help to his state of mind nor to our predicament. She thinks of herself as an empress still and demands of our guards and remaining retinue the respect due an empress. It only makes the guards meaner. An unhappy situation: Papa, until last week, what with gardening and woodchopping, pretending to be a peasant, and Mama pretending to be an empress, and neither of them being truly what they are pretending to be.

Last week I overheard them talking. "You should have been strong," she scolded. "You should have been Peter the Great, Ivan the Terrible. The people would have responded with love and respect. Russia loves to feel the whip. Now it is too late."

And he replied, forlorn. "You speak to me as if I were a child, your poor, little, weak-willed Nicky." And still there is great affection between them. They are like the right hand and the left hand of a single body. And they are, like my sisters and my brother and me, figures in limbo on a bumpy train, en route from a past that is no longer relevant to a future that is vague and uncertain.

And maybe that, too, is why my pencil would appear to be guided by a trembling hand. I am frightened. I dare not tell my brother and my sisters for each of them I am sure is enduring their portion of fear, and I don't want to add to their burden any more than they, it would appear, care to add to mine. But I can confide to these pages that I want to cry out, weep and scream like a lost or abandoned child.

Where are we going? What is this Tobolsk that they are sending us to? Away from Petersburg, away from the river and the sea. A thousand miles away. Beyond the Urals. Eastward into the fearful emptiness of Siberia. Why? And what will await us there?

Mr. Kerensky has told us he is doing it for our protection. I would like, ever so fervently, to believe him. But if he really wants to let us go, why doesn't he just put us on a boat and send us to England?

# CHAPTER TWELVE

The abrasive bark and cadence that constituted the litany of command drifted across the Horse Guards' yard through the partially opened window in the Prime Minister's study. There was a clatter of hoofbeats, then silence, then more commands.

Lloyd George turned away from the window in disgust. "The Twentieth Century!" he growled in his rolling burr. "The world in upheaval. And we play these games. Horse Guards! What use would they be, done up in all their finery, mounted like tin soldiers on all those aristocratic animals, if someone chose to set up a Vickers gun in the yard? Why do I tolerate it?"

Heckart remained respectfully silent. He knew the P.M.'s moods well enough to know that this question required no answer.

The Prime Minister threw himself into his chair and sat profile to Heckart, arm extended, impatiently drumming his fingers on his desk. Heckart waited. He sensed that the P.M.'s outrage was directed not so much at the Horse Guards as against all institutions and circumstances over which he could exercise no control. There were the usual several dozens of annoyances nipping at his equanimity today, and one of them was the case of Aldonby, certain disquieting information relative to his most recent activities having filtered down through military intelligence.

Another shouted command came drifting through the window, followed by another clatter of hoofs. The P.M. spat, scoring a bull's-eye from the sound of it, in the spittoon to the right of his desk.

"Why do we permit this nonsense, Heckart?"

This time Heckart knew a response was expected. "Because it pleases the people, I suppose."

Lloyd George hrumphed. "I suppose. Same as we support a whole bloody royal family—a sinful extravagance, if you ask me. But it amuses the people. Which brings me to this harebrained friend of yours."

"A classmate, sir."

"Aldonby. Is that his name?"

"Yes, Minister."

"You know he's gone to the King, don't you?"

"Yes, Minister. There is a family connection there; he chose to take advantage of it."

"*And* us, Heckart. And us."

"Yes, Minister."

"You made it absolutely clear to him that we would sanction no move that could be read as a move against the Provisional Government in Petersburg?"

"I did, sir."

"Then he has deliberately gone over our heads."

"I believe he only requested that the King have him restored to civilian status."

"So that we would have lost the control over him that we had while he was a soldier."

"I would guess that to be his motive, sir."

"And do you think that the King knew his motive?"

"I would guess that he did, sir, and that it worked in Aldonby's favor. There are family ties there, too, sir . . . between the King and the Tsar, as you know."

Another command rang out in the yard. Lloyd George went to the window and slammed it shut. "I'd rather stew in my own sweat than listen to any more of that nonsense out there. So, what can you do about it?"

"About what, sir?"

"Whatever this Aldonby is planning."

"We can't very well order him back into uniform, sir. In the first place he was severely wounded and by all rights should have been mustered out long before this. It was only through his family connection that he was kept in."

"And now it's his family connection that's letting him out." The Prime Minister swung around in his chair, faced Heckart squarely and glared at him with intimidating intensity. "A king, whose only proper function is to stand on a balcony and let the populace bask in the warmth of his presence, who has no real power beyond that, has deliberately turned loose an adventurer whose designs are contrary to the best interests of this government and its allies."

"On the other hand, sir, history would reproach us were it known that we forcibly restrained a man from attempting at his own risk what could be considered a purely humane mission."

"What do you propose we do, Heckart?"

"Well, there is no guarantee he'll ever get his project off the ground. But, should he . . . maybe there's a way that we ourselves can keep hands off and let someone else bear the burden of frustrating his efforts."

"Within the law?" the P.M. asked guardedly.

Heckart neatly sidestepped the question, as he suspected the P.M. hoped he would. "As I see it, we would be saving Aldonby from himself as well as guarding against an embarrassment to His Majesty's government."

The Prime Minister nodded.

"Shall I try to develop it for you now or would you rather have a memo?"

"Not now. And certainly not in a memo. When you have it fully developed, we'll discuss it." The Prime Minister dismissed Heckart and then went to open the window again; the nuisance in the yard had ended.

# CHAPTER THIRTEEN

*From the journal of Anastasia Romanov*

IN TRANSIT
AUGUST 6, 1917

We have been on the train for four days; it seems endless. Colonel Kobylinsky apologizes. He informs us that we should have been in Tobolsk by now. But we are not anywhere. We are waiting in a siding near the village of Kez for a new trainman to drive our engine. The one we had and his fireman deserted last night. Thank God it is still summer or we might all be frozen to death. We have been subject to desertions and sabotage all along the way (and these were from people in whom Mr. Kerensky felt he could place his trust). It would seem that the populace blame us for everything: for the sins of my forebears, dead these hundreds of years, whose abuses were committed not against the individuals who threaten us but against *their* forebears also dead for centuries. And for present hardships: the bread shortages and the continuing casualties at the front against the German armies. But we are powerless and have been for over six months now. How can we be responsible if conditions of life are worse now than they were before Papa laid down his burden?

We are truly helpless now. Our lives depend on Colonel Kobylinsky. And his position is precarious. In the new order of things an officer is not appointed by a higher authority but is elected by the soldiers he will command. Not so bad, one might think. Having elected him they will certainly respect and obey him. Not so. For they elect him to a term of no specific length, and they may strip him of his elected authority at any moment of the day or night. So . . . for *our* sakes, if not for his own, Colonel Kobylinsky must walk a very thin line. Let the deserters desert,

59

for they are potential mutineers, and we are safer with them gone.

So, we wait on a siding, praying for a train crew to come and drive us deeper into exile, because the longer we remain here, immobile, the greater is the danger that the local populace will have time to organize a force against us. And Colonel Kobylinsky is afraid that, should the locals have the audacity to attack, many of his men would join them rather than shoot at those whom they consider to be their brothers.

# CHAPTER FOURTEEN

I n his office in the Russian Embassy in London, Ambassador Josef
Zorbitov sucked on a long, cardboard-tipped cigarette and impatiently waited for a decent interval to pass. In his bowels he could feel
a kind of agitation that invariably signaled the onset of a session of
agonized creative reflection. At last, he flicked the switch on the intercom that connected him with his secretary.

"Has Mr. Heckart left the building?"

"Yes, Comrade Ambassador. Would you like me to see if we can call
him back from the street?"

"No. I just wanted to be sure that he had left; I don't want him
popping back in; I have some thinking to do." He mashed out the
cigarette in a large lead crystal ashtray. "I shall be unavailable for a little
while."

"Yes, Comrade Ambassador." A certain puritan restraint demanded
that the reason for his unavailability remain unmentioned but, of
course, she knew what it would be.

Zorbitov opened the top right-hand drawer of his desk, fished impatiently among the pencils and pens there, pricked his thumb on one of
the pushpins he used for marking his maps, cursed, and sucked noisily
on the wounded finger. He thrust his other hand into the drawer more
carefully, probed, and came up with the item he had been searching
for: a key.

He was aware that certain purists would frown upon this heretical
manifestation of bourgeois vanity. But he coveted the key to the w.c.,
which he regarded as his personal and private sanctuary. While he
controlled the key, he controlled access to the w.c., the use of which he
denied to his fellow comrades. Nobody had complained out loud—yet.
But he was aware that he was risking the stigma attached to elitism. He

wondered if Kerensky himself dared indulge in the luxury of maintaining a private w.c. No matter. Kerensky was in Russia and he, Zorbitov, was in England. And in England such things were possible. Besides which, he used his w.c. as a kind of retreat, necessary to the efficacious performance of his work—a place for constructive reflection, a place where there were no intrusions to distract or disturb him. He did some of his finest thinking in the service of his government in his w.c. They could not fault him for that.

He left his office and went quickly down the corridor, prodded in his haste by the rumbling in his gut. Ah! This really was a moment of portent.

He locked the door behind him, dropped his trousers and, lowering himself onto the seat, assumed the attitude of Rodin's "Thinker."

If what the Englishman, Heckart, had told him was the truth, he had been presented with intelligence of the highest value. And it had been offered to him as a gift. No drain on the petty cash. A young soldier, or former soldier, English by birth but with a mother who was Russian by birth and with family ties to both the Romanovs and the newly named Windsors, was planning an adventure with the object of removing the deposed Tsar Nicholas and his family from Russian custody to a haven in Western Europe or Britain. In other words, concluded Zorbitov, reducing it to the essentials—steal the Tsar right out from under our noses!

But why, Zorbitov wondered, would this Englishman, Heckart, come to him with such news? Why would he betray one of his countrymen who was engaged in an enterprise that much of the world might laud as humanitarian in the highest?

Could it be that, as Heckart claimed, the humanitarian move conceived by this Aldonby was indeed contrary to the policy and interests of His Majesty's government? Hard to believe, since His Majesty was a kinsman of Nicholas. Or, could it be that Heckart had come to him with a mouthful of misinformation. And if, indeed, it was misinformation, to what end had it been dripped like poison into his ear?

Zorbitov leaned toward the conclusion that Heckart's intelligence was false. By all the instincts of his peasant upbringing there was a smell of simmering dung about Heckart's story. And then, with a thunderous voiding of his bowel, the veil of suspicion lifted and Zorbitov saw with blinding clarity Heckart's mendacity for what it was. Had there been any truth at all in Heckart's story it would not have come free. Nobody gives away gratis information as valuable as gold. Heckart had placed no value on it in pounds or rubles because it had no value: it was made up, a phantom, a malicious prank. But could it be that simple? Of course not. Nothing was ever what it seemed to be.

Zorbitov felt a spasm in his abdomen. Why would Heckart play a prank on him? To embarrass him? It made no sense. Why would Heckart want to embarrass *him*? They weren't friends; they weren't even enemies. One does not bother to embarrass a mere acquaintance: there's no satisfaction in it. If only Heckart had asked for cash, a favor—anything in exchange for his information—Zorbitov would not be foundering now in a miasma of doubt. But this! This was truly baffling.

His impulse was to consign Heckart's entire visit to the wastebasket, but his survivor's instinct informed him to hedge his bet. He would put a memo in the next day's diplomatic pouch to the effect that he had chanced upon unconfirmed intelligence alleging the existence of a plot to remove the former Tsar and his family from the jurisdiction of the Provisional Government. He would make special note in the memo of the unsubstantiated nature of the intelligence and add that it had come to him under highly suspect circumstances. He would advise them that he intended to investigate further. He would be covered, and the next move, if any, would be up to Petersburg.

Damned English toilet paper; good for nothing but lining hatboxes. He reached up and pulled the chain. The overhead tank emptied and flushed his troubles away with a satisfying roar.

# CHAPTER FIFTEEN

The two men faced each other across a neatly laid table in a waterfront tavern. Freshly laundered curtains and small, neatly set panes of glass insulated them from the penetrating chill of the autumn rain that pelted the homeward-bound workers. The tidy little establishment, almost feminine in character, was nothing like the waterside pubs Aldonby had known at home. But, then, Oslo itself had been a surprise—more like a charming little river town than the capital of a nation.

The man opposite him, thirtyish, massive and red-faced, nearly bursting the confines of his white roll-neck sweater, seemed out of place in this polite room. But it was he, Lars Dahlgren, who brought Aldonby to The Circe and who was greeted as if he were a well-loved member of the family by a proprietor who was almost Dahlgren's size. The other customers, too, seemed to be ill-matched to the genteel setting; a redolence of fish and fog banks emanated from the woolens and tweeds all around. And the women who moved among them were whores.

Dahlgren was as much a man of the sea as the rest of the company, but he was no simple fisherman. He was an entrepreneur of some reputation. And he was treating Aldonby's proposal with good-natured condescension.

"It is plain to me," Dahlgren declared, "that you have never spent a winter in Russia."

"No. But summers I have."

Dahlgren cut a wedge off the cheese that lay temptingly in the center of the table, balancing his portion on the blade of his knife as he transferred it to his plate. "Summer and winter in Russia are two different worlds. You say your mother was Russian?"

Aldonby nodded. He had come a considerable distance at no small risk to speak to this man, and he had the feeling that he was being treated as a child.

"Didn't you ever wonder why she never sent you to visit in the winter? Entire armies have been swallowed up by the Russian winter, and you want to know the most feasible route *inland* from Archangel? Aside from the railroad, which has become hopelessly unreliable since the Reds took over, there is no feasible route. I can use the railroads in their current state to illustrate for you what the Russian winter is like. Early last March I was in Petersburg. Absolute chaos. The few trains that ran took an eternity to get anywhere. They were so overloaded with human cargo that some passengers had to ride clinging to the steps of the cars. God help them; they froze there. You would see these decrepit trains struggling into the stations, wheezing like asthmatics, with passengers clinging to the sides of the cars like clusters of winter-berries. And you are proposing a venture by motorcar from Archangel across western plains open to the wind, through mountain passes in the Urals, fourteen hundred miles inland to Tobolsk, and then back again? Never mind the hardships, where would you get the petrol?"

"We could carry our own supply?"

"And suppose the supply lorry broke down? Suppose any of your motorcars broke down? How would you make repairs in a land where engine oil turns to gelatin?" He cut the block of cheese in half, picked up his half in his fingers and began to devour it.

"You've traded there most of your life. What do you do?"

"I do my business in the summer, there being very little spring and autumn. And in the winter I sit here and eat and drink and in other ways enjoy the fruits of my labors." He cast a glance in the direction of one of the whores. "I've done a fair amont of trading with Tobolsk too. Lumber. Very good lumber. But the only way to get there is by the waterways. I wouldn't venture to make the trip overland with any kind of heavy cargo." Lars Dahlgren poked a stubby thumb and forefinger into a pocket and drew out a fat soft-leaded pencil. He reflected for a moment while he fed the remainder of his portion of cheese into his mouth and washed it down with half of a stein of beer. Then he moved his dish and the stein aside so that there was a clear place on the table in front of him. He licked the tip of his pencil and then began to draw on the tablecloth.

"This is Archangel, here on the left, where you want to leave from." He made a little circle. "By the way, why Archangel?"

"We have a military installation there."

Dahlgren shrugged and again applied his pencil to the tablecloth. "And here on the right..." some distance away he drew another, smaller circle, "Tobolsk. Some fourteen hundred miles away. And in between..." he made an oblong **X** "... land, too much land. A wilderness, mostly. It will swallow you up. Stay out of it.

"But here..." he inscribed an arc "... across the top of Russia, water." He said it with the appreciation of a thirsty man who had just discovered drink. "You leave by sea from Archangel." He held up a cautionary finger. "But before winter sets in ... or after the thaw." He laid his pencil on the cloth and slowly began to draw a line, running almost parallel to the arc he had peviously drawn. "Across the Barents Sea. It's big and wide and thinly patrolled; the Red Navy is barely functioning; there is very little chance that you would be spotted.

"The Barents Sea gives onto the Pechora Sea as you move eastward. And still, smooth sailing. But now ..." He drew a representation of a knob of land, separated by a narrow strait of water from a long, northward-pointing finger of an island. "In the southeast corner of the Pechora Sea you will face potential difficulties." He labeled the knob of land *Yagorskiy Peninsula*. He labeled the long, finger-shaped island *Novaya Zemlya*. "New Land," he translated, "hundreds of miles long." Now he tapped his pencil point on the narrow stretch of water that separated the *Yagorskiy Peninsula* from Novaya Zemlya. "The Kara Strait. This is easy to guard. Here there might be patrol boats or shore patrols." He cast a wary glance in Aldonby's direction.

"Is it likely that they would expend manpower and matériel to stand guard on a wilderness?" Aldonby asked.

"Suppose they had reason to suspect that someone was coming? Who knows what is likely or unlikely anymore? It is unlikely that this miserable war should have lasted three years already. But, likely or unlikely, it doesn't matter; the Kara Strait is your only way into the Kara Sea. And the Kara Sea gives access to the peninsula that will take you to Tobolsk."

Aldonby studied the diagram on the tablecloth. "Could we avoid the strait? Go due north, parallel to the coast of this Novaya Zemlya, around the northern tip of the finger, and then down into the Kara Sea?"

"You might never come down. You would be above the Arctic Circle in a sea of ice. In the winter absolutely impassable. Even in the summer you could be trapped in the ice packs."

Aldonby grunted. "So we go by way of the strait into the Kara Sea.

And pray that the Comrades have no reason to suspect that anyone is coming."

"If you are able to get through the strait without being seen, you should have smooth sailing across the Kara into Darata Bay on the western shore of the Yamal Peninsula."

"And if we are spotted in the strait?"

"It would depend on how fast and how well-armed you are, and upon what they have to throw against you. It is possible you wouldn't make it into the Kara Sea at all."

Aldonby nodded. "Let's say we reach the Yamal Peninsula."

"You go inland by boat on the Yerkuta River as far as you can. Correction; not quite as far as you can. You could navigate on the Yerkuta maybe thirty miles inland, as far as the village of Yarongo." He made a little dot on the diagram of the land area that represented the Yamal Peninsula, looked up to make sure that Aldonby was following him, and noticed that Aldonby was dividing his attention between the diagram and the waitress, who was standing halfway across the room. She had a look of alarmed concern on her face. Dahlgren glanced around and confided to Aldonby. "She's new here. She hardly knows me. She's worried about the tablecloth." He turned to the waitress and called out jovially, "It's all right, my love. We'll buy the cloth."

Flustered, she turned to the imposing presence behind the bar. To her astonishment, he was grinning.

"Tell her it's all right, Arnie, and put it on the tab," Lars Dahlgren called out cheerfully.

"It's already on the tab," the barman laughed.

"So, where were we?" Dahlgren asked, trying to find his place.

"Navigating the river as far as the village of Yarongo," Aldonby said, laying his forefinger on the appropriate pencil mark.

"Correction," said Dahlgren. "You *could* navigate as far as Yarongo, but you don't want to. You want to moor maybe ten miles west of the village, camouflage the boat as best you can, and then set out on foot."

"For Yarongo? Why not just sail in?"

"They'd be talking about it all up and down the whole peninsula. The word might get to Tobolsk before you did. The Yamal is isolated, but word of mouth travels fast. And south of Tobolsk, in Tyumen, there is a telegraph: the line runs all the way to Petersburg."

Dahlgren began shoving plates and steins into a corner of the table. He looked up and shouted to the barman. "Arnie, we need more room. And more beer. I can't see to think for the mess here."

The waitress came running and cleared the table. Dahlgren lit a small black cigar while he waited for the fresh beer.

"I think," said Aldonby, "that if we're going to hike across the peninsula—by the way, how wide is it?"

"Over a hundred miles."

"As long as we're going to have to go overland part of the way, I'd prefer to go overland all the way. I'd rather moor the boat in good shelter in the bay than go fifteen or twenty miles up the river."

"They're your feet," Dahlgren shrugged.

"They can take a little extra wear and tear."

"It will depend on the time of year how much a little extra wear and tear means. In the summer, blisters. In the spring your boots could be sucked right off by the mud."

"No matter. I don't want to moor the boat upriver; it would make it too damned easy for someone to cut us off. The boat is our way home."

Dahlgren nodded thoughtfully, appreciatively. "Very well. You moor the boat in Darata Bay. I know a perfect place; when we get the charts, I'll mark it precisely."

"What kind of terrain will we be dealing with once we get out of the boat?" Aldonby asked.

"Lowlands mostly. Plains. Low hills here and there. But no high ground of any consequence. Nothing that could be called mountains. An undulating land, not at all difficult to traverse, provided you survive the flies and mosquitoes in summer. The vegetation is mostly moss and lichen. Some pine forests. Nothing impassable."

"What about winter?"

"Ah! Winter is winter everywhere in that nation, except in the south. The peninsula isn't as cold as the main part of Western Siberia because you've got the sea on two sides and as cold as the water is it's a little warmer than the land, and it's never farther from you than sixty or seventy miles."

"How cold is it?"

"On the peninsula? Maybe twenty below zero, Fahrenheit."

Aldonby winced.

"And that's without the winds. The winds can cut you in two. In winter you could find yourself pissing icicles. But surely you don't intend to try this thing in the winter."

"This summer's almost gone."

"*Here* it is almost gone. I can assure you, in that part of the world it is *all* gone."

"Then it would mean waiting till spring?"

"April, at least. May, ideally. In May, once you get across the eastern shore of the peninsula, you could drift down the River Ob all the way to Tobolsk. There's a good deal of traffic on the river once the ice breaks up. In a small local boat or barge nobody would even notice you."

"What about April?" Aldonby asked.

"You are impatient. Nature doesn't deal kindly with impatience; not out there."

"What about April?" Aldonby repeated.

Lars Dahlgren shrugged. "The land is passable. The high winds begin to abate. Temperatures are somewhere below freezing, but at least above zero . . . depending on what time of day it is."

"The river?"

"Early in April, frozen solid. Late in April, thawing out."

"Damn!" Aldonby slammed his fist down on the table. The beer steins jumped and foamed over their lips. He was ready to move. To begin recruiting. Expatriate Russians, preferably. But, according to Dahlgren, the time to move had already passed, for this year, at least. As long as Kerensky held power, the family was probably safe. But Kerensky's regime was growing shakier every day. Military Intelligence didn't give him another six months of control. If Kerensky fell, would his successor be as inclined as he to guarantee the safety of the Romanovs? Did Kerensky have until spring? Did the Romanovs?

"Suppose the river is frozen?" Aldonby asked Dahlgren. "How would one get from the mouth of the Ob to Tobolsk?"

"The same way one got across the peninsula—on foot. Maybe on skis."

"How long would it take?"

"Probably forever. The chances are ten to one against your making it. From the mouth of the Ob south to Tobolsk it is hundreds of miles. Do you think you could go that distance with a party of men, on foot, or on skis in the worst part of winter? Do you think you could muster a group of men who could do it? Eskimos in winter spend most of their time under shelter; you would be exposed most of the time. And then, if by some miracle you got to Tobolsk, do you think you would be doing these royal hostages a service by taking them from the shelter of a house on a trek hundreds of miles northward in that brutal weather? And probably under pursuit? You would save the Comrades a job. *You* would be the Romanovs' executioner."

"There is no railroad line from the peninsula down to Tobolsk?" Aldonby asked.

Dahlgren laughed derisively. "Oh! You dreamer! There is no rail-

road line from Tobolsk to *anywhere*. It is a backwater. Except for the
river it would be totally cut off from the world."

"What about a sleigh?"

"What about a sleigh?" Dahlgren downed his beer and signaled for
more.

"What's the name of the town in the north, at the mouth of the Ob?"

"Khadyta."

"In Khadyta . . ." Aldonby asked intensely " . . . are there sleighs in
Khadyta?"

"Of course, there are sleighs in Khadyta. How do you think the
people get around? But not for hundreds of miles in winter."

"Could we buy sleighs in Khadyta?"

"If not in Khadyta, then in Yada. Of course!"

"And there are horses?"

"Yes, there are horses. Who else would pull the sleighs?"

"Then couldn't we outfit ourselves with sleighs and horses in
Khadyta or Yada? Wouldn't that make the run down to Tobolsk
possible?"

"I said it before; I say it again. You are a dreamer."

"Why?"

"Because. There are no roads from the north to Tobolsk. The river,
as I told you, is the only connection between Tobolsk and the north.
You cannot run these horses through snow over unknown terrain.
They will break their ankles and you will be left to pull the sled. Not
good at all." Dahlgren lifted his beer. "Drink up, my friend. Take your
example from the great Russian bear; he knows what winter is: a time
to store up energy and to sleep. In the spring everything will begin to
move again. And then, so can you, if you wish. There is enough risk
already in this enterprise of yours without attempting to beat the
Russian winter." Dahlgren downed his beer, wiped his lips with the
back of his hand, and belched loudly and with great satisfaction.
"Come, my boy. We have eaten and drunk. It's time to be merry. I'll
find us some girls." He swept the room with his eyes, but the whores
had already been engaged. He pushed the beer steins into a corner of
the table and began rolling up the cloth. "No use leaving this here as
long as we're paying for it anyway. Who knows what big eyes might be
working in the laundry, eh?"

Aldonby put a restraining hand on Lars Dahlgren's arm. "What
about the river?"

Dahlgren looked puzzled. He wondered if the young man across the
table from him had defective powers of retention. "The river? I told

you about the river. The river is frozen solid until late in April. Nothing moves on the river until spring."

"Exactly!" Aldonby cried out triumphantly. "But a sleigh could move on it. Couldn't it? In November. Before the blizzards come. Before winter really sets in. The horses wouldn't break their ankles there. It would be as smooth as a highway."

Dahlgren stared at Aldonby in amazement: Aldonby was right, of course. The river, when frozen, could be used as a road running straight to Tobolsk.

# CHAPTER SIXTEEN

*From the journal of Anastasia Romanov*

The house they have assigned us is no palace, but it is large enough. A comfortable bourgeois house. And that is fitting, for we are bourgeoisie now—if we are anything. The house stands on a street called Liberty Street, which was called Nobility Street before the revolution. And that, too, is fitting, if ironic; like the street, we are former nobility, and on this Liberty Street our freedom is most narrowly restricted.

There is no great park for us here as there was at Tsarskoe Selo, no forests, no ponds, no friendly deer. There are all of these things, I am sure, in the surrounding countryside. But none of it is for us. There is a yard with a fence around it and one or two trees for Papa to cut and saw into firewood. But when they are gone—what? "A wretched vegetable patch" is what Papa calls our yard in one of his rare outbursts of bitterness. Otherwise he continues to be passive, cuts what wood there is to cut, and plays the role of handyman. He put up a swing in the yard for Alexei to play on and upset mother most fearfully with this bit of handiwork. "What if Alexei should fall . . . and bleed?"

Mother still believes that Alexei will fulfill his destiny: that he will be Tsar one day—if we can but protect his fragile body from harm. She has never given up hope of escape and begs us to be prepared, though there is no evidence whatsoever that any of her couriers reached his destination.

On her command, for she is still very much the Empress in the circle of her family, we spend hours each night sewing items of value into the hems of our clothing: jewelry, gold, coins, so that when the time

72

comes, as she fervently believes it will, we can carry our fortunes on our backs as we flee toward freedom. And so we will have enough, when the time comes, to finance our return and place Alexei on the throne. This is mother's dream.

As for Papa, he takes photographs with his camera when he isn't chopping wood. Pictures of the house, the rooms, when enough light comes in through the windows: pictures of Alexei on his swing and playing with a toy bow and arrow that Papa cut for him from a birch branch: pictures of Mama in her chair (she spends a good deal of time in that chair, not so much because she is playing the Queen as because her health is failing. And I wonder, should her dream of rescue come true, could she survive the hardships of such an effort?). And Papa has taken photographs of Olga and Marie and Tatiana and me standing in the yard, sitting on the porch steps. Pretty pictures. Pretty girls. Doing nothing. Waiting. There is a vacancy about our look, the look of those who have lost their purpose.

So maybe Mama is right. Maybe our only hope is to hope for escape. And if we fail to escape maybe all that will be left of us will be these wistful, vacant images on photographic paper and closets of clothing worth their weight in gold.

TOBOLSK
SEPTEMBER 14, 1917

Papa looked out the sitting-room window this afternoon and gave a joyful shout. Startled, we all rushed to his side and saw, waving from the street, Baron Bode, big as a stallion, mustached like a walrus, trumpeting his greeting like a friendly elephant. (Oh! Good Baron Bode, forgive me for comparing your splendid person to all the animals of God's creation.) In the street behind him stood a cart loaded with all manner of nice things. Silverware, books, clothing, wine— some of the treasure that had been left behind in Tsarskoe Selo. He called for two of the sentries to unload the cart and bring the contents into the house. And they did.

And the Baron is only the latest—though surely the grandest—of the arrivals of the past few weeks. Old servants and courtiers, ladies-in-waiting, secretaries, physicians, cooks—all former members of the household and their families from Petersburg and Tsarskoe Selo have made their way on their own by the dozen to Tobolsk. With each new arrival Mama and Papa's spirits have lifted. And my sisters' spirits too.

And mine. And Alexei's. And I begin to think that no small part of the gloom that weighed us down and caused the vacancy in our eyes in those photographs that Papa took had to do with the feeling that we were universally despised . . . that we must have been monsters indeed to have inspired such hatred and disgust in others. But the new arrivals belie this. Those who knew us did love us and must have loved us dearly to have undertaken individually and on their own this arduous journey to be at our side. It is almost as if we are a family again. And we have reason to hope.

TOBOLSK
SEPTEMBER 17, 1917

Well, the picture is not so absolutely rosy as I had thought. Among the things that dear Baron Bode brought were four cases of Papa's favorite wine. A Comrade Nikolski, a local official of the Provisional Government and a gentleman hostile to our family, as most residents of the town are not, heard about the wine and declared that such a luxury on our tables was not to be tolerated and sent a squad of reservists to demand of Colonel Kobylinsky that we give it up.

The good Colonel was embarrassed and dismayed . . . and was forced to consent. He explained to Papa that to resist this demand might give Nikolski a basis for stirring the locals against us. And how important were four cases of wine anyway?

So, while Papa impotently watched and while Mama ranted upstairs in her bedroom, the wine was carted away and, we were told, poured into the river. It would not have been quite so bad if only *somebody* had drunk it.

SEPTEMBER 20, 1917

This is my day to shout for joy. Leonid is in Tobolsk. He arrived this morning to rejoin his detachment and stood before our window and hoped that I would see him. And I did. And I dared not tell Mama or Papa why I spent the morning running aimlessly about the house, and giggling to myself, and going out into the yard, and turning right around and coming back in.

Finally I told Marie, who jumped up and down like a child and joyfully embraced me. And that settled me down. I think I needed to be hugged. I needed to share my happiness.

But that was not the end of it. Because Marie told Olga and swore her to secrecy. And she came in and hugged me. And then she must have told Tatiana. Because she hugged me too. Thank goodness Tatiana told no one else. Because I don't think I would have got a hug from Mama or Papa if the word had reached them. So it is a secret, just between the girls. And between Leonid and me. Though I have not yet spoken to him. But that will come.

For now, it sufficiently lifts my spirits just to know that he has kept his word.

# CHAPTER SEVENTEEN

K erensky had the look of a whipped dog. He sat slumped at his desk, head down between his shoulders, hands on top of his head as if shielding it from blows. He had been up all night, pleading with the Duma for the special powers he would need to quell the Bolshevik uprising. The Duma had debated until dawn. And in the end Kerensky came away empty-handed. If extraordinary powers was given, even temporarily, they had decided, who will have the strength to take them back?

Kerensky reached out and irritably tore the top page off his desk calendar, crumpled it, and threw it away. November sixth was gone, lost, wasted in fruitless pleading. It was fourteen hours into November seventh now. And as days go, it looked even less promising than yesterday.

From the Duma he had returned to his office and ordered that the bridges that spanned the Neva be raised, cutting the city into sections. He had hoped by that measure to halt, at least temporarily, the Bolshevik momentum. Throughout the day he had been working, doing what he could with the limited powers he possessed. But it was like standing in the way of a stampede.

If only he could break up their leadership, there might be hope; but they were like phantoms, forever on the move, issuing orders and edicts from this hiding place or that. Lenin had gone underground in July and had not surfaced since then. How could one defeat such people? They would not stand and fight.

Wearily Kerensky rolled his red-rimmed eyes up until they settled on his aide Pietor Grodin.

Rabbit-eyed, Grodin thought: the rims all red and the whites all pink.

Too tired even to bother to put his glasses on and see me properly. "You look terrible," Grodin said.

"So the midwife remarked on the day that I was born."

"You should go home and go to bed."

"And who can guarantee that I would make it through the streets? Who is the government in this city today? Who is the law?"

"Lenin made an appearance today."

"Ah!" said Kerensky. "Is that my answer?" With some effort he managed to sit erect in his chair. "So the rat has come out of his hole."

"He showed up at a meeting of the Petersburg Soviet and announced the beginning of a new era."

Kerensky smiled bitterly. "How long ago was it that we made an almost identical announcement? Eight months?" He sighed. "Eras are growing more and more transient these days."

He levered himself out of his chair and moved stiffly to the window. "Shall we order his arrest? Would there be anyone to carry out the order?"

"It would be treacherous. The soldier who received the command might turn on the officer who gave it."

Kerensky stood gazing out over the wintery city. "Something of a monster we've created here, eh?"

"Lenin?"

"The whole thing."

"He has promised them he'll sue for peace with Germany, give the land to the peasants, the factories to the workers, and the stocks of food being hoarded by the wealthy to the poor."

Kerensky shrugged. "The usual promises. Easier said than done. God knows, I wish there were hidden stocks of food. *I* could feed the hungry." He noticed the file folders that Grodin was carrying. "What have you got there?" he asked.

"Reports. All manner of discouraging reports." Grodin opened one of the folders. "The Bolsheviks have taken control of the telegraph offices and the telephone center."

Kerensky stiffened. "I ordered the bridges raised."

Grodin shook his head remorsefully. "Somebody didn't listen. Somebody closed them."

"I should have ordered them blown."

"Would they have carried it out?" Grodin shrugged helplessly.

"Any more good news?"

"More government offices have been occupied. Almost all of them . . . except the Winter Palace."

"God help us. This is how Nicholas Romanov must have felt last March when he pushed all the familiar buttons—and received no response."

"Since you speak of Romanov, there's a memo in one of these files from London. The Ambassador sent it via the diplomatic pouch. It came through just before everything was cut off." Grodin found the folder and opened it. "He claims to have got wind of an effort to, in his words, 'steal the Romanovs out from under our noses.' "

Kerensky stared in disbelief at Grodin. But only for a moment. And then he began to laugh—too loud, too hard, the news didn't warrant such a reaction. Grodin looked concerned. Kerensky caught the look and checked himself.

"The Romanovs may not be the only ones in need of rescue," he said. "Get me a car. Is it still possible to get a car?"

"Of course." Grodin blanched.

"And a recent report on road conditions to the Western Front."

"We're running?"

"Running? No! We're fighting."

"To some observers it might not look that way."

"To hell with some observers. What we need here are a few regiments of cossacks to put these bandits in their place. And I can't just tap out a message on the telegraph to General Krasnov asking for support. Or have you forgotten what you just told me: the bandits own the telegraph."

Grodin left the file folders on Kerensky's desk and moved quickly toward the door. "I'll see if I can find a recent report on road conditions."

"And a car."

"Of course."

"And don't use the telephone for any of this business; the bandits might be listening."

# CHAPTER EIGHTEEN

*From the journal of Anastasia Romanov*

This afternoon Colonel Kobylinsky asked us all to join him in the sitting room. There was a look on his face as if someone had died.

He is usually a friendly and loquacious man. Today he seemed withdrawn and ill at east. He fidgeted and paced restlessly until we had all gathered. He must have been grinding his teeth, too, because his mustache kept twitching. His discomfort was contagious and soon we were all filled with the direst apprehension.

At last the Colonel cleared his throat and solemnly announced: "It is my duty to inform you that the Provisional Government under whose orders we have all been functioning these past eight months has fallen."

Alexei let out a cheer. Papa remonstrated with him for his rudeness. To my embarrassment I, too, was clapping my hands. We thought, you see, Alexei and I, that a group loyal to our family must have regained control in Petersburg and that it would not be long before we would be on our way home. And in that instant of misguided hope, for the length of those four or five hand claps, I envisioned Papa surrounded once again by the splendor of the court, giving a special decoration to Colonel Kobylinsky for his courtesy to us and, at my special request, a decoration to Leonid, too, and a special appointment for him to enter the officers' school.

They were like a fairy tale, those few moments, before we learned the truth.

There were no friends of the family in the seat of power. Men whom

79

Colonel Kobylinsky called Bolsheviks had taken charge. They were far more radical than Mr. Kerensky and far less kindly disposed toward us than he had been.

Colonel Kobylinsky told us that it was fortunate that we were here in Tobolsk and not in Petersburg in this wild and tumultuous time. He said that he thought we would be safe under the new regime as long as we remained far removed from the great centers of population.

How horrid to think that we are so despised that, like some loathsome bacillus, we must be kept at a distance or be destroyed.

Colonel Kobylinsky says that the new government, which calls itself The Soviet, will try to sue for peace with Germany and for that reason will dare not harm us. Because Mama is a cousin of the Kaiser and therefore we, too, are related to him and this Ulyanov or Lenin, or whatever, would not want to antagonize the Kaiser by harming us. He might even want to use us, this Lenin, for bargaining: to exchange us in return for a more generous peace treaty than the Kaiser might otherwise agree to.

He assured us that for as long as he, Kobylinsky, was in charge no harm would come to us.

Later in the afternoon I was standing alone in the little yard in my overcoat with the fur collar up and my hands deep in my pockets against the cold. Great flakes of snow had begun to fall. The world beyond our house and our yard had disappeared from view, vanished into ghostly whiteness.

Leonid was on duty on the other side of the fence, and we stood close together, with the wooden slats between us, talking through the spaces between the boards. I told him everything that the Colonel had told us and, with my cheek close to the fence where I knew that his cheek would be pressed on the other side, I began to cry. He took off his mittens and worked his fingers through the space between the boards, trying to take my hand to comfort me. But we could only just touch the tips of our fingers. We stood that way, silently touching, until our hands began to grow numb.

# CHAPTER NINETEEN

The dust had barely settled on the ruins of the Kerensky regime when Borodnev was back in Petrograd in control of his former precincts. He was not one to let a political vacuum go unfilled or old insults go unanswered. So it was his source of deepest frustration that Kerensky was beyond his reach, for the time being anyway.

He had slipped away in a stolen motorcar—while his cossacks were being cut to pieces by Trotsky and the Red Guard at Gatchina—to fight another day, he had declared as he fled. According to the best intelligence available, which granted was not very good and which was a problem that Borodnev would have to attend to now that he was reinstalled at the Peter and Paul Fortress, Kerensky was already across the border. He had probably got out through the Crimea, that open sewer through which the flotsam of monarchists, Mensheviks, weak-kneed right-wing socialists, kulaks, and bald-faced traitors flushed themselves clear of the people's retribution and into the flaccid embrace of decadent western Europe.

So maybe Kerensky had escaped temporarily. But Borodnev's memory was long and so was the arm of the revolution. There would come a day, if Borodnev had his way, when no traitor could lay his head down peacefully to sleep anywhere in the world.

Borodnev shut the file folder that had lain open on his desk; he already knew its contents by heart as well as the contents of all the files that Kerensky, in his haste, had left behind in his office. Obviously Kerensky had been certain that he would return. To have such arrogance and such weakness in one body was truly an anomaly of nature, Borodnev thought.

Borodnev got out of his chair and moved ponderously toward the door of his office, shouting as he went: "Golov! I'm waiting for you."

The door was opened from the other side by a rumpled looking Red Guard, rifle slung over his shoulder. An abashed and timorous young man stood behind him in the doorway.

"Forgive me, Commissar," begged Viktor Golov. "I was on time, I assure you. I was asked to wait outside. I thought they would have told you I was here." He glanced uneasily at the armed doorman.

Borodnev shoved past the Red Guard and hooked a heavy forearm around Golov's shoulder. The slender, fine-featured young man blanched and allowed himself to be fairly dragged into the office.

"They didn't have to tell me you were here," Borodnev jovially roared. "I knew. When Borodnev invites an individual to be here, he will be here . . . unless he is a fool!" In the neighborhood of a wooden armchair he released his hold on Golov. "And you are nobody's fool, are you, Viktor?"

Golov dutifully and warily shook his head no. With Borodnev one could never tell whether one was about to be patted on the cheek or squashed.

Borodnev patted Golov on the cheek. It was meant to be an avuncular, reassuring gesture, but Golov saw stars. Either Borodnev didn't know his strength, or the sadism that lay at the core of his nature was uncontrollable—or both.

"Sit!" Borodnev commanded and released his hold on Golov's shoulder. Gratefully, the younger man slid down into the chair. But he didn't surrender to the reflexive desire to bring his hand to his face and rub away the sting, not even while Borodnev had his back to him as he waddled around the side of the desk to his own chair. Borodnev had eyes in the back of his head.

"So, how's married life, Viktor?" Borodnev roared. "You getting fucked regular?"

Golov blinked and nodded eagerly. He couldn't figure out what Borodnev was after. Georgi Borodnev wasn't known to waste time and small talk with effete young men whose manners and pretensions he despised.

"So, Uncle Georgi fixed you up good, eh? No complaints?"

"No complaints." Golov tried to smile, but he could feel a tic in the corner of his mouth. He wondered if it showed. Borodnev had fixed him up all right. Even before the collapse of the monarchy Borodnev had recruited him from the decaying fringes of the bourgeoisie, had apprised him of the direction in which the winds of the future were blowing, had planted him close to the imperial court. He had paid a faded courtesan to instruct Golov in the art of wooing and to engineer an introduction to the plain and insecure daughter of a bankrupt count. Golov had ingratiated himself with the girl and her circle of friends, and Borodnev had, quite literally, a sleeper agent in the bedrooms of the court.

"How would you like to leave the country?" Borodnev asked.

Golov looked up in startled apprehension. There was nothing he would like better; nothing a lot of people would like better. But who would dare admit it, and to Borodnev of all people? This had to be a trap. "Why should I want to leave the country?" Golov warily asked.

"You shouldn't want to. But I would like you to."

Golov squirmed uncomfortably in his chair. "Have I done something wrong?"

"Nothing that I've heard about . . . yet." Borodnev laughed disquietingly at his own joke. Golov smiled nervously and adjusted his collar: suddenly it seemed too tight. "Maybe you have something to confess?" Borodnev couldn't resist taunting him.

"Certainly not." Golov swallowed hard, trying to keep a rein on his unsettled stomach.

"Then stop behaving like a guilty man," Borodnev trumpeted reassuringly.

Golov was not reassured. There was something about the Borodnev presence that nourished anxiety.

"Perhaps," Golov desperately offered, " . . . my wife?"

"What about her?"

Golov was drowning in fear and desperately flailing about for something to hang on to. "Perhaps my wife has done something," Golov suggested. "If she has, I cannot be held accountable." The surprising thing was that Golov had grown reasonably fond of his plain dumpling of a wife in the ten months of their marriage, and she absolutely adored him. But affection was one thing and survival another. He, Viktor Golov, was not about to put his neck in a noose for anything that Tania might have done . . . or even for anything that Borodnev might have imagined that she had done.

"I'm glad to see you so ready to throw her to the wolves," Borodnev noted. "It will make the separation that much easier."

"Then she *is* mixed up in something," Golov shouted triumphantly.

"Forget her."

"In a moment's time," Golov eagerly volunteered.

"God help us," Borodnev rumbled. "I wish I had someone else with your credentials to send on this mission. Unfortunately, Viktor, you are unique."

"Mission?" Golov blinked. He could feel himself growing giddy with relief.

"I want you to go to England."

"England?"

"You look pale," Borodnev teasingly observed. "The prospect of leaving mother Russia is that disturbing, eh?"

"Of course," Golov gasped, weak with relief.

Borodnev waddled over to a sideboard upon which stood a steaming samovar. "You want tea? It'll bring you around." He had business to do with Golov and he didn't want him passing out.

"Thank you." Golov's reply was barely audible.

"Then settle down," Borodnev advised, as he filled the glasses. "If your hands are shaking, you'll scald yourself."

"I'm quite all right," Golov assured him. But his voice was still a whisper.

"Maybe now. You didn't look so good a few minutes ago." Borodnev grinned malevolently and put the glass of tea down on the desk in front of where Golov was sitting.

Golov kept his hands on the wooden arms of the chair; he wasn't in a hurry to pick up the glass. His hands *were* shaking, and he didn't want to embarrass himself any further. "Why do you want me to go to England?" Golov asked, his voice getting back to normal.

"I want you to assist in a fund raising venture."

"For the Party?"

"No. For the butcher Romanov."

Golov's jaw dropped. Was this a joke? Or was it a trap after all? He began to shift uneasily in his chair.

Borodnev held up a file folder. "I have intelligence here that speaks of an effort led by an Englishman and supported by emigrant monarchists: they escaped Russia with a good deal of their wealth in the criminally lax days of the Kerensky regime. Now these vermin are attempting to organize and finance an effort to free the butcher Romanov and his family before the new Soviet people have an opportunity to exact justice. I want you to leave Russia just as they did, join this group, assist in the fund raising efforts, work energetically with the Englishman . . . and see to it that none of the money they raise is spent for the purpose for which it is intended. I want that mission to die for lack of funds."

Golov swallowed hard. "That's a very large order, Comrade."

"Not for an unbridled opportunist like yourself. This job is custom-made for you. It is merely a constructive extension for the public good of what you have been doing for private gain all your life: kissing all the right asses. Surely you're not going to tell me that suddenly you don't feel up to it? I would have to regard such an attitude as dangerously antisocial."

"Of course!" Golov gasped. "It's just that the prospect of being entrusted with such a—"

"Entrust?" Borodnev roared. "I wouldn't trust you out of my sight. I certainly wouldn't trust you if it were my prime interest that the money you help raise be diverted to us. But that isn't important to me. What is important is that this effort to free Romanov be crippled. You can burn the money, bury it, or keep it yourself. The more funds you divert, the wealthier you become . . . and that should be enough to motivate you to go about your business with the necessary cunning and diligence. You can buy yourself a castle in England and a title and become truly one of the nobility to which you have always aspired. It makes no difference to me. What does matter to me is this: that you stay on the job for us until the end."

"And how will I know when the end is?" Golov asked, hoping his greed didn't show.

"When you hear the news that justice has at last been meted out to the Romanovs. That they are dead. Every one of them. From the butcher father to the invalid son. And lest you falter before the word comes down, remember this: you will be functioning in the open, posing as an emigrant monarchist doing what he can to help the Tsar. But there will be others working for us cloaked in secrecy. They will be watching you, and they will be empowered to eliminate you should you waver in any way before the job is done. In short, if you prove yourself to be of no use to us, you will be dead."

"Will my wife come with me?"

"No. She will be arrested before you leave."

"Why? You said before that she was guilty of nothing."

"Since when must one be guilty of something? Half the wretches in the cellars here are guilty of nothing. It's a thing we learned from the Romanovs. Tania must be arrested in order to validate your flight. The word will go out that we had gone to arrest both of you for monarchist activities but that you escaped. The best credential you could carry."

"Will she be harmed?"

"My poor Golov. I didn't know you cared."

"A man has some feelings."

"But that's wonderful. An extra check on you that I didn't realize we possessed. No, she will not be harmed . . . as long as you follow instructions. Do well and maybe some day you can buy her way to England to take up residence with you in your castle. Lord and Lady Golov!" Borodnev slapped his thigh. Golov tried not to wince as Borodnev's laughter filled the room.

As Golov left Borodnev's office and entered the corridor, he passed a pale and frightened young woman standing between two brawny guards. She was shuddering so badly that she might have been standing exposed on the street on a freezing January day. But it was November, not January. And she was wearing an adequate, if shabby, coat and the corridor was overheated.

As Golov hurried away he heard Borodnev shout: "So, you've found the bitch!"

Borodnev took a few steps down the corridor, the better to fix his good eye on the terrified young woman's face. The bruises were gone, of course; many months had passed. But the broken features were as good as a brand, as was the steel bridgework that had replaced her missing teeth. This was the slut. Her image had been engraved on his memory on the day she had sat in accusation against him in Kerensky's office. He turned from her to one of the guards.

"How many men have we got between watches in the barracks room across the yard?"

"Twenty-four, Commissar."

"Do you think your Comrades could make use of her?"

The guard stared at him, speechless with astonishment.

"Take her down there and let them have a good time. When they're done, if there's anything left, throw her down in the cellars. And then call me. I'm not finished with her yet."

He turned away and waddled back toward his office. At the door he turned and roared: "And if there's any man down there who's too pure, or too squeamish, or too queer to use her thoroughly, I want his name."

Borodnev slammed shut his office door. As he moved toward his desk he could hear, ever so faintly, a plangent wail as they dragged the young woman away. Borodnev thought that she must be screaming at the top of her lungs; otherwise, he wouldn't be hearing her at all through the thickness of the door. With a satisfied grunt he dropped like a sandbag into his chair.

Stubby fingers, round and fat as nickel stogies, peeled a sheet of blank paper from the top of a pile on the right side of the desk, then curled themselves around a pencil. Thick tongue, coated with a yellowish scum, like the tongue of a dray horse after a strenuous haul, licked at the point of the lead pencil.

He composed his thoughts and began to write in a simple word code that would be understood by the addressee in England.

> *Dear Nadia,*
>
> *I am arranging today to send to you a package: an item associated with the household of the late Baron Prinzup. (In case you didn't know, his daughter has been taken into custody by the Reds and his son-in-law, Golov, has fled.) This item has no great value in itself, which is undoubtedly why it is being allowed to leave the country, but its past associations will undoubtedly be of sentimental value to a number of our beloved compatriots in exile. I would hope that you will take a personal interest in this item when it arrives and that you will see to it that it is not misused or sold to any outside parties.*
>
> 

*Affectionately,*
*Your Uncle Georgi*
> 

Nadia Demanova, to whom the letter was addressed, was neither Borodnev's niece nor a monarchist in exile. She had been, for two years, employed as a personal maid to the Princess Stepanova, a cousin of the former Imperial Family. (God! thought Borodnev: there are more of them than there are fleas on a rat.)

Beautiful, young, delicate, intelligent, Nadia had served her Princess well and the Revolution even better. Daughter of a bourgeois merchant, she had been a Bolshevik since her days in the gymnasium. Upon graduation with honors, she had offered her services to the Party and had submerged herself into the murky, duplicitous world of the secret agent.

Nadia would understand that Golov was the package that would soon arrive in England, and she would know how to keep a discreet eye on it in order to make sure that it didn't sell out.

Borodnev addressed the envelope, licked it with an almost lascivious pass of the tongue, and sealed it shut. One day Nadia's special services would no longer be required by the Revolution. He looked forward to establishing a different kind of relationship with her then. He leaned back in his chair and closed his eyes: the bitch who had betrayed him to Kerensky was still on his mind.

To hell with appearances! He decided to go down into the barracks room and watch the fun.

# CHAPTER TWENTY

T he dinner table was fourteen feet long and beneath the silken cloth was the color of oiled chestnut. The service was gold, dazzling in the candlelight. The entire room was aglow with it, so that the faces of the begowned and tailcoated diners appeared to be bathed in a glorious sunset.

The bottles of claret, Margaux '06, were almost empty. The guests were sodden with food and awash with wine. The men tugged surreptitiously at their stiff wing collars, their faces pink as borscht. The women fanned their bosoms and squirmed inside their corsets. Foreheads were pearly with sweat. Backsides, cleavages, and crotches were clammy. Count Orlov pressed a linen napkin to his lips and muffled a belch; only the slightest spasm of his Adam's apple gave him away. The foreigner, Lars Dahlgren, was either a boor or had been listening so attentively to the monologue of the Duchess Petrova that he had taken no notice of the expanding bubble in his gut. He belched unceremoniously in the Duchess's face.

Only the Englishman, Aldonby, had not made a pig of himself. He had tasted sparingly of each of the dishes set before him and had fastidiously arranged the food remaining on his plate so that it would appear that he had eaten more than he actually had. He had sipped sparingly of the wine. As far as he was concerned, the meal had been a thing to endure, a tedious and unavoidable precursor to the main business of the evening.

Standing attentively behind the Princess's chair at the head of the table, Nadia Demanova had taken it all in. She thought to herself that she really ought to open the window a crack and let in some air before they all died of heat prostration, apoplexy, or gluttony—a more likely cause of death in this company. But then she decided not to touch the window unless she was asked to. The Princess, not she,was the mistress of the house. Whatever unpleasantness they were enduring, they deserved. You could feed a small village for a week on what this dozen had consumed in a night.

The Princess, a frail, avian creature, encrusted in brocade, half turned to Nadia, placed a damp palm on her wrist and in what was to Nadia's mind her most offensively patronizing tone said, "Darling. We'll take tea and sweets in the parlor. I am afraid if we stay imprisoned behind the table for another minute, we will all expire."

After dessert the Princess clapped her hands for attention. "Dear friends," she announced and then, with fingers to lips, tittered with chagrin. "I almost called you Comrades but that fine word has forever been corrupted. We have with us tonight two distinguished guests: Lord Charles Aldonby, whose late blessed mother some of you may have known as Katerina Simonev in Petersburg in a better time. Lord Charles has recently been discharged from His Majesty's Engineers and is here in the capacity of a private citizen for reasons that will soon become apparent. So we welcome Lord Charles to our circle."

There was a dry, polite clapping of hands from the ten exiles in attendance. They prepared themselves for another of the endless pleas for money—to send packages to those less fortunate who remained behind, to which they always complied, resentfully, but too embarrassed by their own good fortune to refuse.

"Our second distinguished guest," the Princess continued, "is a man wise in the ways of the sea and in the geography of a part of our country to which, I daresay, few of us have ever ventured. And which, most sadly, has recently become the home of our beloved Tsar and his dear family. And so we welcome Captain Dahlgren."

Lars Dahlgren held up his right hand to acknowledge the same brittle applause that had greeted Aldonby.

The Princess, with an encouraging nod to Aldonby, sat down.

Aldonby got out of his chair and crossed to the center of the room.

He began by greeting them in flawless Russian. He had meant the greeting in their native tongue to serve as an icebreaker, a warm and friendly gesture with which he hoped to disarm them. When he saw the looks of amazed delight and heard the hearty outburst of truly spontaneous applause, he decided to do the entire speech in Russian; he spoke it like a native.

He told them of the dead pedagogue, Malenovsky, who had carried across thousands of arduous miles a message from the Imperial Family. He told them that had the plea arrived sooner or had His Majesty's government not been subjected to bureaucratic delays a rescue might have been effected without undue difficulty or danger while the Romanovs were still at Tsarskoe Selo. Now, however, they had been moved deep inland across the Ural Mountains. With each eastward mile they are moved, the task of mounting an expedition to bring them out becomes more and more difficult, more and more costly, and more and more time consuming to plan and to provision.

At the mention of costs, certain members of the group began to shift restlessly in their chairs. The Princess darted them reproachful looks. Lars Dahlgren observed the movement with a wry smile. It was what he expected. People were the same everywhere. Full of goodwill and good intentions—until it came time to unbutton the purse.

"Yes," Aldonby said, acknowledging their unspoken reaction, "I am here to ask for money. And not for any comfortably small amount, not just a few rubles to lighten the burden back home and your guilt here. I am going to ask for substantial sums—enough to mount an expedition, the ordnance and budget of which Captain Dahlgren will outline for you when I am through. So costly will this undertaking be that I doubt that those gathered here could support it entirely on their own. . . ." He waited until the murmur of relief and the nods of agreement had abated. "You who are here have been chosen as a kind of phalanx to go out among the many hundreds of your compatriots in England and anywhere else you can reach them, and through them as well as through yourselves to raise the necessary funds."

Aldonby paused for a moment to give them time to absorb what he had said and to comment in whispers among themselves. They seemed somewhat relieved to realize that whatever it was wasn't going to come entirely out of their own pockets, that everybody would have to carry at least some of the economic burden or bear the shame of having turned their backs on their Tsar.

Nadia Demanova moved about the circle of displaced nobility, refilling teacups, offering cakes from a silver tray. She found the Englishman the more attractive by far of the two newcomers to the Princess's home but instinct informed her that the Scandinavian would be a better target of opportunity. So she was particularly attentive to Lars Dahlgren, and her special attentions did not escape his notice.

"Now," Aldonby continued when they had all settled down again. "In a way the funds are the lesser half of our problem. . . ." The ex-nobility exchanged more uneasy glances; a few teacups rattled apprehensively against their saucers. What problem could there be that would be greater than the acquisition of funds?

"I will need men," Aldonby said. "Volunteers."

To this statement there was no audible response, no whispers, no coughs, no shifting of chairs; there was just silent, gaping astonishment.

"The political and pragmatic considerations that prohibit His Majesty's government from lending financial support to this expedition also prohibit any commitment of manpower. We are on our own. And I must advise you that, with the change in regime in Petersburg, with the flight of Kerensky, and with the Bolsheviks in the seat of power, the hazards of the expedition have increased—as has the need grown more urgent for its implementation. Kerensky was not personally hostile to the Imperial Family. The Bolshevik leadership is. While the family was merely displaced and discommoded under Kerensky, they are now in mortal danger."

The room reverberated with alarmed whispers. And then, before Aldonby could begin again, bald, red-faced, mutton-chopped, old Count Andriev rose slowly from his chair, pendulous rows of medals setting up a clatter on his dinner-coated chest.

"Sir," the Count announced in a booming bass voice, "I should like to be the first to volunteer."

There was more buzzing from those in the chairs as one by one all the men in attendance rose and offered their services. Apparently, Lars Dahlgren silently observed, it is easier to risk one's neck than one's cash. Or, safer to volunteer a commodity that nobody wanted than something of value.

"Gentlemen," Aldonby said, "I am moved. And I know that the Tsar would be both moved and heartened if he could witness this display of loyalty and sacrifice. But, gentlemen, how can I state it without risking offense; regretfully the burden of your years would render you all ineligible."

From most of the volunteers, the Count Andriev being the notable exception, there was evidenced by a certain subtle relaxation of the body an involuntary expression of relief. Only the old Count stiffened, bristled, grew even more red in the face than before and declared: "Young man, I should like to have a minute alone with you. Later."

"Of course, sir," Aldonby replied and wished that the Count were forty years younger.

Count Andriev grunted and sat with the same martial erectness with which he had come to his feet. The other men, who were still standing, gratefully retreated without another word into the unexposed safety of their chairs, hoping that Andriev would speak only for himself and not attempt to include them in whatever he might have to say later to the young Englishman. They now began to feel that if a tapping of their pocketbooks was all that resulted from this meeting, they would have got off easy . . . and with a clear conscience to boot. They would have done all that they were capable of doing to help their Tsar.

Aldonby continued. "What I would ask you gentlemen, and ladies, to do is to act in the matter of manpower as I hope you will act in the matter of funds. I would ask you to search out from among your expatriate group those young men, none over the age of thirty, who would be willing to join an expedition at considerable hardship and risk in the hope of delivering your Tsar and his family from their enemies. You need not evaluate the qualifications of any potential volunteers; I will do that. And Captain Dahlgren will brief them thoroughly on the hazards that they are likely to encounter. But you must be absolutely discrete in your inquiries. If I wished this mission to receive wide publicity, I could advertise in the newspapers. In the matter of recruiting, speak only to those whom you know you can trust. Your closest family. Your dearest friends. I'll need no more than six or eight volunteers. But I would like a pool to draw from. I regret that I must come to you this way, hat in hand, pleading for men and money; but it is the only way. This must be as totally as possible a Russian enterprise. It must in no way be construed to be sanctioned by His Majesty's government."

"Sir!" A quavering male voice interrupted him. Aldonby stopped and looked around the room. A wizened old gentleman at the end of the first row laboriously raised a tremulous, blue-veined hand from the walking stick braced between his knees. He succeeded in partially uncurling an arthritic index finger and pointing it almost directly at the ceiling, as if he were trying to register a bid at an auction. Having succeeded in attracting Aldonby's attention, he proceeded to identify himself. "Baron Vorinsky. And forgive me for not rising."

"Of course, Baron."

The Baron slowly returned his upraised hand to its resting place on the head of his cane; the lowering of the hand seemed to require as great an effort as did the raising of it. "You say, sir, that this must be a Russian enterprise. . . ." He paused and silently worked his lips.

"Yes, Baron?" Aldonby asked encouragingly.

"Yet," continued Vorinsky, "you are not Russian nor is Captain Dahlgren."

Aldonby smiled. "You're quite right, Baron. But Captain Dahlgren is not a British subject, and that is the important thing: he is a citizen of Norway and is operating as a disinterested entrepreneur offering his services, his skills, his knowledge of certain terrain, and his vessel for our use. For a price. In the name of this Russian group I am contracting for those services."

"And you, sir, are British, are you not? What is your interest in this matter when the Crown has none?" The last words were uttered with contempt.

"The Crown is not disinterested. If it were, I wouldn't be here tonight. It is simply unable to act in accordance with its interest. As for me, I will not be operating as a British subject. My mother was Russian. I was born in Yalta. We returned to England while I was still an infant. But I have a dual nationality. In this enterprise I will assume a Russian name and identity."

Baron Vorinsky was working his lips again. It was as if he had to lubricate his tongue before he could speak.

"Yes, Baron?" Aldonby asked again.

"There is the question of funds."

"Yes, sir."

"You are asking for large sums of money. Captain Dahlgren is by your description a mercenary. For all we know, your claim to a Russian birthright may be to the contrary; you may be a charlatan. Forgive me, sir. But I must question the wisdom of putting such vast sums directly into your hands."

The room began to buzz. Baron Vorinsky worked his lips vigorously. Princess Stepanova, sitting at the back of the room and a little apart from the others, caught Aldonby's eye and nodded knowingly. Aldonby returned her nod and waited until the hubbub had subsided.

"Baron," Aldonby announced, "I heartily agree with you. And, in truth, I will really have too much on my hands to tend to the very important and time-consuming business of bookkeeping. I have already mentioned this matter to the Princess and she has succeeded in recruiting from among your circle a volunteer who has agreed to take on the heavy burden of treasurer for this enterprise. He will be responsible for collecting and disbursing funds. None of the money will come directly into Captain Dahlgren's hands or mine except that portion which will be due Captain Dahlgren for his services. All other monies will be paid directly to our suppliers of armaments and equipment by the gentleman who has so graciously volunteered to act as keeper of the treasury."

The room buzzed again. Baron Vorinsky again raised his gnarled finger.

"Yes, Baron?" Aldonby asked.

"I think, sir, that you have satisfied my inquiry, and I wish you luck."

A domino chain of approving nods circled the room.

"Good, then," said Aldonby. "Perhaps Princess Stepanova would be kind enough to introduce our treasurer."

The Princess moved to the front of the room and stood beside Aldonby. She cleared her throat, thanked Aldonby for his efforts in all of their behalfs, and introduced: "A member of our group most recently arrived from the motherland, upon whose consciousness was engraved more deeply even than on all the others the barbarous nature of the new regime. By his service to the group he hoped to justify his good fortune in having escaped and to assist those most in need of assistance at this time: the Imperial Family.

"May I ask for a round of grateful applause for our dedicated compatriot, Viktor Golov."

Golov rose to an enthusiastic clapping of hands and bowed humbly to those assembled.

# CHAPTER TWENTY-ONE

When the meeting had ended, the guests had departed, and the Princess had gone to bed, Nadia Demanova sat alone in her room, thoughtfully, at her writing table, formulating in her mind the composition of a letter to her Uncle Georgi. Upon reflection she had less to tell him than she had hoped.

When the evening had begun, she had thought that this was to be another tiresome gathering of the expatriate clans. After the true purpose of the meeting had been revealed, she had been astonished. When Aldonby had begun to speak, she had felt that at last her months in exile with these detestable people had been justified. Surely by the end of the evening she would have a spectacularly detailed report to send home to Borodnev.

But Aldonby had revealed very little, except that he needed men and money. And Dahlgren had not been much more specific. To be sure, she knew that a boat would be used, that a certain amount of arms and ammunition was hoped for in the event they ran into patrols, that horses and carts or sleighs would have to be hired, that bribes would have to be considered, and so on and so on. But the specifics had been left out and deliberately she thought; this Aldonby was no fool. A boat could land at any one of a thousand places on the Russian coast. It had not even been specified whether the approach would be by the Baltic in the north or the Black Sea in the south. For all her hopes at the evening's outset she knew very little. She knew only that an attempt was to be made with no specific date given to free the ex-Tsar, and that the approach to the Russian borders would not be made by railroad train or motorcar. She could not add much to what Borodnev already knew of a prospective rescue attempt, thanks to Heckart's interview with the Russian Consul.

Nadia dipped her pen into the ink bottle on her table and began to write. When she had finished, she sealed the letter inside an envelope addressed to Georgi Bokoff, a made-up name at an address that had been established specifically for Borodnev to receive communications such as this.

Work done, she filled a basin with water and placed it in front of her full-length bedroom mirror. Then she undressed. She dipped a cloth into the water, stepped into the basin and, standing naked in front of the mirror, began to sponge herself off. It was a daily ritual from which she derived a truly sensual delight. A delicious body, she thought: a virgin feast of round breasts, swelling hips, and straight, plump calves. One day soon she would be called upon to employ it in the name of the toiling classes, a duty that she anticipated with mixed feelings of delight and trepidation.

She wet a fingertip, tapped at a nipple, and watched it bud like a tea rose. She smiled. She wondered if she dared approach Aldonby to learn more specifically what she needed to know about the expedition. Aldonby was certainly the better-looking of the two foreigners. But there was a forbidding air of reserve about him. Dahlgren, on the other hand, had gobbled her up with his eyes every time she had come near with the service of cookies and tea.

# CHAPTER TWENTY-TWO

*From the journal of Anastasia Romanov*

TOBOLSK
NOVEMBER 18, 1917

During the night one or more of the soldiers drew crude pictures on the walls of the w.c.—a figure representing Mama, nude, performing indecent acts with another unclothed figure representing Rasputin.

I am an early riser, and so I was the first to see the defacement of the wall. I wakened Tatiana. She is not the eldest of my sisters, but she is the one who most takes charge of things.

She turned pale when I showed her what was on the wall and, for a moment, looked as though she might vomit. Then she ordered me to look away, to run hot water in the sink, and to dissolve soap in it.

Of course, there was no hot water at this hour, but I managed to make a soapy solution with the cold. Then Tatiana began to soak towels in the soapy water.

She ordered me to leave the w.c. and to erase from my memory what I had seen, as she was about to erase the images from the wall.

By this time Olga and Marie, aroused by the commotion, were standing outside, tapping softly at the door, demanding entry, demanding to know what was happening. They rushed in as I left. I heard them gasp before the door closed behind them. Then I heard the sound of the towel scrubbing down the wall.

I was back in my bed with the covers pulled up to my chin trying to comprehend what I had just seen: my mother, lying on her back, naked, save for the crown on her head, legs thrust skyward. All those horrid lying stories that were circulated around Petersburg last winter by our enemies were here filthily depicted on our wall.

Tatiana came and ordered me to use Mama's and Papa's w.c. for the rest of the day. She had been unable to completely efface the deeply etched pencil markings. They would have to be covered with plaster and paint.

But, horror of horrors! When I used Mama's w.c. later that morning, I found a towel affixed to the wall with pins, and when I looked behind it, I saw to my dismay obscene drawings like the ones in our w.c. These, too, were faded, as if someone, either Mama or Papa, had tried and failed to completely scrub them away.

Early in the afternoon I overheard raised voices in the study: Papa demanding that the perpetrator be identified and punished. Colonel Kobylinsky, most apologetically explaining that this would be almost impossible, conditions deteriorating as they are. How awful for Mama and Papa, and for Colonel Kobylinsky. He is afraid that to make much of it among the men might make matters worse. But he did order paints and brushes so that the walls could be covered over immediately. He said that it might be wiser to have one of our loyal retainers do the job than the men of his guard. And sadly Father was forced to agree.

So now the walls are painted over. But there is a strong smell of wet paint in our quarters. And it reminds me of what I saw this morning. And I am most disturbed, in a most ambivalent and unsettling way: repelled by the meanness of the monster who did such a thing and intrigued by the acts that were depicted. I had never before seen, so explicitly described, what it is that men and women do together. I am infected with a shameful excitement. And I wonder if Leonid and I will ever have a chance to do those things together.

# CHAPTER TWENTY-THREE

W hy! Captain Dahlgren!" Nadia Demanova exclaimed, pressing her hand to her bodice as if to contain her surprise.

Lars Dahlgren interrupted his unsteady progress across the sidewalk, turned inquisitively, blinked, and grinned bemusedly at the shapely young woman who had so delightfully materialized beside him. He knew her from somewhere, he supposed. He must: after all, she had called him by name. But in his present pleasantly boozy state, he could not quite recall whether she was the wife or daughter of one of his business acquaintances or one of the girls from Madam Frangione's bordello in Applegate Road. He decided that until he properly placed her, he had better wipe the smile off his face lest it degenerate into a leer. And he did so, quite literally, drawing the back of his hand deliberately across his mouth and achieving what he hoped would be a soberly questioning expression.

"Nadia Demanova," the young woman offered helpfully.

"Miss . . . Madame Demanova." Lars Dahlgren exclaimed and not too loudly he hoped. "Of course." Of course he still hadn't placed her, though the exquisite face was unforgettable.

She smiled meltingly. "I am Princess Stepanova's personal maid. The other night—"

"But of course!" he roared, remembering now and only too well. "What a pleasant surprise." She was neither the wife of a friend, the daughter of a friend, or a whore.

"Yes, such a surprise," Nadia ingenuously replied.

She had found his address in the Princess's directory and had been following him, discretely, through most of the afternoon as he made his rounds. She had been waiting in a cab across the way from the White Stag Pub ever since he had entered there almost an hour ago. (The

99

expense had been frightful, but no woman pretending respectability could safely spend an hour loitering on a corner in a run-down neighborhood.) Dahlgren's rounds until then had been strictly business, with stops at the establishments of various tradesmen: map sellers, provisioners, and ships' chandlers. He had walked into The White Stag sober as a judge. When he came out, walking with noticeable ambivalence of gait and with a pleasantly vague smile on his face, she let escape a soft sigh of relief. Things would go that much more easily.

She paid off her cabby, who was astonished that after all that waiting she decided to go nowhere. The cabby watched her cross the street and bump into the burly man who came out of the pub, then he shrugged and drove off. Easiest fare he had ever earned.

Dahlgren, head bobbing and steadying himself with one hand resting lightly on Nadia's shoulder, examined her features. "Of course, the other night. All those old aristocrats."

"I'm only a maid," Nadia demurred.

"Well, I'm only a sailor, myself," Dahlgren drawled, "so we're both as common as oatmeal, if you want to look at it from the point of view of social classification."

"Oh, you're not so common," said Nadia, eyes alight with admiration. "No ordinary man would have volunteered to lead a dangerous mission of the kind on which you will soon embark."

Dahlgren smiled and leaned close to Nadia in a confidential attitude. His breath came at her whiskey-soaked and steamy in the chilly evening air. And while he chose not to dilute his leadership role in the mission, he did deprecate his nobility a bit. "Tell you the truth, Miss Demanova," he whispered, "I'm a businessman, a damned successful one too. I'm in it for the money."

Nadia allowed her jaw to drop in astonishment and tried not to flinch in the face of the powerful undigested whiskey fumes that were wafting her way.

"Which is not to say," Lars Dahlgren assured her, "that I won't do a proper job. I'll do the damnedest most proper job you people have ever seen. And I'll do it right just because I'm in it for the money; I have a reputation to uphold as a businessman who gives full measure."

"I'm certain that you will, Captain Dahlgren," Nadia agreed. And decided that maybe it was time to move things along a little.

She hugged herself and shivered.

"Oh!" declared Lars Dahlgren. "How thoughtless of me, detaining you out here in the cold, philosophizing and such. My lodgings are just a few doors down. Would you come in and have a cup of tea with me? Warm you up a bit?" He laughed.

Nadia brought her fingertips to her lips in a gesture of dismay. "Oh, Captain Dahlgren! Really! I don't think that would be correct, do you?"

Dahlgren cleared his throat. "Of course not. Forgive me. What could I have been thinking? Can I invite you to share a little supper with me in a public house?"

"Well . . ." Nadia hesitated.

"It's just across the way," Dahlgren persisted. "You see?" He pointed. "The White Stag."

"A pub?" Nadia asked in a scandalized tone.

"Perfectly respectable," Dahlgren assured her. "They have a family room around at the side. We'll go in there."

"Well . . ." Nadia considered. "If you're certain. It *is* getting a little chilly out there, and I am getting a little bit hungry." And, she thought, with a sherry in her she would no longer smell the whiskey on his breath. "I'll accept your generous offer, Captain Dahlgren."

"Call me Lars," the burly seaman grinned, as he took her by the arm and piloted her across the street.

An hour and fifteen minutes later, ballasted with kidney pie and afloat with alcohol, they came tacking back across the street. But on this trip it was Nadia who was piloting the Captain. She had been drinking sherry to his whiskey, and at a pace so calculatedly sluggish that when they left The White Stag there were still untouched glasses of the wine on her side of the table. In his cups Dahlgren either had not noticed or had not cared. Which is not to say that Nadia was stone-cold sober. She had had to make some concessions to an image of creeping abandon, and her head was slowly spinning. But not so badly that she didn't know where she was going or where she had been or that, for all the alcohol that Lars Dahlgren had consumed, he had told her very little of value beyond the name of his ship. And she had dared not press him; he may have had a weakness for women and for drink, but he was nobody's fool.

She listened for over an hour while he regaled her with stories of the sea and of his inland journeys and escapades in ports of call along the Baltic and the Arctic, with heavy emphasis, in the interest of aphrodisia, on the lewder habits and customs of certain of the women he had encountered along the way. At the outset he had begged her pardon often and invited her to stop him if she felt that his anecdotes were out of bounds. As the hour progressed he had lost all sense of circumspection.

It was during the course of one of these stories that he had mentioned *Elena,* which at first she had thought to be a woman and which she finally realized was the ship. But when she had teasingly inquired as to where his *Elena* was berthed or when she next would be sailing out, he had dropped the subject, despite all the alcohol in him. He had brought his index finger to his lips, looked suspiciously about, and whispered that such information had been decreed by Captain Aldonby to be a secret of the highest priority. No one was to know where *Elena* was berthed or when she would sail or where she would sail for. Not even the volunteers who would sail on her. There were too many big ears abroad in the land. He had been at fault in the first place even to have let slip her name.

The kidney pie having been downed along with his fifth glass of whiskey, Lars Dahlgren began a tentative manual under-the-table exploration of the skirted length of Nadia's thigh.

"Please! Captain Dahlgren!" Nadia gently rebuked him as his hand cupped her crotch, "this is not the place!"

"Oh . . ." Dahlgren forlornly replied, the words sliding sloppily off his tongue. "I had always thought it was." By this time Dahlgren was so drunk that he had missed entirely the note of suggestion in Nadia's mild rebuke.

After Dahlgren had swallowed one more glass of whiskey, unreeled one more lewd yarn, and gone on one more groping expedition under the table, Nadia declared that she was feeling slightly giddy and wished she weren't so far from home.

This was a cue that Dahlgren even in his drunkenness could not miss; he reminded her that his lodgings were only a few meters away. And so they began their return journey across the street, Nadia unobtrusively guiding the foundering seaman while he occupied himself with the task of keeping his big left hand firmly clamped to her right buttock.

As they labored up the stairs Nadia felt that once she had him in his room, beyond outside distractions, she could stroke him into a state of such euphoria that he would let slip the three elusive pieces of information she had gone to such trouble to acquire: where the *Elena* was berthed, when she would sail, and what her destination would be.

Lars Dahlgren dropped his keys twice as he tried to open the door to his flat. The first time he got down on all fours and padded around like a half-blind hound and had to be helped up by Nadia.

As she grappled with him, trying to put him back on an even footing, she silently prayed that he wasn't one of those weak-stomached types who threw up all over the place when he'd had too much to drink.

The second time he dropped the keys, he spread his arms wide as if clearing a space for himself on the landing and ordered Nadia to stand out of the way; he was going to break down that goddamned obstacle.

While he took three ponderous and unsteady steps backward to build up momentum, Nadia knelt, swept up the keys, opened the door, and then rushed to grab Dahlgren's arm and steady him before he toppled over the banister into the stairwell.

Inside the room Dahlgren fell into a mangy armchair, raising a small blizzard of dust as the seat cushion imploded beneath his weight.

He sat there for a moment, massive in his open topcoat, chin down on his chest, legs spread wide, scuffed ankle-high shoes planted squarely on the soiled rectangle of oriental rug. He looked as formidable and as inanimate as the overstuffed, heavy furniture of which he seemed to have become a part.

Nadia stood a few feet in front of him, panting from the effort she had made to bring him this far. He was breathing so deeply and moving so little that she wondered if he might simply have passed out on her and if the whole evening's enterprise hadn't been wasted.

She went to the door and slammed it somewhat harder than was necessary, hoping that the sharpness of the sound might revive him. When she turned back into the room, she saw that he had not moved. But something had changed. His chin was still down on his chest, but the curve of his mouth had been altered from a slack, drooping arc to a satyr's upturned leer. Dimples had appeared in the florid cheeks, and one open and bloodshot eye was following her progress across the room with the greatest of interest.

"Oh! Captain Dahlgren!" Nadia exclaimed. "I was afraid you had fallen asleep in your clothes."

Dahlgren chuckled throatily, ponderously raised a huge hand from the arm of the chair, extended a thick index finger, and then curled it invitingly in his direction.

"Come over here, my dear. Let's be sociable." The words were badly slurred, but Nadia understood their meaning.

She moved fluidly, seductively she hoped, toward the chair, unbuttoning her coat, peeling it off, letting it drop with abandon at her feet. Dahlgren followed her progress appreciatively with the one open eye. The other eye remained shut and as inert as the rest of his body.

He patted his heavy right thigh with the same hand that had called her to him. "Sit here," he invited.

She sat, sidesaddle, her diminutive body fitting easily into the **V** formed by his spread-eagle legs.

That same right hand that had signaled for her to approach and that had indicated where she should sit now found it way around her torso and applied itself on her right breast.

Nadia sighed as loudly and ecstatically as she could manage, leaned in, and pressed her lips moistly to Dahlgren's forehead, right between the eyes.

Dahlgren acknowleged the kiss with a gentle rotating motion of the big right hand. He was not yet quite dead to the world, and Nadia was determined to keep him awake and voluble.

He was whispering something into her ear, but she couldn't make out what he was saying. His mouth was too close, and the slurred diction combined with the breathiness of the whisper made it hard for her to understand. And her earlobe was getting all wet. She'd had no idea when she'd started out this afternoon that seduction could be such a sloppy affair.

"Yes, Lars?" she inquired invitingly.

"Whiskey," he muttered. "In the cabinet."

She would have liked to have got up and brought him the whiskey, anything to interrupt the rhythmic kneading action of his hand on her breast; it was beginning to arouse her in ways she had not anticipated. And it was he, not she, who was in need of arousing. But to bring him more whiskey now would be to anesthetize him for the rest of the night.

Instead she leaned over and kissed him on slack and unresponsive lips. Only his big right hand seemed to be alive. She was beginning to tingle all over, definitely beginning to melt. Her underclothes would be a mess.

"No more whiskey tonight, Lars. You've had too much already. Would you want to return to your boat in an embarrassing condition?" she leadingly inquired.

"Shit." Dahlgren replied. Or had he said ship? She couldn't tell. And then he asked for whiskey again.

"No more whiskey, Lars. Not tonight." She became aware that his hand was no longer working her breast. To her chagrin she found that she missed the sensation it had produced; to her dismay she saw it lying limp across the arm of the chair.

"Lars . . ." she cooed into his ear.

No response.

A little more sharply she inquired, "Are you awake?" She was near her wit's end. None of her favorite heroines in fiction had ever been confronted with anything like this. It was almost an affront.

"Wake." Dahlgren snorted. "Sure." And then, "Where's the whiskey?"

She kissed him on the ear. "Isn't there something else I can do besides bring you whiskey, Lars?" she suggestively inquired.

Dahlgren thoughtfully smacked his lips. Nadia waited, kissing his ear, his neck, his nose. Trying to be kittenish, trying to be playful, trying to keep the game alive.

"Sure," Dahlgren said at last. "Like Edna from Hamburg."

"Like? . . ." Nadia repeated, hoping for clarification.

"Edna from Hamburg. That was good. Like that."

Nadia gasped. Now she knew what he meant. Edna from Hamburg. She had been the leading character in one of the lewd stories Dahlgren had regaled her with in the pub. Edna with the tongue of a reptile. Edna, the snake, she could swallow men whole.

Nadia drew away from Dahlgren. She had calculated that in order to acquire the information she needed to send back to Russia she might have to sleep with the man. In the normal way, of course, as she had read about in the manuals. And she was willing to do it, for the Revolution. But to do it like Edna from Hamburg? Nadia had not taken into account the possibility of being made a partner to perversion. She stared at Lars Dahlgren in dismay. He seemed to be dozing again. She had to do what was necessary to keep him awake.

"Lars!" she intoned sharply.

The one bloodshot eye opened inquisitively.

"Like Edna from Hamburg!" Nadia heroically announced.

Dahlgren's drooping mouth lazily animated itself into a contented smile.

Timorously, Nadia slipped down between his legs. Following the blueprint laid down for her in Dahlgren's oral memoir of Edna, Nadia addressed Lars's fly.

"Will we ever meet again, Lars?" Nadia cooed, as she daintily undid his buttons, one by one.

"Depends," Dahlgren muttered drunkenly. "All depends."

"I mean," Nadia clarified, "if you will be sailing very soon on so dangerous a mission, we may never meet again."

With her fingers she gingerly parted the flap on his heavy flannel underwear and was confronted with an undergrowth of bright orange hair peppered with gray. Like flame and ashes. At least, she thought to herself, surveying the scene with interest, he keeps himself reasonably clean.

"How soon will you be sailing?" she inquired, as she explored the area with her fingers searching for the proper organ. "Tomorrow? Next week? Week after?"

"Shhh," Dahlgren contentedly responded.

Locating it at last and daintily grasping it with the tips of forefinger and thumb, as if fishing a pickle from a barrel, she brought to the surface what the more scandalous novelists liked to call his manhood. To her surprise she found it to be more nearly the size of a gherkin than a pickle and not nearly as firm.

"Will you be sailing from London?" she asked, puzzling over the slack, wrinkled thing that she gingerly held between her fingers. "Harwich?"

"Shhhh."

"Dover?" Edna from Hamburg, he had told her, had treated him to exquisite delights, licking him into a state of ecstasy, as if he were a lollipop. But this was no lollipop she was examining with growing dismay.

"Dover?" she dulcetly reiterated, as she tapped lightly with fingertip on its head, as if trying to gain its attention.

"Shhhh."

Lars Dahlgren was not responding either verbally or physically and Nadia blamed herself. Pretty as she was, she was not a seductress. In the secret councils and cells of the Revolution, talk had been her aphrodisiac. All those wonderful doctrinal debates lasting until dawn. But all of it was of the mind not of the body. She was temperamentally equipped to throw herself into a seduction of this peculiar sort with the skill or verve of Edna from Hamburg. Never mind! She would just have to do better.

She drew a deep breath, lubricated her lips with her tongue, and, for the first time in many minutes, looked with wide, adoring doe's eyes lovingly up into Lars Dahlgren's face.

"Shhhhh . . ." Lars Dahlgren breathed. His chin was down on his chest again and both eyes were closed.

He was sound asleep.

Nadia backed gratefully away, leaving everything as it was, lest in trying to put things back in place and get them all buttoned up she wake him. She knew that this was only a respite, that sooner or later she would have to complete her intelligence gathering ordeal. Unless, while he slept, she could find something in the room that would reveal where the ship was docked, when it would sail, and for what destination.

In a stealthy frenzy, to the accompaniment of Dahlgren's sibilant breathing and thunderous snores, she went through the chests and the closets and found nothing. If there was any information at all in the room, it might be in the wallet that he must be carrying inside his coat. But she decided that to go through his clothing at the risk of waking him would be less than wise.

She would wait until morning. Create a nice scene of unguarded domesticity. Prepare his breakfast. Chat. She would be more comfortable with that than with physical seduction. And maybe she would be more successful. Perhaps in that unguarded setting she could elicit from him the information she needed. And surely during the course of the morning he would change his clothes, or bathe, or just go to the w.c. Then the wallet would be left, vulnerable to inspection, for a brief—but for her purpose adequate—length of time.

The next morning, when she heard him stirring, she lit the fire on the little range in the alcove, greased a pan, and began cracking eggs.

Lars Dahlgren came awake to the sizzling sounds and mouth watering smells of eggs and bangers frying, came awake with a searing headache, and with an erection of enormous size. He opened his eyes and peered down in astonishment at where Nadia had left his pants unbuttoned and his penis exposed. Wonderful, he decided, remembering very little of the night before, another Edna.

Nadia looked up from her cooking in time to see him coming toward her, massive in physique, and armed with what appeared to be a lance where the gherkin had been the night before.

"Turn off the eggs," he huskily invited. "And take off your clothes."

Nadia gulped. Her domestic scenario hadn't called for this. A cozy breakfast. Unguarded conversation. "The eggs are ready," she sang out bravely.

"So am I," Dahlgren declared. "And I don't have time for breakfast too. I have to catch the ferry at noon for Oslo."

The significance of this last announcement almost eluded Nadia as Lars Dahlgren gathered her up in his arms and carried her to bed.

That evening in her room upstairs in the Princess's house Nadia tried to compose a letter to her Uncle Georgi in Petersburg. But her mind kept wandering. Her body was still reverberating with the aftershocks of its morning engagement. She was still on fire. Lars Dahlgren, sober, had taken his pleasure with her in a more or less conventional way but with such zeal and such frequency that she wondered if she could consider herself to have been raped. And there were blotches and bruises manifesting themselves all over her body. Which is not to say that Dahlgren had abused her. But his caresses and embraces had been applied by a man unaware of his strength. She suspected that her body would carry the purpling souvenirs of those embraces for weeks to come. And she smiled. Because in the middle of it all, despite the cold purpose of her mission, her senses had overwhelmed her mind and she had been swept away. She felt as if in the vortex of a tornado, weightless, sightless, mindless, her total being reduced to a writhing, undulating mass of flesh and ganglia, engulfed in roaring, rushing sounds. Her blood was a torrent, her voice a cry urging him on. She wondered if there was something wrong with her to have allowed herself to surrender with such abandon to the big sailor. In the middle of it all she had even forgotten the purpose of her mission, and it was only Dahlgren's concern for timetables and tides which he discoursed on volubly between bouts of lovemaking that had told her almost everything she wanted to know. She was surprised now—and thankful—that she was able to remember.

And then she had arrived back at the Princess's house in the middle of the afternoon and had mendaciously to explain her overnight absence and tend to her daily chores.

Nadia Demanova sighed as she dipped her pen into the ink bottle. She wondered if she would become part of Lars Dahlgren's repertoire of lewd tales, along with Edna from Hamburg and all the rest.

> *Dear Uncle Georgi,*
>
> *With regard to the shipment of the consignments in which you expressed an interest, there is a boat named* Elena, *home port Oslo, which makes frequent sailings between Britain and Norway and Russia. This ship, before undertaking its next voyage, will be berthed in Oslo for approximately the next three weeks. Then it will sail for Archangel. Its exact sailing date is still unscheduled. Any contact you wish to make should be made in Oslo within the fortnight.*
>
> > *Your loving niece,*
> > *Nadia*

# CHAPTER TWENTY-FOUR

In her berth in the harbor of Oslo the *Elena* rocked gently with the rise and fall of the tide.

In the wheelhouse in a heavy gray roll-neck sweater, Lars Dahlgren took a break from his work, filled a pipe with tobacco, and struck a match. He sucked energetically at the stem until the tobacco began to glow in the bowl and the first hot aromatic jet of smoke billowed into his mouth.

The waters of the fjord were as flat as a looking glass, offering in sequined reflection the gay lights of the city across the way. City? Not a metropolis like London or Hamburg or Amsterdam or Petersburg or any of the great ports of call. Capital of a nation, Oslo was more a cheerful town than a city. A cozy place, embracing its harbor at the head of the long fjord. Bustling but not frenzied. Relaxed but not languid. A good enough home for any man. So why, he wondered, was he forever running off to sea? Lars Dahlgren shrugged. What had driven his Norse forebears to abandon the security of their fjords for the wild and bleak unknown beyond the great waters? He took another deep drag of his pipe and then went to the heater and turned it up a few degrees. There was a whiff of winter in the air, and the cold outside was penetrating his little ship's steel skin.

Dahlgren sat down again at his chart table and finished working on his inventory. The equipment and provisions he had ordered were on board. He had done the first part of his job; if Aldonby had been as successful with his recruiting activities, the venture could get under way at anytime—the sooner the better as far as Dahlgren was concerned. If it was cold in Oslo, benefited as the city was by the tepid Gulf Stream, it would be brutal where they were going, across the Arctic to the Russian interior, even in mid-November.

He wondered why he had agreed to join Aldonby in what was certainly an extremely hazardous, perhaps insane, enterprise. There was the money, of course. But he was comfortably fixed. There were other ways to make money, and he had made it, pots full of it, safely in trade and shipping. The problem was it had all become so routine. The sense of adventure that had drawn him to the sea in the first place was gone. He had traveled the same routes so often that he might as well have been driving a tram on the main street in Oslo. Even the women had become routine. They were all as jaded as he, motivated by habit and inertia rather than by desire—with the notable exception of that Nadia creature in London. What a wildcat that one had turned out to be. What an intoxicating blend of innocence and raw lust. He would see her again, he hoped, when this trip was done. But until then, abstinence. No women, no liquor, no heavy food, nothing that would distract him from the task ahead. This would be no simple trolley run. The Barents Sea he knew, though he had rarely ventured across this late in the year. But the Kara Strait would be absolutely treacherous.

"But you'll bring us through, dear girl, won't you?" he said softly but audibly in the empty wheelhouse. He often spoke aloud when he was alone on the ship, conversed with *Elena* as if she really were a woman. They had a warm and loving relationship, these two. Like a couple who had been married for a long, long time. *Elena* was his bride; the others were merely mistresses of the moment.

He cast an affectionate eye around the room. The spoked wheel, the glowing binnacle, the gleaming brass speaking tubes, the engine telegraph, the barometers, the clocks: all the familiar and friendly pieces of hardware that were to him more than mere fittings of iron and brass; they were flesh; they were blood; they were life.

Dahlgren drafted a cable to Aldonby advising him that all the necessary provisions had arrived and that the Russian, Golov, who was keeper of the war chest, should be instructed to pay off the suppliers. He folded the notepaper and tucked it into the pocket of his shirt. Then he unrolled the first of the new charts he had bought and with pencil, compass, and ruler began laying down a course across the Barents Sea.

It was hours later, 0300 by the clock on the bulkhead, and he was in his bunk in the cabin behind the wheelhouse when he was wakened by the sound of something heavy being dragged across the steel deck outside.

He drew aside the musty old woolen blanket that covered his bunk, raised himself up on one elbow, and listened. Whatever it was, whoever it was, he or they were now moving down the outside ladder to the main deck, humping a heavy load down the steps.

For a moment, his head still muzzy with sleep, he thought that some of the old crew might be coming home to roost after a night on the town. But he had put them on leave weeks ago, before his most recent trip to London; Aldonby's volunteers would man the boat on its run into Russia.

Still, some of the boys may have been out on a bender, lost their way, and, guided by a homing instinct, wound up back on *Elena*. It certainly sounded like one of them wasn't navigating under his own steam and was being helped down to his old berth below decks.

Lars Dahlgren sat upright and listened again. He was still dressed in the heavy roll-neck sweater and moleskin trousers he had been wearing in the wheelhouse hours before. He slipped his feet into his boots and began lacing them up. Damn! It sounded like the gang outside were dragging a barrel or a steel drum down the ladder not a man. He decided he had better have a look.

He cracked his cabin door open about an inch. The sweet, damp, frosty night air came in with a rush, washing his grainy eyelids clean of sleep, and with it came the voices of the men now down at the bottom of the ladder near the cargo hold. And they weren't his old crew at all. They were speaking Russian.

He pulled the door all the way open and ran aft along the upper deck. At the top of the ladder he stopped and looked down. There were two of them, manhandling a heavy steel drum toward the canvas-covered hatch to the cargo hold. The steel drum was squat, black, and evil-looking, like the depth charges he had seen lined up on the decks of British naval ships of war. Explosives!

"Hey! You bastards!" he shouted as he came pounding down the ladder. "Get the hell off my ship."

The two men with the drum looked up wide-eyed with astonishment. "Anton!" one of them shouted.

Dahlgren could feel the handrail vibrating as another pair of feet came pounding down the steel steps after him. He stopped and turned in time to see a heavy dark mass materializing over him. He saw it without really comprehending what it was, certainly without having time to react to it.

Anton's boot caught him high on the side of the face, a hammer blow against his right cheekbone. His nerve endings blew out in a soundless display of fireworks somewhere behind his eyes. He didn't even feel the blow. It was as if he were made of mist and the boot had passed painlessly through him. Nor did he feel the bruising slide down the rest of the steel steps or the impact as the top of his head slammed into the deck at the bottom of the ladder.

Ten minutes later, however, it seemed to him that no time at all had elapsed; after the trespassers had finished what they had come to do, he heard muffled voices. Though the voices lacked presence, he sensed that they were standing very close to him. It was as if his head were wrapped in cotton.

"Is he dead?" Russian again but he understood.

"No."

"Is it Dahlgren, you think?"

"I suppose. He came out of Dahlgren's cabin."

Lars, hearing his name, felt impelled to respond in some way. In his head he said yes a few times, like a schoolboy answering roll call. But he didn't think any sound was coming out. And he dimly thought that that was just as well, especially since the effort required to produce sound seemed to be so great. So he gave it up. He was not uncomfortable.

"Should we finish him?"

"Let the explosion do it. More natural."

"Let him go down with his ship." Subdued laughter.

Now Lars began to worry. They were talking of finishing him with explosives of some kind, and he felt too bundled in lethargy to do anything about it.

"Nadia will get a medal for this."

"And what about us?"

"Finished, Josef?"

"Finished."

"Let's get out of here, then."

Dahlgren could feel the vibrations in the steel plate under his back as they pounded up the ladder. And then there was silence. He guessed that he must still be lying at the foot of the ladder where he had fallen.

"Let's get out of here . . ." "Explosion . . ." The stubby black drum that looked like a depth charge. They were going to blow up *Elena* . . . and him. The timers must already be set and running, which was why they had bolted.

And left him to die with his ship. Which was exactly what he would do unless he got up off his back.

His face began to hurt, a searing, pulsing pain, as if all of his teeth had decided to ache all at once.

First the sound of the voices, then the vibrations of the retreating footfalls, and now the terrible aching in his face. Little by little he was coming back.

He groaned. He heard it. An awful sound. It didn't just stay locked in his head like the responsive yes a few moments ago but passed his lips and rang in his ears like the roar of a wounded lion. He rolled over onto his belly, worked his hands down beside his chest and, with another woeful roar, pushed himself up onto all fours.

Even down on his hands and knees he began to feel dizzy, as if the deck were rolling and pitching under him in a force ten sea. He began to vomit. He felt like returning to the stability of a prone position, flat on the deck. But he knew that would be the way to certain death.

He felt that if he could navigate at all, he should try to locate the explosive and disarm it. Yet he could barely maintain his balance on all fours, and from the haste with which the intruders departed he had to assume that he didn't have time.

He swung his left arm in an arc feeling for the handrail on the ladder and almost toppled onto his side. But his fingers made contact with the rail and he held on and began torturously to haul himself to his feet.

The gangplank connected to the pier from the upper deck near the wheelhouse. Somehow he would have to drag himself all the way up the ladder; in his present condition it would require an effort something like that which a healthy man would have to expend in order to scale a sheer cliff face.

He had managed to haul himself about a quarter of the distance up the ladder when the explosive blew.

Dahlgren felt the pressure of the blast before he heard the sound. *Elena*'s rear deck bucked clear out of the water, and Lars felt himself airborne, felt himself rolling weightlessly over the rail, felt the sharp slap of the water against his back, and then total immersion in the shocking chill of the fjord.

The lethargy and dizziness that had gripped him on the deck just seconds ago was receding. He came up coughing and spitting ice water and his nose was running with blood. He saw the blood in the water but couldn't taste it in his mouth because both the blood and water were salty, and he didn't know which he was swallowing.

He reached down to pull off his boots, but they were gone; the blast had taken them. He supposed that he was lucky that the boots were all that had been blown off. His head and his arms and legs were all in place.

He thrust his arms out in front of him and began to breaststroke for the shore. He would make it. He was certain that he would. He had been thrown sideways, and he could see that the shore wasn't more than thirty yards away.

He glanced over his shoulder and saw his beloved *Elena* being swallowed by flames and settling slowly on her side, like a great soft behemoth that had been struck a mortal blow.

There were tears in Lars Dahlgren's eyes, tears coursing down his face, but he couldn't taste them either.

# CHAPTER TWENTY-FIVE

*From the journal of Anastasia Romanov*

TOBOLSK
NOVEMBER 25, 1917

Why is it that the worst rumors always turn out to be true? Colonel Kobylinsky has been relieved of his command. He came today to bid us good-bye. He will not be leaving for another twenty-four hours, but he wanted to make his farewells now. He feels that tomorrow, when the officer who will replace him arrives, there will be no opportunity for a proper leave-taking. There were tears in his eyes.

He confesses that things may be a little harsher for us now than they were before. He begs us to endure as best we can whatever new unpleasantness and indignities might be heaped upon us. If we can endure the discomforts to come, he thinks we will be all right.

It is his opinion that while there are those among the Bolsheviks who hate us and would wish us all the worst of harm, there are cooler heads among the leadership who are aware of certain advantages to be gained by keeping us from serious harm.

The good Colonel further says that the installation of the new officer in charge may turn out to our advantage as that person will have come from Moscow, under instructions from the Central Council, whereas Kobylinsky was a leftover from the Kerensky regime. For this reason the more radical Red Guards never quite trusted our Colonel; they felt that his sympathies lay too much in our favor. And he, in turn, was finding it increasingly difficult to handle this element among his men. Leonid confirms this.

The Colonel believes that the new officer, while personally less friendly to us, may be more effective in protecting our interests since

115

he will have the authority of Moscow behind him and will be considered by his men to be one of them.

And so the Colonel is gone. And our circle of friends shrinks. Only Mama's maid, Demidova, remains, and Trup, Papa's footman; Nagorny, the loyal sailor who cares so well for Alexei; Kharitonov, the cook; Dr. Botkin, our physician; and, of course, for me, Leonid. But still, as the snow grows deeper and the winds howl through the house around the windows and under the doors, I have the feeling that we are more and more alone; that our family is an island in a bleak northern sea, and the freezing waters are rising all around us.

# CHAPTER TWENTY-SIX

I t was well past midnight.

Nadia Demanova was ineffably weary. As she climbed the servants' stairway to her room at the top of the house, she felt as if she were carrying lead weights on the soles of her shoes. She had spent most of the day grooming the Princess for the party that had only just ended and then had attended to her needs and to the needs of her guests throughout the long evening. Thank God it would be the last for a while.

The exhausting soirées had grown in frequency and length over the past month as Aldonby and Golov's fund raising activities had grown more intensive. Tonight Aldonby had announced that the war chest was full. Those present, he had declared, could take pride in the contributions they had made of both a monetary and personal nature. Their Tsar and his family would be forever grateful.

Among those in the gathering were the four volunteers he had chosen from among the dozens who had offered their services. But the four didn't yet know who they were.

The guests had departed; the servants had cleaned up; the lights had been turned out, the doors locked, and Nadia had begun the long heavy-footed climb to her room.

She sensed nothing out of the ordinary as she entered the room, didn't even notice that the light was already on. With the tunnel vision and single-minded purpose of the very tired, she made a direct line for her bed.

With a sigh she fell back into its billowy embrace. She lay there for a little while, eyes closed, arms and legs dangling over the edges, thinking how wonderful it would be to just allow sleep to take her this way,

117

without bothering to change into her nightclothes, without even troubling to remove her shoes.

A polite cough from a corner of the room startled her. She opened her eyes, protectively drew in her arms and legs, and turned her head in the direction of the sound.

The man sitting in her shabby armchair under the reading light, knees neatly crossed, was Viktor Golov.

"I didn't mean to startle you," he apologized. "But I didn't know how else, in the interest of decency, to apprise you of my presence, Comrade."

She disliked Golov intensely, found him oily and repulsive, found it hard to reconcile her contempt for him with the fact that they were both on the same side. What did a creature like Golov know of the aspirations of the masses?

"Get out of my room," she rasped.

Golov took her rebuke with equanimity. "We are Comrades, Nadia, dear. There is no such thing as your room, my room. Everything belongs to everyone, all together. We have wiped out the degenerate concept of privacy. Isn't that so?"

"Get out."

"Hear me, won't you?"

"Suppose someone should find you here."

"Don't let your guilty conscience betray you. If someone should find me here, their first thoughts would not be of a conspiracy but of seduction: me of you or you of me."

"Never."

Golov shrugged. "If you want to protect your reputation should someone come through the door, cry rape."

"What do you want?"

"To congratulate you. To congratulate us."

"Don't play games with me; I'm very tired."

"So I noticed." He reached into his pocket and withdrew a telegraph flimsy. "It's here. Coded, of course. The outcome of your liaison with Captain Dahlgren. His boat is lying at the bottom of the Oslo Fjord."

Nadia blinked, astonished that her actions had actually produced results. She had spent most of her life talking and dreaming. Words had always been simply words to her. Sounds that touched the heart or the mind. How astounding that words she had committed to paper had resulted in the physical destruction of so sturdy and material a thing as a ship.

"And Dahlgren?" she asked, startling herself with her concern.

"It doesn't mention Dahlgren. It was only the boat that mattered."

"When?" She was breathing rapidly, the rise and fall of her breast betraying her agitation.

"Little victories excite you, I see." His thick lips twisted into a lewd smirk.

She was feeling light-headed and slightly queasy in the stomach as she watched him draw from his pocket the telegraph flimsy. He took his eyes off her long enough to glance at the paper.

"Early yesterday morning. A little more than twenty-four hours ago."

"I saw nothing about it in the evening newspaper."

"Did you read it line by line?"

"I hardly had time. I work," she said pointedly.

"A rather small vessel catches fire and sinks at its pier in Oslo and you think it would be news in England? My dear!"

"Don't patronize me."

"Forgive me. In any event, after I received the cable, I *did* check the newspapers, most carefully, and there wasn't a word about it anywhere, which is not to diminish your achievement. If the newspeople had any idea how important that boat was, you can be sure it would have been on the first page and in a prominent position."

"Thank you," she said, without any warmth, "for bringing me this news." As if that had been the only reason he had come. "And now I would like you to go."

Golov hadn't moved from the chair, hadn't even uncrossed his legs.

"But aren't you curious about the rest of the cable?"

"It was not addressed to me."

"No. The instructions were for me. Wouldn't you like me to share them with you?"

"Not in the least." Of course, she was curious, but she would be damned if she would play along. "If it involved me at all, you would be obliged to tell me."

"But, in a way, it does concern you, Nadia, dear."

"Then tell me how and stop these coy games."

"Very well." Thick-skinned as he was she had stung him. He uncrossed his legs and then recrossed them the other way. Otherwise he remained immobile. "Your part of the checking maneuver having been completed, I have been given the signal to proceed with my part, which will effectively deliver the checkmate."

"Get on with it, Viktor," she coldly demanded. "I don't play chess."

Golov shook his head despairingly. "Considering your hostility, I really don't know why I pursue this. We are two birds far from home in a hostile environment, pretending to be what we are not. A most lonely existence. Human beings, no less than other creatures, were meant to dwell in pairs."

"What *are* you babbling about?" Nadia snapped.

"Only this. My part of the stratagem is to make vanish the money that has been collected in the name of the Tsar."

"So?"

"I am proposing that after a decent interval has elapsed we share that windfall, and that during the interval we share each other."

Nadia threw him a withering look. "Preposterous. Besides, you have a wife."

"She's a thousand miles away in Russia. I may never see her again. And I wasn't proposing marriage."

"I find you repulsive." The words were out, and Nadia wondered if she had not at last gone too far.

Golov's eyelids dropped. He seemed to be staring at the tip of his upraised shoe. Then he shrugged. "There are some fifty-six thousand pounds in that fund. That might help you to improve your opinion of me. It would all be . . . ours. All the comforts of life would be . . . yours."

Nadia's nostrils flared. The man was so offensive she wanted to kick him. "Not for very long. The people you are stealing from are not without influence. Some of them are poorer now than they ever dreamed they could be. Some of them sold off their family heirlooms to raise their share. Do you think that they'd just let it slip away? You're not in Russia now. The law in this monarchist paradise would run you into the ground. You wouldn't last long enough to spend a thousand pounds of it."

"They won't know that I've stolen it."

"Will they think that it just got up and walked away of its own accord?"

"They'll think Aldonby stole it. I've already set up a special account in his name, signed his name with my own hand. As far as that bank is concerned, I am Charles Aldonby. As far as Aldonby is concerned, he doesn't know that the account exists. I put the money in; I'll take it out when it suits me to. Now does my proposition seem more tempting?"

"And will Aldonby just stand silently by when they accuse him of this monstrous theft?"

"Aldonby will say nothing."

"You are a dreamer, Golov. Your head is in the clouds."

"Dead men can't complain," Golov replied.

Nadia gasped. "You've killed him?"

"I will. He will vanish. Just as if he'd absconded."

Nadia stared at him in astonishment.

Golov uncrossed his legs and rose from the chair. He felt that he had at last won a point, and he wanted to leave before she neutralized this small victory with a deprecating remark. He opened the door and turned to face her briefly. "Think about it, Nadia." Then, before she could reply, he left, simply evaporated into the darkened upstairs hallway, letting the door swing shut behind him.

# CHAPTER TWENTY-SEVEN

Aldonby unfolded the telegram from Lars Dahlgren and read it again. "ALL PLANS ALTERED STOP ARRIVE LONDON TOMORROW STOP LARS."

Sara had waited up for him to return from the Princess's, handed him the telegram, still sealed, and learned only that he didn't know what it meant, that he would have to contact Lars. But his face was ashen and tight with concern. She had gone off to bed, at his insistence, knowing from experience that he preferred to face trouble alone, wishing it were otherwise. She lay in bed now, sleepless, listening to his distraught pacing.

Aldonby puzzled over the telegram's point of origin. "PERTH: PRINCE CHARLES HOTEL." What in God's name was Lars doing in Scotland? What had gone wrong?

The flimsy paper tore under the tension in his fingers. He had nervously unfolded and refolded it so often in the forty minutes since he had placed the call to Perth that it was beginning to disintegrate. He shoved it into his pocket and glared angrily at the telephone. Why hadn't the connection been made? The damned operator must have gone to sleep.

He began to pace the room again. He felt that if he tried to sit still he might explode. He had put in one quick call to Golov immediately after placing the call to Perth. But Golov had not yet returned to his flat. That had been over half an hour ago. Surely he must have returned by now, but Aldonby was reluctant to place the call again for fear of tying up the line just when the circuit to Perth might be open. Besides, he wasn't quite sure what he'd tell Golov anyway.

Aldonby pulled a pillow off a chair and hurled it across the room. He wasn't aiming at anything in particular, just venting off anger and frustration. The pillow went crashing into liquor bottles on the side table. Whiskey glasses bowled over and shattered against the wall. A decanter of whiskey tipped onto its side, spun around once, and began dripping Dewar's onto the carpet.

Sara called from the bedroom, alarmed. "Charles?"

"It's all right," he yelled back. "I just dropped a glass. Go back to sleep."

The telephone rang. Aldonby, on his way to salvage the whiskey, stopped in half stride, spun, and grabbed the phone.

"Your call to Perth, sir."

"Yes. Please." He watched the carpet drink up the last of the whiskey. There was a sound of static and gurgling, as if the lines had sprung a leak.

"Hello." It was Lars's voice. Aldonby forgot about the whiskey and the carpet.

"Lars? Aldonby here."

"I can't hear you very well."

"Aldonby here, Lars. I have your wire." He was shouting.

"Ah! Aldonby. You have my wire?"

"Yes, Lars. For God's sake, what's happened?"

"I'm sorry. I'm having trouble hearing."

"I hear you loud and clear, Lars," Aldonby shouted.

The door to the study opened. Sara, eyes screwed up against the light, poked in her head inquisitively, saw the mess around the side table, hurried across the room, tying up her robe, and straightened up the tipped-over decanter. Aldonby waved her away. She ignored him and knelt to pick up the pieces of smashed glass.

"My head is covered with bandages. I look like an Egyptian mummy. I also feel like I've been dead and resurrected. I cannot hear too well. The blast hurt my ears, I think."

Aldonby cupped his hand over the phone and snapped, "Sara, for God's sake, leave it."

She threw him a look, pointedly spilled the shards of glass back onto the carpet, and stalked out of the room. There was a limit to patience and understanding.

"What happened?" Aldonby yelled into the phone.

"Wait. I'm going to pull of some of the damned bandages."

"Lars?"

"They blew up *Elena* in the Oslo Fjord."

"Blew up? Oh, God! Who?"

"Who do you think?"

"Can she be salvaged?"

"Maybe for scrap."

"Christ!"

"I have to go now. My train will be leaving soon."

"What train? What are you doing in Scotland?"

"I escaped from the hospital. The first ferry out of Oslo landed here. I'm taking the train to London."

"Can we get another ship?"

"We'll talk when I see you. It will take time."

"The supplies?"

"They went down with *Elena*."

"We'll reorder."

"You'll first have to pay for the destroyed orders. They weren't insured. How's the money?"

"I'm trying to contact Golov now."

"We are already on the edge of winter. A few more weeks and it's no good until spring. And what about those expatriate Russians? Do you think they'll pawn what's left of their personal treasures to supply a second mission, when we couldn't even get the first one launched? My head is splitting. I have to go."

"Stay where you are and rest."

"I have a score to settle. I can't wait."

"Lars—"

"I have a train to catch. We'll talk tomorrow."

There was a click.

"Lars!"

The line was dead. Aldonby slammed down the receiver. He went over to the side table and poured himself a generous slug of whiskey from an undamaged bottle. He carried the whiskey back to the telephone stand and gave the operator Golov's number again.

This time Golov answered.

"I've been trying to reach you," Aldonby said without preamble.

"It is very late." Golov sounded curt, annoyed.

"You weren't in earlier. We have a problem."

"So? What is it?"

"We'll have to meet."

"Of course." Suddenly Golov was dripping cordiality. "What seems to be the trouble?" Of course, he knew. What surprised him was that Aldonby also knew so soon.

"A problem with transportation. I'll go into the details when I see you. Possible financial problems too. We'll have to work the whole thing out. In any event you must be prepared to start disbursing funds tomorrow."

Perfect, Golov thought. He'll walk right into it. "I'll need a few hours to get everything in order, and nothing can be done until morning. Suppose you come to my flat at noon. We can work there."

"Tomorrow at noon, then."

"Good night."

As he rang off, it occurred to Aldonby that Golov had received the news of a looming emergency with a surprising absence of curiosity and with amazing equanimity.

# CHAPTER TWENTY-EIGHT

The black hansom cab had been parked at the curb in front of the Princess's house for some time. Nadia Demanova had seen it from her window at the top of the house as she dressed to go out for her morning's round of shopping. It was still there some thirty minutes later when she left the building through the service door in the basement. It would probably be there when she returned, she thought. Very few people had the patience for a horse-drawn carriage these days. They were a vanishing species, those tall hansom cabs; only the war and its attendant petrol shortage had given them a brief new lease on life. Still, how charming they were, how quaint. She hoped that the driver, perched in his seat outside, earned enough to feed his horse properly.

Inside the cab Lars Dahlgren saw her coming and about time. Every moment he had spent waiting cost him good money. No matter. The old cab was ideally suited to his purpose. Enclosed. Private. The driver seated outside and in back. Out of sight. He might not be able to lure her to his flat. But he could pull her into the cab before she had time to comprehend the danger.

As she drew parallel to the cab, Lars threw open the door and leaned out. Nadia stopped short and gasped.

"Will you ride with me?"

She stood there nonplussed, eyes wide, mouth agape.

Lars Dahlgren reached out and clamped his right hand firmly around her upper arm.

"I thought . . ." she stammered, stunned into compliance as Dahlgren hoisted her into the cab, afraid that if she resisted, her arm might snap.

"You thought? . . ." he repeated, as he set her down beside him and pulled the door shut.

"Your head!" she gasped, staring at the bandages. She looked terrified.

"Yes. My head. And lucky I was to get away with just this. You were going to say that you thought I was dead, weren't you?"

Dahlgren rapped sharply on the roof with his free hand. The driver shouted a command. The horse whinnied. There was a little jerk as the traces took up the slack. And the cab slowly began to move forward.

Nadia opened her mouth as if to cry out. Lars clamped his big hand over it. Then his other hand released her arm and came up over her shoulder and locked itself around her throat.

"One sound out of you and I'll break it," he warned dispassionately. Nadia rolled her great brown eyes imploringly in his direction.

"Will you be quiet?"

She raised and lowered her lids in what she hoped would be interpreted as an affirmative signal.

Lars removed the hand from across her mouth. But the other hand remained around her throat.

The driver, following Dahlgren's earlier instructions for an aimless ramble, turned into Lowndes Street and proceeded at a walking pace. The faster-moving motorcars behind him bellicosely honked their horns. The cabby proceeded, unruffled. It was his belief that he was taking a pair of lovers on an outing, a wounded veteran, judging from the bandage-wrapped head, and his girl. There had to be some room left in this war-weary, machine-ridden world for the timeless rituals or else what was it all worth?

Inside the curtained cab, hidden from the driver's view and from the view of the agitated motorists, Nadia Demanova pleaded. "Please. What do you want with me?"

"Maybe another night like the last one we spent together," Lars Dahlgren murmured into her ear, his voice hoarse with what she mistook for desire.

"Oh?" She sounded surprised and greatly relieved. Dahlgren could feel her shoulder muscles relax. He felt that he could easily break her neck now. But she would hardly be aware of what was happening or why. And he wanted her to know.

The cab turned left into Chesham Street. At the end of the block he could see the iron fences and the open space of Belgrave Square.

"Well, you needn't have kidnapped me for *that*," Nadia cooed, her voice still slightly aquiver with residual fright.

Lars smiled and tightened up his grip around her throat.

"Lars! You're choking me!"

As if he didn't know it. "Bitch!" he snarled. "That night cost me dearly. Your price is too high."

The naked terror was back in her eyes again, exactly what Dahlgren wanted to see.

"I don't know what you're talking about," Nadia croaked.

"My ship, you bitch. Your friends blew it up." He applied a little more pressure." They think you may get a medal for it."

"Please!" Nadia gagged. "Mistake!"

Dahlgren loosened his grip a little. "Your mistake or mine?"

She blinked and took a deep breath. Tears burst from her eyes, like a just squeezed sponge. They flooded her cheeks.

The cab clip-clopped past the elegant facades of Belgrave Square and turned left again in the direction of Wilton Crescent.

"Please!" she cried.

"Any sound out of you louder than a whisper, I'll snap your head off," Dahlgren warned.

Nadia blinked her consent. Her warm tears rolled off her chin and bathed Lars's wrist and hand.

"My mistake," she gasped. "I didn't know what I was doing. I didn't know what *they* would do," she lied. "I can make up for it," she rushed on, desperate to make a point before he closed the awful vise around her throat again. "I can do you a great favor."

"I can hire a girl for a quid to do whatever you can do."

"Not that," Nadia gasped. "I don't mean that. But we can do that, too, if you want."

"Tell me, you slut."

"Golov."

He thought she was choking and relaxed his grip a little more.

"What?"

"Golov."

"Golov?" His astonishment was so great that his voice rose involuntarily. He waited a moment to make sure he hadn't attracted the driver's attention. Nadia gazed at him, blinking.

"What about Golov?" He tightened his grip for emphasis.

"Please. I can't breathe."

"That's the whole idea," he said. But he loosened up just a little. How fine she felt in his arms, he thought. Like a quivering bird. What a waste it would be to break her.

"What about Golov?"

"They'll kill me."

"I'll kill you."

Nadia rolled her eyes at him beseechingly. "He's one of us. One of them."

Lars Dahlgren glared at her bitterly. "Are you telling me that Golov, not you, was responsible for my ship?"

"No," she pleaded.

"What then?"

"He has the money."

"Yes? So?"

"He's going to steal it."

Lars stared at her, dumbfounded. "Do you know what this will get you if you're lying?"

She shook her head.

"Thirty minutes more," Dahlgren told her. "Maybe an hour. But you'll wish that I had done it now."

"It's true," Nadia pleaded. "It's true. He wanted me to go away with him."

"So you betray him too?"

"No. I never would have gone with him. I told him."

"Where can I find him?"

"Basil Street. Number seventy-eight. He has a flat there."

Lars kept her neck in the crook of his right arm. With his left hand he reached back and rapped sharply on the rear wall of the cab. The little panel slid open.

"Sir?" the driver asked.

"Number seventy-eight Basil Street. How far from here?"

"Quarter of a mile, maybe, sir."

The driver slid the panel shut, shouted "Giddy-up!" and cracked the whip in the air behind the horse's right ear as they headed into Malcomb Street. Those lovers looked as if they had little time to spare.

# CHAPTER TWENTY-NINE

In a second-floor front room at 78 Basil Street, Charles Aldonby sat in a ladder-backed chair at the table that Golov used as a desk. The account books and deposit slips spread out on the table before him were counterfeit. He knew that now. They had been merely the lure that had facilitated the springing of the trap.

Golov sat, or stood, somewhere out of reach behind Aldonby armed with a Nagant revolver. Aldonby actually had no way of knowing Golov's exact position in the room. He had been ordered to remain seated and to keep his eyes front and his hands on the table. In front of him, aside from a disarray of worthless paper, was the window, shut tight. Even had he been able to risk diving through it hoping that Golov's first shot would miss him and the glass wouldn't cut his throat, he was some thirty feet above the street. A headfirst landing would be as fatal as a bullet in the back.

For the moment at least, they were in a stalemate. Golov couldn't shoot him in the back for fear that the sound of the shot might cause someone in the house or on the street to call for the police. Aldonby couldn't move or he would risk Golov's pulling the trigger despite himself.

In the street below Aldonby could see the untroubled progress of the day's activity: tradesmen making their deliveries, a mother rolling her bundled infant about in a wicker pram, two five-year olds at play, hopping about on one foot on the flagstones. War? Terror? Privation? In the worst of times life went on.

Golov coughed. From the sound of it Aldonby guessed that he was still at least halfway across the room, certainly out of arms' reach. That would mean that neither of them had moved since Golov had drawn his pistol; it may have been only minutes ago. It seemed like hours.

Aldonby wondered if Golov's palms were sweating as his were. He also wondered if the floorboards creaked. He hadn't noticed when he had come into the room and sat down; there had been no need. Nevertheless, he kept listening intently for the sound of creaking floorboards; if Golov decided to move up close behind him, he would like to have some warning. If Golov came close, it would probably signal the imminence of a blow to the head with the pistol butt. A silent execution. One that wouldn't alarm the neighbors as would the firing of a shot. Then Golov could dispose of the body at his leisure, whole or hacked up piecemeal; it wouldn't matter. Not if, as he had maliciously informed Aldonby, he planned to make it appear as if Aldonby had run off with the funds.

If Golov chose to kill him silently, as surely he must if he hoped to make good his escape, he would have to approach to within arms' reach. And if he chose the most convenient weapon at hand, the butt of his pistol, there would be a moment, while Golov was within his reach and before the butt came crashing down, when the pistol would be turned around, raised ceilingward, and could not effectively be fired.

So Aldonby concluded that his best hope of coming out of this alive lay in the chance that Golov would decide to bludgeon him to death. That—combined with creaky woodwork and a properly timed move in the interval between when the weapon was raised and just before it came smashing down—was his only hope.

Aldonby had to concede it was a very slim hope, but it was his only hope, and he had to be ready.

So he sat, staring down at the street, and trying to block from his consciousness all sounds but the sounds in the room. He could hear the sound of his own breathing. But not Golov's. For a moment he wondered if Golov might have silently slipped out and left him sitting alone staring out the window, like a fool.

He decided to see what might happen if he ventured very, very slowly to turn his head.

"Remain as you were!" Golov hissed. Then silence again.

So much for vagrant hope. Aldonby resumed his listening and staring out the window.

A carriage drew up at the opposite curb. A burly man climbed down and helped a trim young woman to the sidewalk. They stood very close until the carriage pulled away, he with his arm around her.

Oh, God! Aldonby recognized them: Lars Dahlgren and the pretty young maid who worked for the Princess. Clinging together, they crossed the street toward Golov's house and then disappeared from view.

With an awful sinking feeling Aldonby decided that he had been a dupe. Lars and Golov were working together, and the Russian girl too. He had been betrayed all around. He had failed all the good people who had trusted him, and ultimately he had failed the Imperial Family. He deserved no better than what he was about to get. That slim chance he had held out of saving himself was gone. They had had it all worked out. Alone Golov would never have approached him to club him to death; they would all be there, covering, one for the other, as they finished him off—unless he could do something to throw them off balance before their organized mayhem began.

He realized that it didn't much matter what he did; there was no hope for him anymore. But he would be damned, if he'd just sit there placidly while they butchered him.

Now was the time to act. Now before the others came into the room. He had nothing to lose.

He braced his good hand against the desk and, pretending to examine one of the ledgers, leaned forward ever so slightly to gain leverage. Then he pushed off backward, toppling the chair, landing on his shoulder on the floor, somersaulting and rolling.

He heard the shot explode like an artillery piece in the small room; he heard the glass in the window shatter. He was on his knees now, dizzy, disoriented, almost within reach of Golov with his one good hand. But Golov was stumbling backward, getting out of the way, as he tried to bring the smoking pistol down into firing position again.

Aldonby coiled to leap, but he knew he'd never make it. Golov was too far away, and the pistol was coming down too fast.

And then there was another sound, like a rifle crack, and the splintered door flew open behind Golov.

Golov started to turn.

In came Lars Dahlgren, low, like a charging bull, under the gun hand, hooking Golov under the ribs with his shoulder, driving him back into the room.

The gun erupted again. Plaster showered down from the ceiling. Lars had Golov pinned against the table near the window, wrestling him for possession of the revolver.

Aldonby, struggling to his feet, caught a glimpse of the Russian girl standing in the ruined doorway, hand to mouth, eyes dilated with terror. She turned and fled down the stairs.

There was a crack, like the sound of boxwood snapping, and a scream, as Lars Dahlgren broke Golov's wrist across the edge of the table.

The revolver dropped to the floor, and Aldonby made a dive for it. From overhead there came a ripping sound, like a heavy sail splitting. Then the whole ceiling came down. Sheets of plaster, adhesion weakened by the pistol bullet, became separated from the overhead lath, fell, broke across the heads and backs of the three men struggling in the room below, and disintegrated in a cloud of choking white dust.

The weight of the falling debris was not so great as to cause physical harm, only confusion. Golov slipped out of Dahlgren's grip and scrambled away across the tabletop. Lars, half-blinded by dust, reached out and caught hold of an ankle. With a strength born of desperation, Golov wrenched himself loose. Lars hurled himself on his belly across the crumbled plaster on the tabletop. But Golov was beyond his reach.

On his knees on the floor clutching the pistol, blinking away dust, and paralyzed with disbelief, Aldonby watched Golov squirm away from Lars and scurry like a blind rat across the tabletop and halfway through the wide open space in the shattered window. He saw Lars grab again at Golov's ankle, saw Golov squirm loose. Propelled by the momentum of his effort, Golov went sailing through the bullet-blasted window, an ungainly, flailing quadruped projectile, all chalky white, a ghost even before he died. Down below in the street a woman screamed.

Aldonby picked himself up from the floor, the pistol dangling from his hand. Lars Dahlgren, stretched out across the table, groaned. Aldonby approached the window from an oblique angle so that he couldn't be seen from below and looked down.

"Did he get away?" Lars gasped.

"Not very far. He looks quite dead."

Dahlgren righted himself painfully. He coughed and spat bits of plaster out of his mouth. "Where's Nadia?"

"The girl who came in with you? She ran."

"Shit. I'll never find her now."

"She must have been scared out of her wits."

"First I lose my ship; then I lose her. Shit." With his fingertips Lars Dahlgren wiped plaster away from his eyes.

"Where you in love with her?"

"I was going to kill her." He spat again. "She sold us out."

"When I saw you get out of the carriage, I thought you were all in this together."

"Me? With them? They sank my ship!"

"You looked awfully damned cozy coming across the street together."

"I had an arm lock on her, which I let go when I heard the shot. I should have rammed the door with her instead of with my foot."

"You saved my neck. Thanks."

"Forget it. She's probably halfway to the Russky Embassy by now. I'll never find her again." He sounded as morose as a schoolboy who had lost his first love.

"Let's get out of here before the police arrive."

Dahlgren raked plaster off his bandaged head with his fingertips. "We're a little conspicuous, aren't we?"

"Just lean on me heavily as we go out the door, as if you're hurt and having trouble walking." Aldonby tucked the pistol into his waistband under his shirt. He surveyed the wrecked room and said, "It could very well pass for a natural disaster."

As they came out of the building, a crowd had already gathered around Golov's corpse. A man was running away down the street to bring help.

"What happened up there?" a woman shouted at Aldonby and Dahlgren. "It sounded like gunfire."

"Gas heater blew up. Ceiling collapsed," Aldonby answered, as he hurried past supporting a limping Lars Dahlgren. "I must get this man to hospital."

"Bloody war's the cause of it all," a man in the crowd muttered. Aldonby and Dahlgren rounded the corner and, once out of view, ran for the Underground entrance two blocks away.

An hour later, in Aldonby's flat, washed, changed, and with a bottle of whiskey on the table between them, they tried to decide what their next move would be.

The ship was gone.

The money was gone.

Nadia was gone.

They could check Nadia's room at the Princess's house to see if there were any clues as to where the money might be. They would have to inform the Princess and the other expatriates of the setback.

Setback?

Disaster!

They would have to start all over again. And it was unlikely that the expatriates, having pawned their treasure to fund this aborted effort, would make the financial sacrifice again. And winter was setting in. Whatever happened, they would be unable to move until spring.

# BOOK TWO

# CHAPTER THIRTY

*From the journal of Anastasia Romanov*

DECEMBER 15, 1917

An unhappy development under the regime of Colonel Osmenov, who was sent here to replace Kobylinsky. The soldiers now roam at will through the house at all hours of the day and night. Leonid has told me that they have been expressly forbidden by Osmenov to physically molest us. Orders from Moscow. But mental abuse is another story. Moscow issued no special directives on mental abuse. Osmenov seems to encourage it.

When Papa protested the presence of soldiers in the house, Osmenov replied that it was winter and the men on guard duty needed to get warm now and then. When Papa asked that the men be restricted to finding warmth in one downstairs room in the house, Osmenov angrily demanded to know if we thought we were too good to associate with soldiers of the motherland. There was no reasoning with him because, Leonid told me, it was Osmenov himself who had invited the soldiers to make free use of the house.

We spend a good deal of our time now washing offensive filth off our walls. Pictures and slogans that would once have appalled us are now so commonplace that we take them in stride.

And now Mama insists that we girls wear several layers of underclothes. Even under our nightgowns. Should any untoward advances be made, Mama believes that these extra layers of clothing will give us time to call for help and give help time to arrive. Our muslin chastity belts, Marie jokes. But Mama is gravely serious.

JANUARY 20, 1918

Tobolsk is an ice palace. From my window on the second floor it glistens slickly in the blinding low sunlight of our brief afternoons and glows eerily blue-white when the moon is not hidden by the clouds. The snow is shoulder high in the streets and encrusted on top with an icy glaze. Pathways have been cut through the snow so that the people can make their way about town. They appear to be walking in ditches. I can see only the tops of their heads wrapped in scarves. Not even their noses show as they move like dark, busy beetles past the house.

Of course, we are not privileged to walk these tunneled paths as other people do. We are not like any other citizen, though we are now addressed as citizen all the time. We are confined to our house and our yard. And we do the best we can, playing games in the snow sometimes or sometimes just standing idly on the back porch for a breath of fresh air—even if it's so cold that our breath freezes before our eyes.

We built a snowman the other day and threw snowballs at each other, and laughed until we were breathless and exhausted. Alexei tried to join in. Big Nagorny wold pack the snow into balls for him, and Alexei would throw them at us. And we would throw ours at Nagorny, who absorbed all the hits with great good humor. We didn't dare throw at Alexei for fear that if we struck him we might cause a bruise and that might be enough with his condition to cause a hemorrhage that might be fatal.

How ironic it is that one of the reasons we are prisoners is that the mighty Bolsheviks so fear that this sweet, frail child, who cannot absorb even the impact of a snowball, might one day have the power and authority to restore the monarchy.

# CHAPTER THIRTY-ONE

There was a deafening scream—tortured steel, flange against rail—as the laboring locomotive hauled its burden of passengers and freight, six carriages, eight boxcars, around the last curve in the right of way before the approach to Moscow.

Borodnev, awakened from a sitting sleep by the racket set up by the wheels, shoved aside the stranger on the bench beside him who had slumped against his shoulder. The stranger sagged the other way and came to rest against the side of the snoring passenger on his left. Borodnev looked at them both with disgust. Was this what the Revolution was for?

He snapped up the window shade, flooding the fetid enclosure with the blinding orange light of early morning, and all the residents of the compartment came protestingly awake. Borodnev threw them a one-eyed look so threatening that it blunted their outrage. Had they realized who their fellow passenger was, there would have been no protest at all. In any event his bearing and his scowl were enough to reduce their protests to muted and impotent mutterings.

And they saw the hands—dangling upside down outside the window—at the end of forearms clothed in raveled wool. One of them blinked in disbelief and pointed, speechless with horror, at the dusty pane of glass.

Borodnev had seen the hands when he had snapped up the shade and had absorbed the sight with equanimity. A dead man's hands were no novelty to him, not even when dangling from the roof of a train.

"Is he all right?" one of the passengers asked stupidly but out of simple human concern.

Borodnev pierced him with a look of disgust. Damned fool. Did he

139

think that the owner of those hands was performing acrobatics out there for the sake of his health?

"Maybe we should see if we can help him?" another suggested.

"You want to help him?" Borodnev spat. "I'll show you how to help him." He yanked the window open, immediately turning the compartment into an ice locker. He reached up and grasped the frozen wrists as if he were taking hold of lengths of iron pipe. He tugged hard; but powerful as his arms were, they weren't strong enough to unstick the corpse. "Doesn't anyone else want to help?" he roared disdainfully.

The others backed off into the corners of the compartment and averted their eyes, certain now that they were in the company of a madman.

Borodnev put all his weight behind it this time. There was a harsh ripping sound as the frozen clothing tore loose from the steel roof and a frosted blue-white face came sliding past followed by a torso and legs, all stiff as frozen laundry.

Borodnev, following the corpse down with his eyes, leaned out of the window and laughed as he saw it bury itself up to the waist, head first, legs and feet pointing skyward, in the snowbank at trackside.

Looking to the right and left, he could see the railway workers and Red Guards breaking loose from the train dozens of corpses, frozen in clusters where they had clung to the steps at the entranceways to several of the cars. Unable to find room in the packed aisles and compartments inside the train, the outboard passengers had paid a fearful price for their journey.

Borodnev shut the window and sat down lest the other passengers in the compartment intrude on his place on the bench. He supposed that the train had been stopped so that the corpses could be scraped off outside the city limits. It would have been unseemly for a train to make its entrance into the nation's new capital all garnished with cadavers.

In the distance Borodnev could see the yards and the huge shed of the Nikolayevsky Station and fanning out from the station the vast, squat, mustard-colored city and the candy-striped swirls of color on the onion domes of St. Basil's Cathedral.

He had seen worse cities; the one where Kerensky had sent him had been worse, really had not been what he would consider a city at all in the sense that Petersburg was a city. Moscow at least had some size, some room in which to maneuver and grow. But Moscow was not Petersburg either; he would miss the splendid parks and vistas, and elegantly colonnaded palaces. And the building on Lubyanka Square where they had assigned him offices was not the Peter and Paul Fortress. But it would do. It would have to as would this jaundiced-looking metropolis. Lenin had chosen to move the seat of government here and he, Borodnev, must consider himself fortunate to have been chosen to move too. A man always wanted to be where the reins of power were held.

Two days and three nights it had taken him to make the normal twenty-hour journey from the old capital. Lenin and Trotsky and Sverdlov might be marvelous polemists, but they were, in Borodnev's opinion, inadequate to the task of making things run. Were he, Borodnev, in charge of everything it would be different. Backs might be broken, heads might roll, but things would run.

But that was in the future. In the immediate present was a gnawing need for breakfast and then to arrange an appointment at the Kremlin. It would be his first interview with the Central Committee. It would be grudgingly granted. He was resentfully aware of how peripheral he was to the ruling circle, but he planned to arrive bearing intelligence that would make his presence felt.

There would be a problem with returning prisoners of war if Trotsky ever actually succeeded in concluding a peace treaty with the Kaiser. And the unfinished business with the butcher Romanov and his family had yet to be settled. Golov, before his death last autumn, had succeeded in aborting the Englishman's rescue attempt but that would not be the end of it. As long as the Romanovs remained alive, they constituted a rallying point for all the counterrevolutionary scum running loose across the land from the Caucasus to the Barents Sea. The butcher and his family must disappear from the face of the earth and soon. And to hell with the outcry that such a step might call forth from the imperialist degenerates of the world.

Borodnev spent three days in Moscow. The first day he visited his office and tried without success to improve upon the quarters that had been assigned to him. He spent the second day with dozens of other functionaries on a long, hard bench in a tunnellike corridor, waiting his turn for an audience in the conference room. Even the endlessly irritating ride from Petersburg had been more pleasant; at least there had been a window with scenery passing by. What with the long wait in the corridor and the less than spacious quarters, he wondered if he were being given signals of a fall from favor. On the third day, when at last he entered the conference room, the very center of power, his anxiety abated. If his quarters were less impressive than he had hoped they would be, Lenin's lair was a sweatbox, a hovel, a dungeon. So that was to be the style as dictated by the example of the leader.

Veils of cigarette smoke floated gauzily about the room. Mixed with the pungent tobacco smell was the human smell of sweat from bodies too long confined in a poorly ventilated space.

The furniture consisted of a long wooden table, surrounded by a dozen wooden chairs. Only two of the chairs were occupied. Lenin and Yacov Sverdlov, Chairman of the Republic of Soviets, sat side by side, facing the door, a couple of empty chairs between them at the long side of the table. There were piles of documents and leaves of notes stacked before each of them as there were in front of at least half a dozen chairs.

From the volume of smoke in the room and the stink, Borodnev deduced that he must have been admitted during a recess in what must have been a long, well-attended, and hotly debated meeting.

Lenin, preoccupied with some papers in front of him, barely looked up when Borodnev entered. He simply raised one hand to acknowledge his presence and greeted him by name. "Comrade Borodnev. Sit, please."

Sverdlov greeted him with a nod of the head and a quick appraisal with practiced inquisitor's eyes.

Borodnev crossed the room, pulled a chair back from the table, and sat down across from Lenin and Sverdlov. The chair scraped loudly on the hardwood floor. Sverdlov darted him a look of annoyance. He would have to watch out for Sverdlov. The spade-bearded, pedantic son of a bitch had never been a friend of his.

Lenin, finished with the document at hand, pushed the whole pile of papers a few inches away toward the center of the table, symbolically clearing the way for the next order of business: Borodnev.

Sverdlov began to cough: a dry, sharp, tearing sound. He brought a balled handkerchief to his mouth; the cloth was rust-colored with the stain of dried blood.

Lenin fixed Borodnev with his dark almond eyes, eyes that Borodnev remembered as clear and amazingly gentle, like a doe's. Today they had a clouded and gelatinous look. And his face was puffy and sallow. His hairless scalp shone waxily under the glare from the overhead light. To Borodnev he looked ill.

"You are looking exceedingly well, Comrade," Borodnev heartily announced, trying to mask the dismay he felt over Lenin's appearance. If Lenin went, who would be next in line? Sverdlov? Trotsky? Neither of them bore any feeling of friendship for Borodnev. Not that Lenin really did either. But Lenin, pragmatist that he was, recognized in Borodnev a man doing a necessary job. Borodnev's prime qualification, aside from his doggedness, was a certain fortuitous lack of those charitable and compassionate human instincts that wold have defeated other men in his position. Every revolution required its Borodnev.

"I feel like death," Lenin replied. "But never mind. If I want a report on my health, I'll call on Dr. Medlev. You, I trust, have asked for an interview for reasons other than a medical consultation." Lenin ran a thumbnail down the vertical edge of the documents stacked in front of him. They made a ripping sound, like a pack of cards being prepared for shuffling.

"Two items, Comrade, aside from wishing to extend my warmest greetings to you and to Comrade Sverdlov."

"We're not a vegetable garden," Sverdlov snapped. "We don't have to be prepared with a pile of shit. Get on with it."

Borodnev stiffened. His bull's neck thrust forward. His hindquarters rose out of the chair. He had been goaded beyond the limits of his restraint. Only Lenin's calm, commanding look checked him and prevented him from making what might have been a fatal move. Later Borodnev decided that Sverdlov had calculatedly provoked him.

Borodnev settled back into his chair and waited a moment until he felt composed enough to speak.

"The Romanovs are one reason I asked for this interview."

"And the other?"

"Our prisoners of war who are presently detained in German camps."

"You must be aware, Comrade," Sverdlov patronizingly intoned, "that Comrade Trotsky is in Brest Litovsk and has been for weeks attempting to negotiate a treaty with the Germans."

"I do my best to keep up with current affairs, Comrade," Borodnev tartly replied. He thought he caught a quick glint of amusement in Lenin's dark, tired eyes.

"Then, when the treaty is signed," Sverdlov continued, "and we can assure you that it *will* be signed, it would follow that our prisoners of war in Germany will be released and will be free to return to their homes."

Borodnev triumphantly slapped the table with the flat of his hand. It was the blow he had been unable to deliver a moment ago to Sverdlov. "Exactly! They will be released and allowed to return home." He thrust his head and shoulders across the table and glowered one-eyed into Sverdlov's face. "But do we want them?"

Sverdlov drew back as far as he could without actually shifting his chair. He tried to look commanding, but he merely looked wary. He began to cough again into the bloodstained handkerchief. Lenin cocked his head to the side and waited for Sverdlov to stop coughing and for Borodnev to continue.

"Do we want these men back? These prisoners of war?" Borodnev repeated.

"Make your point, please," Sverdlov muttered into his handkerchief. He knew he was caught, but he didn't quite know the nature of the trap. And he wasn't about to let Borodnev toy with him.

"The point is this," Borodnev said. "We are at this moment engaged in civil warfare with the counterrevolutionary forces in the Caucasus, in the north, in the east. And it is debatable who is winning."

"One more reason this peace treaty will be signed at any cost," Lenin interjected, massaging his temples with the forefingers of both hands. "Once we're relieved of the drain of the war in men and matériel, we can get on with the business of building a socialist state. Our armies will be free to crush the Cossacks. The counterrevolutionaries will be deprived of their main issues. They will atrophy."

"With all due respect," Borodnev said, "that brings me back again to the prisoners of war. Many of them, particularly the officers, will be monarchist symphathizers. Do we want to add to our problem by inject-ing into an already unstable society the catalyst of thousands of trained soldiers who are antagonistic to our cause? Do we *want* these people to return?"

Lenin cast a thoughtful sidelong glance at Sverdlov and then di-rected his attention back to Borodnev. "How can we close the borders to them?" Lenin asked. "Should the word circulate that we are refusing our returning heroes entry into the motherland for which they bled, what would their families say? Their friends? Their lovers? How many millions might rise in the name of the tens of thousands we locked out? You present us with an interesting problem, Comrade Borodnev."

"May I present a solution?"

"Please, Comrade," Lenin invited.

Sverdlov tugged at his beard and had the look of a man who had just been forced to swallow a spoiled herring.

"We might . . . absorb them."

"And exactly what does that mean?" Sverdlov demanded.

"We might welcome the returning prisoners at the borders. Even go so far as to establish rehabilitation camps at the points of entry along the Western Front, a sort of embrace from the motherland. There they will be issued rations, new clothes, and travel passes for their journey home. We will do our best to locate those families who have been moved or dispossessed in recent months and to direct the returning prisoners to the hearths of their loved ones."

"Admirable," said Lenin. "The uncharacteristic spirit of benevolence in your nature overwhelms me."

"Of course, there will be a purpose to all this benevolent effort on our part."

"Of course."

"In these centers we will screen out the officers. Here I am assuming that most of the lower ranks will accept recent events and move with the times. It is in their nature to follow the crowd. Possibly they will even welcome the change in order. But the officers present a threat. Not only are they generally sympathetic to the monarchist cause, but they are men trained to lead not follow. So. All will be welcomed home at the border camps. But only our friends will leave."

"Won't these detainees be missed?"

"By whom? If they are monarchists, most of their families will have long ago departed or in other ways vanished from the scene."

Lenin sat in thoughtful silence for a moment. Even Sverdlov could think of no belittling reply to Borodnev's proposition. The man smelled, looked, and behaved like a swine. But it had to be conceded that the pig was among the shrewder of the domestic animals.

"Interesting," Lenin said. "We'll bring it up before the full committee. It has merit. I believe the other issue was the Romanovs."

"Yes, Comrade. In fact to my mind it takes precedence over the issue of the returning prisoners."

"That may be because you have a personal quarrel with the Romanovs that transcends objective political considerations," Sverdlov interjected.

"Continue, Comrade, please." Lenin took a long cardboard-tipped cigarette out of a box, placed it between his teeth, and struck a match.

Sverdlov coughed.

Borodnev gathered his thoughts.

"You are aware," Borodnev began, "that there have been efforts to set them free?"

"We have received your communiqués and others."

"Tobolsk is not the most secure place in the world. Kerensky chose it for them because the populace has no strong feelings against the Romanovs."

"We are aware of that."

"They could escape."

Lenin exhaled a plume of smoke. "That would represent a consider-able tactical loss to us."

"A tactical loss?" Borodnev was puzzled.

Lenin explained. "When this treaty at Brest Litovsk is signed, we will be roundly condemned by Britain and France. Abandoning our allies. All that nonsense. Their real concern will be that all those German troops that we have tied up on our front will be free to move against their front. But our own people will condemn us too. The Germans will exact a heavy toll in land and resources in exchange for peace. And our people will forget how anxious they have been to be rid of this war. We might reduce this toll by offering the Kaiser something of value in lieu of a region or resource that he covets. Nicholas and his family are what we have to offer."

Borodnev stared at Lenin, speechless. For thirteen years, since Bloody Sunday in 1905, he had nourished the dream of lining them all up against a wall and blowing them to pieces. Nicholas, Alexandra, the daughters, the invalid son—the lot. And maybe raping the women first, before the ex-Tsar's eyes. And now Lenin was willing to set them free?

"We know your feelings, Borodnev," Lenin said. "But this is a time for pragmatism. As circumstances dictate, we shall set them free, passionlessly—or kill them, passionlessly. They are bargaining chips, not people. For the time being we want only to hold them until we come to a final decision as to their disposition.

"And," Lenin added pointedly, "should we decide in favor of execu-tion, we will want a public trial first to legitimatize the act. We do not want to appear repellent to those in the world who might otherwise sympathize with our cause."

Borodnev protested. "As long as they live, there is a risk that we'll lose them. What if your bargaining chips fall into the wrong hands? Tobolsk is rotten with monarchist sympathizers. All they need is for someone to light a fire under them."

Lenin ground out the stub of his cigarette. "The Committee has devoted some time to considering just that point. We have thought of moving them to a more secure place. But a move has its hazards, too, the countryside being in such unstable condition."

"A move could be arranged," Borodnev insisted. "There is a way to minimize the risk."

"Where would you move them, were you in charge?"

Borodnev pressed his lips together, not so much thoughtfully as to suppress a smile. "To an industrial area, Comrade. Not Petersburg or

Moscow, where the population is too dense, too volatile. Somewhere in the Urals: industrial, worker-oriented. Firmly loyal to the revolution. Ekaterinburg," Borodnev suggested. "I can vouch for the loyalty of that town."

Sverdlov looked quizzically at Lenin. Lenin considered Borodnev's statement for a moment. Sverdlov coughed; his fingertips were becoming stained from the handkerchief.

"Suppose you draw up a blueprint for this evacuation," Lenin said. "Bring us a step-by-step outline of the procedures by which Nicholas and his family will be safely moved from Tobolsk to Ekaterinburg. Then we'll see." He looked at Sverdlov.

Sverdlov shrugged.

"Comrades," Borodnev responded with feeling, "consider it done."

"I would prefer to consider it as being considered, if you don't mind," Sverdlov said and indicated with a nod that as far as he was concerned the interview was over.

"I thank you for your confidence," Borodnev said, pushing back his chair.

Lenin held up a hand. "Nothing can move until spring. I will want you to have arranged everything so that as soon as movement becomes possible, we move first before any rescue parties do. There is a great deal at stake here."

"Nobody is more aware of that than I, Comrade," Borodnev stood up and reached out to shake both Lenin's and Sverdlov's hands. Then he left the room.

"An animal," Sverdlov muttered as the door shut. "Do you think it wise to put the Romanovs in his hands?"

"He functions," Lenin replied. "Why is it that so very few of our people seem capable of getting things done?"

"You know the answer."

Lenin sighed. "Because the bureaucrats who got things done in the past were mostly on the other side."

Sverdlov nodded wearily. "They have all either fled or are dead or are residing in one of Borodnev's prisons."

"So," said Lenin, "in this business of the Romanovs we are left with very little choice. We must entrust the sheep to the care of the wolf."

"What has a wolf ever done to you," Sverdlov asked, "that you should malign the species so?"

# CHAPTER THIRTY-TWO

It was not without a twinge of conscience that Charles Aldonby had invited Sublieutenant Mountbatten to dinner at his club. He knew that in the past the younger man had apotheosized him, as a sibling sometimes does an older brother. Although he hadn't seen Mountbatten since the outbreak of the war, he hoped that something of that earlier feeling remained—enough at least to work to his advantage. He was ruefully aware that in eliciting Mountbatten's help he might be exposing a promising naval career to ruin at the hands of a court martial. Still, it had to be done. Aldonby felt that without Mountbatten's help, he would have little hope of launching his expedition in the approaching spring.

Throughout dinner Aldonby had avoided addressing himself to the topic that was uppermost in his mind. But when the meal was done, all the small talk used up, and all the loose ends of reminiscence tied up, Aldonby laid his napkin aside and confessed to the young Sublieutenant that he had had an ulterior motive in inviting him to the club.

Mountbatten's lean, dark actor's face split into a sly grin. "I didn't doubt it for a moment, Charles. Last time we met, I believe it was at Falconhurst, you regarded me as something of a pest. And didn't hesitate to let me know it."

Aldonby demurred. "That was years ago." As if time had effaced it.

"And I *was* something of a pest," Mountbatten cheerfully confessed. "The Romanov ladies were visiting that spring. Attached myself to you like a leech. In the way all the time. Especially in the matter of the Grand Duchess Marie."

Aldonby's face clouded over. "Forgive me. I wasn't much older then than you are now." He took a deep breath and plunged in. "It's the Romanovs I want to discuss with you."

"Terrible, the predicament they're in."

"Perhaps they can be helped."

"Not as far as His Majesty's government is concerned. Shameful that not a finger has been lifted in their behalf in all this time. Nevermind that they're kin; they were the staunchest of allies. His loyalty probably cost Nicholas his crown. You don't just cut off a friend like that. My God, they've been prisoners for almost a year. Don't tell me the Prime Minister has suddenly developed a conscience."

"No. But an effort will be made."

"Unsanctioned?"

"Yes."

"You?"

"I'm involved." Aldonby signaled for the bill.

"That's why you had yourself demobbed?"

"Yes." The table captain approached bearing a slip of paper on a sterling silver tray. Aldonby signed the chit without bothering to look at the figures. The captain withdrew.

"And there's something you think I can do to help?"

"If you will."

"I'm still in uniform. I don't know if I can get demobbed. I don't know if there's time."

"You probably can't. And there isn't."

Mountbatten spread his hands in a gesture of helplessness.

"But it's not your physical presence that's required," Aldonby clarified.

"What, then?"

"Would you mind," Aldonby asked, "if instead of finishing with port in the lounge, we went for a short stroll by the river? Too many ears here. All friendly, I'm sure. Just listening for gossip to liven up the next dull dinner. Nevertheless . . ."

Mountbatten cocked an eyebrow. "Well, now you do have my curiosity at the peak. And to think I have always admired you as one who played the game strictly by the rules."

"Apparently there are no rules anymore."

"Let's get our coats, then," Mountbatten eagerly suggested.

It wasn't truly frigid outside. Winter had relaxed its clammy hold on the city. And there was a redolence along the embankment that was reminiscent of bygone springs. But there was still a chill in the air, and it was so heavy with humidity that it saturated the mens' woolen overcoats and seeped through to the skin, causing them to shudder, putting a tremor into their voices as they made their way along the dark path near the river.

They walked with their hands in their pockets and their backs humped and their breath crystalizing before their eyes. Mountbatten heard Aldonby out. "I cannot help you, Charles." His voice was low and heavy with distress.

"Much as I'd like to, I can't. I know that family too. Almost as well as you do. I share the same blood ties. I have the fondest memories. My heart bleeds for them. I cannot understand how their allies can abandon them to the whims of those fanatics. But I am still an officer in His Majesty's Navy."

"I'm not asking you to take an active role, Dickie," Aldonby reminded him. "I am only asking for certain information."

"Which given would make me party to an act contrary to the national interest. I'm sorry about your colleague's lost vessel and the loss of your funds. And I agree that time is the enemy of Nicholas and his family. But I cannot show you the way to steal, or borrow without Admiralty consent, a motor torpedo boat of His Majesty's Navy. I would be an accessory to an act of treason. We are at war, and those vessels, small as they are, are ships of war. And since no naval combat vessel, no matter how small, is left unguarded, you would have to overwhelm the watch in order to take the vessel. And I don't know that that could be achieved without loss of life or at least serious injury to a British seaman.

"Thirdly, were you to steal the boat, you would be piloting a British vessel of war through waters patrolled by enemy submarines. You are a soldier, Charles. Those Russian volunteers you've recruited may be well-meaning, but they were trained as cavalry officers. They have no knowledge of naval warfare. Even your experienced seaman, this Lars Dahlgren, is not trained in the conduct of war at sea. Should a German submarine pick you up in its periscope, it will not venture close enough, I assure you, to offer you an opportunity for hand-to-hand combat. So odds are you would not make it across the Baltic. But if you did, you would not at this time of year get much farther than Murmansk. A motor torpedo boat is a small, frail craft built for speed and maneuverability, not for smashing through ice."

"If we could get to Murmansk or Archangel, we might proceed overland from there."

"Mmmm," Mountbatten grunted. "Maybe you don't need one of His Majesty's valuable torpedo boats."

They walked in silence for a while until Mountbatten spoke again. "If Archangel were your first objective, there might be another way." He drew his handkerchief out of his pocket and blew his nose. "Damned chill."

A tugboat went puffing past, nudging a heavily loaded barge up-river. Mountbatten rested his elbows on the low stone wall that separated the embankment from the Thames and watched the tug and the barge slowly meld with the darkness. Beside him Aldonby waited.

"Do you know about the Russian war prisoners?" Mountbatten asked.

"Yes. They seem unable to get home. They can't go across Finland because of the civil war there. And they can't get through Germany despite the Bolshevik peace treaty, because Germany is still fighting us. The gates to the camps are open, but the prisoners have nowhere to go."

"You speak Russian, don't you?"

"Yes."

"Well?"

"Like a native of Petersburg."

Mountbatten threw him a puzzled look. "Why Petersburg?"

"My mother's hometown."

"And, of course, your expatriate Russian volunteers do. What about this mariner of yours?"

"Lars? Like a Siberian."

"Then the whole gang of you could pass for returning prisoners."

Aldonby stared at Mountbatten in mute astonishment. He had been bound to a blueprint drawn up months ago in different circumstances, before the Bolsheviks had made peace with Germany. He had been tied to the past. Mountbatten had come to it fresh and with an overview born of noninvolvement. Aldonby could see a slow smile spreading on Mountbatten's lips and a conspiratorial glint in his eyes.

A freighter, its portholes blacked out and engines barely turning over, ghosted past, beating almost silently against the current. The spreading iridescent **V** of its wake rolled out toward the facing shores.

"You'll need papers," Mountbatten said. "Certainly there'll be half a dozen among those prisoners who'd sell their identities for cash as an alternative to returning home."

Aldonby glumly considered that for a moment. "Suppose we get the papers. How do we get into Russia?"

Mountbatten blew his nose again. "Let's walk on a bit. Get the blood circulating again."

They moved away from the river, across the narrow park, between the Houses of Parliament and Westminster Abbey.

"The word I have, through naval sources, is that a route is being opened. We have received instructions that there will be certain ships traversing the Barents Sea between the North Cape of Norway and Archangel that are not to receive our normal scrutiny. Apparently the Russian prisoners have improvised a way home, roundabout but effective. Overland from their camps in Denmark, north through Sweden to the northernmost tip of Norway. Thence by steamer ferry to Archangel.

"So long as our forces are in Archangel, ostensibly guarding our military stockpile there against the predatory Huns, the returning prisoners have an open gateway to their motherland. All you'd need would be papers. As for uniforms, there's no difference between the old and the new except that the Reds strip off the epaulets and braid."

"We are in your debt, Dickie," Aldonby said sincerely.

"Glad I've been able to help. But I would appreciate it if you would take the entire credit for this idea for yourself. I have no business discussing it at all."

Aldonby smiled and dug his hands deeper into his pockets for warmth. A fine, cold drizzle began to fall as they crossed St. Margaret Square.

# CHAPTER THIRTY-THREE

H yde Park was quiet and empty that Sunday morning, the early March chill keeping the lawns and walks free of visitors, the trees still stark and winter bare.

They came at a gallop down the bridle path, neck and neck, handling their mounts with easy authority. They reined in near the Serpentine and dismounted in high spirits, he first, lending her his good hand for support, that bit of gallantry being his only concession to her womanhood when they rode together. His other arm was pinned by the sleeve across his abdomen to keep it from getting in the way during the ride.

As there was nobody around, she clung to him a little longer than decorum would dictate and brushed his mouth with her lips as he helped her down.

"What was that for?" he asked good-humoredly.

"Just storing up memories," she said.

"Against what? Winter's over."

"Yes," she answered and looped her rein around the post. "You'll be leaving very soon, won't you?"

"You know I can't discuss it," he said gently, apologetically.

"Won't."

"Very well, won't. It wouldn't be fair to you, working as you do in the War Office."

"Do you think I'd tell them?" she said, hurt. They had been through this before.

"Of course not. But why should you have to bear the burden of knowledge that you might be duty-bound not to withhold?"

"For God's sake, Charles. It's not as if I'm absolutely in the dark about what you're up to."

"You're only guessing."

"I feel it in my bones."

"That's entirely different from knowing it for a fact. I don't believe in intuition."

"I know when your mind is off somewhere; you don't have to tell me. Even though you're standing here now, I can feel distances opening up between us. You might as well have gone already."

"Shhh," he whispered and drew her to him, shielded by the horses on either side.

"There was a time late last autumn when I was sure you were going to leave. I just knew it."

"But I didn't. You see how reliable your intuition is."

"I might have informed then, if I were going to. But I didn't, even though I saw it as the only way of keeping you from destroying yourself. I was afraid you would never forgive me. And I won't inform now, even though I know by the signals your body sends me that before the week is out you'll be gone. So don't put a wall between us for whatever few days are left. Give me that little bit of time."

He kissed her hair. "You're talking as if I won't be coming back. If I felt that way, there'd be no point in starting out. Because if I don't come back, *they* don't come back. Right?"

"Will you ride with me next Sunday morning?"

He didn't answer.

"Friday?"

"You'll be at your desk on Friday."

"I'll phone in sick. Shall we ride together on Friday?"

"Let's bring the horses back to the stable." He took her by the arm to lead her around to the stirrup.

"Wednesday? Will you be here tomorrow?" Her voice was rising. "At least tell me that, or I *will* inform."

He held her close again, to calm her. "Let's not spoil today."

"And tomorrow?"

"I'll be gone," he conceded. "For a little while."

"And I thought when Craig called you last summer to identify that Russian that it might be a kind of blessing, getting you interested in *something*. Damn Craig anyway," and she sagged helplessly against him.

# CHAPTER THIRTY-FOUR

*From the journal of Anastasia Romanov*

TOBOLSK
MARCH 30, 1918

Spring is almost here.

The ice daggers dangling from the eaves are beginning to drip water. At noontime the weak sun warms them a bit and they begin to glisten, and appear to grow slippery. A drop or two of liquid forms at their pointed tips and falls like a teardrop into the snow. And then the sun, as if exhausted by its labors, tucks itself in behind the overcast and rests for the remainder of the day. And the icicles freeze solid again.

But it is a sign, this first brief melting, of the great thaw to come. The trees will shed their vestment of snow, and the earth will turn green again.

Will we be here to see it? Will we see it if we are here? This morning, as if to rob us of even this small hope of spring, our windows were all whitewashed over. We cannot see out into the town. We have been rendered blind as well as immobile.

The excuse that Osmenov gave was that the whitewashing was done to keep us from making signals to local sympathizers.

# CHAPTER THIRTY-FIVE

On the railroad maps of Norway, Narvik was the end of the line. A lumberman's town of wooden buildings and boardwalk streets, it lay within the Arctic Circle at the northeastern end of the Scandinavian peninsula.

That spring, as it happened every spring when the warming influence of the Gulf Stream overwhelmed the languishing force of winter, its roadways turned to mud. Otherwise it was an immaculate town, its spotless, whitewashed buildings with their gaily colored trim flouting the gloom of so northern and fog-bound a place.

Taverns lined the thoroughfare that led from the railroad station to the harbor to delight the thirsty lumbermen on their holidays from the camps. And down the side streets a multitude of rooming houses and hostelries waited: clean, welcoming, warm. And in some of the hostelries, for those whose hungers transcended food and drink, there were women, clean as the town, crisp as the sheets, gay as the trim on the buildings.

From her window in Olsen's Hotel across the little square from the station, Nadia Demanova engaged in an enterprise of a different kind; with the aid of a railway timetable and a pair of strong field glasses, she kept track of the trains that arrived and their occupants.

The train that was of principal interest to her was the one that came puffing in at two o'clock every second afternoon, splashed with mud and dripping with melting frost; the one that had made the long, long journey from the south through forests and across swollen rivers, had negotiated the mountainous spine of the peninsula, braved blizzards, penetrated tunnels, bored through primordial ice, and had finally snaked its way down the spectacular palisades of the Narvik Fjord and come gliding, gasping from its forty-odd hours of effort, into its berth between the well-scrubbed platforms of the Narvik Station and there, with a sigh, had come to rest.

On some arrivals certain cars of this train carried the soldiers and officers of the former Imperial Army of Russia, lately prisoners of war, on the first long leg of their journey home.

It was not by chance that Nadia Demanova had found her way to this unimportant northern outpost. Nor had her special interest in the trains arriving from the south been improvised as a way of passing the time.

Having fled England after Golov's death, she had passed the winter months in a torturous return to Petersburg. There to her dismay she had found that the laboring classes in whose name the revolution had been made were no better off than they had been under the hated Tsar. They were even worse off, if she were to admit the truth to herself. Rather than commit that error, she indulged herself in a small mental deception and determined that her year in decadent London had corrupted her sense of values and destroyed her perspective. She understood that these horrendous conditions were only a temporary thing, a result of the dislocations that inevitably must follow in the wake of a political upheaval. In this way she denied what her eyes bore witness to and kept her ideals and goals intact. She had faith in the future and in the Central Committee. Though she didn't like Borodnev, she found her "Uncle" of correspondence to be a frightening eminence in person; the closeness of his lumpy, porcine face as he commended her on her work in London had made her flesh crawl. Somehow she had managed to evade his dinner invitation without making it seem like a rebuff. She sensed the danger in the man. She was no longer the naive adolescent who had gone off to England in the service of the cause.

With the signing of the peace with Germany, Borodnev ordered her to return to Western Europe as part of a network of monitors who would keep track of the returning prisoners of war. Perhaps he thought of it as a penalty. To Nadia it was a relief.

In the isolated settlement of Narvik, which she guiltily considered a kind of paradise after what she had seen at home, she watched the trains that arrived from the south and cabled her encoded reports to Petersburg. Other agents like her, stationed in Archangel on Russia's northern rim, augmented her intelligence with information on the arrivals on Russian soil of those returning prisoners who might be considered potentially subversive. The destinations of these individuals inside Russia were noted. As they departed the areas of control of the Allied Expeditionary Force, they were picked up by Borodnev's men—*absorbed* was the word he used—and were rarely ever seen again.

The truth was that Nadia did not fully appreciate the ruthlessness of the action in which she played an initiating role. She thought that she was part of a vast operation aimed at reorienting and indoctrinating those returning heroes who had been so unfortunate as to have been absent from the motherland during the most significant event in her history.

Nadia Demanova set a sheet of foolscap down on the windowsill, picked up a pencil, moistened the point with the tip of her tongue, and wrote down the date: April 2, 1918. Then she picked up the pair of field glasses from the sill, pressed them tight against her eyes, adjusted the focusing ring, and read the number of the train from the plaque on the side of the engine. She made note of the number on the foolscap a little below the date. Having done that, she checked the train number against her schedule to make sure that it was indeed the one from the south. Then she waited until the passengers began to depart.

As usual the windows on the train opened first, and the baggage came spilling out before the passengers appeared at the doors. When the first of the passengers jumped down onto the platform, she raised her glasses again. She was looking for uniforms: officers' uniforms.

Her instructions were to note how many officers' uniforms she saw and to assess their rank. She had been given a color chart to aid her in her observations and she had memorized the various colors and insignia that would be significant. She had also been given a number of photographs of those officers in whom there was a special interest. She had memorized those faces, too, and when one appeared, magnified in her field glasses, she made a check mark against his name.

Not every train from the south carried returning soldiers. And some trains that did carried only a handful. Sometimes the watching and waiting became a terrible bore, but on some days there was such a flood of arrivals that she really was not able to keep track of them all. Then she would just make an estimate of numbers: approximately so many officers and so many enlisted men. Today it looked like there were several dozen.

She scanned the platform through her glasses in an effort to pick out the officers, if there were any. She stopped. And gasped. And searched to find again the face that she had just passed. The crowd on the platform was shifting, too rapidly. Never mind. It was an impossibility. Lars Dahlgren was not a Russian soldier, had not been a prisoner of war, would not be in an Imperial Artilleryman's uniform traveling with a group of repatriates. There was someone down there who *resembled* Lars; all bearded men tend to look alike anyway, and her mind had played a trick on her. During the long dull weeks in this little town at the end of the world, she had occasionally and guiltily entertained herself with thoughts of Dahlgren and this was her penalty. She was seeing things. Best just to count heads as she had been instructed to do and relegate her fantasies to her sleeping hours.

Oh, God! There he was again. And this time she held him in focus. He had been stooped over, picking up his luggage from the platform, and he straightened up right into her lens, looking at her so directly that she flinched before reason took over and assured her that the powerful lenses were playing tricks with her; he was too far away to be aware of her presence. But there was no question about it.

It *was* Lars Dahlgren. He stood on the platform, supporting his pack on his shoulder, looking this way and that, as if he were waiting for someone.

As he moved, Nadia made small adjustments in the focus, holding him prisoner in the lens. Her heart was beating too fast, and her face felt hot. And to her chagrin she could feel a stirring in her loins. Despite her betrayal of him, despite her narrow escape from him with her life, she could not—her body would not—forget the night she had spent with him. Even during that terrifying cab ride to Golov's flat, the closeness of him had excited her physically. She was sure now that had she not fled Golov's apartment, Lars would not have carried out his threat against her. In fact she had fantasized that he would have made love to her instead. She wondered if she were a sadist or a masochist, even though she wasn't sure exactly which was which or exactly how one's behavior qualified one for such a description. But she suspected that it involved the sort of sexual depravity that reputedly had been practiced by the ex-Tsaritsa and the insane monk, Rasputin. She re-called that she had found the stories titillating. She found Lars Dahl-gren exciting. And she wondered, with mixed feelings of concern and revulsion, exactly what that made her.

As she watched Lars now, she had to resist an impulse to wave to him. She giggled. What nonsense. In the first place he could not see her even if she waved. In the second place if he had come to Narvik looking for her, might not his purpose be to finish the business that he had left unfinished in the cab in London?

But would that be to kill her or to make love to her? Her cheeks felt like they were burning up. She could feel her nipples pressing against her brassiere. Her arms began to tremble. Her focus began dancing erratically all over the platform. She lost Lars momentarily and found him again. She had to brace her elbows hard against the windowsill in order to keep the field glasses steady. He was still standing there, pack on shoulder, looking about. The crowd of people around him was beginning to thin. She wasn't doing her job, she realized. She wasn't counting officers. It didn't matter. She began to wonder about Lars.

If he hadn't come to Narvik in pursuit of her, and she reluctantly had to concede that this was unlikely, what had he come for? And she had to confess to herself that his being there was not as extraordinary as it might seem. He was a Norwegian and a sailor: Narvik was a Norwegian port. Perhaps he'd heard of a boat in need of a captain? Or he had come looking for a boat to replace the one that her Comrades had destroyed.

But what was he doing there in a Russian Army uniform? That certainly didn't fit the picture of a ship's officer in quest of a berth. Could the answer simply be that he had been in need of clothes and had not cared about their origins? Had he bought them secondhand from a penniless veteran? Or stripped them from a corpse? Impossible!

This was Norway not Russia. There were no frightful shortages here. Europeans did not buy clothing off the backs of starving men or steal it from the dead.

Abruptly Dahlgren's eyes made note of something. He held up a hand, moved a few yards, dumped the pack from his shoulder onto the platform, and came face-to-face with the Englishman. Aldonby! The meddler who had come to the Princess's house. And Aldonby, too, was in the uniform of a Russian soldier, homeward-bound.

The flush of excitement at the sight of Lars that had so recently brightened her cheeks vanished. Her jaw tensed. The dewy warmth that had so delightfully bathed her loins a moment ago turned clammy and cold. Her nipples withdrew protectively. A frost settled over her body.

Lars Dahlgren's arrival in Narvik alone would have been a happenstance that invited all kinds of interesting speculation. His arrival in concert with Aldonby and both of them in Russian uniforms was decidedly ominous.

As she watched them, standing side by side, looking about for someone else, with straining necks and upraised arms, she felt a chilling sense of loss. None of the things she had imagined in that moment when she had thought that Lars was alone would happen now. By his presence, the Englishman had robbed her of that sweet liaison. She hated him for it.

Now, she could see, others were joining Lars and the Englishman. A small circle of men and packs was forming on the emptying platform. Young men. She recognized some of them from the circle of London expatriates. Igor Kubishev. Boris Alexandrovich. Sergei Trobinsky. And one other whom she could not identify. All boys. Barely out of their teens. But, then, so was she barely more than an adolescent. And all of them in Russian Army uniforms, like soldiers returning home.

She would have to watch them, if she could, without being seen herself. She would have to get word to Petrograd. She could guess the route they would be taking, but she would have to make sure. According to the timetables on the windowsill, the next ship on the shuttle to Archangel would be due the day after tomorrow.

She watched them as they shouldered their packs and left the station. Watched them, as they plodded in a group across the mud-clogged avenue, looking for a place to settle for the night. Never for the next day and a half would she allow them to be far from her sight.

Early on the morning of the fourth of April the ferry from Archangel, the steamer *Albert Michalsky,* ghosted into its slip, veiled in mist. Only its wheelhouse was visible above the soupy water hugging the haze in the harbor.

Nadia watched from her window as the fog dissipated and the ship began to unload its passengers: forlorn-looking men, babushkaed women with guarded eyes, frightened children in threadbare clothes. Hundreds of them. The waste products of civil war, they had worked their way north through Russia, the most valued possessions of their lifetimes on their backs and sewn into the linings of their clothes. Singly and in small family groups, they had found their way to Murmansk or Archangel, their numbers decimated during the jouney, the roads and forests along the way pockmarked with the shallow graves of those whose stamina had failed. Once they had been aristocrats and bourgeoisie; now they were nothing. Had the makers of the Revolution had any use for them at all, they would never have allowed them to reach the ports of embarkation. Let them filter into and infect the corrupt nations of Western Europe—let them be someone else's burden.

Some of the more venturesome of the new arrivals drifted into town. Into the food shops. Into the railroad station. Most of them simply sat down on their bundles on the pier, as if having come this far they could go no farther, too ineffably weary even to evidence curiosity about this new place they had come to. Or perhaps, for them, after so many weeks spent in motion, all places began to look the same.

The cranes on the pier had begun unloading the heavy cargo from the holds. If past experience was any indicator, the steamer would be ready to start loading up for the return voyage in about two hours. By mid-afternoon the *Albert Michalsky* would be gone.

Nadia decided that she would have time for breakfast. Better eat now while she could; half the day would have passed before she might be free to eat again.

When the ship announced with a blast of its horn that it was ready to accept cargo and passengers for the return voyage, Nadia picked up her field glasses and resumed her vigil at the window.

Aldonby, Lars, and the four young Russians were at the head of the line. Nadia went down and sent her cable. Then she returned to her room and watched again. As she had expected, papers were still being checked. The line of passengers had not yet moved. She would wait until they were on board before going down to the pier. And even then, she would remain out of sight until the gangway was up and the steamer under way.

Forty-five minutes later, shuddering with the chill, she stood concealed behind a shed on the pier, waiting for the moment when it would be safe to step out and flaunt her presence before Lars. Had she dressed properly in layers of clothing with a warm shawl covering her head, as the other people on the pier, her teeth would not now convulsively be clicking away like castanets. But then she would have looked like a dowdy bale of wool with feet, undistinguishable from the others and certainly not recognizable as the Nadia Demanova whom he had known and, she hoped, remembered.

The boat sounded its horn again. The gangway was raised like a drawbridge, opening a watery moat between the pier and the ship. Nadia stepped out from behind the shed and scanned the main deck looking for Lars. When last she had seen him, through the field glasses from her window, he and his friends had been standing near the rail in the stern quarter of the ship.

She moved very quickly, half-walking, half-running, down the length of the pier. Her haste and her anxiety would easily have led an uninformed observer to guess mistakenly that she had come to say good-bye to a dearly loved one.

A squat red tugboat burped smoke and treaded water under the stern of the ship. Nadia could feel the throb of the tug's powerful engine transmitted by the water, pulsing through the boards of the pier as she ran.

A line, black and snaky as an eel, darted out over the stern rail, wriggled through the air, and landed soundlessly on the tug. A crewman reeled it in. The fat hawser followed. Thirty yards away Nadia saw Aldonby and three of his young Russians, but Lars was nowhere in sight.

The stevedores on the pier lifted the mooring lines off their bollards, straining under their weight, and heaved them into the water between the steamer and the pier. Somewhere on the deck above, unseen sailors worked their capstans and hauled in the lines.

Nadia was now standing exactly where she had planned to be when the steamer sounded its farewell whistle. But Lars was nowhere to be seen. It was as if he were deliberately thwarting her. Water boiled up around the little tug as it took a strain on the hawser and began to tow the steamer, stern first, out into the channel.

Nadis raised an arm, waved it back and forth, and began to shout his name: "Lars Dahlgren! Lars Dahlgren!" But she was sure that no one could hear her above the tumult of departure; she could barely hear herself.

Maybe it was the gesture, maybe it was her prematurely springlike costume, maybe it was just chance that caught Igor Kubishev's eye. He had seen her at the Princess's house on his occasional visits there, and she was not the sort of young woman that a young man would easily forget. He turned to Aldonby and shouted something to him. Aldonby looked where he was pointing. Nadia could see the astonishment on his face.

But Aldonby was not the one she had come to see or in a sense to expose herself to. Aldonby turned away, raised his hand, motioning to someone on the other side of the deck. The ship was slipping away from the pier. The horn sounded again. And then Lars was there, at the rail, beside Aldonby. And Aldonby was pointing down in her direction.

The steamer was not yet so far away that she could not read the expression on Lars Dahlgren's face: the eyes staring in unblinking disbelief, the mouth agape with bemusement, the head shaking from side to side.

Lars regained his composure, and it was Nadia's turn to be astonished. He spat no curses at her, shook no fists at her, didn't turn away. Instead he spread his arms wide in a supplicant's gesture of embrace, threw back his head, and began to laugh. She couldn't hear the sound, but there was no mistaking it: his whole body shook with laughter.

As the ship drew farther away, when she could no longer define his features, he raised his powerful right arm and slowly began to wave to her, the fingers on his hand spread wide, a benevolent gesture. He was as surprised by his reaction to her as she was. He had no idea that her presence in Narvik was more than a coincidence.

And now, to her surprise, she was waving back, eagerly, and smiling. An ecstatic giggle escaped her lips as her mind manufactured an image of him on that morning in London when he had come at her like a lancer. And then, as the ship began to turn, he pressed his hand to his mouth and blew her a kiss, and then she could see him no more.

She stood there for a while, until the ship was out of sight around the bend in the fjord. And when she turned away to walk back to her rooming house, there were tears in her eyes. She had come to taunt him, and he had left her desolate. She wanted no more of this place or of the work she was doing. She wanted no more of the insane destructiveness of well-meant causes. She wanted only one thing at this moment, and she couldn't have it, because it would mean performing the impossible, turning back time, calling back the cable that had already been sent.

She sat down on one of the hard, cold, pitted iron bollards, cupped her face in her hands and began to sob like a child.

Taking into account her scant nineteen years and the sordid affairs in which circumstances had involved her, she had every right to cry.

# CHAPTER THIRTY-SIX

S he's just a child," Lars Dahlgren said and laughed, remembering. "Some child! Anyway, you can't spend your life expecting the worst of people. It's bad for the digestion." He drained his mug of beer, plunked it down on the table, and called for another.

They had rounded the North Cape an hour before. Their four cadets, as they had begun to call their young Russian volunteers, had gone below to sleep. It was well past midnight, but dusk still hung on.

Aldonby sipped thoughtfully. "I'd still like to know what she was doing in Narvik." He was a couple of pints behind Lars, and he intended to keep it that way. He didn't have Lars's capacity. And he had no intention of becoming engaged in a contest.

"Probably stranded. Probably trying to get home."

"She's had damn near six months to do that, since we last saw her in London."

"Maybe she's run out of money. Maybe that's why she waved at us. Saw familiar faces and was overwhelmed. She must be terribly lonely."

"I can't believe that," Aldonby declared. "You might have killed her in London. Why would she wave to you now? If I were she, I'd have kept well hidden if I saw you pass by."

"I can't hold a grudge. If I'd killed her then so be it. But who can stay angry for half a year? Maybe she knows that."

"I think she had something else on her mind."

Lars gazed boozily across the top of the head on his fresh mug of beer. "We spent a night together, remember? But how could you remember, you weren't there. I was there. She was there. We remember." He raised his mug to salute his memories and began to drink.

"Take it easy," Aldonby said. "We don't want to have to pour you off the boat in Archangel. We are relying on you."

"Don't worry," Lars assured him. "I stop drinking at sunrise."

"And how can you tell when that is?" Aldonby asked, glancing through the porthole at the pearly sky outside.

"Ahhh!" replied Lars, contentedly, and emptied his glass.

An hour later Aldonby stood at the porthole watching a sky that had at last begun to darken. Lars sat snoring in his chair. Aldonby sensed someone standing behind him and turned.

"Captain Dahlgren?" the steward softly asked. He was holding an envelope, tentatively offering it.

"Captain Dahlgren is asleep over there," Aldonby answered. "Is that for him?"

"Yes, sir. Shall I wake him?"

"I'll take it."

"Thank you, sir."

He took the envelope. The steward hurried away. Aldonby crossed the lounge, thoughtfully tapping the envelope against his thumbnail. It wasn't sealed; the flap was merely tucked in. He decided to have a look, rather than wake Lars unnecessarily.

The slip of paper inside was from the radio room: a wireless message. Aldonby unfolded the piece of flimsy and read: "My Comrades are expecting you. Take care. Apologies. Signed—Nadia."

# CHAPTER THIRTY-SEVEN

*From the journal of Anastasia Romanov*

TOBOLSK
APRIL 5, 1918

Last night I escaped.

I don't know why I did it. I achieved nothing and only brought more suffering on my family. Had I thought even for a moment before I did it and then decided to do it anyway, I should have consulted first with Leonid and enlisted his aid. Then maybe *something* would have come of it. But I acted on impulse, alone, without forethought, and without considering the consequences. I can blame the months of confinement, the oppressiveness of winter. I only know that suddenly the opportunity seemed to be there, and I took it.

The night was clear; the snow was a cushion four feet deep beneath my second-floor window. The other members of the family were reading and sewing in the parlor. It is always warmer that way, with everyone gathered together in one place. Alexei was asleep in his bed. The soldiers assigned to guard the house this night were gathered in the foyer, keeping warm, I supposed. Nobody would want to be outside on a night like this. I could hear them laughing and joking at the foot of the stairs.

I looked out the window and could see no one in back of the house. And I thought to myself, what an excellent opportunity. I could just leave. It was as simple as that.

I put on several pairs of woolen stockings, my warmest boots, more layers of petticoats than usual, an extra sweater that Mama had finished knitting for me just last week, and a scarf would round and round my face. I looked like pictures I have seen of Turkish women. Only my eyes showed between my scarf and my hat. And then I simply opened the window and jumped.

I allowed myself to fall, as I have seen circus trapeze artists fall into a net, in a sitting position, hands crossed on my chest, feet straight out. How free I felt, like a bird in flight, weightless, careless. I had to restrain myself from shouting with delight.

I landed on the snow as on a great white pillow. The most difficult part was crawling out of the drift. I crossed the yard to the fence and then made my way up another drift that was almost as high as the fence. I crawled over and slid down the other side, like a child in a playground, and I was free.

I felt no need to be furtive, no need to run; I simply walked away from my prison. It was like a dream.

Once outside the compound I found the path in the street that had been cut through the snow. I didn't know quite where it would lead me; I simply followed it, rejoicing in my liberty, in my ability to walk more than thirty paces in any one direction, in the swift movement of the moon gliding over my head.

I wandered through the town, the streets eerie and empty and glistening blue white, the windows on the houses opaque with frost.

I found myself near the river, which was frozen as solid as a glacier. The steamer that had brought us to Tobolsk was tied up at the pier, imprisoned in the ice, in a nest of logs and branches that keep the frozen waters from crushing its sides. The gangway was a bridge of ice topped with snow. I crossed onto the steamer and walked round and round the empty decks, looking for a way in. By now I was very cold. The part of my face that was exposed to the frigid night air had lost all sensation. When I touched it with my fingers, it felt as brittle as Christmas candy.

A door yielded and I found myself in what I remembered was the ship's saloon. It was not much warmer in there than it was outside, but at least there was no wind. I sat down in one of the big, soft chairs, which was stiff with the cold, and I curled up there and waited. For what? I didn't know. Did I think that I could wait there until spring when the steamer would leave for the south?

The soldiers found me there. And just as well that they did, otherwise I surely would have frozen to death. Marie told me later that I hadn't been gone for quite half an hour. The wind rushing in through my open window had alerted the household. The soldiers had simply followed my tracks in the snow.

But today the high snowdrifts near the fence have been cleared away. And the fence has been topped with wire. And the windows have been nailed shut. And guards no longer prowl about the house at their whim; they are now stationed inside as well as outside, one man on each floor. And they are growing meaner than ever because of the discipline they suffered for having let me walk away in the first place.

# CHAPTER THIRTY-EIGHT

They hadn't known how it would come. But when it came, they recognized it for what it was thanks to Nadia's warning. And they were ready.

They had decided that there were three possible ways in which they might be intercepted: while still at sea; in port as they went through customs; on the train as they left Archangel. And they had developed a plan of action to deal with each of these contingencies.

Sergei Trobinsky saw the Russian gunboat first, when it was still four or five miles away, his eye drawn by the staccato flash of a heliograph signaler. He alerted Dahlgren, who could read Morse code. The *Albert Michalsky* was being ordered to heave to and take on a boarding party. By the time the boat had pulled up some three-hundred yards away and dispatched its skiff bearing an officer and five seamen, Aldonby and his people were ready.

Lars watched through the porthole as the Russian crew rowed across the flat, gray stretch of sea. "Six of them," Lars counted. "That's probably about half their roster. Those Russian gunboats are usually manned by twelve officers and men."

"Why so many men for such a small vessel?" Aldonby asked.

Lars shrugged. "War is wasteful. I suppose they have to have spares."

"By what right do they stop us in the open ocean?" Vasily Stanovich asked.

"I would guess," said Lars, "that we have just entered Russian waters. They have a right to do any damned thing they please. They may have been following us for hours. Waiting."

"Will they call a muster on deck or come to the cabins?" Boris Alexandrovich wondered.

"No matter," Aldonby reminded him. "We stay in the cabins and

170

make them come to us. All except you." They could hear the voice of the Russian coxswain now, clearly, setting the cadence for the oars. In a matter of minutes they would be alongside.

"Boris," Aldonby quietly said, "it's time. Get up to the wireless room."

Boris Alexandrovich nervously drew his Nagant revolver out from under his coat, broke it open, and checked the load.

"It's all there," Aldonby admonished him. "You checked it five minutes ago."

Boris nodded, snapped the revolver shut, and tucked it under his belt. "We'll meet later," he said, almost interrogatively. The wave of fear had swept over him suddenly, surprisingly. He could feel his heart pounding in his throat. He had never thought he could be so frightened. It embarrassed him.

"We'll pick you up," Aldonby assured him.

Boris nodded affirmatively, pulled open the door, and left. He hoped that he looked sure of himself and of his purpose, and that his hand wouldn't betray him by trembling when next he drew his revolver.

The Russian's skiff had vanished in the lee of the steamer. But Aldonby could hear their voices and the shouts from the wing of the bridge as they tied up alongside and began to clamber up the boarding ladder.

"All right," Aldonby said, very quietly, very coolly, through a jaw locked with tension. "We all know what to do."

Kubishev, Trobinsky, and Stanovich nervously checked their weapons, as Boris had done, wished luck to Aldonby and Lars, and went to their cabin, which was directly across the narrow corridor. They closed their door without turning the lock.

Aldonby shut his door, went to the porthole, and looked out. He could see the gunboat marking time a few hundred yards away. The commotion on the ship's boarding ladder had ended; the Russian crew must be on the main deck now, stating their business to the captain or first officer. If in the next few minutes there was no general call to muster, Aldonby would assume that the Russians would have obtained their cabin numbers from the purser and would be coming down directly to find them.

"Any minute now," Aldonby said to Lars. "Into the bunk and cover up."

"I think I have to shit," Lars complained.

"Don't we all," Aldonby replied.

They could hear heavy footfalls hammering down the companion-way at the end of the corridor.

# CHAPTER THIRTY-NINE

Aldonby positioned himself against the bulkhead beside the cabin door so that when it was opened the door itself would screen him from the view of the intruders. His revolver rested easily in his hand, cocked and ready to fire. Lars lay on the bunk, covered from his chin to the soles of his feet with the heavy, gray, moth-eaten ship's blanket. He, too, was armed with a revolver. The Russian seamen who broke into the stateroom would find themselves trapped between Aldonby and Lars. If the Russian crew were judicious and left several of their number in the corridor, those could be taken from behind by Kubishev, Trobinsky, and Stanovich. Whichever of the two cabins the Bolsheviks chose to enter, they could be trapped, if the timing was right and if the inexperienced cadets in the room across the corridor didn't freeze at the critical moment.

"You look positively ill," Aldonby whispered to Lars, somewhat alarmed.

"I'm supposed to."

"But you really look like you're going to pass out."

"Wouldn't you, if you were lying here with a cocked Webley between your knees? One pull the wrong way on the blanket and I've blown my balls off."

"Keep that thought," Aldonby whispered. "The sicker you look the better off we are. Remember to groan at the proper moment, and quiet!"

Aldonby could hear the footsteps approaching the door, then shuffling around outside, then silence. To his great relief he didn't hear any bolts being thrown on whatever weapons they might have been carrying. They, too, were counting on the element of surprise.

He heard a whispered command. Then there came a polite rapping at the door. It was very disarming. Aldonby wondered why they had not simply burst in. He tried to hear whether they were knocking on the door across the way as well. No! Apparently their plan was to take Aldonby's party piecemeal.

Aldonby nodded to Lars. Lars groaned woefully and called out, "Come." The door was opened from the outside, as deferentially as it had been rapped upon. For effect Lars groaned again and stirred under the blanket, so that their eyes would be drawn to him in the darkened stateroom.

They rushed in silently, swiftly . . . three of them, carrying rifles, of all things, into these confined quarters, and at port arms, as if they were performing a close order drill.

They moved quickly up to the bunk, the spokesman in front, two men behind, and loudly declared that Lars Dahlgren was under arrest. Aldonby hoped that the declaration was loud enough for his friends in the opposite room to hear, because there were probably three Reds standing in reserve in the corridor. He could see at least two of them through the crack between the door and the frame.

The spokesman for the three in the stateroom rudely pulled back the blanket on Lars's bed and then recoiled, bumping into the two sailors behind him, jamming them so that neither of them could bring their rifles into firing position. By this time Lars was sitting up, and they all could see the mean-looking Webley in his fist. The sailor on the right turned his head, looking for some help from his comrades in the corridor. Instead he saw the cabin door slam shut behind him, revealing the man who had shut it, Aldonby, also armed.

"Lay down your rifles," Aldonby ordered with quiet authority and prayed that his cadets across the corridor were functioning according to plan; if they weren't, he would have the door in splinters beside him in less than three seconds' time.

There were two Bolsheviks in the corridor, not three. They were darting uneasy glances this way and that, like fidgety lookouts protecting an illegal dice game against the discovery by the law.

Startled by the sudden slam of the door, they cast questioning glances at one another. One of them reached out with his left hand to try the knob. The other shifted over behind him, the better to see into the room when the door was reopened.

He was the one who felt the pistol barrel in his back. The force of it, as it was rammed in just above his kidney, caused him to grunt. The other sailor turned and saw his partner, rigid and pale with fright, and a man directly behind him and two others fanning out into the corridor from the room across the way. And they were all armed with revolvers.

"Set your weapons down against the bulkhead and get into the cabin," Vasily indicated the open door behind him. "Quickly. And not a sound out of you, please."

"Lay down your rifles," Aldonby repeated. "Your Comrades outside will be of no help." The silence in the corridor allowed him to hope that he was right.

There was a knock at the door.

Aldonby tensed.

"All right?" It was Igor's voice.

"Check," Aldonby replied, trying to conceal his relief.

The three Russians in the room slowly lowered their rifles to the floor, butt first, hands around the barrels, as if completing the drill they had begun when they had rushed in.

They released their grips on the barrels, and the rifles toppled to the floor.

"We have control here," Aldonby called through the door.

"Here too," Igor replied.

"Keep them in your stateroom. How many have you got?"

"Two."

"There were six in the boat." Aldonby sounded alarmed.

"Maybe one stayed in the boat to fend off," Lars said. He returned to one of the Bolsheviks. "Did you leave a man in the boat?"

The Russian nodded agreeably. He seemed eager to please.

"All the same," said Aldonby warily, "let's make sure he's not at the top of the companionway when we go up."

They took their time tying the Russian sailors into the bunks and gagging them. They knew that the knots and lines wouldn't hold forever. But forever wasn't important; the next thirty minutes were. They wanted to be as certain as possible that the Russians would not break loose for at least the time it would take to collect Boris in the wireless room and then to row across to the patrol boat.

In a frenzy of tugging, adjusting, exchanging, they dressed themselves in the sailors' uniforms and locked the cabin door behind them. Carrying their captured rifles so that from a distance they would appear to be those whom they were pretending to be, they moved along the corridor and up the companionway.

"Remember," Aldonby admonished them, "move quickly and in a

businesslike manner. Someone across there on the patrol boat may be watching."

"We have no uniform for Boris," Igor reminded him.

"Bring him down from the wireless room at gunpoint, as if he were a prisoner."

To the others he said, "When we go down the boarding ladder into the small boat, go fast and with your faces averted. We want to be in that boat before the seaman they've left behind realizes what's up. We want him to see only uniforms, feet, and asses as we come down. And when we take him prisoner, let's do it subtly. Don't wave your weapons around. We don't want to precipitate an alert on the gunboat."

With Boris between them they swiftly crossed the main deck, past the steamer's first officer, who seemed as relieved to be rid of these Reds as he was grateful that they had managed to find only one renegade to take back with them.

The sailor in the skiff was so busy trying to keep his small craft from damaging itself against the flank of the steamer that he didn't realize that anything was amiss until the first two men down, Lars and Sergei, were in the boat with him. He looked up then to ask a question and was confronted by a revolver, pointed at him but shielded from the view of those across the water by the invader's body.

"You're doing very well," Lars said approvingly. "Continue until we're all down and then shove off and take your place on the bench and row with the rest of us."

"Where are my Comrades?" the frightened seaman asked, rather bravely, considering the circumstances.

"Do you want to join them?" Lars replied menacingly.

The sailor shook his head.

"Then do as you're told."

When they were all in the boat, they took the oars in hand and all, except Boris their "prisoner," rowed as swiftly as they could toward the mother vessel. They prayed that the lines and knots would hold on the men they had bound and gagged and left behind. And they hoped that no steward attending to his chores would wander into the cabins that contained the hostage Russians.

With each pull on the oars they fearfully anticipated a sudden shout of alarm from aboard the steamer and involuntarily tensed their backs against the fusillade of machine-gun fire with which the gunboat would greet them in the event an alarm was raised.

# CHAPTER FORTY

W hen they had gone a little more than half the distance, to their immense relief the *Albert Michalsky* began laboriously to get under way, turning its stern to them, as if they were an unpleasantness that the steamer's captain wished to forget as soon as he could.

As they drew up alongside the gunboat, Lars again warned the captive sailor to keep his mouth shut and his head bent. The ladder was already down and waiting. Two sailors, elbows on the rail, were peering down waiting to take their line. Only Boris returned their gaze.

Instead of casting the line up to the waiting hands, Lars stepped quickly onto the boarding ladder and secured the line there. Aldonby and Igor raised their rifles and ordered the sailors to remain still and quiet. Lars clambered up the ladder followed by Boris and Sergei Trobinsky. They came onto the deck facing away from the wheelhouse. While Lars pretended to guard his "prisoner" Boris, Sergei ordered the two sailors at the rail to get down the ladder into the small boat.

In the wheelhouse the helmsman turned to his captain and asked, "Have they brought back just one prisoner? We were told there might be as many as six."

"There'll be more," the Captain assured him as he watched his two boatswains start down the boarding ladder. "Maxim and Arbat are going down now to help bring them up. Hold her steady."

Lars began marching Boris toward the wheelhouse, staying close behind him, using him as a screen. The captain looked puzzled. The man behind the prisoner was wearing the uniform of his first officer, but there was something wrong about the gait . . . the physique. . . .

He opened the wheelhouse door and stepped out onto the narrow wing to have a better look. By this time the prisoner and his first officer were just below, and he was staring down into the lethal-looking barrel of a Webley revolver in the prisoner's hand.

"Please keep your hands at your sides and step down here, Captain," Boris ordered.

The captain's chest sagged. "Who are you?"

"Just move," Lars commanded. He could see the Captain's jaw muscles working as he came slowly down the four steel steps to the main deck. By this time Aldonby was on deck and running toward the wheelhouse.

"Helm above," Lars shouted to him. "Wireless room behind that."

"Is that all?" Aldonby asked.

"Unless I've forgotten how to count."

"You take the helmsman. I'll do the wireless room."

"Be careful. The operator may be watching and ready."

"Let's go."

Lars started up the ladder. "And don't damage the equipment," he reminded Aldonby. "We may want to use it." He burst into the wheelhouse and ordered the startled helmsman to get out. The sailor, hands raised, hurried down the ladder, stumbled on the bottom step, and almost fell on his face at his Captain's feet.

By this time all of Aldonby's crew were aboard the gunboat. Igor was running toward the wheelhouse to see if he could help, while Sergei and Vasily stood at the top of the boarding ladder aiming their rifles down into the small boat to make sure that their prisoners behaved.

When Aldonby broke into the wireless room, he found that the operator was indeed ready for him, arms raised submissively and a nervous smile on his face.

One of the deck crew of the steamer, a seaman chipping rust off the stern rail, was the first to see the heliograph signal from the Russian gunboat. There were several miles distance between them now. The deckhand called his boatswain over and pointed to the flashes of light coming from the gunboat.

"I'm not a signalman. How the hell do I know what that means?" the boatswain replied in response to the seaman's question.

"Do you think they can see it on the bridge?" the deckhand asked.

"You keep on chipping; I'll make sure. We don't want them to start shooting at us."

The boatswain went forward at a trot. The deckhand went back to work. But he kept an eye on the incomprehensible flashes of light, concerned that if the steamer didn't promptly comply with whatever it was the gunboat was signaling, they might wind up with a cannon shell down their stack.

On the bridge the breathless boatswain saluted and made his report. The captain stepped out onto the wing, but he was no more able to read the flashing signals than was the boatswain. He wondered why in hell they didn't just use their radio instead of this primitive device and ordered the boatswain to run down the corridor and bring up the wireless operator.

Moments later the wireless operator, rubbing his wrists and trailing yards of line from his ankles, appeared on the ship's wing and reported that his radio had been rendered inoperative.

"By whom?" the captain roared.

"I'm not sure."

"What do you mean, you're not sure? What the hell happened to you?"

"I was tied down. He was in a uniform of the Imperial Artillery, one of the returning prisoners of war. Then he broke up the radio room. He and one of the sailors from the gunboat."

The captain peered with suspicion into his radio operator's eyes. "Are you sober? I saw the Red sailors take him off the ship under guard."

"Well, the man who came up to take him away under guard was treating him like an old friend all the time they were in the wireless room. They worked together to break everything up."

"Stop making up stories and read what they're sending with that light of theirs," he ordered. "Boatswain, get back into the wheelhouse and bring out my field glasses."

"They say—"

"Yes?"

"Stand by."

"Go on. Go on."

"I'm reading it, sir. 'Sending . . . across . . . a . . . boat . . . load . . . of . . . men.'"

"Where are those damned glasses?" The boatswain came with them on the run. "What else?"

"That's all," the wireless operator reported.

"They're still flashing the damned light."

"Same message. They're just repeating it, over and over."

The captain pressed the glasses to his eyes and began adjusting the focus. And now he could see the small boat and the six men in it laboriously stroking away from the gunboat.

"Engines quarter-speed," he yelled into the wheelhouse. "Rudder hard-a-starboard."

The steamer began to turn in a slow, wide circle that would bring it three hundred sixty degrees around to a point somewhere near the laboring small boat.

"Uncover our light," the captain ordered, "and signal them message received." He trained his glasses on the gunboat searching for a clue as to what had prompted this return visit.

Interestingly the view through his glasses confirmed the story that the wireless operator had told him. The seamen who had marched the Imperial Artilleryman off the steamer under guard were behaving on the torpedo boat as if they and their captive were comrades of long standing.

"Do you know," he remarked to his boatswain, "I would be willing to bet that if we made a search of this vessel we would find trussed-up somewhere below and in their underclothes six very angry Reds."

"I don't understand, sir," the boatswain replied.

"No need for you to."

"Do you want me to search the ship, sir?"

"Not just yet. They'll keep."

A smile crept across the captain's face as he watched the small boat's oars dipping in and out of the water. He really had little sympathy for these Red fanatics. He wondered whether the commandeering of the gunboat had been a purely defensive act or whether it had been done as part of some larger plan. And he hoped that, whoever they were, they had some knowledge of the sea.

"Sparks," the captain called to the wireless operator, "you might add a word or two to that message of acknowledgement."

"Yes, sir?"

"Tell them on the gunboat, Good luck."

# CHAPTER FORTY-ONE

*From the journal of Anastasia Romanov*

TOBOLSK
APRIL 8, 1918

We are never out of their sight. The soldiers now have orders to keep us under constant surveillance, and they make the most of these instructions to make our lives miserable. Not *all* of them, of course. Certainly not Leonid. But those who do take advantage of their orders harass us beyond reason and more than make up for those who do not.

Leonid begs me not to despair. He tells me that it was not my brief escape alone that brought these latest miseries down on us but also the persistent rumors that rescue plans are being made somewhere.

And the White armies have beaten the Bolsheviks in many parts of the country. The Red armies are growing very uneasy. If the Whites can maintain their momentum, they could sweep the country in a matter of months and sweep the Bolsheviks out.

Leonid has told me of great estates in the Caucasus, where hordes of peasants have driven out the landowners and looted the manor houses and stripped the fields. These dispossessed landowners are now returning with the White armies, and the peasants in the way of their advance are cravenly trying to restore the loot they have taken and trying to make everything as it was before.

Will anything ever again be for us as it was before?

# CHAPTER FORTY-TWO

Greasy gray water, pewter sky, dead seascape. A world leached of color. Not even a breeze to whip up whitecaps on the slick flat surface. Only the creamy wake boiling up behind them, a long, white plume undulating into the distance, relieved the monotony of the changeless vistas and engine's drone.

Boris stood at the helm, steering strictly by the compass on a course plotted for him by Lars Dahlgren. Aldonby and Lars worked at the chart table in the wheelhouse. Igor manned the cramped wireless room, monitoring the radio traffic, listening for a word about them. So far, to everyone's relief, there had been none. Sergei kept an eye on the gauges in the engine room. And Vasily had gone below to sleep. Aldonby and Boris would join him in a moment.

They had been under way, speeding eastward across the Barents Sea, for a little over eight hours. They had shared the first two watches familiarizing themselves with the boat and its weapons. Now they were ready to begin a cycle of four hours on, four hours off.

Lars dug his calipers into the chart and spanned a distance equal to the miles they had already covered. "A few more hours and you'll begin to see some ice."

"How much?" Aldonby asked.

Lars shrugged. "It's hard to tell at this time of year. Not much at first. Some loose floating stuff—growlers—broken off from the main pack."

"And the main pack?"

"A couple of hundred miles north of us."

"Then it'll almost be a relief to see the ice. Anything with some shape to it and some color."

"Oh! You'll see it, I promise you. But it will be no pleasure."

"You're taking us north?"

"No. But look here, where we're heading. Remember the map I sketched in the tavern in Oslo? We can do in this gunboat what we had hoped to do in *Elena*. Sometimes what man's mischief takes away the good Lord gives back." He brought his finger down on the chart. "Our objective: Darata Bay and the Yamal Peninsula. But before we reach Darata Bay . . . an obstacle. This island of hundreds of miles in length lying south to north. Nova Zemlya. A virtual roadblock."

"But there's a channel here. Between Nova Zemlya and the mainland."

"Ah! Yes. The Kara Strait."

"That looks like the simplest and most direct route."

"Of course. That's where we are headed. You are a born navigator."

"Then what's the problem?"

"Maybe ice. The channel is narrow. It tends to freeze over until later in the year than now. The passage becomes stopped as if with a cork. We were going to take *Elena* through before the first freeze, remember?"

"Then we would be blocked?"

"*If* there is ice in the channel and there very well might be, we will be blocked. We will have to disembark and make our way overland several hundred miles more than we would have had to do had we been able to go through the channel. There is no railroad to Tobolsk from the north or from the south for that matter. Nor is there any river on that side of the peninsula—not until we reach the River Ob. And between where we would land and where we would be heading would stand the Ural Mountains, like a fence barring our way. Those several hundred extra miles could very well destroy us."

"And if the Red sailors we sent packing to the steamer reach Archangel before we reach the Ob, we are liable to be cut off by Bolshevik troops. How long will it take that steamer to reach Archangel?"

"The steamer is slower than we. They'll probably reach the White Sea at about the time we reach the Kara. They will probably face the same obstacle in the White Sea, which is the gateway to Archangel, as we may face in the Kara Strait. Ice."

"How does the steamer get through?"

"Usually there is an icebreaker waiting at the entrance to the White Sea. The icebreaker leads the traffic in and leads it out."

"What about an icebreaker at the Kara Strait?"

Lars shook his head. "Not enough traffic there to warrant it."

"Then how does the occasional shipping there get through?"

"They radio for an icebreaker. It comes. Sooner or later."

"We have a radio. We could call an icebreaker to our assistance in the Kara Strait."

Lars threw him a dubious look. "I think that would not be wise, considering who we are."

"Think about it, Lars. Who are we?"

"I don't have to think about it; I know right away. We are a mixed bag of mercenaries and romantics who have decided to give aid to a defunct Tsar. If the steamer hadn't been intercepted, if we had landed in Archangel and traveled most of the way by railroad, we might have succeeded. As it is now . . ." he shrugged. "If there is ice in the Kara Strait, we might as well turn back; we will never get to Tobolsk."

"We are the crew of a Bolshevik gunboat," Aldonby reminded him. "Suppose we radioed the icebreaker. Told them we were on a special patrol and had become locked in ice at the entrance to the Kara Strait. Wouldn't we take priority over a steamer ferry?"

Lars looked up from his charts, cocked an eyebrow and smiled. "We could try. We could hope that the Reds on the steamer haven't been able to spread the alarm. Because if they have, we could be met by more than just an icebreaker at the Kara Strait.

"Boris," he shouted. "I hope you did a proper job on the wireless on that steamer."

"It will never function again. I tore its guts out."

"Let's hope they don't carry enough spare parts to rebuild it," Lars said to Aldonby. "Otherwise when we call the icebreaker, we may be committing suicide."

The steamer ferry *Albert Michalsky* sat dead in the water at the narrow entrance to the White Sea, waiting for the icebreaker to take them through. They had been waiting for two days.

"Where do you think it could be?" the first officer asked.

"Your guess is as good as mine," the captain replied. He didn't seem at all concerned over the nonappearance of the icebreaker or by the delay.

"We can't sit here forever," the first officer complained.

"Not forever," the captain replied. "But for a little while longer. The weather is fine. The galley informs me we have enough food for a week. We aren't burning any coal except for heat. If it weren't for the fact that there are probably a couple of hundred refugees camping on the pier in Archangel waiting to get out, I would be inclined to turn around and head back to Narvik."

"I don't think the Comrades we took aboard from the gunboat would accept that with equanimity."

"I don't expect they would, but I don't give a damn. If they raise too much hell about it, we'll clap them in the brig and sail them back to Narvik in irons."

"They were raising hell with the wireless operator this morning, demanding he send a message through to Archangel or Murmansk."

"Can't they see that the wireless is wrecked?"

"They can see it. But they insist that he is not doing all that he can to repair it. One of them confronted me on the boat deck this morning. Accused us of deliberately stalling in order to help a criminal gang of capitalist pirates and subversive infiltrators."

"Rude lot, aren't they, considering that if we hadn't picked them up they might still be drifting around in that lifeboat. Probably be eating each other by this time."

"I reminded then that it has been the absence of their icebreaker that has stranded us here."

"Send Sparks up here, will you."

"Yes, sir."

When the wireless operator arrived on the bridge, the captain asked if the harassment from the Bolshevik sailors had unduly upset him.

"Not at all, sir. I am continuing to do my best to repair the wireless with the parts and equipment at hand, as you ordered, sir."

"And what about the spare parts in the hold?"

The wireless operator coughed and cleared his throat. "I have disposed of those, over the side, as you suggested, sir."

"Thank you, Sparks."

"You're welcome, sir."

The wireless operator saluted and left the bridge. The captain could hear him whistling a cheerful tune as he went down the ladder to the main deck.

The captain was smiling as he picked up his binoculars and scanned the featureless sea for a sign of the icebreaker. He decided that he would wait one more day and then turn around and make steam for Narvik.

# CHAPTER FORTY-THREE

B orodnev held the telegram under his good eye and read it again—as if reading it again could diminish his disbelief. Or his rage.

"From: Commander White Sea Fleet . . ."

"White Sea Fleet!" Borodnev snorted. A few run-down gunboats and icebreakers.

" . . . To: Director Security Western District. Gunboat commandeered by subjects of search. Icebreaker Gorki reports gunboat last seen crossing Kara Sea in easterly direction."

What the telegram artfully avoided saying, but what Borodnev nevertheless understood, was that the icebreaker must have unwittingly assisted the gunboat in its eastward passage. Borodnev crumpled the paper in his fist and with a thunderous expletive hurled it across the room. "Imbeciles!" he shouted to the four bare walls. "Incompetents!"

Borodnev's aide rapped urgently on the door. "Is something wrong, Commissar?" he called.

"Something?" Borodnev roared, crossing to the door and yanking it open. "Everything! Our brilliant Navy has made it possible for six saboteurs to sail clear across our northern coast in one of our own gunboats, headed without a doubt for the Yamal Peninsula. And what is on the Yamal Peninsula, a few hundred miles down from where this stolen boat no doubt will land?"

"I'm afraid I am not familiar with that part of Siberia—"

"Tobolsk!" Borodnev roared.

"Tobolsk?" The aide now looked properly concerned. "They are going for the Tsar?"

"The ex-Tsar, imbecile. There is no longer a Tsar in Russia. Only Citizen Nicholas Romanov and his degenerate brood."

"Of course, the ex-Tsar. They are going for him?"

"Cable the commandant at Tobolsk. Immediately. 'Monarchist party on Yamal. Heading south. Six men. Armed. Maybe more will join them. Object—' Are you getting this?"

The aide continued to scribble furiously, trying to keep up. "I'm doing my best, Comrade."

Borodnev yanked the pad out of his hand so that the word *objective*, only half finished, trailed off into a wavering pencil line. Borodnev read what was written and thrust the pad back at his aide.

" 'Objective: To free Romanov. Fortify against intruders. Stop them. More to follow. Borodnev.' "

He waited until the aide had finished writing and then ordered, "Send it immediately."

"Immediately, Commissar," the aide echoed and stood waiting to be dismissed.

"Immediately!" Borodnev roared.

The aide fled. Borodnev wheeled and stormed back into his office, slamming the door behind him. In his rage he kicked out at a side chair near his desk, breaking the chair's leg with his boot, feeling no pain at all in his toes. He kicked the ruined chair once more, sending it smashing into a wall. Then he reached across his desk and picked up the telephone.

"Connect me to the office of Comrade Sverdlov. Double urgency."

He sat down and waited. Maybe the imbeciles in the navy had done him a service, allowing the invaders to get through. Maybe this would be just what he needed to persuade the Central Committee of the importance of resolving without delay the question of the Romanovs.

His good eye began to search the room for the crumpled piece of paper which in his rage he had hurled away. He spotted it in a corner, lay down the telephone earpiece, and went to retrieve the crushed telegram. He brought it back to the desk, sat down, and carefully, almost lovingly, began to smooth it out.

# CHAPTER FORTY-FOUR

I am dying," Aldonby gasped. "I have never been so cold."
They were unharnessing the horses from the sleighs for the night at a point on the River Ob almost midway between where they had made their landfall and Tobolsk.

"Nonsense," Lars assured him. "If you were dying, you wouldn't feel cold at all. Besides it is practically springtime. Hardly anyone freezes to death in the spring."

Aldonby draped a blanket across the horse's back and wiped his watering eyes with the back of a mitten. "I don't believe it's spring."

Dahlgren laughed. "Once you wanted to come here in the winter. Remember? What would you have done if I had let you come then?" He reached into the sleigh and took out an armful of the hay, which they sat on by day and slept on by night but, most importantly, with which they fed their horses. They had bought the horses and the sleighs in Yada, near where they had landed. After that at each village or farmhouse they passed they had stopped to replenish their supply of hay. They kept their sleighs filled with it. It was vital: the fuel without which their mission would be doomed.

"If it is springtime," Aldonby protested, "why is the river still frozen? Why is there snow on the trees? In the springtime everything is supposed to turn green."

"In springtime in Russia everything turns to mud. Be glad the river is still frozen. Be glad the snow is still on the trees and on the ground. In two or three weeks the sun will burst through and thaw everything, all at once. The mud will swallow you to the knees; the river will become a torrent: the land will become practically impassible until the summer. And in summer there are the flies. Don't ask me to tell you about the flies. Just believe me when I tell you that we are traveling at one of the better times of the year. Not really cold enough to freeze you and not really warm enough to drown you."

The horses whinnied, stamped their feet, and exhaled steam through their nostrils, like friendly dragons; then they lowered their heads and began to feed.

"I've spent summers in Russia. It was never like that. My mother grew up in Russia. I've never heard her speak of it that way."

"Your mother grew up in Petersburg and wintered on the Black Sea. You spent your summers in Tsarskoe Selo. It is a different world. We are in Siberia. Western Siberia, to be sure, but Siberia nonetheless. It has earned its reputation, believe me."

Off to the left, a few yards away, there sounded the pop and crackle of tinder catching fire. A low cheer went up from Sergei, Igor, and Boris, huddled in the shelter that they had set up for the night.

Patiently, expertly, despite frost-numbed fingers, Vasily nursed and fed the hopeful flame until it took hold on the fat birch logs. Aldonby and Lars moved closer, beating their hands together to stimulate circulation. It sounded like applause.

Vasily unpacked the food, filled a cauldron with snow, and prepared to cook dinner.

"Better?" Lars asked Aldonby as they stood around the fire.

"Just like home. You're sure we'll reach Novoje tomorrow night?"

"Before night, unless one of the horses breaks down. We have to. We have only enough hay left for twenty-four hours."

"You're sure we can get hay there?"

"Have I failed you yet?"

They had been traveling south toward Tobolsk, using the frozen river as a highway, for four days now, and Lars had not failed them. His knowledge of the flat, densely forested peninsula was phenomenal. He knew the villages and the villagers, and they trusted him: he had traded with them for lumber and furs for almost a decade. The Revolution was far away; their lives went on almost unchanged. They assumed that he was here on business again: a few months earlier than usual, that was all. He had arranged for the purchase of the sleighs, the horses, and the provisions. He had plotted their southward journey so well that, if they didn't always have a farmhouse or barn to sleep in, they were never without their most vital necessity: hay for the horses.

He had proven himself to be as able a captain on land as he was on the sea. Aldonby had reason to be grateful to him and had not hesitated to let him know it. Sometimes Lars would shrug and reply, "You owe me nothing. I am being well paid, and I owe those bastards something for sinking my ship." Other times he would reply, "Never mind. Let's get the job done. I have an itch to get back to Narvik."

"Nadia?"

Lars would nod affirmatively.

"Do you think she'll still be there?"

"It'll be a starting place. If she's moved on, I'll find her. We have unfinished business, Nadia and me."

"I don't think you have it in you to harm her anymore. I saw the look on your face when we steamed out of Narvik."

"I didn't know then that she was in the act of betraying us again."

"And regretted it. And warned us. And saved us in her way. I think she saw the look on your face too."

"Do you know what I think we are destined to do?" Lars would ask, a wicked gleam coming into his eyes. "I think we are destined one day to screw each other to death, Nadia and me." And then he would roar with laughter. "Can you think of a happier fate?"

They reached Novoje the next evening, as Lars had said they would. Established for the night in the loft of a barn situated just outside the village, with plenty of hay for their horses and the body heat of the farm animals for extra warmth, Lars turned command over to Aldonby.

"Tomorrow night we should be in the neighborhood of Tobolsk. Whether we camp outside and wait for daylight, or enter at night is up to you."

"It will depend."

"On what?"

"On a number of things. For example the crew of that gunboat. What do you suppose became of them?"

"Unless they chose to walk on the ice on the White Sea, I would guess that they stayed with the steamer until the icebreaker returned and led them into Archangel. I would guess that they landed two or three days ago."

"And then raised an alarm. How would they send the word out here? By courier from Petersburg or Moscow?"

"By telegraph, more likely."

"I haven't seen any telegraph lines since we landed."

"They haven't run them this far north. At least there weren't any when I was here last year. And I think that the Reds have been too busy holding their revolution together to expand the old communications system. There are lines running west to east along the route of the

Trans-Siberian Railroad. Either Omsk or Tyumen, which is a little closer to us, would get the cable and send a courier with it up to Tobolsk. Too bad the lines don't run up this far; we could tap them and maybe learn something."

"So they know we've landed?"

"By now they must know."

"It might work to our advantage."

Lars smiled wryly. "The mousetrap might work to the mouse's advantage, if he can get to the cheese and get out again without getting his neck broken."

"That's how we planned it. To get in and get out."

"We hadn't planned on their being on the lookout for us."

"They're on the lookout for an assault force of armed guerrillas who've been reported to the north of them. We're going to circle and come up from the south, not an armed band, just you and me, armed only with smiles. We're just a couple of Comrades, arriving from the direction of the rail line from Moscow, with written orders from the Central Committee to remove the Romanovs to the Kremlin for trial. Of course, we'll add that the move is particularly urgent, in light of reports of armed insurgents descending on Tobolsk from the north. And for the commandant at Tobolsk, this will be relief from the Romanov headache."

"May he wet his pants for joy. And may your high-priced London forger be worthy of his fame! So we have the Romanovs. But by now the Red Navy also has a couple of warships in the Kara Strait. The exit is blocked. What do we do? Pray for a quick White victory?"

"We go out the back way. Remember?"

Lars made a face. The original escape plan, made before they had taken the torpedo boat with its promise of a quick, clean sea run back to Norway. Now it would again be eastward by rail, all the way to the American military enclave in Vladivostok on the Pacific. "Weeks on the damned Trans-Siberian Railroad."

"It will be a holiday after Omsk," Aldonby assured him. "The Bolsheviks control nothing beyond Omsk, remember? And Omsk is just a few hundred miles from here. Then, it's a joyride all the rest of the way."

Lars sighed. "And I thought I had managed to avoid adding train robbery to my menu of sins."

"But you have," Aldonby cheered him. "Train robbers usually make off with the train's treasure. We'll just be making off with the train."

# CHAPTER FORTY-FIVE

T he telegram from Archangel lay between them on the desk.
Borodnev waited, impatiently, while Sverdlov brought a spasm of coughing under control. The Chairman of the Republic of Soviets clearly was not a well man. Borodnev hoped that he was managing successfully to mask the disgust he so overwhelmingly felt for illness of any kind. Not that Sverdlov would have noticed; he was too busy examining the folds of his handkerchief, looking for an unused place into which to spit. This accomplished; he balled up the handkerchief again, carefully wiped the righthand corner of his mouth, then the left, then the little beard under his lower lip. He held the balled handkerchief in his right hand and motioned for Borodnev to proceed.

Borodnev hoped that the Chairman would neglect the courtesy of a handshake at the meeting's end. "I propose," he said, "to go myself to Tobolsk to supervise the removal of the Romanov clan to a more secure locale."

"Because six infiltrators are reported to be moving in that direction?" Sverdlov asked skeptically. "We have a garrison of well over a hundred in Tobolsk. You don't think that a hundred Red Guards is sufficient defense against six troublemakers? Assuming that their mission is indeed what you guess it is."

Borodnev struggled to quell his rage. He did not like being lectured to, not even by the Chairman of the Republic of Soviets. "As I have pointed out on other occasions, Tobolsk is crawling with monarchists. We can't be certain even that all the Red Guards in the garrison would remain loyal to us. Maybe these six agents in the Yamal hope to serve as catalysts to stir the monarchists in the area into a counterrevolutionary uprising. Who can say for certain? But I can assure you of this: given

191

the threat and given the political climate, it would be wise to move the family to an area where we know they will find no friends."

Sverdlov dabbed at his lips with his handkerchief and dubiously asked, "Given the political climate, what area would you consider totally secure?"

"I made a proposal weeks ago for their removal to Ekaterinburg. I would hope it has been under consideration."

"There is no small risk in making a move, even a move to the Urals. Central Russia is riddled with White raiding parties."

"The greater risk is to leave them where they are."

"I'm thinking of their safety as well as their security. We may need them for barter. We would want them to meet with no accidents along the way. Do you take my meaning?"

"I take your warning."

"We are aware of your special feelings of hostility toward them."

"You are also aware of my loyalty to the Revolution. If the Central Committee has decreed that they must be preserved for the time being, then I will preserve them. You have my oath on it."

"We'll have your neck if you break your oath. I'll present your case to the Committee."

"I may need extra military support. Perhaps a hundred fifty men."

"You don't think the garrison at Tobolsk is sufficient?"

"Not for such a move. As you said, the country is infested with White units."

"Because of that, we have very few men to spare. We are being pressed everywhere by Kolchack. Besides, the rails being what they are, can you imagine the problem we'd have moving a hundred fifty men from the west through the Urals?"

"We could get them from the garrison in Omsk. It's practically in the neighborhood of Tyumen and Tobolsk."

"I'll put that suggestion before the Committee as well."

Borodnev wondered who would get credit for the idea if it proved acceptable: Sverdlov or he?

Two days later Borodnev was entrained for Tyumen, armed with a letter of authority signed by Sverdlov, giving him power as a Commissar Extraordinary to operate across regional lines and move the Romanov family from Tobolsk to more secure quarters in Ekaterinburg.

# CHAPTER FORTY-SIX

Kossirev, boss of the Omsk Soviet, showed the telegram from Moscow to his military aide, Captain Ospensky.

"Can we spare a hundred fifty men to go to Tobolsk with this Borodnev?"

"We *can't* spare a hundred and fifty men. Not armed and equipped. What is Central Russia doing in our territory anyway? They sent their Commissar out from Moscow; why don't they send troops from Moscow?"

"They would never get here. Their railroads are hopeless."

"And should we then be required to make up for their deficiencies? Because our Siberian railroads run should we be penalized?"

"There's a party of infiltrators moving down the Yamal toward Tobolsk. The Central Committee wants to move Romanov and his family."

"There are Red Guards in Tobolsk. Can't they be trusted?"

Kossirev didn't reply.

"How many infiltrators are we defending against?"

"Six that we know of."

Ospensky looked dismayed. "Six infiltrators? And they can't handle it with their garrison?"

"The six may just be a spearhead."

"I say they should shoot Romanov and be done with it."

"That is forbidden by the Central Committee."

"I don't know what they're being so scrupulous about. Shoot Romanov and you remove the motivation for these infiltrators. End of the problem."

"They want a public trial. They don't want us to look like a gang of barbarians before the world."

"If they try Romanov before they shoot him, will the result be any different?"

"No. But it will be respectable."

"A number of my men are from families who came to Siberia under Romanov exile. You want these men to have to guard them? They would as soon kill them."

"They would have to answer to Moscow if they did."

"Moscow is far away. And its arm isn't that strong."

"They're flexing their biceps. They're sending out this Borodnev. Do you know him?"

"How would I know him?"

"This Borodnev will be their muscle. Quite a muscle from what I've heard. Round up as many men as you can who can be equipped and who will make a good showing. One doesn't play games with this Borodnev."

"How much time do I have?"

"He left Moscow yesterday. The way things are it will take him maybe three more days to get to Tyumen."

"He'll be tired."

"And cross. So be there when he gets there. Impress him with our efficiency."

"We could get to Tyumen on foot in three days."

"Save your strength. We have freight cars in the yards for the horses. Take one of our excellent trains."

# CHAPTER FORTY-SEVEN

*From the journal of Anastasia Romanov*

Tobolsk
April 18, 1918

Leonid tells me that the commandant has been advised that a rescue party is reported to have landed at the northern end of the peninsula.

Can this be true? Or does Leonid make up fibs to lift my spirits? The commandant has fortified the house and the grounds as never before. If there is a rescue force, how will they ever penetrate this ring of armor? And how will we survive the onslaught?

Sometimes I feel so guilty because Leonid tells me so much more than the other members of my family know. And I never know how much to tell them. Sometimes they don't believe what I tell them anyway.

And Mama grows so angry whenever I mention him at all. She swears she'll report him to the commandant. She warns me that he is probably a spy. I plead with her. I break down in tears. She turns her head away, but she doesn't make good her threats.

Let us pray for those brave men, whoever they may be, who are coming to save us. If they are coming.

# CHAPTER FORTY-EIGHT

On the twentieth of April some thirty hours' journey south of Tobolsk, they made camp just outside the settlement of Vinzili, east of Tyumen on the Trans-Siberian line. They had found a railroad siding that would serve as their rendezvous and point of eastward departure four days later if all went well.

Aldonby had given Tobolsk a wide berth on the day before. His great concern now was not that the commandant would balk at ridding himself of the Romanov burden but that one of the Romanovs might doom the entire enterprise by betraying his, Aldonby's, identity with a look or word of recognition. He would have had even greater cause for concern had he been aware that Borodnev was on his way, operating under authentic and almost identical orders.

While Aldonby and the cadets warmed themselves by a fire, Lars Dahlgren climbed one of the telegraph poles that formed a colonnade stretching into infinity along the right of way. He had spent intermittent hours during the day perched like a great dark bird near the top of the pole, tapping the line, patiently gathering data on the movement of trains through the region, clarifying the emerging pattern. The schedules were hopeless coming from Central Russia to the east. Somewhere in the great, crowded industrial areas transportation broke down. Lost trains seemed to be more the rule than the exception. But the return journeys from Siberia were taking place on a quite reliable schedule. On April twenty-sixth it would be the job of Aldonby's cadets to commandeer the westbound freight that came through every night at 2230 hours, run it into the siding, reverse its direction, and wait approximately twenty-four hours for the arrival of Aldonby, Dahlgren, and the Romanovs.

Lars Dahlgren scrambled down the pole for the fifteenth time that day.

"He looks as if he had been born in a tree," Igor remarked, as Lars dropped to the ground and began slogging toward them through the decaying snow that was the first sign of spring.

"He spent his youth on sailing ships. If you can climb a mast at sea, you can climb anything," Aldonby said with admiration.

Lars slipped once and almost fell, righted himself, and continued toward them waving the notepad on which he had been jotting the telegraph transmissions.

"Stir up the fire a little," Aldonby told Boris. "He looks like he's going to need thawing out again."

Dahlgren came puffing into the encampment and thrust the notepad at Aldonby.

"Sit down and warm yourself," Aldonby told him.

"Sit down, my ass! I am not cold, you damned thin-blooded Englishman. Read that. It's no timetable."

With his teeth Dahlgren pulled off his mittens and warmed his hands over the fire. With a sideward glance he watched Aldonby slowly turning the pages of the notepad, reading and then rereading the clumsy scrawl, just a few words to each sheet of paper. When he had finished, Aldonby looked grim. He walked away from the fire to the edge of the encampment and stood with his back to the others, shoulders high and tense.

"What is it?" Vasily asked Lars.

"Trouble," Lars replied. "The message is in response to another message sent some days ago from Moscow. Apparently Moscow is sending a special agent here to help protect the Tsar from us. This special agent has asked for extra military support. That's what this message is about. And we are caught in the middle."

When Aldonby turned back to face them, there was a trace of a smile about his mouth and a wicked glint in his eyes. "This message was sent from Omsk to the station just west of us at Tyumen. When the train stops there, it will be delivered to a special commissar on board named Borodnev. I'll read it to you:

> *From: Kossirev, Commissar Omsk*
> *To: Borodnev, Commissar Extraordinary. En route Tyumen. Train number 41R672. Reference your troop request. Ground conditions prohibit infantry. Forty-five cavalry meet you Tyumen 4/23.*

"That's three days from now," Lars said. "What are we to do? If we haven't been shot in Tobolsk, we'll be en route with the Romanovs, and this Borodnev and his cavalry will be in position to cut us off."

"We're going to send a message to Kossirev in Omsk. Can you rig a device?"

Lars shrugged. "I can. But what would be the purpose? To tell this Kossirev where we are and throw ourselves upon his mercy?"

"No. To tell him that Borodnev is a couple of days ahead of schedule and that he wishes to be met tomorrow, April twenty-first, fifty miles or so closer to Omsk, in Vinzili, rather than on the twenty-third in Tyumen."

The others stared at him in mute astonishment.

"What could be more commanding and persuasive than for us to arrive in Tobolsk with a Red cavalry escort?" Aldonby pulled off his mittens and began to write on the pad.

> *To: Kossirev, Omsk.*
> *From: Borodnev, en route.*
>
> *Ahead of schedule. Imperative cavalry meet me Vinzili, 4/21. Require horses for myself and one aide.*

They were coming on at a walking pace, miniaturized by distance so that they looked no more formidable than gnats on the snow. Against the glistening white backdrop Aldonby could count twenty-two distinct little figures in a line and supposed, therefore, that it actually was a double line, except for the leader. Through his field glasses he could see that a couple of supply sleighs brought up the rear. And behind the sleighs were two riderless horses. It was April twenty-first and they were right on schedule.

Aldonby smiled. They had received his message and were acting in compliance with his instructions. In a sense he was already in command. He dug into his pocket and took out his watch. It was a little after two o'clock in the afternoon. He turned to Lars. "We'll tell them our train came through here four hours ago. Let's stand up and start pacing in case they can see us. Look impatient. Work up some steam. We want to appear angry as boils when they come riding in here. We want to keep them off balance right from the start."

He looked off to the south of the tracks where a copse of birch sheltered his four cadets. He wanted to make certain that they were well out of sight. Certainly by now they, too, had seen the riders from Omsk.

If for some reason the meeting at the siding between Aldonby, Dahlgren, and the horsemen failed to go according to plan, the other four were to make no attempt to save their leaders. That would be futile. If the mission seemed hopeless, they were to flee eastward to Vladivostok and the Pacific and save themselves.

But if things went right, they were to have an engine and at least one car capable of carrying passengers waiting on the siding on April twenty-seventh.

When the horsemen were only a quarter mile away, Aldonby stopped pacing and kicking at the snow and turned to face the troop, legs set wide apart, hands on hips, jaw thrust aggressively forward. "How do I look?" he asked Dahlgren.

"Formidable," Lars assured. "Like the coxswain on a Roman galley."

"Good."

"The only question is have any of them ever actually seen this Borodnev?"

"I'm betting that they haven't. You know the size of this country. Administration is local. Communication is poor. They probably don't even know Lenin's face out here."

"We'll find out in a minute."

The riders were barely a hundred yards away now and had changed their gait to a canter. They sat their horses masterfully, moving with fluid elegance. But the riders' faces were pinched, their beards unkempt, and their clothing shabby.

"Just try to look meaner than they do," Aldonby counseled.

As the horsemen wheeled into the clearing near the tracks, Aldonby stepped up onto a stout log, using the extra height to lend authority to his bearing, to give whoever was in command of the troop a point of focus as he brought the riders to a halt.

Aldonby waited on his improvised platform, impassive, imperious, stonily patient while the troopers arranged themselves in two long rows in front of him, as if they had already accepted his leadership.

The horses restlessly pawed the ground. The dry, cold air became saturated with the smell of sweat, animal and human. The riders sat their mounts, waiting, glancing uncomfortably from side to side, wondering what would come next.

"Who's in charge here?" Aldonby shouted.

A rider at the end of the first row dismounted and began to trudge through the snow.

Aldonby waited, tight-lipped. Rather than watch the approaching officer, he let his eyes pass deliberately from one rider to another, inspecting, appraising, as if they were passing in review in front of him rather than just sitting there shivering in their stirrups.

Their officer now stood before Aldonby. "Comrade Borodnev." He saluted. "I am Captain Chernovsky. Commissar Kossirev has placed us at your service."

Aldonby hoped that Lars had not just sagged with relief. As for himself, he stared grimly at a point some six inches above Chernovsky's head.

"We have been waiting in this wilderness for almost five hours," Aldonby snapped in his flawless Russian.

"I beg your pardon, Commissar. The telegram that informed us of your schedule change did not afford us sufficient time."

"I'm sure you've done your best with what is available, Captain. Conditions are less than perfect everywhere."

Chernovsky nodded gratefully, relieved to have been forgiven his tardiness by the special Commissar from Moscow. Aldonby felt that he had Chernovsky neatly in hand; there was no point making an enemy of him. Just keep him on a loose rein, like a well-trained stallion. "You and your men have earned some food and rest."

Chernovsky thanked him.

"Make a temporary camp here. Feed the horses. Break out your rations. In three hours we'll begin moving north."

He stepped down from the log and placed an arm in comradely fashion over Chernovsky's shoulder. Even without the platform he towered over him. "And meanwhile," Aldonby added, "why don't you introduce me to each of your men. I want to tell them what a fine picture they made coming over the hill."

Chernovsky smiled and nodded agreeably.

Toward dusk, two days later, on the afternoon of the twenty-third, while the rest of the troop fed and watered their horses, Aldonby, Lars, and Captain Chernovsky climbed to the crown of a knoll and looked down at Tobolsk, a forlorn-looking little enclave of dilapidated buildings and snowbound streets.

From their vantage point three miles away it looked like little more than a bald patch in the forest. Aldonby held out his hand, palm up, and Chernovsky turned over his field glasses. "They are housed in the former governor's residence," Chernovsky said, "so it will be the biggest house in town."

Aldonby traversed the town with the glasses until he came upon a white, two-story structure that stood out above everything except the onion-domed church. The building, facing the street with blind white-washed windows, was surrounded by an unpainted wooden fence.

"I think I've found it," Aldonby said. He could see sentries posted outside the fence. Across a square there was considerable activity. Garrison headquarters, Aldonby decided.

They came into the square at a canter, kicking up snow and blowing steam like a squadron of dragons, and drew up in front of the garrison headquarters in a double line. The Red Guards of Tobolsk stood about, gawking, and confused.

Aldonby swung down from the saddle and began plowing on foot across the few yards of snow between the horsemen and the head-quarters' building. He was almost at the door when Osmenov, the Commandant, came storming out, pulling on his overcoat, demanding to know what was going on.

Aldonby didn't break stride and, towering over Osmenov, loudly introduced himself: "Borodnev, Commissar Extraordinary." He clapped a hand on Osmenov's shoulder and turned him around so that he was again facing the building from which he had just come.

"We are here under the special direction of the Central Committee to remove Citizen Romanov and his family to more secure quarters in Moscow," Aldonby declared as he guided Osmenov into the building and swung the door shut behind him.

# CHAPTER FORTY-NINE

As the old train creaked to a halt in front of the station in Tyumen, Borodnev appraised the scene with a jaundiced eye. He was in a veritable wilderness: a station that might be mistaken for a public toilet in Moscow or Petersburg, a few weathered buildings, fewer people. A wasteland. The locals lacked the curiosity to give even a passing glance to the train.

No porters. No guards. No cavalry! He had expected to see neat rows of eager horsemen lined up across from the train, waiting to salute him, to take his inspection, to escort him to Tobolsk. And there was nothing.

True, he was a day late, thanks to the hopeless mismanagement of the internal transportation system. But being a day late was all the more reason that the cavalry should have been there.

He dropped his baggage out of the window into a foot of soggy, porous snow. Disgusted, he stormed up the corridor and climbed down from the train. He drew out his Nagant revolver and checked the load. For all he knew he might have dropped down into a nest of monarchists. He shoved the revolver back into its holster and went sloshing through the snow to pick up his bag. The damned cavalry troop, he decided, must have spent the previous day waiting, guzzling vodka. Now, though it was already almost noon, they were probably sleeping it off in an encampment on the edge of town.

Well, he decided, he would teach them the meaning of discipline before they arrived in Tobolsk, if he had to hang a few of them along the way.

He stormed into the railroad station, hurled his bag into a corner, and like a half-mad bull descended on the petrified attendant cowering behind the ticket window.

"Where is the cavalry from Omsk?" he roared.

The stationmaster blinked and drew back a little behind his barred window, as if he were afraid that the one-eyed lunatic before him might extend an arm between the bars and throttle him.

"I don't understand, sir," the railwayman stammered.

"Sir?" Borodnev thundered. "Is this a Tsarist stronghold I have come to?"

"Comrade." The railway man corrected his error. "I know of no cavalry from anywhere."

Outside there was a lazy clanging of bells and a sibilant discharge of steam as the train started up again. The railway man shifted his eyes right and left, as if looking for an exit.

"I won't hurt you, you worm," Borodnev growled. "But I want some answers."

"I know of no cavalry," the railway man repeated. "There would be no need. There have been no military engagements here in a hundred and twenty years."

"You saw no horsemen around here yesterday?"

"No, sir. I mean, Comrade."

"And there are no horsemen presently encamped in the neighborhood of this wretched village?"

The railway man shook his head.

"Imbeciles!" Borodnev spat.

The railway man licked his lips nervously and backed off another foot or two. The stranger had both fists wrapped around the bars now, knuckles white, muscles bulging on the backs of his hands. The railway man was afraid he might rip the bars out of their sockets.

"Is there a telegraph here?"

"Of course, Comrade."

"Is there a message for me? Borodnev. From Moscow."

The name didn't bring any more terror into the railwayman's eyes than was already there. Clearly he had no idea who Borodnev was. He only sensed that he must be someone to be feared.

"No messengers. I mean—m-messages," the railwayman stammered, blinked, and waited.

"Get the telegrapher. I want to send a wire to Omsk."

"I am also the telegrapher," the railway man whispered. He was choking with fear.

"Then send this, you maggot!"

The railwayman nodded and backed hurriedly away.

"Where the hell do you think you're going?" Borodnev roared.

The railwayman froze. "For a pencil, Comrade. I mean, sir . . . " He dove for the desk at the back of the room and came up with a pencil and a pad. "I'm ready, Comrade," he huskily announced.

"I doubt it," Borodnev sneered. "But we'll try anyway."

> *To: Kossirev, Omsk.*
> *From: Borodnev, Tyumen.*
>
> *Demand whereabouts cavalry. Reply immediately.*

The railwayman had not heard of Borodnev but he certainly knew the reputation of Kossirev in nearby Omsk. If this Borodnev had the temerity to speak so severely to Kossirev, his worst fears were well-founded.

"I'll send it immediately, sir—er—Comrade."

"How long will it take?"

"It will be in Omsk instantaneously."

"For a reply, idiot! Which means how long will it take for them to carry the message from the telegraph station to Kossirev and from Kossirev back?"

"I'll add my own most urgent to a request for delivery. If Comrade Kossirev is in his office, you may have a reply within thirty minutes."

Borodnev nodded approvingly. "Do that." The savage edge had gone from his voice. The railwayman smiled, significantly relieved.

"Would you like some tea, Comrade?" the railwayman ventured in a quavering voice.

"Send the damn message," Borodnev roared.

"Yes, Comrade."

"Then the tea."

Twenty minutes later Borodnev was pacing restlessly near the stove, a glass of lukewarm tea in hand, when the telegraph in the office began to click away.

Borodnev set the glass down on the stove and crossed to the barred window. The railwayman was bent over the machine, transcribing the message on a pad. Borodnev strode a few paces to the right and pulled open the door to the office. The railwayman turned, alarmed, and missed part of a word in the message. Borodnev pointed a stubby finger at him, directing him to get back to his work. The railwayman tapped the key and asked for a repeat of the word he had missed, while Borodnev read over his shoulder.

*To: Borodnev, Tyumen.*
*From: Kossirev, Omsk.*

*Forty-five riders dispatched Vinzili 4/20 await your arrival and further instructions.*

"Vinzili!" Borodnev shouted. "Where in hell is Vinzili?"

"A few miles down the line, Comrade," the railwayman said, as he signed off.

"More incompetence!" Borodnev roared. "Why were the riders sent to Vinzili when I told them to meet me in Tyumen? Does nothing function properly in this wilderness?"

"Do you have a response for Omsk?" the railwayman asked weakly.

"To hell with Omsk. Send a message to Vinzili."

"Begging your forgiveness, Comrade. But there is no station in Vinzili. Only a siding." He sounded apologetic, as if the lack of a station and a telegrapher were his fault.

"When is the next train?"

"Seven o'clock this evening if it is on schedule. I cannot guarantee that it will be."

"I must go to Vinzili," Borodnev roared menacingly.

"Would you consider a horse and sleigh, Comrade?" the railwayman timorously inquired. "I could perhaps arrange for a horse and sleigh."

He hoped he didn't sound too eager to get Borodnev out of there.

# CHAPTER FIFTY

W hile Captain Chernovsky found food and quarters for his men and horses, Aldonby and Lars walked through the snow toward the former governor's house, setting a breathless pace for the shorter, older, fatter Colonel Osmenov; he trailed behind, puffing, stumbling, occasionally running to catch up and then losing ground again when he paused to catch his breath.

"Should we slow down for him?" Lars whispered to Aldonby. "We don't want him to start getting cross with us."

"Cross?" Aldonby answered, picking up the pace a notch. "The poor bastard is feeling too inferior to dare get cross. Let's keep him feeling that way."

When they arrived at the governor's house, they stopped out of earshot of the first sentry and waited for Osmenov to catch up. "This may be the most difficult part," Aldonby whispered to Lars. He pulled his collar high up around his face. "If Marie or the Tsaritsa betray by so much as a blink that they know me, we're done."

Osmenov arrived, panting. Without allowing him time to catch his breath, Aldonby motioned for Osmenov to lead the way. The Commandant nodded to the sentry who stepped aside so that they could pass. Inside the foyer another sentry stood lounging against the newel post, his rifle carelessly slung, chewing on a piece of sausage. When he saw Osmenov, he adjusted his posture and achieved a stance resembling that of attention.

"Where are they?" Osmenov demanded, trying to control his panting.

The sentry waggled the stub of sausage in the direction of the back of the house. "Old Romanov is in the study with the doctor."

"Is he ill?" Osmenov asked, without alarm or even real concern.

"No. It's the boy again. He's always ill. It's a wonder he's still alive. The doctor was just upstairs with him."

"The daughters?"

"They're all upstairs. The German bitch too."

"The ex-Empress," Osmenov explained. And then to the sentry, "Bring them down."

"Wait!" Aldonby stopped him. "I'll go. I want to see for myself whether this boy is really ill or if he isn't just malingering."

"I assure you," Osmenov protested, "we would allow no malingering in this house. The boy is a certified invalid. Something wrong with his blood."

Aldonby was already halfway up the stairs. He stopped and turned. "Take my Comrade to the room with Citizen Romanov and wait. I'll bring the whole lot down."

He turned away to foreclose the possibility of further debate and continued up the stairs. He stepped into the second-floor hallway breathing a sigh of relief. Now he could confront Marie out of sight of Osmenov.

There was a sentry leaning against the sill of a window at the far end of the hallway. The sentry looked at him with only passing interest. Aldonby began trying doors.

Alexandra Romanov, pale and drawn, looked up with alarm from the story she was reading aloud to her son. Alexei was sitting up in bed, waxen-faced and rheumy-eyed with fever, his back propped with pillows set against the headboard, his hair plastered wetly to his forehead.

A tall, ramrod-postured man in a shabby remnant of a uniform stepped defensively between Aldonby and the bed. Aldonby froze: he hadn't counted on this. Sentries in the family's private rooms.

"Get out," Aldonby ordered him.

The man didn't move. Instead he asked, "Who are you?" His voice was firm, almost defiant.

"Borodnev," Aldonby snapped. "Commissar Extraordinary. Moscow."

"What do you want here?" the soldier sullenly demanded, barring Aldonby's further entry into the room. Stalemate.

The Empress, having overcome her initial alarm, had begun to examine Aldonby's features with special interest. The perilous confrontation was imminent. Unless he did something quickly one of the family would betray his identity in the presence of a Red Guard.

From where he stood across the room, he risked making eye contact with Alexandra and with an almost imperceptible side-to-side movement of his head tried to warn her to be silent.

Alexandra brought a clenched hand to her mouth and gasped. There was no doubt about it now. She had recognized him. Aldonby decided to retreat before she could speak. It would mean losing authority over the guard in the room and that might be the beginning of the disintegration of his entire masquerade. But that was a risk he would have to take. If he allowed her to speak his name, everything would be lost.

He looked away from Alexandra and pointed a menacing finger at the tall figure before him. "You," he spat, "have not heard the end of this."

He turned to go, had his hand on the doorknob, was almost out of the room and out of the way of disaster when Alexandra's voice rang out, strident, slightly nasal, but still haughtily imperious despite her beggarly circumstances, "Aren't you Katerina's boy?"

Aldonby stiffened. The woman was stupid beyond belief. If he was Katerina's boy, what did she think he was doing here and why didn't she have the sense to keep the news to herself?

"You are mistaken, Citizeness," he shot back, without turning. He had only two options now: he could leave the room and hope the Empress's outburst hadn't registered on the man who stood between them, or he could turn back, kill the Red Guard, and try to think of some way to justify it.

"Of course," the Empress excitedly exclaimed. "Charles Aldonby. But what are you doing here?"

Aldonby whirled, drawing his pistol. He felt like killing her as well as the guard.

There was a strained smile on her pinched face, a smile so thin and tight that it seemed as if she were trying to recall, one by one, how to make the muscles work. The child in the bed was staring, frightened and bewildered at Aldonby's drawn revolver.

"It's all right, Alexei," she assured the child. "He is a friend." Then to the guard, "Help me, please."

To Aldonby's astonishment the tall guard rushed to her side in the most solicitous and respectful manner and helped her from her chair. Aldonby let his gun drop and flicked on the safety. Alexandra and the Red Guard were so close together that he couldn't shoot in any event.

Once on her feet the Empress shrugged the guard off. "I'm all right now, thank you."

"Yes, Tsaritsa," the guard replied, as he watched with concern her arthritically enfeebled progress across the room.

"I don't get up and down very well. But I manage to get around," she said.

She came very close to Aldonby and examined his face. Her eyes were sunken and dark-ringed, as if set in perennial shadow, but they weren't defeated. There was autocratic steel there yet, and fierce indomitability. "You *are* Charles Aldonby, aren't you?"

"Yes, madam," Aldonby quietly conceded. It was all over. "Who is he?" he asked, nodding in the direction of the guard.

Alexandra turned, puzzled, as if wondering to whom he could be referring, as if wondering if there were a fifth person in the room. "Do you mean Trup?" she asked. "He is Alexei's nurse now since Nagorny was sent away, the Tsar's former footman, our most loyal friend and subject."

"Forgive me, m'am," Aldonby begged, recalling how he had mentally condemned her a few moments ago and the thing he nearly did.

"For what, Aldonby? Are you with *them* now? Have they enlisted the youth of England in this bloody business of theirs?"

"I am not with *them*, m'am, I promise you. We've come to bring you out, if we can. Until we all are out I must be known to you as Borodnev. And you must by no word or look betray the identities of any of the others in our group whom you might recognize. When we are in the presence of anyone connected with the Bolshevik regime, I will speak to you and any other members of your family with disrespect, even contempt. You must bear with me and forgive me. It must be done."

"Alexei is ill," she said softly, plaintively, with no trace of her characteristic arrogance in her voice. "He cannot travel."

"We'll see," Aldonby replied. "Somehow we'll manage."

Alexandra gripped his arm imploringly. Clung to him.

Gently he disengaged himself. "I have to speak to the others now." He hadn't counted on an invalid boy or an empress who behaved in these circumstances no differently from any other concerned and doting mother.

"Olga and Tatiana are in the room directly across the hall. Marie and Anastasia are two doors down. The Tsar is downstairs with Dr. Botkin. Shall I go to the girls' rooms with you?"

"No, thank you. I would like you to begin the procession downstairs. Can you manage the stairs?"

"With Trup's help."

"Then, when I order you downstairs, please obey."

"Alexei can't be moved. . . ."

"I understand. Trup can help you down and then return to sit with Alexei."

Aldonby opened the door, took a step out into the hallway, and shouted back into the room. "You! Woman! Downstairs! Immediately! The boy can stay in bed."

The sentry at the end of the corridor remained slouched against the windowsill but nodded his head approvingly. Aldonby pounded on the door across the hall, the one belonging to Olga and Tatiana. There was no response. The sentry looked amused.

Aldonby kicked the door open and rushed into the room.

There was no one there.

When Aldonby came out, the sentry was grinning and pointing to the other door. He seemed to regard the proceedings as an entertainment. Anything to relieve the tedium of life in this backwater.

Aldonby hammered once on the next door and, for the sentry's benefit and approval, kicked it open before there was time for a reply.

The four girls were standing around the bed. They had been using the mattress as a card table, playing a game of patience. Their faces were all turned in Aldonby's direction now. Alarmed. Alert. Alive. No evidence here of the wan visage and hollow eyes, no husks of former great personages such as he had encountered in the Tsaritsa's room. The young Grand Duchesses, even in their momentary fright, were radiantly alive, aflush with youthful womanhood. Neither the drabness of their clothes nor their dismal surroundings could diminish their abundant beauty or their charm.

Marie, who had held him in thrall years ago, suffered not at all by comparison to the creature he had built in fantasy in the intervening time. Somehow this astonished him. He had been certain that she would be something less than he recalled. He wanted to go to her, to embrace her, but he restrained himself lest a sudden move in their direction terrify them all.

Marie had so occupied his thoughts that he had forgotten how lovely the others were—even the little imp, Anastasia. Which one was she? She had been just a child when last he had come to Petersburg.

But it was Anastasia who was the first to recognize him. Her eyes grew round; her lips parted in amazement. Speechless, she extended her arm and pointed a forefinger in his direction.

Almost simultaneously Marie gasped and called his name. Aldonby held a silencing finger to his lips. Overwhelmed by a confusion of feelings, the girls stood immobile around the bed, staring at him.

"Some months ago," he said, as softly and as reassuringly as he could, "your mother sent a courier to London. I am here by way of reply." He moved toward them, arms extended. Marie rushed into his embrace. She tucked her face tight into his shoulder. He buried his face in her hair. Tatiana pressed close, and he found room for her too. Anastasia threw her arms around his neck. They remained that way for a moment, a warm, throbbing cluster. Olga, the oldest, stood a foot or two away, hands clasped under her chin in an almost prayerful attitude, her eyes glistening.

Aldonby raised his head, and there were tears in his eyes, too, as he began to disengage himself from the tangle of clutching arms and bodies.

"In case the door should open, we must not be seen this way," he whispered. They stood back, stood apart from each other. The girls looked frightened again.

"We thought they had set us free," Marie said quietly, her voice heavy with disappointment.

Aldonby wanted to reach out and take her hand, but he didn't dare. "They have not set you free. But you will be free," he promised, "in just a few days' time. We will all leave here tomorrow, in sleighs, accompanied by an escort of forty-five horsemen. We will travel as quickly as we can, and it will not be an easy journey. To Vinzili, south of here on the railroad line. Four friends, loyal to your family, will have a locomotive and at least one car waiting at the siding. We will take this train eastward through Siberia, to Vladivostok."

"But," Marie interrupted, "you said they had not freed us. How can we go from here to Vinzili with a cavalry escort?"

"Because," Aldonby explained, "and this is most important, the Commandant here has been led to believe that I am someone other than myself. From this moment until we have passed through Omsk on the train, I must be known to you, as I am known to the Commandant, as Commissar Borodnev. It will be necessary for me to treat you rudely, harshly, callously." He placed both his hands on Marie's shoulders and held her eyes with his own. "This most necessary conduct will not come easily to me, I promise you."

He stepped back, resisting an impulse to embrace her again. There would be a time for that. Then he turned away and went to the door. He pulled it open, stepped into the hall, and shouted back into the room. "I have advised you of the rules. I will expect you to abide by them. Or you will suffer for your disobedience. I will expect you downstairs in the study in three minutes." He strode down the hall without even according them the courtesy of closing their door. The sentry nodded approvingly.

As Aldonby went down to the study, he hoped that Lars had managed a private word with the Tsar. Those years ago in Petersburg and Tsarskoe Selo he had met the Tsar only briefly, certainly had not been known to him as he was to the Empress and her daughters. But he put his hat back on, low on his brow, and pulled his collar up around his face. Just in case.

# CHAPTER FIFTY-ONE

A t Vinzili the cadets had found shelter in a stable near the edge of
town but within sight of the railroad tracks. So without unduly
exposing themselves to the elements, they had been able to maintain
round-the-clock surveillance of the rail line, the siding, and the com-
ings and goings of rolling stock.

They had noted that the trains rarely stopped at Vinzili except when
flagged down by a signalman. This individual seemed to eat, sleep, and
tend to his business for the railroad out of a tiny, tar-papered shed at
the side of the tracks. Through observation the four cadets had learned
the procedure used by the signalman when a train had to be called to a
stop: some fifteen minutes before an expected arrival, the signalman
would leave the shelter of his tarpaper hut and hoist a pennant to the
top of a twenty-five foot pole beside the tracks. Presumably the driver
of an oncoming train could see this notice of an impending stop from
some miles away. The signalman then withdrew into his hut until the
train was in sight. Then he stepped out, unfurled a hand-held flag, and
with a series of flourishes waved the oncoming train to a halt.

The cadets had also validated by observation the schedule of the key
train on Lars Dahlgren's intercepted timetable: a short freight that
came through from the east without stopping every night at about 2230
hours. It carried no passengers, so there would not be large groups of
people to contend with—only the crew.

They felt secure and comfortable in their hideaway on the outskirts
of the town, and if the few locals who were seen on the streets cast
questioning glances at one or the other of them when they came in to
purchase food or supplies, they were left alone. There were so many
refugees on the loose these days that they were taken for granted.
Nevertheless, when they did go into town, they never went all four

together. They took turns making this trip, once or twice daily, and whoever's turn it was always went alone.

Igor was carrying a sack of potatoes over his shoulder, the only man abroad on the snow-covered wooden sidewalk of Vinzili's one short main street, when Borodnev's sleigh came through.

The Commissar was sitting beside the driver, scowling fiercely and tongue-lashing the poor man mercilessly. Finally he tore the reins out of the hands of the distraught driver and brought the sleigh to a stop in front of Igor.

"You!" he shouted. "Halt!"

Igor had never seen Borodnev before. But the man's manner and tone of voice were alarming.

"Yes, Comrade?" Igor asked, as ingenuously as he could.

"Where are the mounted troops?" Borodnev demanded.

"Mounted troops?" Igor repeated, batting his eyes like an imbecile.

"The horsemen. From Omsk. They were to be waiting here."

A shudder of apprehension ran through Igor. This must be the man from Moscow, Borodnev.

Had Igor come into town armed he might have killed the Commissar on the spot. But he had left his weapon in the stable rather than generate questions among the townspeople. He wondered if he would have been capable of killing an unsuspecting man, even one as potentially dangerous as this one, in cold blood.

"There are no horsemen here, Comrade," Igor replied. He was alarmed by the tremor in his voice, and then decided that it didn't matter; it only reinforced the image of the bewildered bumpkin.

"I can see that, idiot. Maybe they have camped near the town. Have you seen them at all?"

Igor thought for a moment of telling this Borodnev that the mounted troops had been here and had returned to Omsk. But it occurred to him that, if all went well, their party would be traveling through Omsk on the train in a day or two with the Tsar and it would do them no good to have Borodnev there ahead of them.

His next thought was to tell Borodnev that they had departed in a southerly direction. But, should Borodnev check with another local, Igor would have been shown to have lied and questions would be raised.

Igor could feel pinpoints of sweat breaking out in the small of his back and turning to ice against his spine.

"There were horsemen here. But they are gone now."

"Which way?"

Igor shrugged. "I didn't see them go."

"Moron!" Borodnev snarled. And whipped the horse into motion.

Igor continued on his way, fighting the impulse to break into a run. Borodnev would question someone else and learn that the mounted troops had gone north. He would probably assume that anyway since that was the direction of Tobolsk. Igor only wanted to get quickly back to the others so that they could decide what to do. But even without consultation he knew that there was little they could do. To attack Borodnev in Vinzili would be to compromise their mission—to pursue him into the countryside would be to abandon it. Aldonby was counting on them to carry out their assigned task. They could only pray that Aldonby would succeed in his: to bring the Tsar and his family safely to the railroad siding.

Pounding on doors and bullying those unfortunate locals who happened to be at home and in the path of his progress through town, Borodnev learned that the mounted troops had indeed been in Vinzili and had been seen heading north. The fools, instead of waiting for him, had taken it upon themselves to go on to Tobolsk in the erroneous belief that he must already have gone that way. So much for independent thought and initiative! It will lead most people astray most of the time.

And now he had more frustrating independence to deal with. The damned sleigh driver. When Borodnev ordered him to head for Tobolsk without delay, the driver protested. His horse was old and not really up to such a journey. Even if they dared venture such a trip, they would first have to find hay and fill the sleigh with it. Besides, he, the driver, was weary and in need of rest. Perhaps they could find another horse and set out tomorrow.

The driver, though he was wise enough to keep silent on the matter, was also weary of Borodnev's company. The great hog of a man terrified him; his foremost wish was to be free of Borodnev forever. His hope was that if they rested for the night in Vinzili, he could slip away before dawn and leave Borodnev to find another poor soul to take him to Tobolsk.

"You spend the night here, you spineless kulak," Borodnev snarled. "I have matters to attend to." He reached under his coat and drew out his revolver. "Spend the rest of your life here for all I care."

The terrified driver began to scramble over the side of the sleigh.

Borodnev swung the heavy pistol as if it were a scythe. The trigger guard caught the driver high on the face, shattering his cheekbone, and he tumbled, semiconscious, into the snow.

Borodnev picked up the reins and shook them and swore loudly at the horse. The poor animal, as if aware of what had befallen his master and sensing the threat of further violence from the new man at the reins, took off at a trot in a northerly direction.

# CHAPTER FIFTY-TWO

At five o'clock on the morning of April twenty-seventh under a velvety black sky, the horses and sleighs were brought into line outside the former governor's mansion in Tobolsk.

Inside the house the family waited apprehensively. They had agreed to go off into the unknown with an audacious young imposter whose only credentials were a tenuous family tie and the fact that he had managed to get to Tobolsk at all. Against this they had to balance their lives, exile, and survival. Life was all they had left now: the dynasty had come to an end. There was no future for them in Russia. If they stayed they would either die or live their lives as prisoners. If there were risks involved in their flight, there were risks taken in the interest of life. If their escape attempt failed, their situation could not be much worse than it now was.

Their greatest concern was for Alexei. His fever had broken but he was still weak. He had never been strong, never would be, and they prayed that the journey would not prove too great a hardship for his body to bear. His fever aside, there was the chronic problem of his bleeding. Severe jostling or bouncing could be disastrous.

Once before months ago in Tsarskoe Selo, a lifetime ago it seemed, Kerensky had been ready to send them north to Archangel and freedom. But one of the children had been ill, and Nicholas had begged Kerensky for a delay and then the moment had passed. If this moment in Tobolsk were allowed to pass, there might never be another. They would take the risk.

The horses and sleighs were brought into line. The pre-dawn stillness was ruptured by the clatter of bridles, a clangor of arms, and the sounds of restless animals anxious to move.

Aldonby stomped the snow off his boots and came into the house followed by Osmenov and Lars Dahlgren. He ordered the family to put on their warmest clothing. The convoy was ready to leave. Due to the health of Alexei, Aldonby announced that Trup, the nurse, and Dr. Botkin would make the journey with the family to their new place of confinement. The services of the maid, Demidova, and the cook, Kharitonov, would be required as well. Room for them had been allocated in the sleighs. In this way Aldonby and the Tsar had arranged to save as many loyal and devoted members of the household as they could.

"Begin loading the sleighs," he ordered. Trup picked up two heavy valises and moved toward the door. Kharitonov followed with two more. Osmenov watched disapprovingly while the rest of the family stood by, fidgeting. He looked at Aldonby.

"Dammit!" Aldonby snapped. "Are you all helpless? Move the baggage out." Osmenov nodded, satisfied.

The former Tsar, his sad hollow eyes like those of a figure on the cross, bent and gripped the handles of the two valises nearest him. Despite his tragic visage his arms and back were strong, as strong as Trup's, and he straightened up and carried the baggage out with no difficulty at all. Dr. Botkin struggled with his bags but made his way to the door.

With malicious delight Osmenov pointed at the women. "Are you such parasites that you will not help your men?"

Tatiana fixed him with a killing look, bent to the bag nearest her, and clamped both hands around the handle. All of the bags were heavy, packed not only with clothing but with what family treasures they had managed to salvage, and she was unable to lift it. She began to drag it across the floor. Olga followed, as did Anastasia and Marie.

Osmenov smiled and glanced at Aldonby to make sure that he, too, was enjoying the irony of it: the former rulers of Russia, once the wealthiest family in all the world, dragging behind them, packed into a dozen valises, the pathetic remains of their empire. Aldonby nodded and smiled appreciatively, but he focused his eyes at a point in the room beyond the struggling women so that he couldn't really see them.

His glance settled on Alexandra, as unbending and imperious as ever despite her failing health and her months in exile. Beside her sat Alexei, heir to a deliquescent empire, who would probably not in any event have lived to rule. Determined not to let his sisters bear their burden alone, Alexei struggled from his chair and began to move painfully toward the cluster of luggage. Alarmed, Alexandra moved after him.

"You!" Aldonby shouted at the boy in the hope of preventing him from injuring himself and keeping Osmenov from heaping verbal abuse on Alexandra. "Go back to your chair and wait until we are ready to leave. And you, Madam Citizeness, go tend to your child!"

Alexandra's eyes narrowed. For a moment it looked as if she might physically attack Aldonby. But she subdued her aggressive reflex, turned away, and put an arm around her son. As she helped him back to his chair, it was difficult to tell who was supporting whom.

When the sleighs were loaded, Lars Dahlgren came in and told Aldonby that the convoy was ready to leave. With the time for departure imminent Osmenov began to grow uneasy. He began to reflect on gloomy possibilities. If anything untoward happened to the caravan en route to the new place of confinement, if they were intercepted by White guerrillas and escaped, a share of the blame might fall on him. "God only knows what forces may be infesting the forests to the south of us," he warned. "I have heard that the damned Whites are popping up everywhere."

"We've just traveled north through those very same forests," Aldonby assured him. "They are secure."

"The situation might have changed in twenty-four hours," Osmenov protested. "Remember the infiltrators who landed in the north."

"I remember," Aldonby said. "That's why we are here. And that's why I have cavalry support. The Central Committee has determined that there is less risk in moving the Romanovs than in keeping them here. We are traveling with riflemen in the two lead sleighs. A machine gun in the rear. Armed riders between each of the sleighs bearing the Romanovs. I will be in the third sleigh with Nicholas. And," he added, to Osmenov's great relief, "when we leave this house, the burden of responsibility is lifted from your shoulders."

"I wish you well," Osmenov said.

Aldonby turned and ordered Lars to start putting the people in the sleighs, two to a sleigh. Romanov and Aldonby. Alexandra and Marie. Alexei and Dr. Botkin. Tatiana and Olga. Anastasia and the maid, Demidova. Trup and the cook. Lars was to bring up the rear with the machine gunner.

As the passengers boarded their sleighs, Osmenov began to fidget again. Aldonby wanted no last-minute obstacles. "Would you like a written document relieving you of responsibility?" Aldonby asked.

Osmenov nodded. "It is always best to have something in writing. Who knows? You may not live forever. Someday somebody may accuse me of allowing them to leave this house."

"I will give you a receipt for them," Aldonby said agreeably. He crossed into the study, took a sheet of paper from the desk, dipped the pen into the inkwell, and wrote under the date April 27, 1918: "Received this day of Colonel Osmenov, Commandant Tobolsk, the persons of Nicholas Romanov, his wife, his son, his daughters, and four members of their household staff. Signed: Borodnev, Commissar Extraordinary."

Aldonby blotted the paper and presented it to Osmenov. The Commandant read it over carefully, nodded approvingly, folded it, and tucked it into his inside pocket. Much relieved, he shook Aldonby's hand and wished him again a safe and uneventful journey.

Osmenov stood on the porch and watched the convoy depart. It was as Aldonby had said it would be, a traveling fortress: two sleighs up front with two riflemen in each sleigh, in the third sleigh sat the ex-Tsar and the Commissar Extraordinary from Moscow, the German woman, Alexandra, and her daughter Marie were in the fourth sleigh, followed by the sick boy and his doctor; the other daughters and the rest of the household staff followed. All the passengers were wrapped to their chins in blankets and furs. Flanking the sleighs were the cavalrymen from Omsk. And bringing up the rear, in a sleigh mounted with a machine gun, were a gunner and the officer who had arrived from Moscow with the special Commissar.

It certainly looked secure to Osmenov. And, as added insurance, he had his receipt signed by Borodnev relieving him of any further responsibility. But still he had misgivings. These were treacherous times. Today's Commissars could be tomorrow's fugitives. The Central Committee itself could be replaced by another committee, another set of leaders.

The street was empty now. All that was left of the bristling caravan were the runner tracks in the snow and the horses' hoofprints. Osmenov reached inside his coat and withdrew the letter of release that Borodnev had given to him. He went back into the house and unfolded the letter and read it again. Without a doubt he had been relieved of responsibility. Nonetheless one couldn't be too cautious. Perilous times.

He decided that he would mount a troop of riders and dog the tracks of the caravan. At a distance. Always discreetly out of sight. Remembering the machine gun mounted in the last sleigh, he was uncomfortably aware of what the consequences of a sighting might mean if the gunners were nervous or if there was not time for a proper identification.

On the other hand while trailing the caravan, he might be of help should they be surprised by a force of counterrevolutionaries. And that effort might bring him a hero's medal and recognition in Moscow.

He refolded the letter, tucked it back into his pocket, marched back to his headquarters, and began to issue commands.

# CHAPTER FIFTY-THREE

**B**orodnev kicked the horse. Hard. In the belly. There was no response. No whinnying protest. No outraged baring of teeth. He might have been kicking a football.

The animal had grown increasingly sluggish and unsure of foot in the last few hours, stopping abruptly to lick the snow, or gnawing on the bark of nearby trees in search of nourishment. The few scraps of hay that had been on the floor of the sleigh when he had left Vinzili were eaten up hours ago. Finally the horse had refused to move any farther, no matter how mercilessly Borodnev had attacked it with the whip, no matter how loudly he had cursed.

The horse had exhausted itself. It had simply stood there for a while and borne the blows, head down between its shoulders, the tired neck seeming to get longer and longer, legs braced wide. Then, with a groan, its forelegs began to buckle and it went down, slowly at first and then with a crash, an avalanche of flesh, flaccid muscle, and flying snow. That was when Borodnev, livid with rage, leaped down from the sleigh and began kicking. He drew his revolver and prepared to shoot, to no end except for the satisfaction it would afford him to pump bullets into that unresponsive hulk. But he remembered where he was and that it ill behooved a man alone in a wilderness to waste ammunition.

He shoved his pistol back into its holster and began to pace back and forth in the snow while he considered how he might salvage a very bad situation. He guessed that he was less than halfway to Tobolsk. He could butcher the horse to provide meat to sustain himself, and then he could go on to Tobolsk on foot. Or he could return to Vinzili or Tyumen, demand a fresh escort from Omsk, and then begin his northward journey all over again.

He knew the terrain over which he had just come. What awaited him between here and Tobolsk was a vast unknown full of hazards for a lone individual traveling on foot. Even now the weather looked ominous in the north; the sky was the color of slate and clouds of snow could be seen swirling and rising from the ground on a hillock miles away, as if freezing cyclones were blowing there.

When he looked again a few minutes later, the snowy tumult in the distance appeared to have settled down, but a thin, dark fissure seemed to have opened like a wound in the hillside facing him. He watched it, puzzled, squinting with his one good eye. The fissure seemed to be moving down the hillside, the snow sealing itself over in its wake.

He cursed himself for not having thought to bring field glasses. But then the fault wasn't entirely his. He had expected to be traveling north with a cavalry escort. He watched until the dark fissure in the distance had moved out of sight into a valley and the wound in the snowy hillside had been completely healed.

A little while later the next nearest hilltop was split by the same advancing dark line. But now Borodnev could see it more clearly. There were men on horses, and sleighs, a line of them. It occurred to Borodnev that these might be the cavalrymen from Omsk. Having traveled north and not found him in Tobolsk, they were returning to look for him in Tyumen where, had they kept their rendezvous with him in the first place, they would have spared themselves a pointless round-trip journey and him this present hardship.

The presence of sleighs among the cavalry puzzled him. Were they carrying supplies? Or had the cavalrymen taken it upon themselves to carry out Borodnev's mission: move the Romanovs to a more secure location with or without Borodnev? Borodnev didn't like that at all. Less still did he like a third possibility: that the riders coming his way might not be Red Guards at all, but instead might be monarchist partisans stirred up by the infiltrators who had landed in the north.

He had been standing still now for some time, ankle-deep in snow, and, despite his lined boots, his feet were growing numb with the cold. He decided that he would leave the sleigh and dead horse in the middle of the track. It would be to his advantage to do so. The obstruction would bring the caravan coming down from the north to a temporary halt, giving him time to appraise the situation and to act.

If they were the Red Guards from Omsk and if they did have the Romanovs in the sleighs, he would give them a scorching tongue-lashing for their fecklessness and then join them on their trek south to the rail line that would take them west to Ekaterinburg.

If the caravan was made up of partisans, he could shoot Nicholas and the German bitch before their escorts realized what was happening. The action would probably cost him his life, but what satisfaction he would have experienced before they cut him down.

He climbed up into his sleigh, undid his boots, and began massaging life back into his toes. He estimated that it would take the approaching caravan an hour or two to reach this place in the road.

He heard them before he saw them, announced by the shouts of the sleigh drivers, the thud of hoofbeats, the creak of carriage work.

He hid himself in a copse of trees a few yards from the right of way, drew his revolver, and flicked off the safety. And then he saw them, sweeping up out of a depression in the landscape, red stars on their hats and red armbands on their sleeves. Comrades. He slipped his pistol back into its holster.

At the head of the column Captain Chernovsky saw the dead horse and abandoned sleigh. He reined in his mount and raised his hand high, signaling for the rest of the caravan to halt. So unanticipated and abrupt was this signal in the middle of nowhere that the riders almost ran over each other before they could stop. The riflemen in the first two sleighs reined in their horses and stood up on their benches, peering around, weapons at the ready, looking for signs of an ambush.

From his place in hiding Borodnev saw the ex-Tsar in the third sleigh, wrapped to his chin in blankets and looking like a cadaver. But it was Romanov, without a doubt. Borodnev could feel his heart pounding. He had never been so close to the monster. He could rush forward ten paces and put a bullet into the middle of his face. The temptation was almost overwhelming. But if he did it, he would have to answer to Lenin and Sverdlov. He almost wished that these were not Red Guards in the convoy but partisans. Then he would have perfect justification for doing it. As it was, he would have to carry out his mission, odious as it was: escort the Romanovs to more secure quarters so that they could safely await a people's trial. He consoled himself with the thought that the trial could have only one outcome. There would be a time then for shooting. He would give the command himself.

A man in an officer's uniform jumped down from the ex-Tsar's sleigh and walked through the snow to the head of the line demanding to know what was going on. Apparently he was the commander of this caravan.

From his hiding place in the trees Borodnev called out "Comrades!" Called out so that he wouldn't surprise them and be shot by mistake.

Then he stepped out, arms held high, and moved forward toward the caravan.

The lead rider and the officer who had jumped down from the ex-Tsar's sleigh stopped, turned, and warily watched him make his approach. The riflemen in the first two sleighs trained their weapons in his direction and waited.

Borodnev laughed. "No, no, Comrades. Lay down your arms. It's all right."

"Halt!" The officer who had been in the sleigh commanded. "Who are you?"

Borodnev kept coming. "I am the one you have come to meet," he shouted congenially. "I am Borodnev."

Aldonby's jaw knotted. His stomach convulsed. From his saddle Chernovsky looked down at him, puzzled. Why should the man advancing toward them claim to be Borodnev? Borodnev was the officer who had met him in Vinzili, had led his troopers to Tobolsk, and stood beside him now.

Aldonby turned to face Borodnev, who was now barely three meters away. "Don't take another step," he ordered and drew his revolver. "You are a liar and an imposter."

Borodnev's face grew dark; the congenial visage of a moment ago transformed itself into an angry mask. He began to lower his hands.

"Keep your hands above your head," Aldonby warned.

"Who are you to tell me what to do, you kulak!" Borodnev roared.

Aldonby could feel his pulse throbbing in his temple. He was in grave danger of losing control of the situation, losing everything. He didn't know if this boar of a man standing across from him truly was Borodnev, though most likely he was. And if that were the case, there was only one thing he could do. And it was imperative that he do it quickly.

He glanced at the riflemen in the nearby sleighs, their weapons aimed at the man at the edge of the woods. "I am Borodnev," Aldonby shouted, "and you are a provocateur."

Borodnev seemed to swell like a blowfish. His face turned plum colored. His one good eye narrowed menacingly. His hands moved to the holster at his side.

"Open fire," Aldonby shouted and prayed that the riflemen would, knowing it would be far better for them to bring his adversary down than for him to have to do it himself.

Borodnev had his revolver unholstered. Aldonby was bringing his own weapon into firing position. The four rifles to his right discharged, startlingly, almost unexpectedly. Four sharp cracks, not quite in unison.

Borodnev's revolver went flying. His limbs splayed out in several different directions, as if invisible tormentors were pulling him four ways at once. He flopped backward into the snow and lay still. The echoes of the four rifle shots came bouncing back from the forest. Then everything became very still.

Aldonby turned to Chernovsky. "Let's move out of here."

"What about him?" Chernovsky asked.

"We don't have time to bury him. There may be more. Let's move on without delay." He didn't want anyone going through the dead man's pockets and discovering authentic credentials. Chernovsky gave the command and the caravan began to move.

"Keep your eyes on the woods," Aldonby shouted to the convoy at large. "We may be traveling through partisan country."

As the procession moved forward, Aldonby worked his way back among the sleighs, reassuring as best he could each member of the Romanov family. They were shaken and frightened, as they had every right to be. They stared in horror-struck silence at Borodnev's body as their sleighs slid past. Anastasia began to cry.

Lars Dahlgren had jumped down from the rear sleigh and came forward to meet Aldonby. "Who was that?" Dahlgren asked.

"It may have been Borodnev," Aldonby answered, very quietly, so that no one else could hear.

And just as quietly Lars told him that whoever the man at the edge of the woods had been, he might not have been the last of their troubles. Every now and then, very far to the north, perhaps four or five hours journey behind them Lars had caught a glimpse of movement. The convoy was being shadowed. But he had no way of knowing by whom.

# CHAPTER FIFTY-FOUR

Borodnev lay still in the snow, spread-eagled on his back, half submerged in the icy crystals, half conscious, half comatose. Aldonby's caravan passed out of earshot and out of sight. The sleigh track and the woods fell silent.

It was the pain that caused Borodnev to stir, otherwise he might have lain there exposed for hours and frozen to death, quite comfortably. But the pain was so sharp it cut through the coma and brought him to moaning wakefulness. It was as if molten lead were being dripped into his veins, spreading, white hot, up his bullet-shattered leg, down his splintered arm, through his torn gut.

He moaned again, rolled over onto his belly, screamed again, and began to vomit into the snow. Gasping, whimpering, he began to comprehend what had happened. He had stumbled upon the monarchist infiltrators. And they were fleeing south with the ex-Tsar. And one of them was using his name. Disgrace heaped upon defeat. He had to stop them. He had to survive. If for no reason other than to clear his name.

He began to drag himself forward through the snow to where the dead horse lay. He cried out pitiably with each movement, allowing himself to give full voice to his agony only because no one was there to hear him. Unable to assess how badly he was hurt, he knew only that he was in excruciating pain. As he dragged himself through the snow, he became aware that a leg was broken and an arm. Maybe that was the extent of the damage. He was encouraged by the observation that there seemed to be very little blood. But he could not determine if that meant that his wounds were superficial, or if the snow in which he had lain had acted as a cold pack, staunching the flow. He knew that he had to find shelter.

227

When he reached the place where the horse lay, he drew his hunting knife from the sheath on his belt; even using his good arm, it seemed a monumental effort, and he had to stop and rest. Perhaps he had not fully assessed the gravity of his wounds. Perhaps he was freezing to death and didn't know it.

With a grunt he thrust the knife into the horse's belly. Whimpering like a whipped child, he dragged the blade the length of the animal's underside from the rib cage to the groin. The belly flapped open, disgorging a steamy avalanche of entrails.

Borodnev left the knife in the snow and with his good arm dragged the guts out of the abdominal cavity; then he crawled inside, curling up like a fetus in the bowels of the dead beast.

Hours later, after the sun had set and the wild animals of the forest, smelling prey, had begun to signal to each other that there was meat at hand, Osmenov found him there, reeking of death and gangrene and moaning hideously.

They pulled him from his macabre shelter, built a fire, and splinted his arm and his leg. There was nothing they could do about the wound in his abdomen. Painfully he gasped out his story, inviting the skeptical Osmenov to find in his inside pocket the papers that would establish his identity.

Trepidatiously Osmenov unfolded the papers, read the letter signed by Sverdlov, studied the identity card, examined the railroad permit that had secured him passage from Moscow to Tyumen and the copies of the telegrams exchanged with Omsk en route arranging for a cavalry escort.

The documentation of Borodnev's identity seemed irrefutable. But the other man had had papers, too, and an escort of Red Guards. If this was Borodnev, then the man who had ridden into Tobolsk yesterday and in whose hands he had placed the Romanovs was an imposter. If that were the case, he had delivered the Romanovs into the hands of monarchists. Unless he could intercept them and bring the ex-Tsar back he, Osmenov, would become one of history's buffoons. But before that happened he would have paid with his life for his lapse of judgment. He tucked the papers into his own coat pocket, not allowing any of his soldiers to see them.

He became aware that Borodnev was demanding, between dumbfounding bouts of pain, that he go as quickly as possible to Tyumen, cut the rail line there, and telegraph Omsk to warn Kossirev that the partisans might make a break to the east. And the garrison at Ekaterinburg must be ordered by telegraph to send a party of Red Guards out to block the road to the south, should the fugitives try to flee to the Caucasus by horse and sleigh.

Nearly delirious, the man made sense. He was certainly no unfortunate traveler who had been shot without cause by the fleeing caravan. He must be Borodnev. Osmenov ordered four of his men to trim branches to make a litter that could be slung between two horses.

Feverishly Borodnev whispered, "Romanov must not escape!"

Osmenov was as desperately aware of this as he. And Osmenov also became aware of something else as he listened to the sound of his men hacking at the birches and to the sound of the wounded man's breathing. If he succeeded in saving Borodnev, the whole story would come to light. Borodnev would bring it to light. Then he would be exposed as a dupe who had placed the whole damned family in the liberating custody of an imposter. Whether or not the Romanovs made good their escape, it would be the end of him. But if Borodnev died here in the forest, the true story would die with him, and Osmenov could tell it his own way. In fact all he need do is report the incidents as they happened, leaving out only the wounded man who lay at hs feet: he had turned the ex-Tsar over to Commissar Borodnev who had come to Tobolsk. He had witnesses, his own soldiers, who had seen Borodnev ride in at the head of a troop of mounted Red Guards and ride out in a convoy with the ex-Tsar and his family. If that Borodnev then allowed them to escape, it was Borodnev, not Osmenov, who had betrayed the Revolution. It was Borodnev's name that would burn in infamy.

Osmenov knelt close to Borodnev and told him that he thoroughly agreed. Romanov must not escape. Regretfully, the burden of carrying a wounded man to Tyumen might slow the pursuing party. . . .

"Romanov must not escape," Borodnev rasped again.

"You will be remembered forever as a hero of the Revolution," Osmenov promised him. "Children generations from now will praise you for your sacrifice." He looked about uneasily as the cries of the wild animals grew louder and more insistent. To leave Borodnev here now was to make him food for the wolves. He drew his revolver and placed it in Borodnev's hand.

Then he ordered his soldiers to stop cutting wood and to mount their horses. They had a mission of surpassing importance to carry out.

They left the clearing without Osmenov once mentioning the identity of the gravely wounded man he had consigned to the forest. Ten minutes later the sound of a single pistol shot echoed after them.

Osmenov smiled to himself. If he recaptured the Romanovs, he would be a hero. If he didn't, Borodnev would bear the blame.

"What was that?" one of the soldiers called out.

"That was the way he wanted it," Osmenov replied. "He was already as good as finished, and it was only a matter of time."

But Borodnev wasn't finished yet.

In the clearing where they had left him wrapped in blankets and propped against the runners of the sleigh, he let the pistol come to rest in his lap. He had lacked the will to employ it as Osmenov had intended that he should.

He had watched the wolves fanning out among the trees around him, heard their hungry howls, seen their gleaming eyes. He had raised the pistol to his head and squeezed the trigger, but in the instant before the hammer had descended, he had jerked the barrel away so that the bullet had gone rocketing skyward.

The report had frightened the wolves and they had retreated. And he began to entertain the notion that he might just manage to survive.

He had five shots left. If he could use them sparingly and tellingly, he might live through the night and who knew what the next day might bring? He had hope.

Weakened by his wounds, his blood growing sluggish with the cold, he began to doze. And was wakened by the abrasive sound of rapid breathing among the trees. He found himself staring into the golden eyes of the leader of the pack, dispassionately examining him from less than ten yards away.

Borodnev raised the revolver, not to his temple this time but straight out before him, trying with his failing strength to keep the barrel from wavering.

The wolf growled deep in his throat and moved cautiously forward, toward the outstretched arm. Borodnev let him come. The closer he came, the less chance there would be of a miss. He was beginning to grow ecstatic with the prospect of a kill, grinning foolishly, a froth of pink saliva forming at the corners of his mouth.

He was concentrating so intensely on his target that he was unaware that a ring of animals was forming around him or that one particularly enterprising creature was now perched above him on the bench of the sleigh.

The wolf facing him crouched to spring. Borodnev tightened his finger on the trigger. The wolf on the sleigh seat growled. Borodnev began to turn his head, but the animal had already launched itself.

The pistol discharged, once, aimlessly, the bullet spending itself in the snow, while the animal above him locked onto his throat, and other tore at his groin. His screams becamed choked with blood, and the rest of the pack closed in.

For a little while he writhed there, like a worm on a hook, while they gutted him. And then he became meat on the table for the wolves and later for the more timid creatures of the forest, for whom the wolves had made the gift of a meal.

# CHAPTER FIFTY-FIVE

I t was almost midnight when Aldonby's caravan arrived at the out-skirts of Vinzili. On a hilltop a mile and half from the slumbering village, Aldonby called a halt, got down from his sleigh, and walked through the snow to the front of the line.

Blue-white moonlight gave an otherwordly look to the settlement, its scattering of houses standing out in stark relief against the snow, casting inky trapezoidal shadows. And everything was engulfed in silence. In the railroad siding a locomotive engine waited with its coal tender and a string of freight cars. It certainly wouldn't provide first-class transportation for an ex-monarch and his family, but it would serve. It would take them across the great emptiness of Siberia to the Pacific, freedom, and life. The cadets had carried out their assignment.

Or had they? From where Aldonby stood there was really no way of knowing. His four young volunteers might be prisoners—or dead. And the dark, silent train might be a trap, bristling with guns.

Aldonby sent someone to bring Lars Dahlgren to the front of the line so that he would be present when Captain Chernovsky received his instructions and would see to it that they were properly carried out.

With Dahlgren standing beside him, Aldonby told Chernovsky that the train appeared to be the one that he had ordered. But, considering the political instability of the countryside, one never could take any-thing for granted. Counterrevolutionaries might have moved in and taken over. He would ride in alone and appraise the situation. If it was safe, he would turn away from the train and begin riding back toward them. That would be their signal to proceed through the town to the siding. If he gave them no signal, it would indicate that the train was hostilely occupied. In that event eight men should be left behind to guard the Romanovs, and the rest of the troop should attack the train.

Captain Chernovsky rode down the line to pass the word to his men. Lars held the reins while Aldonby prepared to mount his borrowed horse.

"Do you think our cadets are in charge down there?"

"I hope so." Aldonby swung up into the saddle. "We don't want to have to shoot our way out of here. We don't want bloodshed."

"There'll be plenty," said Lars, "if the train is full of Reds. Our Reds killing those Reds."

"Should such a catastrophe come to pass, may our Reds prevail."

"If they don't? . . ."

"If an attack is ordered, I want you to stay behind with the Tsar. The family's safety will be in your hands. If things go sour, arrange a bloodless surrender. As long as they're alive, there is hope." He spurred his horse and cantered down the hillside toward the town.

He was spotted the instant he left the cover of the forest: a dark, rapidly moving object against the gleaming white hillside.

They had been watching for him for hours from the shelter of the first of the freight cars. They had been sleeping in shifts so that they could keep an eye on the approaches to the village all through the night if necessary and still be alert when alertness was called for. They had known he would be coming; they just hadn't known when.

It was Igor's turn at the lookout when Aldonby broke out of the forest. "Boris! Sergei! Vasily!" he urgently whispered. "Someone's coming."

He heard the stirrings of awakening behind him as he brought his field glasses up to his eyes and tried to bring the rider into focus.

"Where?" Sergei was kneeling beside him.

Igor pointed without removing the glasses from his eyes. "There."

"Just one man?" Sergei sounded alarmed.

"Can you see him?" Boris asked. "Who is it?"

"Hard to tell. He's got his head down behind the horse's neck."

"There must be others," Vasily insisted. "I'm going to look out the other side."

"It's Aldonby!" Igor joyfully exclaimed.

"Where are the others?" Boris asked anxiously, as Aldonby climbed down from his horse.

"Safe," Aldonby assured him. "Back in the forest. Waiting for a sign. You did a fine job."

"Is the Tsar well?"

"They're all well. What became of the train's crew?"

"Locked up in the last freight car. They and the flagman."

"Good. Detach it before we leave. In fact detach all the cars after the coal tender except the first two. That's all we'll need. No point hauling deadweight. Did you learn how to fire up the engine?"

"Before we locked up the crew."

"Then do it, so it'll be ready to go when the others get down here. The sooner we leave the better."

Captain Chernovsky watched Aldonby riding toward them. He turned to Lars Dahlgren. "It looks secure. Borodnev is coming this way."

"Let's go on down then."

When Aldonby met them halfway and led them toward the siding, smoke was already beginning to rise from the locomotive's stack.

# CHAPTER FIFTY-SIX

A ldonby gave the order to move the train. Boris released the brake and slowly opened the throttle. The great steel wheels strained to find traction on the icy rails. Boris opened the sand reservoir; the wheels bit in and began slowly to roll.

The Romanovs had been installed in the car directly behind the coal tender. A bed of straw from the sleighs had been laid down in a corner of the car to soften the ride for Alexei.

Captain Chernovsky and his riders stood in a double line at trackside as the train pulled out, still aglow with the compliments that Aldonby had heaped upon them for a job well done. The cavalrymen had decided to rest themselves and their horses for the night in the neighborhood of Vinzili and then return to Omsk in the morning. Aldonby had assured them that their efforts would not go unnoticed; the word of how well they had carried out their mission would precede them to their home city. Aldonby personally would commend them to Kossirev.

In view of the fact that Captain Chernovsky had decided to camp for the night in Vinzili, Aldonby decided to keep the entire train intact for a while, including the last boxcar containing the bound and gagged railwaymen. After they were well under way, somewhere between Vinzili and Omsk, he would cut them loose from the train. In fact he decided he would cut everything loose beyond the first boxcar. They could all live in there, crowded though it might be. The more densely packed with bodies the car was the warmer it would be.

"They look like a bloody honor guard," Lars Dahlgren said to Aldonby as the train chugged past the lines of horsemen.

"They're good soldiers," Aldonby sighed. "I'm rather sorry for the way we had to use them. They'll catch hell when it all comes out."

235

"Just pray it doesn't start coming out until we're well on our way."

"Amen to that," Aldonby said as they left Vinzili behind.

An hour and a half later in the dead, windless chill of the Siberian plain, Aldonby climbed over the tender into the locomotive and told Sergei, who was handling the throttle, to stop the train. It was time to cut loose the hostage railwaymen and the unwanted cars.

Sergei applied the brake, too hard at first, and the wheels grabbed. The train began to skid down the track. He let up on the brake and tried again, eventually bringing the locomotive to a lurching halt that nearly sent Aldonby and Vasily, who was tending the coal, crashing against the firebox.

"A little more practice," Aldonby cheerfully called out as he jumped down into the snow, "and you may qualify for a driver's position on the Green tram line when we get back to London."

Lars, Igor, and Boris, having already left their places in the boxcar, were jogging toward the rear. When they reached the last car, they drew their revolvers and waited for Aldonby, who had the key to the large padlock that sealed the heavy sliding door.

"That was some rough stop," Lars Dahlgren complained as Aldonby arrived. "I hope he learns to drive before we reach Vladivostok."

"We'll all have to learn," Aldonby said, as he fitted the key into the lock. "Once we get past Omsk, we'll be working in teams of two, in four-hour watches. Nonstop." He turned the key in the lock and with an assist from Igor rolled back the heavy door.

The four railwaymen inside lay like cast-off garments, in a heap on the floor of the car. As the door slid open, they struggled to right themselves, despite the handicap of bound hands and feet. Their gags made it appear as if they were wearing masks as they stared fearfully out into the beam of Aldonby's torch.

"It's all right, Comrades," Aldonby assured them. "We haven't come to harm you, but to set you free."

He vaulted up into the boxcar, followed by Lars, Igor, and Vasily. "But you must behave," he cautioned, as he began untying the first man. "We are armed, and we will use our weapons if you attempt to take advantage of your freedom. In short, you do us no violence and we will do you none. You go your way; we'll go ours."

Igor was untying a second man. Lars and Vasily stood off near the door to the car, pistols leveled, to underline Aldonby's warning.

The first two freed men backed themselves against the wall of the boxcar farthest from the guns. They stood there nervously, hands half raised, although they had not been asked to raise their hands, waiting while Aldonby and Igor freed their two companions.

There was a sound of running footsteps in the snow outside. Aldonby turned. Lars and Vasily tightened the grips on their weapons and waited, one eye on the open door, one on the railwaymen in the car. Marie's face appeared. She was breathing hard. Small white streamers of condensated breath came in bursts between her parted lips as she tried to speak. "We can't leave," she gasped.

"What?" Aldonby ran to her and knelt. Thee railwaymen darted concerned looks at each other.

"Alexei has fallen." There were tears in her eyes. From the cold? From anguish? Aldonby couldn't tell.

"He was sitting up when the train stopped. He was thrown against the side of the car."

"Oh, God!" Aldonby turned to the others. "Keep everything as it is here. I'm going to the front."

"He's bleeding," Marie whimpered.

Aldonby jumped down, put his arm around her to support her, and led her forward toward the engine.

"Dr. Botkin says he might die. He must be kept still or he might bleed to death. The train cannot be moved." She was panting and crying. Twice she lost her footing as she tried to keep up with Aldonby, and it was only his strong supporting arm that kept her from falling face down into the snow.

When they arrived at the front of the train, they found Trup out on the embankment, along with Olga, Anastasia, and Tatiana, making packs of snow and passing them up into the car. From a distance they might have appeared to be playful children making snowballs by moonlight. But close up their faces betrayed their anxiety and their concern.

The Tsar himself was carrying the snow packs from the doorway of the car to the corner where his son lay, attended by Dr. Botkin and Alexandra. They were encasing the child's arm and shoulder in snow, wrapping the rest of him in blankets, trying to keep half of him cold and the other half warm. He was as pale as a corpse and still as death except for the shallow rise and fall of his chest. And the part of his arm that showed through the snow pack was swollen and purple like a great long bruise.

Aldonby helped Marie up into the car and told her to rest and get warm. Then he stood aside until the ice pack on the boy's arm was complete and the doctor could speak to him.

"He is hemorrhaging," the doctor said, so quietly it was almost inaudible. "He cannot be moved."

"How long?"

"How long until what?" the doctor asked angrily. He was exhausted. And the Tsar was standing beside him, listening. And he thought that Aldonby was asking him how long until the boy would die. The Tsar looked so drawn and anguished that it might have been he, not Alexei, who was moribund.

"How long until we can move?" Aldonby said.

"Oh." The doctor blinked. "We'll have to wait until the bleeding stops. The jostling of the train—"

"How long might that be?" Aldonby interrupted him.

"It might be hours. We'll see."

"Is there no way that he can be cushioned? . . ."

"We will not move until the bleeding stops," the Tsar declared. His face was haggard, but his voice was iron. "Is that understood?"

"It is, sir. But you must understand. The cavalry troop that rode with us from Tobolsk will be riding into Omsk in the morning. The man who stopped us on the road from Tobolsk may be missed. Word may come from Moscow. We may be cut off. We are in a very precarious position. Every moment that we delay increases your danger, your family's danger, builds a barrier in the way of your freedom."

"I will not sacrifice my son."

"With all respect, sir, there are other members of your family to be considered."

"We are a family. We are one. No one of us is valued any less or any more than any other. We will survive together. Or we will not. But we will not take it into our hands to decide which of us will live. We are in God's hands."

And mine, Aldonby wanted to say; but he didn't.

"Maybe in a few hours," the doctor said hopefully.

"Maybe," Aldonby agreed. He was thinking not of a deposed Tsar or a dying child or a ruined dynasty. He was thinking of the pale, beautiful young woman shivering with cold and worry in a corner of the bare wooden boxcar. He was thinking of himself and Marie. Well, they were all in his hands no longer; the Tsar had made that decision.

He jumped down from the boxcar and ran to the back of the train and told Lars and the two cadets and the frightened railwaymen that, unfortunately, nobody would be going anywhere for a while.

And then, regretfully for all of them, he ordered his men out, leaving the railwaymen inside, and again locked the door of the boxcar.

# CHAPTER FIFTY-SEVEN

The stationmaster at Tyumen was jarred awake by a hammering at his door. He propped himself up on an elbow and squinted at the big clock beside his bed. He hadn't overslept. It was just thirty minutes past midnight. No train was due for four hours. Then what was all the hammering about?

Pulling the blankets around his shoulders, he sat up and probed with his feet for the felt boots that were somewhere on the floor in the neighborhood of the bed.

The room was like an icebox. After he had dealt with the lunatic at the door, he would have to light the stove or he would never be able to get back to sleep.

"Lunatic!" Pummeling the door at halfpast midnight! "Madman!" Oh, God! A terrifying consideration seared his groggy brain. Had the fat hoodlum returned? The one from Moscow? The special Commissar who had frightened and bullied him two days before?

Halfway across the room the stationmaster hesitated, afraid to open the door, afraid not to. The latter fear prevailed and he shuffled the rest of the way to the door, tripping over the blanket.

He slid the bolt aside and opened the door a crack, half expecting to be knocked down by the presence outside. Instead, he found himself the recipient of an apology from the man standing there who was in uniform and wore the insignia of an officer of the Red Guard and whom he had never seen before.

"Forgive us for waking you at this unholy hour, but we have an emergency. May I come in?"

Overwhelmed with relief by the officer's courtesy and by the fact that the bully from Moscow had not returned, he opened the door wider.

And saw behind his visitor what appeared to be a whole troop of cavalry.

"What is the trouble, sir... er... Comrade?" the stationmaster asked.

"Close the door, please. No point in everybody freezing." Osmenov looked around the sparsely furnished room. There was a bed, a chest of drawers, a chair, a small table with a kerosene lamp on it, and a stove. He pointed to a closed door at the opposite end of the room. "Where does that go?"

"To the station. My quarters are attached to the station. There would be nobody there at this hour."

"I know. We looked in through the windows."

"The last train came through two hours ago. There was nobody there then either. It was a freight, east to west. In fact, nobody has been in the station all day; we have very little passenger traffic here at this time of year. In fact, the last person to come off a train here was two days ago, I think. A special Commissar. From Moscow." He emphasized the latter two points. He feared and detested Borodnev, but he felt that the fact that he had entertained a personage of such high standing would impress this officer of the Red Guard.

"Was the Commissar named Borodnev?"

"I think he was," the stationmaster replied. He couldn't really remember the name, but it sounded right and how many Special Commissars came through his station anyway? "He sent a message. I can find his name on the copy if you'd like."

"What did he look like?"

Like a hog, the stationmaster wanted to say, but he was afraid that that might sound disrespectful. Instead, he held his arms out, as if he were measuring the circumference of an immense vat, and said, "A rather large man."

"With only one eye?"

"Yes, sir... Comrade. Only one eye. And steel teeth. A smile of silver, one might say."

Osmenov sighed despairingly. The stationmaster's description perfectly fit the wounded man he had found in the forest and did not sound even vaguely like the officer who had ridden into Tobolsk and taken the ex-Tsar away. He had not the slightest doubt now that he had turned the Romanovs over to an imposter.

He walked over to the lone wooden chair and sat down. He braced his elbows on his knees and rested his forehead in the upturned palms of his hands. He felt very tired.

Without raising his head he said, "Please open the station. My men need rest and shelter."

"Are you all right, sir . . . Comrade?" the stationmaster asked.

"We've just had a long ride. You have a telegraph?"

"Yes, sir," the stationmaster answered proudly. And then realized that the officer had not upbraided him for saying *sir* instead of *Comrade*. Maybe officers didn't mind.

"After you've opened the station for my men, come back here. I will have some messages for your telegraph."

While the stationmaster was out, Osmenov tried to think. They could not have come west through Tyumen. After leaving Borodnev in the clearing, he had deliberately taken a diagonal route so that he could cut them off at Tyumen if necessary. Most likely they had continued southward, in the hope of reaching territory controlled by the Whites near the Caspian Sea. But it was a long way to the Caucasus, and a search party from Kurgan, two hundred miles to the south, could set up a screen that would stand between the Romanovs and their objective—unless they had decided to flee directly to the east. But that would be madness. Where would they go in the east? There was nothing out there but thousands of miles of Siberian wasteland.

A sudden draft of frigid air informed him that the stationmaster had opened the door to the main building. He could hear the voices of his men and the tumult as they stumbled into the shelter.

Traveling by horse and sleigh, the Romanov party would become meat for the bears in Siberia. Their only hope would be to reach the Pacific Coast, but they could never make it. The imposter who had duped him into giving up the Romanovs would never attempt such a long and hopeless journey. He was too competent, too smart. The only way anyone could survive a journey across Siberia would be by train.

Osmenov slapped his forehead and sprang to his feet. In the other half of the building he could see his men milling about, trying to get warm. The stationmaster was fumbling with the stove.

"Old man!" Osmenov shouted.

The man looked up, startled by the urgency in Osmenov's voice; he had been so amenable just a few minutes before. "I'm lighting the fire, sir," the stationmaster called.

"Now!" Osmenov shouted. "I want you here now!"

The stationmaster looked up, bewildered, dropped his armload of tinder, and hurried to the back room. Osmenov slammed the door shut behind him.

"Nobody boarded the midnight train to the west?"

"No sir. I'm sorry, sir. Do you mind if I call you sir? It's such a habit."

"Call me what you damn please. Just tell me about the trains. The last train that came through heading east into Siberia?"

"It was a freight. Just a handful of trainmen aboard."

"When was that?"

"About four hours ago. Eight o'clock."

"And that was the last train in that direction?"

"Yes, sir."

Osmenov looked relieved. The imposter and the Romanovs hadn't boarded that train in Tyumen nor could they have intercepted it at some point down the line. At eight o'clock at night they would still have been in the hills, miles from the railway line.

Since he had no way of knowing that Aldonby had left a detail in Vinzili to sidetrack that train and hold it for the fugitive party, Osmenov considered that he had an excellent chance to save the situation. A net had to be cast and slowly drawn in.

"I want you to send two telegrams."

"Tonight?"

"Immediately."

"They may not be answered until morning. The whole world is asleep."

"I'm not asleep. You're not asleep. And I know a number of fugitives somewhere on the road tonight who, I'll wager, are not sleeping."

"Yes, sir."

"Put on those telegrams, Most urgent. Immediate action." If they acted immediately, the situation could be saved. If they delayed, the blame would fall on them.

"Yes, sir."

"Do you know how to write?"

"Yes, sir."

"Then why aren't you writing?"

"I'm sorry, sir. So much is happening. We're not accustomed . . ." The stationmaster hastily crabbed sideways to the table, opened a drawer, and withdrew a pad and pencil. He pulled the chair up to the table, sat down, and licked the pencil point. "I am ready, sir."

"Number one."

"Yes, sir."

Osmenov began to pace. "To Commissar: Kurgan. From Commandant: Tobolsk. Most urgent. Immediate action. Nicholas Romanov and family believed traveling south by sleigh under questionable escort." He paused and waited for the stationmaster to catch up. "Block routes south. Detain caravan for questioning." He had the stationmaster read back what he had written.

The stationmaster stared at him pop-eyed. "Has the Tsar escaped, sir?" Then he bit his lip, appalled at the tone of his voice. He had sounded almost pleased, certainly excited.

Osmenov ignored him and proceeded. "Number two. To Commissar: Omsk. From Commandant: Tobolsk."

"Yes, sir." The stationmaster's hand was trembling. He wondered if he could manage the telegraph key. There hadn't been such excitement in Tyumen since the ex-Tsar had come through last summer on his way to Tobolsk.

"Most urgent. Immediate action. Nicholas Romanov and family believed traveling east by sleigh under questionable escort." Osmenov waited again.

"I'm ready, sir. 'Questionable escort . . .' "

"If you breathe a word of this, I'll stand you up against a wall," Osmenov warned.

"You can trust me, sir. All messages that pass through my hands are absolutely confidential."

Osmenov knew, of course, that the stationmaster would begin gabbing the minute the troops left town. To expect otherwise would hardly be realistic. And, in truth, Osmenov didn't care, as long as the man kept quiet for the next eight or ten hours. After that it wouldn't matter. Nicholas would have been recaptured and Osmenov would be a hero; or the family would have made good its escape, and Osmenov would be the one who would be standing against a wall, unless he could firmly fix the blame on the dead Borodnev as a betrayer of the Revolution.

" 'Questionable escort . . .' " the stationmaster prompted.

"Yes. Questionable escort. Block all routes between Vinzili and Omsk."

Osmenov leaned against the doorjamb and sighed. The net had been cast. He had the stationmaster read back the telegrams, and then ordered him to send them in the sequence in which they had been dictated.

The stationmaster left the room. Osmenov lay down on the bed. The next few hours would tell.

# CHAPTER FIFTY-EIGHT

At five-forty in the morning Dr. Botkin wakened the sleeping Tsar and informed him that Alexei's condition was stable. The hemorrhaging had stopped. They might chance moving the train.

Nicholas thanked the doctor, got to his feet, and, stepping carefully around the sleeping bodies of his wife and daughters, went to the corner of the car where his son lay on a cushion of hay. He knelt beside the sleeping child and placed a hand gently on his forehead, so gently that, though the boy stirred, he did not waken. His flesh felt warm but not fevered, color had returned to his cheeks, and his breathing was steady and strong.

Stepping around the sleeping figures again, the former Tsar joined the doctor near the door to the car.

"Are you sure he'll be all right?"

"There is nothing in this world of which we can be absolutely sure. You must know that better than I. But if we keep our speed down, the ride should be tolerable. I think it reasonable to believe that if we keep him on his back, the normal motion of the train will cause no further injury."

Nicholas nodded, rolled back the door wide enough so that he could slip through, and dropped to the ground. He took a deep breath of the chilly predawn air. Spring was definitely on the way. Then he made his way forward through the slushy snow to the engine, and told Aldonby who was standing watch that it would be all right to move the train, but that they must keep the speed down to avoid jostling Alexei. He begged him to do his best to achieve a smooth ride, although he was perfectly aware that Aldonby had no control over the condition of the track.

"I'd like to ride in the engine for a while, if you don't mind," the ex-Tsar said.

244

"Of course," Aldonby said. But he looked surprised.

"I haven't had much exercise lately," Nicholas explained. "The want of it puts me on edge. I could help feed the fire."

"As you wish, sir." It occurred to Aldonby that Nicholas wanted to ride the engine in order to be able to call a quick halt should the ride become too rough.

"I'm really quite strong, you know." And added with a wry smile, "I've spent a good deal of the past year chopping wood."

Aldonby told Vasily to get up steam. Then he went back to the car where the others were sleeping and woke Boris and told him to go to the engine and take the throttle. They were getting ready to leave.

He jumped down into the snow, moved to the rear end of the car they were all living in, and removed the linchpin that connected it to the rest of the train. Then he ran back along the trackside to the very last car, where the railwaymen were locked up. He drew his revolver, opened the lock, and pulled back the door just a crack. He held his torch up so that he could see inside. The railwaymen were all huddled together again for warmth, and just rousing themselves from sleep; none of them was hovering near the door or in a position to attack him.

"Now listen to me," he announced. "Are you awake enough to understand what I say?"

They nodded groggily, sullenly.

"I'm taking the lock off your door so that you'll be able to fend for yourselves. We're leaving . . . and leaving you behind."

The railwaymen exchanged guarded looks of relief.

"Once we are out of sight you are free to do as you wish. But I warn you. The first man who attempts to leave this car while we are still within rifle range will be shot. To insure against any such unfortunate occurrence I recommend that you stay right where you are for at least fifteen minutes after you hear the engine leave. Remember . . . any man leaving the car while we are within rifle range will be shot."

The railwaymen stared at him resentfully.

"We are now situated some twenty-five miles from Vinzili. Your best chance for food and shelter would be there. It should not be too arduous a journey, not even on foot. I wish you luck."

He stepped back, slid the door shut without locking it, and hurried forward. Boris told him that the engine was ready. The Tsar stood beside the firebox, face grimy, shovel in hand, looking in better spirits than Aldonby had seen him since their odyssey had begun. Apparently hard manual labor did agree with him.

"Let's go then," Aldonby said. "But easy does it."

The Tsar watched anxiously as Boris gently nudged the throttle forward. The locomotive began to move, though barely perceptibly at first. Boris was indeed being very careful.

Aldonby leaned out the side and looked back along the length of the train to make sure that the cars separated properly and that the railwaymen stayed put.

The locomotive, tender, and first boxcar drew slowly away from the rest of the train. As the track followed a slight curve, Aldonby could see the door on the last boxcar slide open and a head peer out and then withdraw.

Everything was perfect.

# CHAPTER FIFTY-NINE

On a hilltop across from the railway line on the road between Omsk and Vinzili, Lieutenant Zavitsky observed the movement of the train.

He had first spotted it, dead on the tracks, some fifteen minutes earlier as his troop of cavalry, dispatched from Omsk in response to Osmenov's telegram, moved in a westerly direction on the lookout for a caravan of sleighs.

There was nothing extraordinary about spotting a train dead on the tracks. One had reluctantly to acknowledge that breakdowns of every kind were becoming a national epidemic. But he had wondered if he might be able in some way to help the stranded crew. It would be no great trouble for him to ride down there, inquire what sort of help was needed, and then have his telegrapher tap the wire and send a message for assistance. But that might take him off the road at the very moment when the ex-Tsar's caravan appeared, if they were on the road at all. But if they *were* on the road, and if they found their way through his area of vigilance, there would be hell to pay. So he had just kept an eye on the train and continued his westerly progress. But now the train was moving and, strangely, seemed to be breaking apart. The engine, tender, and one freight car were moving slowly toward Omsk; and ten or eleven other cars, perhaps packed with sorely needed staples, were being left behind.

Surely the engineer would quickly become aware of the mishap, back up, and put his train together again. But no such thing was happening. The moving part of the train was beginning to accelerate. There was already a gap of nearly a mile between the head and the severed tail.

Lieutenant Zavitsky raised his field glasses and focused on the runaway engine, but his angle was such that he couldn't see inside the cab.

247

The stranded cars presented a picture of lifelessness. Perhaps, Zavitsky reasoned, they were empty, and the engine was partly disabled and unable to pull the extra weight.

He had lowered his glasses and was about to give the order to ride on when a movement along the side of the last car in line caught his eye.

He raised the glasses again, focused, and saw that the door in the side of the car had been opened and a man had jumped down into the snow.

Now he saw others following. Four in all. They seemed to glance furtively this way and that, and then they began to make their way along the tracks in a direction opposite from that which the engine had taken. Thieves? Saboteurs? Revanchist partisans? All possible. But he saw no evidence of weapons.

Zavitsky decided that he had better investigate. He left half of his company on watch on the road. With the other half he rode down the hillside toward the abandoned freight cars and the four men fleeing on foot.

Five minutes later the trainmen were on their way up the hillside, doubled up with four of Zavitsky's riders.

Zavitsky's signalman climbed one of the telegraph poles that stood along the trackside and began splicing his transmitting unit into the line that ran to Omsk. An hour later, having failed to raise Omsk, he came down to warm his numb fingers by the fire.

"We'd have done better to have tried to chase the locomotive on horseback," Zavitsky complained.

"We'd never have caught them," the shivering signalman answered. "I can't understand why Omsk won't answer."

"Maybe the runaways stopped a few miles down and cut the telegraph line," Zavitsky decided.

"They were stopped here for hours according to the train crew. If they were going to cut the line, why didn't they cut it here?"

"Maybe they had other things on their minds. Maybe they just didn't think of it. If men could be trusted always to consider the appropriate action at the appropriate time, the world would not be in the mess it is most of the time."

He turned and took stock of the other troopers who were hovering near the fires. Then he pointed to one whom he particularly trusted to function on his own and shouted, "Yuri! Take your horse and ride with Josef."

"You want me to ride with Yuri?" the signalman asked. "Where to? Omsk? To deliver the message by hand?"

"If you had to go all the way to Omsk, you might as well sit down and eat the message. They'll be long gone by then."

"Where to then?"

"For about twenty minutes down the line."

"What for?"

"To see if maybe they did think to stop and cut it."

"Why twenty minutes? They might have stopped thirty minutes down the line. Or forty. It's hopeless."

"Twenty minutes is all that's necessary. You had started transmitting less than fifteen minutes after the train left here. If they hadn't cut the line by then, your first message would have gone through. So, if twenty minutes down the line, you find it still intact, the question will be why wasn't it received in Omsk. But there's nothing we can do about that. We will all bear witness for each other that we tried.

"Take your equipment and your tools. If you find the line cut, mend it, and begin sending again; you must know the message by heart by now. If the line is intact, get onto it and begin sending immediately. Maybe the receiving problem in Omsk will have been cleared up." Zavitsky turned to the company at large. "Finish feeding yourselves and your horses. We'll be moving back to Omsk."

Yuri rode up, leading Josef's horse. Josef wearily climbed into the saddle. Zavitsky patted his thigh. "In an hour or so you can rest all you want. If we haven't raised Omsk by then, they'll have passed through the yards and be scot-free."

"Free? There's nothing out there beyond Omsk. Nothing but wilderness."

Zavitsky shrugged. "Exactly! If they get past Omsk, we'll all have a lot to answer for." Then he slapped Josef's horse on the flank, and the riders set out at a canter.

# CHAPTER SIXTY

The communication problem was rooted not in the line or in malfunctioning equipment at Omsk. The problem lay in the person of Constantine Yelenov, whose habit it had become to sit through the lonely watches of the night in the company of a bottle of vodka. Usually there was so little activity between the hours of two and eight A.M. that a few drinks didn't get in the way of his adequate performance of his duties. Usually a few of the Red Guards who had the night duty dropped in to share the bottle or tell a story or play a game of cards. But tonight they were nowhere about. Half of them had been assigned a few days ago to accompany a Special Commissar to Tobolsk. The other half had been sent out an hour or so before he came on watch to patrol the road to Vinzili looking for the Tsar, Constantine had been told by the man whom he had relieved. And they had both had a good laugh over that. The few soldiers who were left in Omsk were all foot soldiers and asleep in the barracks across the way. So he had no one to share his bottle with and had been particularly lonely and bored. So he drank a little more than was his custom.

By four in the morning the bottle was three-quarters empty, and he had begun singing songs to himself, softly at first and then with noisy abandon. All kinds of songs: bawdy songs, love songs, lullabies. By five o'clock in the morning he could barely hold his head up long enough to drain the last drops from the bottle. He was very dizzy and very sleepy. Thank God there had been no messages to copy. Thank God his relief would be coming by in just a few hours.

How many hours to eight o'clock? He couldn't concentrate well enough to count. And all his vodka was gone. Feeling totally alone and abandoned, he lay his head down on the table and began to cry softly.

At six o'clock, though he couldn't really see the time, he thought he heard a faraway clacking sound as if the telegraph were being worked. But he couldn't determine whether or not they were his call letters; they seemed to be going by too fast. He thought he had better signal whoever was calling to repeat the sign, just in case. He raised his head to look for the key, and the room began to tilt. He tried to hold onto the sides of the table, but it was no good; he was falling.

At eight o'clock when Rudolph Nicolaiev came in, he found the chair tipped over and Constantine sprawled on his back on the floor. Were it not for Constantine's ear-splitting snores, Nicolaiev might have believed that his comrade was dead. He was certainly not responding by so much as the quiver of an eyelid to the insistent clatter of the telegraph. And they were Omsk's call letters, too, repeated over and over again. God only knew for how long they'd been calling.

Nicolaiev stepped over the body of his stupefied friend, set the chair upright, sat down, and keyed a response to the call. Then he drew up a pad and pencil and began writing down the message as it came over the wire.

When all the words were down and he reread what he had written, he found himself in a state of panic.

The ex-Tsar and his family had abandoned their sleighs and were attempting to escape by rail—on the line that would take them through Omsk. Lieutenant Zavitsky had been trying for the past two hours to get this message through. Depending upon the speed at which they were traveling, the train may well have passed through the yards already.

Nicolaiev's first thought was for himself. Would he be linked in blame with Constantine? Would they both be shot for Constantine's dereliction? He fled the shack, message in hand. He felt a strong urge just to keep running. But that would be the way to certain death. He thought of turning around and sobering up Constantine before he delivered the message and decided he couldn't spare the time. Besides, with Constantine still asleep on the floor, the evidence was indisputable. Constantine alone would take the full measure of blame.

He ran across the square to Kossirev's quarters and began banging on the door.

# CHAPTER SIXTY-ONE

I n the hours before dawn Marie, in her turn, had watched over her invalid brother. Aldonby sat with her, his back to the car's planked walls, his good arm around her, her head tilted and tucked into his shoulder, his cheek nesting in her hair. The others not engaged in driving the engine slept, depleted by exhaustion, wedged between the bags and parcels that held their refugees' belongings, undisturbed by the steady rumble of the wheels or the creak and swaying of the car, unconscious of the huddled pair who had made Alexei's straw-cushioned corner their solitary paradise.

They hardly spoke as the hours passed, cherishing in mute delight the wonder of their being together again. She, in the welcome custody of his embrace, feeling the terrors of the past months slowly draining away, as if his body were absorbing them, disarming them, transforming them into harmless memories. He, as he held her, feeling his ties to England relaxing, as if Sara were there, absolving him, understanding that this had to be. Though no one knew better than he that his debt to Sara could never be repaid.

Once, as the train wobbled through the night, Charles and Marie kissed, without preamble and lingeringly, as if Tsarskoe Selo had been only yesterday. "Did you know that my little sister saw us?" Marie asked. Charles darted a glance at the sleeping Anastasia. Marie set a forefinger against his chin and turned his face back to hers. "Not now. That night, in the maze. She was spying from the window. She teased me without pity the next day. She threatened to tell—unless I told her everything."

"And you did?" he asked in mock dismay.

Marie shrugged insouciantly. "I was at her mercy. And besides, each

253

time I told her, I could live it again. I told her—every time she asked."

"I despaired of ever seeing you again."

"To the Revolution! It has freed me of my chains," she declared, but not so loudly as to waken the others or with such abandon as to have forgotten what their new freedom had cost. "Where will we go after Vladivostok?" Marie asked.

"To America, I think. The homeless and dispossessed do very well there, I'm told."

"And we speak the language," Marie said.

"But we'll both have to work on our accents."

Marie laughed delightedly and buried her face in his shoulder, so that no one would hear. And Charles thought, all we need do is pass through Omsk.

Just after sunrise a shout from Lars Dahlgren in the engine sent Charles scrambling.

# CHAPTER SIXTY-TWO

Aldonby slipped through the partly open doorway in the freight car and climbed the ladder to the roof. There he paused momentarily, flat on his belly, orienting himself to the movement of the train. The gentle rock and sway, so rhythmically pleasant below, presented certain hazards to an individual perched alone and exposed on the narrow spine of the car.

Eyes slitted against the backward rush of icy morning air, Aldonby tried to take advantage of his lofty position to assess their situation. A snow-swept plain fanned out all around, forested with birch and pine, pierced by the steel rails that ran straight back behind him as far as he could see. The only animate object in the flat, still countryside was the train itself.

Some miles ahead, but not so far ahead as to be lost in perspective's vanishing point, the tracks appeared to begin a gentle curve to the left. And somewhere beyond that there was a smudge on the scrubbed pink face of the morning sky. Perhaps smoke.

He scrambled forward, made the crossing onto the tender, and then moved down into the locomotive. Lars Dahlgren was at the throttle. Sergei was feeding the fire. Lars, who seemed genuinely to be enjoying himself, was so absorbed in the running of the train that he didn't notice Aldonby's arrival.

Aldonby patted him on the shoulder to let him know that he was there. "You seem awfully carefree for a fugitive."

"Fugitive? What's that? I'm driving a train. That's every boy's dream."

"I saw smoke ahead on the horizon. Could another train be headed this way?" Aldonby asked.

Sergei looked at them, concerned.

255

"Maybe," Lars said. "But more than likely it's Omsk. If I remember this country, we should be almost there."

"That's what I was hoping," Aldonby said.

"Can we believe it?" Lars Dahlgren shouted exultantly above the roar and rush of the engine. "Can we really believe that we've done it?" He let out a joyous whoop.

"Shhh," Aldonby good-humoredly remonstrated. "They might hear you."

"Who? The Red Guards of Omsk? If they get in my way, I'll roll right over them."

Aldonby laughed. Sergei laughed. Lars Dahlgren reached for the whistle cord. Aldonby grabbed his arm. "No. They might hear *that*." Lars looked petulant, like a child deprived of a treat.

"Wait until we're out of earshot on the other side of Omsk."

"We'll take turns at the whistle then. The Tsar, too, I'll bet."

"What about the fuel?" Sergei asked soberly.

"What about it?" Aldonby sounded annoyed. He was still in a festive mood. After weeks of tension and bare moments of release, he resented being brought back to earth. He was like a man on a binge.

"It won't last forever. Maybe half a day."

"Then we'll stop and cut down some trees. The Tsar is a woodcutter of some experience, isn't he?"

Sergei looked affronted. The Tsar was the Tsar, whether he reigned in Petersburg or on a fugitive train. The festive spirit died. There was only the sound of the wheels and the pistons and the fire. Chastened, Aldonby threw his arm around Sergei's shoulder. "Would I have come all this way to commit a lèse majesté?"

Sergei nodded, accepting the apology.

"We talked at great length coming down in the sleigh, the Tsar and I. He is more a man than even you may realize."

Sergei nodded, mollified.

Then Aldonby thumped him on the back. "And he told me himself that he could cut wood better than any peasant, and he sounded damned proud of it."

This time, even Sergei grinned.

And Lars interrupted them with a shout. "I see it now. I see the smoke. It must be Omsk."

# CHAPTER SIXTY-THREE

In the railyards of Omsk, Kossirev anxiously gnawed on his mittened knuckles while a railway crew nursed a trackside fire, trying desperately to build up enough heat to melt the frozen switches. Overlooking the scene from the vantage point of his saddle, Kossirev could see a disaster taking shape.

With Zavitsky on the road and Chernovsky God-only-knew where, he had only twelve soldiers to deploy. He also had sixteen spare rifles with which he could arm a few civilians, if he could round up sixteen ablebodied civilians in time. But of what use would that be? What was to be gained by putting rifles into the hands of people who did not know how to shoot?

If he couldn't stop the train before it got through the yards, if it was able to come through at speed, then the screen of fire his soldiers could lay down for the few brief seconds that the train would be within range would be as good as useless, barring a lucky shot.

They had to stop the train in the yards. And the only way to do it would be to switch it from the main line into a dead-end siding as it came through. And the switches were frozen solid.

Beyond the curve, behind the fringe of pine that ringed his town, Kossirev could see smoke: dark, brownish, greasy locomotive smoke. He rode up behind the nearest trackman working on the switch and kicked him, sending him sprawling. The man rolled onto his back and lay there cowering.

"Get on your feet and get back to work," Kossirev yelled. "If that switch stays frozen, we'll dig your grave right here beside it."

He rode at a gallop back to where half of his dozen soldiers were deployed along the trackside. The other six he had dispatched to the

257

dead-end siding to capture the fugitives, should the switches be thawed in time. Altogether it seemed hopeless.

"Remember," he shouted, "don't waste your fire. Don't look for special autocratic targets. We're offering no bounty for the Tsar's hide. Just try to kill the engine crew. That's the only way we'll stop them if the switches don't thaw."

A mile away the engine poked its broad black snout around the curve. They saw it before they could hear it, swathed in a dirty brown veil of smoke, looking soiled and breathless and tired, advancing with astonishing lethargy for a vehicle bearing fugitives. Only its cow-catcher, sheathed in ice, and glinting like a silvered shield under the early morning sun, evidenced any sense of life at all.

Kossirev couldn't believe his eyes. In the first place, it was hardly a train at all: just an engine, tender, and freight car. There were no passenger cars at all. Would the former Tsar of all the Russias be riding in a freight car like a common tramp? And the train was moving so slowly. Would fugitives be fleeing at a crawl?

Was this the train? Or was it just a maintenance vehicle that happened to be on the track? If the switches remained frozen and he was forced to give the order to fire and if his men hit their targets, as well they might considering how surprisingly slowly the engine was moving, would he be responsible for the murder of an innocent railroad crew?

They could hear the engine now, gasping like an overweight babushka who had just climbed too many stairs. Kossirev began to make the sign of the cross and then stopped. Habit. One didn't do that anymore.

"Ready!" He shouted to his men and waited while they raised their rifles and laid their cheeks down along the stocks. "Wait until I give the signal."

Then he rode at a gallop to the western entrance to the yards to see if the switchmen had made any progress. He hoped, too, that from the head of the yards he might be better able to assess the true status of the train before it became necessary to give the signal to open fire.

In the engine, standing behind Lars Dahlgren who was still operating the throttle, Aldonby could see the Red Guards, rifles raised, deployed along both sides of the track. Somehow they had been warned, unless it was their custom to greet the arrival of every train with a six-gun salute. But why only six riflemen? Could the whole town of Omsk be guarded by so few Red Guards? Or were there others waiting in ambush farther down the line?

The occupants of the freight car had been ordered to lie flat on the floor until they had passed through the yards. But even then, could they risk running a gauntlet of rifle fire and the chance that a stray bullet or bullets might destroy one or more of the very people they had come to save? He saw an officer detach himself from the group of riflemen and ride toward the engine, to the head of the yard, where a couple of civilians had built a fire on the tracks.

"What are they trying to do with that fire?" Aldonby yelled to Dahlgren.

Lars shook his head. "What's the difference? A little fire like that won't stop this machine."

"The marksmen might."

"Not unless they can hit me. And I can tell you I'm going to be sitting on the floor with all this steel plate around me when we go through there."

"What about the passengers? The freight car is wood."

"If we go through fast enough, I don't think they'll hit anything. They've got us timed at a crawl. They're down at track level. They'll be shooting up at a difficult angle. The passengers are flat on the floor. If we do a real job of acceleration as we go through the yard, we'll be past them before they have time to adjust."

"We risk hurting Alexei if we accelerate."

"The boy is lying down, on a cushion of hay, not sitting as he was outside Vinzili. We take a greater risk if we don't speed up. But you're the captain of this ship."

Aldonby turned to Sergei, who was tending the fire, and yelled, "Let's feed the furnace!" Then he moved over beside Sergei and picked up a shovel. "Let's keep shoveling until we come abreast of the troops. Then everybody down."

Lars let out a whoop and shoved the throttle to the wall.

Kossirev, bending over his straining switchmen, looked up with alarm. Something about the sound of the oncoming engine had changed. The gasping, puffing wheeze had become a roar. The track ties began trembling with the vibration. The locomotive was bearing down on them at a velocity approaching the speed of an express.

He pulled out his revolver to give his soldiers the signal to fire. Suddenly the locomotive was almost on top of him, emitting ear-splitting blasts of its whistle. Kossirev's horse reared. He threw himself clear of the saddle to get out of the way. The pistol went flying. The switchmen, making one last desperate heave at the lever, pitched forward and went tumbling into the trackside snowbank.

"Jesus!" Lars yelled as he pulled back on the throttle and groped for the brake.

The engine lurched sharply and veered to the right, knocking Aldonby and Sergei to the floor. Lars managed to stay upright only because he had the side of the cab to cling to. "They've thrown the switch!"

The train was off the main line now, speeding into the siding.

As he frantically worked the brake, Lars could see a dead-end abutment looming a quarter of a mile ahead. And a cluster of armed Red Guards deploying themselves on either side of the track where the train would have to stop.

# CHAPTER SIXTY-FOUR

*From the journal of Anastasia Romanov*

Tobolsk
May 1, 1918

They took us from the train in the railyards at Omsk and did that thing which Papa had feared and fought against for over a year: they divided the family.

Papa, Mama, and Marie were placed under guard and put on the next train west and sent to Ekaterinburg.

Tatiana, Olga, Alexei, and I were sent back to Tobolsk.

Mama and Papa were half out of their minds with concern for Alexei. God only knows why we were so cruelly divided. We are like chaff in a whirlwind.

I don't know what has become of the brave men who tried to rescue us. I saw them being led away under guard. I pray for their safety and for us all.

Papa told us, as we were saying good-bye, that we had come within minutes of being free.

# AFTERWORD

On May 23, 1918, the Romanov family was reunited in Ekaterinburg for the fifty-five days of life that remained to them.

On July 17, with the Revolution in disarray and with the boom of the advancing White artillery sounding in Ekaterinburg, the Tsar and his family were taken to the basement of the house that had been their last prison and were shot. By the bitterest of ironies it was the irrefutable evidence that rescue was at hand that had sealed their fate. Had the Revolution enjoyed an early and universal success, they might have survived, held hostage for a while until they could be traded in the interest of diplomatic advantage. But in the summer of 1918 the Revolution was dying, and it was decreed that the Romanovs must die with it.

Regarding Charles Aldonby, unofficial inquiries were made by Arthur Craig in Sara McKenzie's behalf.

As far as could be determined Aldonby never betrayed his true identity to the Bolsheviks. His captors assumed that he was as Russian as his cadets and they were all branded traitors to the Revolution. They were imprisoned for a time at Omsk and then transferred to Moscow for more specialized interrogation. They attempted to escape from the train en route. Aldonby succeeded. Igor was shot and killed. Boris, Vasily, and Sergei were recaptured and returned to the train. They were never heard of again.

When the White armies liberated Ekaterinburg, it was reported that a soldier fitting Charles Aldonby's description was seen riding in the advance guard. Craig's sources reported no trace of him after that. He became one of the millions who vanished ignominiously in the great upheaval.

Of all the principals in this story only Lars Dahlgren was known to

263

have survived, imprisoned for a time at Omsk, released eventually upon the intercession of the Norwegian Ambassador.

In his ninety-third year he could be found in a home for aged seamen, frail of body but clear of mind, particularly concerning events of long ago, easily moved to live again through reminiscence his great, doomed adventure, supporting his narrative with the evidence of yellowing snapshots stored in a water-stained shoe box: a robust, shaggy-bearded, young seaman in a heavy roll-necked sweater poses proudly beneath the bows of a sturdy little ship named *Elena*; a lean, intense youth of military bearing bends over a map, his body radiating authority and purpose, except for the one arm, lamely dangling; the cadets are seen grouped like members of a rugby team, dauntless adolescents who would be octogenarians now, had they lived.

One photograph is kept always in sight, at his bedside: eight-by-ten, sepia toned, formally posed, protected by a frame. The Lars Dahlgren of this photo is a young burgher, gazing solemnly at the lens: clean shaven, carefully groomed, dressed in a morning coat, starched collar, and necktie. The fancy clothes are of awkward fit, borrowed for the occasion. Beside him, in a white gown, clutching a bouquet to her bodice and smiling with her eyes, stands a lovely, diminutive, dark-haired young woman.

His frail, knotted finger settles like a caress on the glass that shields his bride. It is Nadia.

He senses rather than sees astonishment and chuckles, contentedly. Thinking back. All that unfinished business. His face is alight with the most delicious of memories.

There is one more souvenir, a glassine envelope, to keep newsprint from turning to dust. Inside, a half-dozen clippings, news photos of the Soviet leadership and its retinue over the years. Stalin. Khrushchev. Kosygin. Brezhnev, in his prime. The principals change as the date-lines advance, but one individual remains constant. He stands always just behind, close and attentive to, the man at the center of power. Part of his face is masked by a trim little beard; his hair is cut in the Russian style, but there is a look about him that one has seen before among the snapshots in Lars's collection. As the years pass the beard becomes flecked with gray, as does the hair; the firm, fine features thicken. But the look in the eyes is unfaltering. And there is something about the attitude of the left arm that hints that it is lame. He is identified in some of the captions as Anton Zagorsky. But he is someone else, a figure from a lost world who has found a way to avenge the murder of his beloved.